"Absorbing . . . poignant, often heartbreaking . . . Schwarz is a vivid storyteller."

—*The New York Times Book Review*

"Expertly magnifies the characters' desperation and intertwines the excitement of eluding the law with their magnetic sexual attraction. Schwarz's rich narrative brings fresh life into the notorious tale of two American outlaws."

—*Publishers Weekly*

"The novel's opening offers even those who remember the movie a fresh, touching view of Bonnie before Clyde."

—*Kirkus Reviews*

"Bodies fall, blood flies, Bonnie and Clyde sleep in stolen cars and can't eat in restaurants but so long as they are in the headlines all is well. In *Bonnie*, Schwarz has created a mesmerizing portrait of a young woman who longs to live a larger life and who almost always acts in her own worst interests. A stunning novel."

—Margot Livesey, *New York Times* bestselling author of *Mercury*

"Bonnie Parker is better known for how she died than how she lived, but Christina Schwarz remedies that with her magnificent new novel. In exploring Bonnie's complex inner life and fascinating story, Schwarz makes this iconic figure relevant to the world we inhabit today. An evocative and absorbing read."

—Greer Hendricks, *New York Times* bestselling coauthor of *The Wife Between Us*

ALSO BY CHRISTINA SCHWARZ

The Edge of the Earth

So Long at the Fair

All Is Vanity

Drowning Ruth

BONNIE

A NOVEL

Christina Schwarz

WASHINGTON
SQUARE PRESS

ATRIA

NEW YORK LONDON TORONTO SYDNEY NEW DELHI

WASHINGTON SQUARE PRESS

ATRIA

An Imprint of Simon & Schuster, Inc.
1230 Avenue of the Americas
New York, NY 10020

First Washington Square Press / Atria Paperback edition February 2021

WASHINGTON SQUARE PRESS **/ ATRIA** PAPERBACK and colophon are trademarks of Simon & Schuster, Inc.

For information about special discounts for bulk purchases, please contact Simon & Schuster Special Sales at 1-866-506-1949 or business@simonandschuster.com.

The Simon & Schuster Speakers Bureau can bring authors to your live event. For more information or to book an event, contact the Simon & Schuster Speakers Bureau at 1-866-248-3049 or visit our website at www.simonspeakers.com.

Interior design by Kyoko Watanabe

Manufactured in the United States of America

1 3 5 7 9 10 8 6 4 2

Library of Congress Cataloging-in-Publication Data is available on file.

ISBN 978-1-4767-4545-9
ISBN 978-1-4767-4546-6 (pbk)
ISBN 978-1-4767-4547-3 (ebook)

To Ben and Nick and to my parents.

In the end, they still have the driving, her scar-shortened leg tucked under her bottom, his stocking feet caressing the pedals, the warm, moist air, like a swift current of dry water, rushing into the car. The cordoba gray V-8 remains a decent machine; the paint is dusty, but they haven't wrecked any essential parts yet. Its big engine luxuriates in the gas he feeds it. Tires entrenched in well-worn ruts, the car whips around the bends, causing her stomach to rise and fall with the hills. Dallas is comfortingly within reach, but this piney pocket of northwestern Louisiana is softer, sweeter smelling, more often dappled with lacy shade, than any place she's been in Texas.

They've bought bacon, lettuce, and tomato sandwiches and two bottles of Orange Crush for breakfast at the café in Gibsland. She struggles to unwrap a sandwich and keep an open bottle of soda pop upright with the Remington in her lap and the Colt strapped around her good leg, but he won't let her transfer the guns to the floor, even for half an hour. He doesn't trust this place, with its narrow, rutted, curving roads, the way he does the squared-off farm roads of the middle states, where he can push the accelerator to the floor and leave any of the law's four-cylinder machines far behind.

She, however, feels safe enough—the thick trees hide them from view and, if they're spotted, plenty of crossroads offer getaways. She's wearing a pair of spectacles, round with wire frames, that she found in the Ford's glove compartment and that happen to have just the right prescription to correct her nearsightedness. The sharpened, brightened view they afford is still new enough to amaze and delight her, and she is enjoying the illusion that she can see distinctly what lies ahead.

PART 1

CHAPTER 1

"Ashes, ashes, we all fall down!"

"*You* fall! *You* fall!" The children, reverential even as they commanded, lifted their eyes and their arms, plumped with sweaters against the chill spring twilight, to the woman who stood over them.

Although she was tiny—not even five feet tall and slight as a finch—she was twenty-one years old, and she might have dipped like a lady and sat on her heels to save her skirt or merely laughed and clapped her hands (that's what the children's stout mother generally did). Miss Bonnie, however, had a penchant for the dramatic. Throwing her head back and her hands in the air, she crumpled to the ground and lay as if dead.

"Agin! Agin!" One of the little boys drummed his feet.

Indulgent, she pushed herself up and gathered two grubby hands in her slender fingers.

But the back door opened, and the children's mother stood in it, unknotting her apron strings. "It's time." Her east Texas accent stretched and softened the terse statement, but she was a confident, orderly person, and her tone, while not unkind, was firm.

All four tousled figures obeyed, although the young woman was obviously reluctant, hanging her blond head and not hurrying, as she resettled her loose dress, a slinky thing some of her friends had brought her, and the plaid jacket that drooped over it. The mother had lent that out of her own closet.

"Go on and find yer daddy. He'll give y'all some milk." The mother bent to give the last of her children a playful tap on the bottom as he disappeared into the house. She folded her apron over her arm. "I'm sorry, Mrs. Thornton," she said, "but it's time."

"All right, Mrs. Adams."

The young woman scuffed her shoes—broken, brown things, shapeless as cow pies, donated by the Ladies Benevolent Society—as they walked over the lawn.

Dragging her feet like a child, Mrs. Adams thought, but she couldn't blame Mrs. Thornton for savoring the out-of-doors. They crossed the yard to the building immediately next door, a stern brick square, its tall windows barred.

"Does every town in this goddamned state have a jail?" Mrs. Thornton had snarled the morning they'd brought her in. They'd taken her cigarettes, and she was twitchy and querulous. Not to mention filthy from the hours she'd spent in that dirt-floored calaboose in Kemp. And barefoot.

"Pret' near." Mrs. Adams had been the one to answer. She was the sheriff's wife, as well as a mother. "There's a good portion of Texans don't keep to the right side of the law. Always plenty of work for a sheriff."

◆

"Is it fixin' to storm tonight?" Mrs. Thornton said now, anxiously studying the sky.

Mrs. Adams glanced up. "Could be. Wouldn't surprise me if the Lord saw fit to send us a flood, times being evil as they are."

The heavy door, painted black, swung easily to admit them, and Mrs. Thornton waited, downcast, while Mrs. Adams lifted the iron ring of keys from behind the desk where her husband did his paperwork. The space was high ceilinged and made of stone, so the sounds that issued from the cells, in the back, echoed throughout the building.

"Who there? Jesus? Is that you, Jesus? Have you come for me, Jesus?" The Negro woman in the cell beside Mrs. Thornton's beat her cup and sometimes her head against the wall.

"Here I come." The voice belonged to a man Mrs. Thornton had never seen, but she believed that the sharpest of the foul smells that permeated the place must come from him. "I'm Jesus coming to fuck you, bitch. You better watch out. I'm comin'. I'm comin'."

The voice of the oldest of Mrs. Adams's little boys, begging his daddy for a glass of water, carried through the damp air into one of the jail's open windows. Mrs. Thornton concentrated on that piping sound and closed her ears to the other, as she obediently followed her jailer into the dimness, the racket, and the stench.

"You really think it's fixin' to storm?" she asked again.

"What difference does it make, honey? You ain't going to get wet in here."

Mrs. Adams had told her husband to give Mrs. Thornton the first cell, so she wouldn't have to walk past the others. Mrs. Adams wasn't generally easy on prisoners; she was a lawman's wife, after all. But she believed she was a good judge of character. She knew that letting the young woman out in the evenings to play with her children was the right thing to do; it brought out her sweetness. And she was happy to supply some empty pages from an old account book and a pencil, when Mrs. Thornton said she wanted to write poetry. Some, Mrs. Adams knew, were born vicious, but most slipped into trouble by degrees. It wasn't too late for this one to scramble out.

That's what she'd told Mrs. Thornton's mother.

"Now y'all don't pay her bail," she'd admonished the thin woman whose hair and skin and even eyes were faded like old cotton and who'd had to take a bus down to Kaufman from Dallas. She'd seemed bewildered to find her daughter in such a place.

"To tell you the truth," Mrs. Parker had said, lighting a Chesterfield unsteadily, "I don't know how I could git the money just now."

"Best not to," Mrs. Adams had assured her. She'd offered sugar and cream for the coffee she'd poured, mutely lifting the bowl and pitcher in turn. "They won't convict her—there's not enough evidence. Let her stew awhile. That'll learn her."

"They won't send her to the pen?" Mrs. Parker's voice had quavered. She'd fit the cigarette to her lips and treated herself to a deep pull, reinforcing the grooves that radiated around her mouth, while she'd cast her eyes haphazardly around the room, as if searching for something to grasp on to. She'd released the smoke with slow reluctance. "It's not like her to lie to me. In fact, I don't believe she ever has before. Not a real, outright lie, anyway."

◆

"I got me a job in Houston," Bonnie had said the very moment Mrs. Parker had come into the house the previous Tuesday evening. The small green cardboard case was already packed and waiting just inside the door. Mrs. Parker, who'd trudged home from work, her mind on the jar of liniment she kept on her dresser top, had been struck by how fresh her daughter looked in her best skirt and jacket, her fluffy blond hair clean and curling around her jawline.

"In Houston? How would you know about a job in Houston?" The pinch in her back had made her voice sharper than she'd intended.

"Ida Jeffers's cousin knows a lady says they're looking for girls to sell cosmetics."

"You don't know how to do that."

"Your skin absorbs all the trials of your day." Bonnie had placed her fingertips on her mother's face. "But I've found that Princess Cream gets deep into the pores and smooths away those tired lines. It brings out your natural radiance. I've been using it for a month now, and I can't tell you how many people have said how well I look." She touched her own fresh cheek.

"But Houston is so far away."

"I don't want to leave you, Mama. But there are no jobs here. You know that." All of these statements were true.

◆

However, it seemed there'd never been a job in Houston or anyplace else. Mrs. Parker hadn't been able to get over it. She'd kept thinking that somehow there'd been an accident along the way, maybe a case of mistaken identity. She couldn't see how her lively, loving daughter—her bonny Bonnie!—could have been involved in anything that would cause her to be locked in a jail cell.

"She made the honor roll, you know," she'd said to the sheriff's wife. Revisiting in her memory the evening Bonnie had gone off, wondering what she could have done to keep the girl safely at home, Mrs. Parker had forgotten her cigarette. She'd tapped the long worm of ash into her saucer and then sucked another calming draft into her lungs. "She got all *As*," she'd breathed with the smoke.

This had been quite a few years ago—in fact, at fifteen Bonnie had given up on school and married her sweetheart because she'd been in love and why wait, she'd argued, when a person was in love? That was Bonnie all over: big dreams, no patience. Her mother had given in, worn out from arguing, but also, secretly proud as ever of her daughter's energy and persistence, the pure willfulness that had always made her more vibrant and winning than other girls and that, in the end, always got her what she wanted.

But Mrs. Parker had been right about the marriage. That love hadn't lasted, although Bonnie'd kept her husband's name and still wore his ring. It seemed a dirty trick, she'd said, to divorce a man when he was in the pen. That was Bonnie all over, too; she was almost as eager to be moved by other people's feelings as by her own.

Mrs. Parker had shaken her head to clear it of this frustrating and futile line of thought and had returned to the bolstering recollection of Bonnie's school record. Even if that was far in the past, it still said something about the kind of girl Bonnie was: conscientious, bright. A girl who could make something of herself, maybe get a job in an office with a lunch hour that allowed her to sit down in a café and order a tuna fish sandwich and a cup of coffee.

Bonnie had scorned that notion of success: "Who from Cement City works in an office?"

But to be different from the kind of person who came from Cement City was the point, Mrs. Parker had retorted, and Bonnie had agreed with that. Bonnie was going to be a singer or a movie star or a poet.

"Can I see her?" Mrs. Parker had asked.

The sheriff had thought to let Bonnie out when her mother came, so they could talk more comfortably, but his wife had cautioned against it. "Let the both of 'em feel what she's got herself into."

She'd let the tired woman into the jail, making a show of jangling the heavy iron key ring. At the sight of her mother, Bonnie had slumped onto her cot. She'd looked pathetic, her shoulders hunched, her hair hanging in greasy strings around her little heart-shaped face, her eyes puffed nearly shut from crying.

"My poor baby." Her mother had pressed her thin cheek to the bars and reached one arm through. She'd squeezed the hand her daughter gave her and had done her best to ignore the incessant keening from the next cell. "You're not going to see him again." She'd tried to say it firmly, but all three women were aware how close her statement came to a question.

Bonnie had pinched her sore eyes shut, the emotion that stabbed at her from inside more punishing than the jail. "I won't," she'd promised, childishly shaking her head with such vigor that the ends of her dirty hair flew out around her ears like a bell. "I hate him, Mama."

"Plenty of boys go to the pen, and then they make good when they come out and don't never have cause to go back again," her mother had pressed on. "But he doesn't seem to care about going right . . ."

"Stop it, Mama! I told you I don't want nothing more to do with him," Bonnie had interrupted, her face folding into outright weeping.

The sheriff's wife had nodded to herself as she'd led the way out, but Mrs. Parker had been less sure. She believed Bonnie's feelings were sincere, but that didn't mean that her daughter had learned her lesson.

CHAPTER 2

Four-year-old Bonnie had been spanked for touching the gramophone, so she did so only when no one was looking, climbing onto the divan and poking her fingers as deep into the horn as she dared. Once she'd gotten her hand stuck in there. She turned the crank to make the table spin, but she knew better than to set the needle down. That would make the music and give her away. Instead she sang, pretending her voice was coming from the machine, and she danced on the very narrow stage that was the back of the divan, so she could watch herself in the mirror on the opposite wall.

> *He's a devil, he's a devil,*
> *He's a devil in his own hometown!*

At night, when the-devil-in-his-many-guises lurked, she was afraid, and Buster, who slept easily, was no help. To steady her tearing heart, she traced with her eyes the spiraling colors of the small braided rug beside her bed and re-whispered her prayers. Yellow strands were wishes; she'd wished for a baby and they got Billie Jean. Dark greens were "sorries"—kicking Buster in the shin and making him cry. She hated it when people cried; it made her go squishy inside, like melted ice cream. The blues were the "Godblesses": Mama and Daddy and Buster and Billie; Granny and Pop-Pop up by Dallas; Uncle Pete and Scamper and all the kitties in the world and all the doggies in the world . . .

◆

God-in-heaven-above lived on the silver roof of the First Baptist Church, blinding bright in the sun, sober gray in the gloom.

Buster stomped into the house ahead of Bonnie. "I'm never being in charge of her again!"

"Don't care!"

"She was supposed to sing a church song! Like 'Jesus Loves Me.' That's what I sang."

"You're not the boss of me!"

"You just want everyone to say, 'Oh, that Bonnie Parker!' "

Bonnie had thought that "He's a Devil in His Own Hometown" was a good church song. After all, the preacher talked about the devil every Sunday. But Buster was right; she did puff up when people said, "Oh, that Bonnie Parker!"

CHAPTER 3

Bonnie Elizabeth Parker was born in the compact, pleasant town of Rowena, Texas, which, like most places in central and western Texas, was far from everything, except, in this case, the tracks of the Atchison, Topeka, and Santa Fe. If you didn't count the clutch of cemeteries about half a mile to the south, the whole of the town—its three churches, its school, its depot, its smithy, its feed store and grocery, and all of its squared-off houses—was inscribed within a neat triangle, its legs two roads, one running east to west, the other, north to south, and its hypotenuse the railroad tracks.

The triangle was divided by the straight streets such flat country allows, five lying one direction and seven the other, with simple names like Depot Street and School Street, Mary Street and George Street. The land beyond the streets was planted mostly with cotton. In winter the landscape presented an ugly, unrelieved corduroy of bare earth, but in spring it glowed like green silk, and by the end of summer it was a Swiss dot of brilliant white that fluffed and clumped in the ditches like a southern snow. Rowena had been named for the wife of a Santa Fe Railroad clerk.

"When I grow up," Bonnie told her mother, "I'm going to live in a town called Bonnie."

She spent hours on her back, staring at Rowena's endless sky, its blue the color of heaven in the stained-glass windows of the church-that-Daddy-was-building. Lying on the patchy grass behind their house, she stretched her arms upward, snagging for a moment a colossal, mottled cloud on her fingertips.

◆

Emma and Charles Parker had settled in Rowena right after they'd married. The Czechs were erecting a large, new church and needed bricklayers.

"That's the church that Daddy's building," Emma always said when they passed the construction site on their walks. Emma, whose own father had been a farmer, was proud to be married to a skilled laborer. She was giving her own children a cleaner, more stable start than she'd had.

"When Daddy's done building it, will we go there?"

"Of course not."

"Why not?"

"Because we're real Americans."

◆

Emma's father was, in fact, a German, and her mother was from Louisiana, but Emma had found her own religion, Southern Baptist, by following a girl she'd admired in school. She'd met the man who would become her husband among the congregation, so she'd never doubted God's guiding hand.

While Charles cemented bricks into straight rows for a living, Emma liked to think she was doing much the same with her three children, laying a solid foundation—dressing them neatly, seeing they were well-fed, teaching them to love and fear God and to know right from wrong. If she was too zealous, unable simply to enjoy them, as Charles wished she would, perhaps it was because she couldn't shake an inchoate belief that some lapse in her vigilance had allowed their first-born, Coley, to cease to breathe at some hour of the very early morning during the sixth week of his life. She understood that each—solemn, reliable Buster; effervescent, unpredictable Bonnie; easygoing, malleable Billie—was a treasure to be cherished and guarded. As if to stamp these three babies onto the world, she'd bought each a christening gift of precious metal and had it monogrammed. Hubert Nicholas (no son of hers would be christened Buster) had a silver cup; Billie Jean, a silver spoon; and Bonnie Elizabeth, a gold bracelet.

"*B.* That spells Bonnie."

Bonnie, only three years old, had butted in on Buster's lesson—as usual—and understood before he did the rudiments of reading. It must have been a Sunday morning, because the bracelet was around her wrist. She stroked the engraving with the tip of her miniature finger.

"That's right," Emma said, amazed. Maybe her daughter was a prodigy, like that Wonder Girl in Pittsburgh she'd read about in *McCall's*, who could speak seven languages. "*B. E. P.*," Emma said, pointing to each letter, "Bonnie Elizabeth Parker. That's you, all right. My bonny Bonnie."

◆

The bracelet wasn't for every day but only for special, like Sunday mornings with the big blue bow and white shoes. When they got to church, Mama wiped the toes of those shoes with a handkerchief she'd drawn across her tongue.

Sitting in the pew, Bonnie fiddled with the gold band, opening it wide and squeezing it tight, according to the rise and fall of the preacher's voice. Buster, bored, let his head fall to one side in church and Billie Jean sometimes cried; but Bonnie watched and listened as the preacher flung his arms and his voice around. She studied the black-ink words as they ribboned behind the square, thick finger Daddy passed over the page, like the shine trailing a snail. And whenever it came time for the singing, she sang *out*, so even God could hear her.

◆

Most of those early years would become amorphous in her memory, as if viewed through the bottom of a drinking glass, even the day her daddy went away.

"Daddy, don't go!"

She swings upside down on his forearm, her hands tight around his wrist, her ankles locked around his elbow. Her milkweed floss hair brushes his knees.

"Let Daddy go to work," Mama says, but she's distracted, feeding the baby, who isn't a baby anymore. "Big bite, Billie."

"No, Daddy. Stay and play."

She wants another yesterday.

Yesterday was Christmas Day but warm in the way that Texas can sometimes be in the middle of winter, the cold West wind stopping to catch its breath, so that the damp air can sponge up the sun. Bonnie and Buster were after Daddy, the moment they got home from church.

"Fly me! Fly me!" they both demanded. "Fly us!"

"Let Daddy rest. He has to work tomorrow." That was Mama, jiggling the baby, trying to spoil the fun. Bonnie wouldn't let her.

"C'mon, Daddy! Fly us!" She spun herself and toppled sideways. She couldn't get off the ground without him.

He *thunked* his bottle down and cleaned the foam from his lips with his finger and thumb. Done.

One hand around her ankle, the other around her wrist, he spun to make her fly, around and around, the air flowing over her face like cool water, the grass and the trees blurring and blending into a river of green and gray, like Little Black Sambo's tigers turning to butter. He dipped her low, so that her fingers brushed the blades. "My Bonnie lies over the ocean." High until she felt that if he opened his hands, she would keep on flying. "My Bonnie lies over the sea." But his fingers were clamped tight. "My Bonnie lies over the ocean." Her arm would pull right off her body before he'd let her go. "Oh, bring back my Bonnie to me."

Yesterday is done.

"Your daddy has to go to work, Bonnie." Her mother's words are crowding now, her hands around Bonnie's waist, tugging. "Let go."

"Goddammit, I won't!"

Her mother's hands jerk away, as if they've been burned. "Bonnie! Don't talk that way! Charlie, really! How could your brother?"

Daddy's brother is Uncle Pete, who'd brought a sky-blue ribbon to tie in her hair and nickels for ice cream when he came to visit. "Now what do you say when you don't want your peas?" He'd tilted his head when he asked a question, just the way her daddy did.

"I won't eat these goddamn peas!" she'd repeated, perfect in one go. His words in her fluty voice had made him laugh, so she'd said it again. His laugh was like her daddy's, too.

Later, the peas had glistened on her plate. She'd been amazed and impressed that he'd known they would be having peas for dinner. He'd winked at her, and she'd given the table a smart bang with the butt of her fork for attention. "I won't eat these goddamn peas!"

Mama and Daddy had stared at her and then Daddy and Uncle Pete had laughed their twin laughs. "I won't eat these goddamn peas!" Daddy'd laughed some more, just like he was laughing now.

"I won't, goddammit! I won't let go!"

But he gives his arm a little shake. "Off now, monkey. Be my bonny Bonnie." He unlocks her ankles easily with his free hand, so that her feet drop to the floor. "I'll be home in plenty of time for some of Mama's delicious red beans and rice." Over Bonnie's head she sees him wink at Mama, and Mama smiles back. Love hangs between them, shimmering like a spider's web in the early morning.

And then he's gone.

CHAPTER 4

If only she'd napped. Then the man would not have come.

But naps were for babies like Billie Jean and, no, Bonnie wouldn't lie down for just ten minutes; she wouldn't close her eyes. Bonnie wanted to play with Mama.

"Come on, Mama. Baby needs her bath." Bonnie emptied the chipped blue bowl of its oranges and plucked her own damp washcloth off the edge of the washstand. "Baby," in fact, is quite clean, having been bathed half a dozen times since Santa delivered her yesterday morning.

"Do it yourself like a big girl." Emma frowned at the pink fabric that humped and slithered on the table. "I have to finish this."

Bonnie dipped the washcloth in the empty bowl and touched it to Baby's face. "Oh, no!"

"Ow!" Startled, Emma had poked herself with a pin and her voice was cross. "Bonnie, what is it?"

"You didn't remind me to test the water and it was too hot." Bonnie rocked Baby petulantly, glowering at her mother.

But Bonnie never stayed mad. She ducked under the table. Mama sometimes let her push the treadle with her hands. "Now? Can I push now?"

The machine had jammed again. Emma yanked the fabric out, snipped the trailing thread with tiny scissors, and flipped the material to expose a matted snarl.

"When can I push it?"

"Oh, go outside and play, Bonnie, please. Mrs. Olsak needs this for New Year's Eve."

"Then let me help you, Mama. I'll make it go very fast." Bonnie pressed the treadle experimentally and the needle whirred, furiously stabbing nothing.

"For heaven's sake! Go outside. Here, let's put your coat on."

◆

This day was nothing like yesterday. The air was cold and the clouds ran together and sunk low around the steeple of the church-that-Daddy-was-building.

Buster had gone down the alley, pulling the wooden wagon that had been his Christmas present. If she'd gone looking for him, then she wouldn't have seen the man and then the man would not have come. But she wasn't allowed to leave the yard.

She could have stayed in the backyard, singing Christmas Baby to sleep in the wash basket, drumming on the hollow tub of the wringer, bossing a class of clothespin students into a straight line, hooking one hand around the cold iron of the clothesline post and leaning away, twirling until her palm burned from the friction and came away orange with rust. If she'd stayed in the back, she wouldn't have seen the man and the man would not have come. But playing in the back alone got dull.

There wasn't much to do in the front, but people sometimes passed, and she could watch them. And, if she skipped or stood on one foot or rolled a somersault or even just waved, she could get them to smile and sometimes even stop and talk to her.

For some time, the street was empty. Bonnie traced with a stick the crooked mortar lines that cemented the stones of her house. The Parkers' house and the Janceks' next door were the only two in town made of crooked rocks in shades of red and brown and yellow, pieced together like a crazy patchwork. Bonnie never tired of following their patterns and admiring the miraculous way such uneven borders could be arranged to fit perfectly together. Her fingers were cold, and her cheek, when she pressed one hand against it, was colder still and felt as slick as the pink silk Mama was sliding through her machine. She wished for someone to come, having in mind a friend of Mama's, baby on hip and child in hand; or next-door Mrs. Jancek, carrying a plate of *dulkove kolacky;* or a preacher with a Bible tucked tight over his heart;

or a drummer in a smart suit and a stiff hat, a heavy case stretching one arm long. *Click, click*, would go the latches and the case would open to reveal rows of shiny razors, lumpy sacks of coffee, brown bottles of medicine, or, Bonnie's favorite, boxes and boxes of colored buttons.

◆

The man emerges from behind the Kriegels' house on the corner.

For less than a second, not even long enough to fully form a thought, her heart quickens. The man wears work clothes just like Daddy's: brown trousers and jacket, a gray cap. But then she sees that his walk is wrong—heavy, as if he's dragging Buster's wagon full of rocks. And his shoulders are bulky; they're not the shoulders she rides to church on, so she's the tallest of all with her chin on Daddy's cap.

This man is neither a drummer nor a preacher. He takes meaty hands from his pockets and hangs them empty at his sides. He doesn't see her, even though she's right there, half under the porch he's about to walk on. She lifts her stick, a baton with which to command attention, but he doesn't smile and nod. Instead, he stares and frowns, as if he's angry to see her crouching there.

She should have run at him with her stick and driven him off. She should have run into the house ahead of him and held the door shut. But she does nothing but watch as he lifts his heavy hand to knock and then raises it to remove the cap that he bunches, puny and limp, in his thick fingers.

CHAPTER 5

"Give Daddy a kiss," Mama said, and Mr. Olsak hoisted her up, his big hands under her arms and around her ribcage. He held her well away from his body, as if she were a wet puppy, not tight against his chest the way Daddy would have. Inside the box, Daddy was hollow, like a jack-o'-lantern. God had scraped his insides out.

Sears, Roebuck sent the front room clock on the train in a long box like this one, but you couldn't get to heaven that way. You had to wait underground, where God would find you by your name carved on the flat stone.

The walk was long behind the wagon that carried the box that held the husk of Daddy. Bonnie stepped on Buster's heel, so Buster pulled the bow from Bonnie's hair. Bonnie punched him in the arm. Buster punched her back. The punching felt good; it helped Bonnie to breathe. But Mrs. Jancek caught her wrist.

"Children." The word wasn't scolding but plaintive, like melting ice.

Daddy fit next to Baby Coley, who'd been Bonnie's brother before Buster but had been too good for this earth. Bonnie kicked the toes of her white shoes into the dirt, so God would see she wasn't that good.

◆

Mrs. Jancek gave Bonnie a green cardboard case with a brass latch and a brown handle that had belonged to her daughter Jeannie, whom it was not polite to talk about. Bonnie hoped there would be buttons inside, but the case was empty.

A man with a big stomach turned the insides of their house upside down and sideways to puzzle them into a wagon and draped the rug from the front room over the whole pile for Bonnie and Buster to sit on.

They rode backward, so their eyes were on their patchwork house, until they turned the corner that set them on the road along the railroad tracks, and the place they'd lived in with Daddy was gone.

Bonnie flexed her bracelet. It was only for special, for church and for walking to the cemetery behind the wagon with the box of Daddy on it, but Mama had forgotten to take it off and put it away. Bonnie stretched the thin gold wire and pulled it over her hand. She threw it into the road the wagon had just traveled over.

"What'd you do that for?" Buster said.

"So Daddy can tell which way we went."

Buster twisted in his seat. "Ma!"

But the wagon's wheels ground through the dirt, and the stuffing from their house jiggled and creaked in its bed, and Billie was wailing in Mama's arms. Mama didn't hear him, or at least she didn't bother to turn or answer.

◆

The first night was fried potatoes, lemon pie, napkins wide enough to drape over Bonnie's head like a veil, and sleeping in a strange-smelling room with the door in the wrong place, and the next night was beans and rice on the dirt and sleeping on the mattresses they'd sat on all day. Snuggling under the wagon, peeking through the spokes at the swirling sky so thrilled Bonnie that she forgot to say her prayers, so God cracked open the sky, trying to flush her soul from her skin. Placid Billie looked around, wide-eyed and open-mouthed, but sensitive Bonnie was so undone, she couldn't even cry, and she clung silently to her mother with a grip that would leave blue dots on Emma's neck in the morning.

By the third day, Emma didn't climb on the front seat but curled with Bonnie and Buster on the folded-over rug or lay on the mattresses, under the tarp. The world as far as Bonnie could see was dirt, which changed color as the days passed from dark brown to red to gray. They bumped and juddered and swayed, until the stillness whenever they paused felt strange.

◆

Finally one morning, as they were finishing their breakfast beans, the driver lifted his arm, releasing a stink from under his coat, and pointed far ahead. "There's yer Cement City."

Six towers rose dark against the fresh peach of the rising sun. Emma dipped a flannel in the water left over from breakfast and washed all their faces and hands. She flattened Buster's hair and painstakingly untangled the knots that days in the wind and nights on the mattress had tied in Bonnie's cottony strands. She dressed Billie in a white sweater with pink rosette buttons and put on fresh stockings and Sunday shoes. Then she climbed out of the wagon bed and, carrying Billie, got back on the front seat with the driver.

◆

As the sky lightened, the towers grew, and soon plumes of black smoke became visible, then tasteable. The air had a sharp, unpleasant tang to it by the time the driver finally *whoa*ed the horse in front of a house the color of old wash water set among hard, brown winter fields.

Almost immediately, the front door opened and a woman no bigger than a girl, with head and hands and feet protruding from a garment so shapeless it might have been a flour sack, stepped out. Limping slightly, she came down the few steps off the porch and hurried across the yard, her palms pressed to her cheeks and her head swiveling left and right on its stringy neck.

She seemed almost to try to lift Mama off the seat, but she settled for Billie, who took up nearly the whole of her front—as Mama got carefully down, keeping her good stockings well away from the splintery wagon. Then the woman had Billie with one arm and Mama pulled tight against her bosom with the other.

"Oh, Emma!" she said. "I ain't got room for all this junk. You shoulda sold it and took you a train."

Buster got out of the wagon bed in the deliberate way that he and Bonnie had taught themselves—first, rolling over on his stomach to dangle his feet as far down as they would reach and then pushing himself off the side. Bonnie had positioned herself to do the same, when a girl came banging out of the house, in two great leaps covered the length of the porch, and, not bothering with the steps, hurled herself off the edge of it. Her hair, cut straight across the jawline like Bonnie's and nearly as pale, lifted on either side of her head like feathery wings.

So Bonnie drew her legs under her, balanced on the backboard, and launched herself. She didn't think to go off the side, where she might have landed on the winter-brown grass. Instead, she hit the packed dirt and pebbles of the drive and fell forward onto her knees and palms, tearing her stockings and her skin and staining her skirt with blood.

CHAPTER 6

If she'd kept her family in Rowena, Emma often thought, maybe Bonnie would have found a different boy, someone with whom she could have settled down and been happy. ("Happy" was a word Emma and Bonnie both used to describe a quixotic state of contentment.) But God had yanked the foundation out from under what Emma had built. What choice had she but to give up and bring her children home to Dallas?

Well, not Dallas, exactly. Not the city east of the Trinity River with its turreted bloodred courthouse and arcaded, marble-floored hotels; its department stores selling Japanese silk and French perfume; its theaters bejeweled with lights; and its dim, cool banks in which tellers fingered bills with manicured hands; but rather the haphazard region west of the river, far enough out that their section of the metropolis was no longer called Dallas or even West Dallas, but had its own name, derived from the industrial product at its heart.

Obviously, Cement City was not named for a woman. Its official name was merely Cement, the "city" being a nod to the humans who toiled to feed the blast furnaces with stone from the jagged-edged quarries, like Dark Age peasants propitiating dragons.

The widest and best-maintained roads in the district led to the Trinity and the Lone Star cement factories. At the foot of these, six rows of identical double houses, built for the workers, were packed like barracks along straight dirt streets. The remainder of Cement City spread west, a weedy confederation of fields and wire fences and stands of straggly trees littered with wooden farmhouses and all manner of outbuildings—lopsided barns, coops for chickens and geese, equipment sheds and mule sheds, pumps and outhouses.

Even at the outer limits, where Emma moved her children into her parents' low-slung house, the pounding of steel against rock, the pulverizing of limestone and shale, so that they could be ground fine, heated literally beyond endurance, and spit out as clinker to be ground again, was ceaseless. "That's just how it is," Mama said, when Bonnie complained about the noise. "You have to get used to it."

Bonnie did get used to that pulse underneath the other sounds of the day and night. She got used to the sulfurous taint of the smoke, too, which clung to the air like gauze. Bonnie wanted to sleep with Mama, but Grandma said it was time she quit being a baby and made her sleep with Buster in the attic, where nail points studded the sloped ceiling. No one knew what had happened to the braided rug, so when Bonnie felt afraid in the night, she had to turn her face toward the little window under the eaves and find comfort in the blast furnace glowing orange in the darkness.

◆

Mama and Billie shared a tiny room tacked onto the back of the house. That was all right, Mama said, seeing as she was all alone now. Bonnie took hold of her mother's hand to remind her that she certainly wasn't alone. She had Bonnie and Buster and Billie. She had Grandma and Pop-Pop. And there were so many Krauses. Curly-haired Uncle Wylie and Aunt Elvina in the yellow bedroom, and Uncle Frank in the attic room across from Bonnie and Buster's. Plus, relatives who seemed to live down every road in Cement City.

Those first days, Dutchie—the cousin who'd flown from the house— tossed names like apples at Bonnie and Buster, as she took them around to meet their kin. Bud, Russ, Everitt; big boy brothers who spilled off a porch and ran for the woods. Aunt Pat, who was Dutchie's mama and Mama's sister, wore trousers and was really named Lily. Uncle Fred, his head fresh pumped, shook droplets like a dog. Up the road were mustachioed Uncle Dink and gap-toothed Aunt Millie with more cousins— LeRoy and Sally Ann, Clora Jean and Floyd. Big John and Wilma Rae had Little J—who was big—Monroe, Gladys, Alma, and baby George P. And—Dutchie flung her hand toward a dirt track that disappeared into the woods—Lela or Lula (or possibly Lela *and* Lula) with more husbands and children lived down over there.

All these people—distracted uncles, sharp-eyed aunts, and running, climbing, kicking cousins—had to love Bonnie, because they were her family. She couldn't wait to be just like Dutchie, knowing all the names and all the shortcuts. She wanted to walk right in those kitchen doors without knocking first.

◆

Grandma took to Billie Jean, who was easy to appease with a crust to gnaw or a yarn doll to finger, and was impatient with Bonnie, who followed her, telling, showing, begging to be noticed.

"Bothersome as a gnat," Grandma complained, waving her hand in front of her face.

Billie hummed softly to herself, but Bonnie sang loud and liked to stand on furniture when she did so. She raised her arms and spun.

"No feet on the table! No feet on the settee! No feet on the bed! No dancing in the kitchen!" Grandma snapped and shooed. "Keep your voice down! You're a little show-off, ain't you?"

Bonnie tried to be more demure, less herself, but in an hour or so, she felt so hemmed in that she hung by her knees over the end of the bed and fell on her head or two-stepped with the cat until a chair tipped over or a canister of flour spilled or the tiny glass donkey from Mexico plunged from Grandma's dresser top and broke two legs.

"Ain't you learned her nothing?" Grandma asked Mama.

"Mama scolds me way more than you do," Bonnie said, standing up for her mother.

But that turned out to be wrong, too, because it made Mama cry.

◆

Mama was different in Cement City. In the mornings now, instead of standing at the stove in her soft robe with her hair uncombed, she sat at the table in a stiff skirt and hairpins and ate what Grandma put in front of her, before leaving the house to sew overalls for the men who worked in the factories. It was a good job, Mama confided, better than stitching bags for cement, like Aunt Elvina did. Was it better than making dresses, the way she had in Rowena? Bonnie wanted to know. This also made Mama cry.

◆

Bonnie cried, too, when Mama went out the door, so loudly and long that, finally, Grandma gave up petting her and paddled her instead, because enough was enough and she might as well have something to cry about. "Time you grew up," she said, giving Bonnie a flannel cloth of her very own with which to wipe the cement dust off the furniture.

Bonnie always started in Mama's room.

"Goddamn slippers!" she said, collecting the flannel house shoes Emma had abandoned haphazardly in the middle of the floor—in this way, too, Mama had changed her ways—and lining them up under the bed. "Stay put where you belong!"

She scolded the crumpled nightgown, as she lifted it off the floor: "Mama doesn't have time for this nonsense." She pressed it to her face and breathed Mama's smell, the smell of before, and then stuffed the gown under Mama's pillow.

She poked her finger into the blue glass jar of Oriental Cream that Mama had left open on the nightstand, leaving a sizable divot.

"Mama will be home soon," she promised, closing the door behind her.

CHAPTER 7

On summer mornings, Bonnie lay half-asleep on the sweat-dampened sheets in the sweltering attic, waiting for Dutchie's hoarse voice, incongruous in the throat of a pixie-faced, yellow-haired girl, to carry up the stairs and start her heart.

"Bonnie! Buster! You up?" Dutchie opened the screen door with a yank that made the hinges squeal and let it bang behind her.

Instantly, Bonnie would be pulling on the flour sack dress Mama had made for her to play in, so her wash dresses would stay nice for school. Grandma didn't have time to feed no layabout kids—she had to get out in the garden before the heat kilt her, and she kept Billie with her—so it was just Bonnie and Buster and Dutchie, with the kitchen to themselves, slicing the biscuits with the sharp knife and lighting the stove to melt whatever was left of the gravy. After that, they ran, through high weeds in fallow fields, plant guts leaving sticky trails on their legs and fingers, into the cool, shadowy woods.

On Saturdays, Aunt Pat gave them dimes for the Orpheum, where behind an unassuming brick storefront, a dark cavern flickered with exotic scenes involving elephants and hoop skirts, chandeliers and batting eyes, in which love was passion and sadness was desolation and bad behavior was outright wickedness. Even milk wagons and washbasins were arresting in the ghostly light and the deepened shades of the pictures. Those vibrant worlds hovered, tantalizingly inaccessible behind Bonnie's eyes long after she'd returned to the pallid Cement City evening. She and Dutchie did their best to elevate ordinary life to the level of dreams.

◆

"Ow! It's hot!"

"Well, quit touching it, Bonnie, for heaven's sake!"

Bonnie sucked her burned fingers, while Dutchie lifted the potato out of the dirt and ashes with a fork.

They'd made the wigwam of feed sacks, draped over a framework of sticks, a house of their own between the garden and the barn. The sun shone through the loose weave, giving the inside a soft, yellow glow. Buster didn't have much use for it, except as a prop to surround or squat behind for cowboys and Indians, but that was just fine with Dutchie and Bonnie. They didn't want any old boys in there anyway, and no baby Billie either, pulling at the sticks, making the whole thing fall down.

They liked it with just the two of them, lying on the matted grass and weeds and staring up at the buttery light, smelling the corny-molassesy smell of the feed sacks and the bitterish, green smell of the crushed weeds, floating in a world apart from Grandma scolding and aunts finding chores.

They were Indian squaws, wrapped in wool blankets, warming their hands around a real fire, tying the chamois clothes Pop-Pop used to wash his wagon around their feet as moccasins. Whose idea was it to take matches from the can next to Grandma's stove and actually light the little pile of tinder? It never occurred to them—Dutchie could say this with certainty—that this was what was meant by playing with fire. They weren't playing; they were roasting potatoes. Bonnie had read how you could bury them under the blaze and taste the fire in their powdery flakiness when they were done.

"Dutchie! Bonnie! Run down to the Coakers' for some meal!"

"In a minute, Grandma!"

Bonnie loved fire, the mesmerizing motion of the flames, repetitive, yet unpredictable, their patterns always shifting. She put her bare palms close to test how long she could stand the pressure of the heat. That day they'd built the fire higher than they'd ever done before, not just a thin, tentative flicker, but a flame-leaping, green-twig-popping mini-conflagration with two bakers underneath.

"Right now, girls, or I'm coming in there and draggin' y'all out."

They threw off the blankets that made them Indians and ran as little girls the half mile to the Coakers' and waited on one foot and then the other for Mrs. Coaker, who moved slow as a slug, banking up the dirt around her potato hills, leaning the shovel up against the fence post, putting one deliberate foot in front of the other all the way into her kitchen.

"You ain't brought no sack? How about a bowl? You got you a bowl? Well, what am I gonna put the meal in, then, I wonder?" She scanned her kitchen walls dreamily, as if a sack might slither out from between two boards if she happened to fix her eyes on the right spot.

"Here, Miz Coaker, just pitch it in," Bonnie said, making a sling by holding up the hem of her skirt.

Bonnie moved her legs as fast as she could, never minding that her drawers showed, but the fire was so strong and fast that it had already eaten through the wigwam, torn across the yard, and was attacking the back fence, where Grandma Mary and Aunt Pat were beating at it with brooms.

Bonnie was too big by then to lie over Grandma's tiny knees, so Grandma held her tight to her chest with one arm, while she reached around with the other to wield the brush. "I'll learn you!"

◆

Bonnie would pass her fingers through flame and swallow stuff that scorched her throat and tasted like poison. She would throw herself into water of any depth or darkness and climb into the high, fragile branches of any tree on which she could get a purchase, but she wouldn't touch the gun.

◆

The gun sleeps under Pop-Pop's pillow.

"Pop-Pop," Bonnie thinks, is a foolish name. It bears no more relation to her heavy-browed, eight-fingered grandfather than Buster's popgun bears to the pistol in the old man's bed. To Bonnie, her grandfather is Krause. At least, in her mind, she calls him Krause; to his face, she doesn't dare call him anything.

◆

"Come on!"

Dutchie's fingers are locked around Bonnie's wrist.

Bonnie hangs back with her shoulders, making Dutchie pull, but she lets her feet lead her forward. She likes feeling a little bit scared; it's an opportunity for daring.

The bedroom embodies Grandma and Krause. Its two plain-framed windows, hung with yellowed curtains trimmed with old-fashioned lace, are stern and correct. Under the bed's dark wooden headboard, the mattress sags in two ditches, as if ghosts are resting on the faded Lone Star quilt. On Grandma's bedside table is no pretty jar of Oriental Cream, but a gray ceramic pot half-full of foul-smelling ointment, a brown bottle that reads "Paine's Celery Compound" in raised lettering, and a tin of tablets.

"Go on."

As usual, Dutchie has claimed Grandma's side, so Bonnie has to go over to Pop-Pop's, where the ditch is deeper and the table holds just a hurricane lamp and a *Farmer's Almanac*.

Giggling nervously, both at the thought of Krause's head lying on the pretty puff, edged with crocheted lavender blossoms, and of what lies beneath it, Bonnie raises the pillow with two hands.

The pistol's single black eye stares. The gun is meant to be feared and obeyed, like her grandfather himself, who to Bonnie's mind is the very image of God, with his cold, blue eyes and the sharp hairs that poke from his nostrils and ears, and the fury in his voice when he shouts.

"Pick it up."

Grandma has taught them how to make the beds together, one girl on each side. But before the plumping and the tucking, the gun must be scrupulously removed.

"Baby!"

Holding her breath, Bonnie slides her hand very slowly toward the pistol, but when her fingertip brushes against it, she yanks her hand back. "I can't!"

Tears prick her eyes. Her arms tremble.

"Baby."

Bonnie squinches up her eyes, while her scornful cousin slides her palms flat under the gun and lifts. She places it on the dresser top, safely out of the way, while they pound the pillow back into shape—Bonnie's favorite part—and pull the sheet and quilt up. When Dutchie brings the gun back, Bonnie cautiously traps it with the pillow. Sometimes she puts the almanac on top, for good measure.

CHAPTER 8

"Do they call it Chalk Hill Road because of the chalk they use at school?" Dutchie didn't know and Buster didn't care, but this was the sort of question Bonnie liked to think about. "Or maybe the name of the road made them think it was a good place to put a school."

Chalk Hill School was almost directly across the street from the entrance to the Lone Star. The pounding of the pulverizer that retreated into the background at home stood out here, a regular wallop of metal against rock, the beat beneath the shrieking and yelling of the schoolyard before the bell.

In the schoolyard, Dutchie became Dodie and loosed herself from Bonnie to join the bigger girls. Bonnie ran, swooping and bellowing with the other children, throwing her head back and stretching her arms wide, soothing herself with the pump of her muscles and the rush of air over her skin.

◆

"Girls here!" A big-knuckled hand closed around her arm, changing her trajectory so that she staggered against another little girl with brown curls and a crutch. The grand front entrance, with its exotic concrete pointed archway like the entrance to the church-that-Daddy-built, was for teachers only. The children jostled through smaller doors on either side. Almost at the top of the stairs, the girl with the crutch stumbled and dropped her dinner pail. A single potato rolled out.

"I'll get it!" Bonnie scurried after the spud, but it was tricky to bend and grab and run down steps all at once. A couple of times, she could just about have snagged it, but aware of the laughter coming from the line of girls watching the chase, she missed, a little bit on purpose, so that there would be another step, another miss, more laughter that lifted her like a warm wind.

At the bottom, the spud rolled away, and a big girl raised her black boot and brought it down hard. The flesh spattered against Bonnie's ankles.

The big girl scraped the white paste from her shoe onto the dirt. "You gonna cry, crybaby?"

Bonnie, standing alone at the bottom of the stairs, as the rest marched into the building, obliged.

♦

When Bonnie was angry, she made other people cry. Noel, with ears that pinked when she talked to him, offered her Black Jack gum every morning, pulling a stick halfway up and then holding out the pack, a nicety that impressed her. But when he was captain for Red Rover, he didn't choose her until there was no one left but her and crippled Florence. That afternoon, when she saw him in front of the drugstore where he bought his damn gum, she was on his back with her legs clamped around his waist and a scrap of metal at his throat before she could think. She relished his blubbering.

"Crybaby," she said. "I'll learn you."

She'd cried herself later, in her attic bed. She'd expected him to pick her first. He ought to have known that even though she was small, she could hold on tighter than any of them. They'd have to tear her hand off before she'd let go. Or break her arm, at least.

When she did things like this, Grandma said she'd "flown off the handle," and indeed, in the midst of her fury, Bonnie felt she was whirling through the air, like the head of Krause's hatchet the time it came loose from its shaft and stuck so deep in the side of the outhouse that they'd had to rip the board out of the wall to free it.

♦

Bonnie loved to practice the Palmer method, which connected the letters like the stitches that ran from her mother's sewing machine. Writing forced her to quit looking around the room—which was exhausting—and turned her inward instead. She savored all aspects of words: their rhythms and sounds, and the puzzle of their structures—syllables and letters, bases and prefixes and suffixes, the way rhyme made sentences waltz.

Bonnie's favorite class was elocution with Miss Gleason, who came on Thursday afternoons and didn't frown and sigh like the regular teachers. Instead of the necktie the others wore, Miss Gleason pinned a cameo brooch at her throat, and she touched the tips of two fingers to it with an attractive, sorrowful look, whenever a child's performance especially moved her. Bonnie's often did, as when she recited "Gertrude, or Fidelity till Death":

> And bid me not depart," she cried: "my Rudolph, say not so!
> This is no time to quit thy side; peace—peace: I cannot go.
> Hath the world aught for me to fear, when death is on thy brow?
> The world—what means it?—mine is here; I will not leave thee
>   now!

"She was marvelous! Such a talent!" Miss Gleason tilted forward, as she expressed her approbation to Emma Parker after one school performance, and Bonnie, beside her, unconsciously mimicked her stance. "Won't you let me take her home next week after school? You see, I promised her ice cream, if she could do it all the way through without a single mistake and, as you saw . . ." Miss Gleason lifted her hands, palms upward, while Bonnie clasped hers together—like Gertrude—in the proper elocutionist's gesture of pleading.

◆

Miss Gleason wasn't the only one who singled Bonnie out.

"What I need," Mr. Godfrey said, "is some of that there charm."

Mr. Godfrey was Mabel Jean's father, and he'd approached Bonnie after another school program. He was running for city council, he explained, and he wanted a girl to ride along with him the next afternoon "and just look cute as a button."

"Hadn't you better take Mabel Jean?" Bonnie asked.

Mabel Jean stood beside her father, one hand masking her face from nose to chin. Her recitation, though accurate, had been monotonous, and if she resembled a button, it was the dull metal kind that Bonnie's mother attached to the tops of overalls.

"I've got to save Mabel Jean for the speech," Mr. Godfrey said in a booming voice that made his daughter wince. "When the family's up onstage."

The upholstery in Mr. Godfrey's car was a soft, tufted red, and he was a more skillful driver than Miss Gleason. He crooked his elbow around Bonnie's knees to steady her, while he steered with one hand and held a megaphone to his lips with the other. "Godfrey's your man! Win with Sam!" he boomed through the neighborhood.

People stopped and turned to see what the ruckus was about. When Bonnie waved, they waved back and smiled.

"Thata girl! That's the way to get 'em!" Mr. Godfrey said. "Blow 'em kisses, why doncha?" So she did that, too, and they cheered and clapped their hands around her kisses and loved her.

◆

Bonnie reached the pinnacle of her public success as the youngest member of the subjunior team representing Cement City in the Dallas County Scholastic Literary Contest. She'd filled three notebooks with words, four columns to a page, by the day of the contest, when the whole family traveled to Fair Park to watch her compete. From the streetcar, she watched the little slipshod, unpainted wooden houses and the dirt streets of West Dallas give way to a stretch of green and brown marshland and then the viaduct, that triumphant monument of cement that she'd learned about in school. Cement City was geographically close to Dallas, but a young girl from that town could have no business in Dallas proper, and this was the first occasion on which Bonnie had crossed the Trinity River.

On the far side, the sudden rush and crush of buildings seemed to explode at her. Downtown Dallas was too full and too brilliant to take in, with automobiles darting around the streetcar and people streaming past big windows that flashed with colors. Tall, block-long structures, important with columns and fanciful with curlicues, were studded with windows that hinted at hundreds more people behind them. She stored the details to examine later, along with her impressions of the region that lay beyond, where the buildings thinned, and houses, as big as her school, took their place behind neatly shaped trees planted in even rows.

Waiting for the competition to begin, Bonnie ate cold fried chicken and bread-and-butter pickles from the picnic basket and cuddled and cooed at babies and let a boy buy her a Ward's Orange Crush. On the stage, she spoke into a microphone, over and over, until she was the very last one standing, and she saw Pop-Pop down below jump to his feet, cheering, and Mama and Grandma hug each other. Then a man whose hair had the oily scent of Brilliantine hung a blue ribbon around her neck and announced her name to the entire world: "Bonnie Parker of Cement City."

Despite Bonnie's victory, when all the events were finished, the Brilliantined man awarded Highland Park, which had gotten firsts in lots of categories, the silver cup. No one questioned the results; after all, Highland Park, newly built "Beyond the City's Dust and Smoke," as its developer claimed, was lovely. The children who lived there were obviously winners, Bonnie thought, fingering her ribbon and seeing in a new light those who'd accompanied her from Cement City with their greasy food wrappings and loud voices.

When they got home, Grandma made Bonnie's favorite red beans and rice and Pop-Pop was the show-off, taking the grosgrain loop around to all the neighbors.

"Just think, you're the best in all of Dallas, Bonnie!" Mama said. "All of Dallas!"

"Well, the best subjunior speller," Bonnie said. She could afford to be modest in the face of such praise, but she was also sincere. She knew already that spelling wasn't everything.

Nevertheless, it was a great deal to be the best at anything. She was proud. Her daddy, Mama assured her, would have been very proud.

The next day, the *Dallas Morning News* announced that Highland Park's award had been a mistake. In fact, Cement City had the winning seventy-one points, to which Bonnie Parker, first in subjunior spelling, had made a significant contribution. Bonnie clipped the article and slid it into the bottom of her drawer.

For many nights after that, Bonnie lay in bed with her eyes on the glowing hive of the Lone Star across the fields and dreamed that winning the spelling bee had marked the start of her real life. She reviewed the awkward, triumphant walk across the stage to collect her ribbon, when the tallest buildings of Dallas had been visible in the west and the applause from the crowd rolled out a carpet of sound to carry her forward. She was convinced she'd reached a launching point from which it wasn't difficult to imagine herself on the far side of the windows set in the green roof of the Adolphus Hotel.

CHAPTER 9

As it turned out, however, the glory of the Literary Contest was an apex above which no further handholds were evident. The heat that in previous summers had acted as a sort of engine, driving her and Dutchie over the countryside, oppressed Bonnie that year, while at the same time, she felt distracted, as if the black crickets that were everywhere—glancing with their hard shells against arms and cheeks, gripping at ankles and necks with their hooked feet, and landing with horrid plops on plates of food—were also scrabbling inside her head.

The household loosened and shifted around her. Wylie and Elvina . moved out, and soon after that Grandma woke to find Krause's body still and cold in its mattress ditch beside her. Aunt Millie and Uncle Dink moved their family to New Mexico from which they sent a postcard of the entrance to Carlsbad Caverns. Strange, spiky plants with huge blossoms like clusters of jewels surrounded a natural fortress of orange rock, which had at its center an open stone mouth, like the cave of Ali Baba. Bonnie pinned the card to the wall beside her bed.

She had hopes for Cement City High School, and she liked the bustle and scramble of it, the streaming through the halls that was a more grown-up version of the swirl of the playground, but she couldn't find her footing there. The high school teachers were impatient with her ready emotion. In English, when she interrupted a presentation of meter once too often to express her raptures over some unrelated aspect of the poem under discussion, the teacher shut her up. "I think the class could stand to hear a little less often from Miss Parker," he said.

She might have been discouraged had she not been distracted by her own body, which was engaged in a process at once mundane and miraculous. There was nothing vague and insubstantial about becoming a woman. It was an earthy affair that demanded endurance and attention. Monthly, Bonnie rocked over waves of ache while she stared at Aunt Millie's postcard. Sucked in through the stone mouth, she wandered through dark, subterranean passages, dreading whatever she approached but irresistibly drawn deeper into increasingly narrow spaces.

"That's just the way it is," Mama said, although she promised it wouldn't be so bad later on. Womanhood, like a colt, apparently required breaking. Grandma clucked, expressing both sympathy and satisfaction that another wayward child had been tamed by initiation. Hers, she confided, had hurt like the dickens, too, and she swelled with advice: a hot water bottle pressed against the abdomen, deep breaths to fill the womb with oxygen, a thick book—the Bible worked well— tucked under the back. But the only real relief, she warned, was a baby. And God knew that brought its own problems.

◆

"It's just the pink part you want to color," Dutchie said in the tone in which she'd once instructed Bonnie to hop between jumps as she turned the rope. She conveyed a glistening drop of lacquer onto Bonnie's fingernail with a brush the size of a toothpick. She'd already filed the five long nails Bonnie currently possessed—three on one hand, two on the other—to form points. "When it's dry, I'll put a little white on the moon and the tip." Dutchie splayed her own fingers to demonstrate. The white bits were uneven, but that had no bearing on the overall effect of feminine allure.

In school, where nail enamel wasn't allowed, Bonnie kept her fingers curled and her hands in her lap. At home, she spent far more time examining her pores and rearranging her hair—amazed she'd never noticed these features before—than conjugating verbs and turning numbers inside out. She read less and wrote more, diary entries and fragments of poetry that scratched ineffectively at an overwhelming itch of feelings. Performing well in school seemed a childish exercise when compared with the serious occupation on which she'd now embarked: love.

CHAPTER 10

Bonnie tucked herself against Roy Thornton, as they drifted down the halls, so his six feet could pull her above "the madding crowd," as she put it. She hadn't read that book, but she liked the sound of the title. Being with Roy made her think of the song: "When I am king, dilly, dilly. You'll be my queen." She sang it softly, tipping her head back so she could admire his profile. "Roy means king, you know."

He didn't. French was for girls and sissies.

While Mr. Ranzo labored at the blackboard, demonstrating how to find the area of a cone, Bonnie bent a corner of her paper, pressed the folds sharp with the back of her shell-pink nail, and tore off a perfect, equilateral triangle.

"Let's get married!" she wrote in red ink. She drew a heart around the words, folded the paper, and slipped it to Roy.

Her mother tried to talk Bonnie into taking time to grow up before becoming a wife, but Emma's resolve was weak. With her own brief marriage forever bathed in the light of happier days, Emma remained as romantic as her daughter. Besides, caring for a husband and children was a worthy ambition—it had been Emma's own. Most of all, however, she was somewhat in awe of her bold daughter's certainty and her determination to snatch what she desired, qualities Emma had never possessed in any great quantity. In a test of wills, Bonnie was the stronger. She would be just like all the others, like Emma herself had been, married the minute she could pass as a woman.

◆

Bonnie wanted a real wedding dress.

"Just to wear the one time?" her mother said. "When you find the tree the money grows on, let me know."

But Emma had been secretly delighted to provide this luxury and bought a pale yellow fabric—more sunrise than lemon pie, she and Bonnie agreed—and sewed a special gown from a *McCall's* pattern. A few days shy of her sixteenth birthday, the new Mrs. Thornton was drinking grape juice to toast the church ceremony, keeping her chin well forward to avoid stains.

While aunts and uncles wished her happiness, she twisted the unfamiliar-feeling ring on her fourth finger. She'd chosen a pink quartz solitaire that caught the light, flanked by gems cut in modern rectangles that could pass as diamonds. Roy had insisted on a tungsten band—"Harder than steel," he said. "Made to last."

Roy extended his part-time job slinging bags of cement into full-time hours, and on the strength of his paycheck, they rented a little house. Bonnie had the fun of furnishing it with wedding gifts—a rag rug from Grandma and a secondhand divan from Roy's parents; a tablecloth patterned with bluebonnets from Dutchie and a set of glass dessert bowls that her girlfriends had bought at Kress's. She supplemented these items with jelly jars and a few chipped plates, a mattress purchased on layaway, and the candlewick spread from the bed she'd shared with Billie.

Once everything was in place, however, she was uneasy. When she was by herself, with nothing to do but chores, the hours dragged, gummy and unsatisfying; she felt colorless and out of focus, like Dallas's gray-tinted sky. At the end of the day, she perched on the edge of the divan, flipping through magazines she'd looked at so often that she'd worn the ink off the pages, waiting for Roy, but when he finally came in, he smelled not like himself but of the factory and drink. She began to notice the way he bent over his plate to shovel food into his mouth and his habit of laughing through his nose. What had they talked about back at school? She felt trapped in a tiny house with a dull and distasteful stranger, and anxiety turned her saliva acrid and quickened her heartbeat.

"Let's go visit my mama," she'd say, as soon as she'd cleared the supper dishes.

It was even worse when he stayed out at night doing what all.

By eight o'clock, she would give up on being a wife and go home to Olive Street, where she helped her sister study for her history test—" 'Give me liberty or give me death' will be on for sure, Billie"—exclaimed over Buster's new girlfriend's new shingle, or just visited with her mama about any old thing. There was nothing exciting going on in that house, but at least there were human beings doing something!

When Roy finally came home at three or four in the morning, he'd throw a wad of bills on the table—fifteen, twenty, once even sixty-eight dollars, as if he were a hunter unshouldering his kill—and the next night he'd squire her out for fried chicken or chicken-fried steak and to see a picture at the Old Mill, and for a few hours she felt proud to be a grown-up married woman. But in bed, she might have been any old mound of flesh; he seemed no longer to care that she was Bonnie. Afterward, alarmed by his sprawling, heavy form, she would panic.

"Wake up, Roy!" She pushed at him with both hands. Her heart was beating so hard she was surprised that she couldn't see it pushing at the skin of her chest.

His eyes opened only a slit.

"I dreamed my mama died. Go and see if she's all right. Please!"

He flung one sleep-heavy arm over her, pinning her to the bed. "She's all right. It was just a dream."

But the fear had her like a runaway horse. "I'll go myself, then. Let me up!"

"Now, c'mere, honey," he mumbled. "I'll make you feel better." He wrapped his arms around her and began moving his hips against her, but she thrust him off.

"No! Roy! I need my mama! Go get her, please!" She was crying now, gasping for breath.

When she opened the door to the two of them, her relief was instantaneous. "Aw, Mama, I'm sorry. You look so tired. You c'mon into bed with me, now. Roy won't mind, will you, honey?"

And he didn't mind really, just rolled himself into a blanket on the divan and went back to sleep, while the "girls" whispered in the bedroom.

Bonnie did her best to forestall her anxiety. She'd ask her mother to come over after work, complaining that no one had bothered to teach her to cook, and Emma sighed, thinking of how often she and her own mother both had tried. Even now, Bonnie was clearly more interested in the company than in the cooking.

While the tough hocks and shanks were breaking down and the dry beans were softening in the fatback drippings, Bonnie brought out cards, and she and Mama and Roy played rummy on the front room rug and sipped the moonshine Roy brought home. And then, of course, Mama had to stay and eat with them in their tiny kitchen. Bonnie ate her own dinner leaning against the stove because they only had the two chairs and, anyway, they couldn't fit more than two plates on the little wooden table. When Emma stood to go, Bonnie ran to the bedroom for an extra blanket.

"Don't you want to stay, Mama? You don't want to walk all that way home now."

Her mother had to laugh. "All that way home" was only two blocks, but often she stayed anyway, although it meant sleeping in her slip and hurrying home at dawn to fix herself for work. It was hard to refuse Bonnie when she needed you.

"You two might as well just move on back home," Emma finally said, after two months of such sleepovers.

Bonnie and Roy didn't hesitate. They were both relieved to quit playing house and have a mama again.

◆

Bonnie had intended to have a big family, eight children at least, maybe twelve. She loved babies so much that she and Billie regularly went around the neighborhood collecting them, so they could host baby parties. Babies were so darling, lifting their plump arms to be held, staring at whatever caught their attention, touching things with their clumsy, insistent fingers. Bonnie knew that a baby of her own would be a bundle of love that was all hers and would stay with her always. Not like her husband, whose dalliances stretched to ten days in August and eighteen days in October. He left again in December, and in January, when he still hadn't returned, she got a job waiting tables at Marco's Café in downtown Dallas. It wasn't until the following January that he finally showed up, having given Bonnie plenty of time to rage, stew, grow self-righteous, mourn, and finally shrug. Although his heavy brows accentuated the pleading in his eyes, she couldn't dredge up an ounce of the feeling that once had propelled her.

"You're lucky you didn't have no babies," Emma said.

But later, Emma would wonder if a baby might have saved her daughter. A baby didn't make you forget what you wanted for yourself, but it got in the way of those wants so often with its crying and its gurgling and its smiling and its needing to be fed and needing to be picked up and needing to be changed and needing to be rocked and needing to be soothed and needing to be carried and needing to be taught and needing . . . well, everything, that it made you see that there was no point in wanting for yourself. Maybe wanting for yourself was a childish dream better grown out of.

Emma believed that Bonnie would have been a good mother—doting, energetic, fierce. But she understood her daughter well enough to know that Bonnie's never-born children had been spared a mother who could not have found happiness in helping babies through their helplessness. And at least, Emma would think bitterly, Bonnie had had no daughter to make her suffer.

CHAPTER 11

At Marco's, around the corner from the massive red courthouse, Bonnie became acquainted with a number of policemen. Laws, in her experience, were no different from the laundrymen who'd yelled their orders across the alley back when she worked over at Hargraves. Laws were just boys who wanted her to smile at them. She let them call her "Blondie" and "Doll" and "L'il Bit" and caught their jokes and tossed them back, so they could consider their cleverness duly appreciated. It amused her to keep the ball in the air.

"Hey, Two Sugars, how come you ain't a law? You look like one."

Ted Hinton always reddened when Bonnie used the nickname she'd coined for the way he doctored his coffee. "As a matter of fact, I'm considering a job in the sheriff's office."

"What's wrong with the PO?"

"I'd just as soon get around more, do something different every day."

"Me, too."

"Too bad you can't work for the sheriff."

She shrugged. "I hate anything to do with a gun. Tuna fish on white?"

He nodded.

He was ready, when she set the plate in front of him. "Bet you could make it in pictures."

"I'd hate to leave my mama and go way out there alone. But," she added over her shoulder, "I'll do something. And when I do, you'll know, because I'm going to write poems all about it."

◆

Men of all sorts asked her out, producing a dime, as if that slight, silver disc was the moon. Their eyes would tell her to take note of the coin being slid under the tilted saucer, while their mouths said, "How about that dance over to the Ridgeway later on?" or "Would you like to see the picture show?"

"Which show? *The Wild Party*?" She could be a blond Clara Bow; everyone said so.

"Any show."

She generally went with him—any him. She hoped for love, but she wasn't expecting it. At least going with boys gave her something to do.

Bonnie and Emma consulted each other about her outfits and makeup, and they agreed that Emma's answering the door added a touch of elegance. "Your beau's here, Bonnie."

Usually they had fun; she wasn't fussy. She liked a show or a dance, but she was happy to have just a walk through Fair Park or a fast ride under the stars. She wasn't any good at judging which were nice boys, though. If they liked her and their manners were decent enough, then she went along, grateful to be asked.

"You shountna gone with that boy," Emma would say later, when certain ones made Bonnie cry. But she didn't know any better than Bonnie who was nice and who would turn out to be "a disappointment," as Emma put it, until it was too late.

Like that fellow Tom Ketchup-and-Eggs. He'd been all right while they walked down Elm Street, quaffing the fizzy, frothy, inexhaustible cocktail of light and color, admiring the shopwindows, festooned with hats and jackets and hair tonics and wedding cakes—all the bounty of the sleek city, assessing the coming attractions at the Ritz, which advertised iced air, and the Capitol, crowned with an angel of lacy white lights. Bonnie acted clingy and cool, swaggering and simpering by turns, for the fun of it, assessing her performance by means of her reflection in every bright windowpane. He bought her pork chops and black-eyed peas at Minette's and knew how to get into the back room afterward to drink whiskey. But when he opened the door for her at the Pantages with a flourish, she wasn't sure if he was playing along or mocking her.

When the movie let out, Bonnie nearly tripped over a woman—Mexican or Indian or Negro or maybe just dirty—who'd plopped herself in the middle of the sidewalk. She had a baby in her lap, and she stretched out a filthy hand palm up.

"Oh, look at that darling!" Bonnie opened her own hand, clean and red-nailed, to her beau. "Give me two cents."

"Give your own money," he said.

She had some coins—her mother had taught her never to be without carfare—and she dug them from her purse and put them in the woman's hard palm.

In the streetcar back to South Dallas, where Bonnie now lived with her mother and Billie, she sang softly bits from the picture, but she knew from his sideways look what he was up to.

They'd barely walked a block beyond the light under which the car had dropped them, when he said, "I seen you, you know."

"What are you talking about?" Bonnie lifted a foot to push a finger between her new T-strap and her pink toes, where a blister had begun to sting.

"I seen you giving away food in the alley. Behind the café."

"So? What are you? The manager's stooge?"

"You're a soft touch, ain't you?" He reached one hand around her neck to pull her to him. Normally, she enjoyed necking, but she didn't like him, and his fingers felt disgustingly rubbery on her skin.

"Sorry, honey," she said, twisting away. "The bank's closed." She held up her left hand and touched the ring around her fourth finger. She still wore it, even if Roy Thornton was long gone, having sold her down the river when he went up the river. That was the clever way she was thinking of describing her marriage in a poem, although the statement was more poetic than accurate, seeing as how Roy had several times wandered off from married life before he'd ended up in the pen.

But he laughed. "The faithful little wife? I'm not buying it." He pushed her into a doorway and pinned her between his arm and his chest, while with his free hand, he began to hike up her skirt.

She kneed him hard, where she knew it would hurt, but although he crumpled, he didn't release her. Instead, he dragged at her, yanking her to the ground with him.

The idea that he thought he could take advantage of her, that he believed he was powerful enough to make her weak and scared and vulnerable, angered her even more than his pawing. The piece of razor blade she kept in her compact came easily to hand. She held it to his jugular and pressed to slit the skin, so that he grabbed at his neck in shock and pain.

Her blisters burned as she ran, but she savored the sensation as an expression of her fury. In a block or two, however, the tears began, and she stopped, exhausted. Sniffling, she slipped off her shoes and soothed her soles with the soft dirt. He'd been too surprised to follow her. They were always surprised at what a fluffy little thing like her could do.

The wooden floor at Marco's was pale along the stretch where every waitress's path converged, the varnish rubbed off by so many Mary Janes treading the same dozen boards. Some days, Bonnie knew that she was going to be a waitress for the rest of her life; she was going to wait and wait and wait until she died.

"You best hang on to that job. You're lucky you got someplace to work at," her mother said, whenever Bonnie complained of the go-nowhere, do-nothing quality of her life, which, to her credit, was not as often as might be expected of someone with her aspirations and temperament. "And, by the way, you best quit playing Lady Bountiful with Marco's food. He's told me twice now that he's had enough of it."

But she couldn't give up the feeling she got from giving away a meal to someone that she could see didn't have enough money to fill his hunger.

"How many slices of chicken come on the sandwich? If butter's extra, I don't want none. No tea; just water for me, thank you." Their tongues would sneak out and work around their lips as they watched other people's food come out of the kitchen.

"Never mind this old check," she'd say, tearing it off the pad with the flourish of a drum majorette and stuffing it into her apron pocket. "You're today's lucky winner. Your meal's on the house."

They'd gawk and sometimes protest but finally would look up at her with a gratitude that was almost love, adoring subjects of a generous queen. The best was snitching rolls and scraps of meat from the kitchen for the kids who came prowling around the alley.

Marco didn't fire her, but she lost her job all the same when Marco's joined the other cafés and bakeries, the millinery, the hardware store, the notions shop, and the butcher that had already closed. Bonnie baby-sat; she cleaned some houses; she accepted a little something from the men who took her out, a thank-you for pleasure supplied. She needed money, but she wasn't desperate for it. She was young; she had no children to feed; she lived with her mother who still had her job sewing overalls for the men who made the cement. But she was desperate in a more general way about her prospects.

Her dreams had been grandiose and gaudy, if predictable and in-substantial. They'd tended to involve wailing jazz and fuchsia silk, arm-loads of red roses and dramatic close-ups. She'd practiced shuddering her shoulders in case she was called upon to weep on cue. She'd also designed a cover—powder blue—in anticipation of her first collection of poetry, with the title—*Texas Treasures*—and her name embossed in florid golden script.

Although she continued to work on her poems, she'd learned to accept the fading of those bright dreams as the price of adulthood. But with the closing and shuttering, the painting over of picture windows, and the boarding ups, even her more realistic hopes had become scruffy. All around her, life was squeezing in and grinding down.

As in that summer before high school, a discontented, wearisome feeling permeated her days, except when she could get a pop of sweet dreams. She didn't let herself do that too often. She could see where that would get her: a spot on a street corner, like those sagging floozies, hideous Sleeping Beauties who closed their eyes and let themselves be taken by the men and the drugs and the booze in turn.

And then her friend Barbara, who'd been supplementing her modest income from a Dallas hairdresser's by inviting men into her bedroom, ended up with a broken arm and needed help. Bonnie and Emma agreed that at least this would be something different.

◆

Mostly, staying with Barbara had been fun, like playing house, but sometimes Babs pushed too far. "Get the door, would you, Bonnie?"

"All right," Bonnie answered. "Although," she said to the pot of beans she was boiling with chopped onions and a ham bone, "I don't see why having an arm in a sling keeps a person from answering a door."

The caller's hat was in his hands, and his dark, wavy hair was parted and slicked back in the way of all young men. He ran her up and down with lively brown eyes. "Hey. You ain't Barbara."

"No, I'm afraid I'm not."

"Don't be afraid." He grinned and one cheek dimpled roguishly, as if his whole face were winking at her.

"Who is it?" Barbara called from the bedroom.

"Some boy," Bonnie answered.

"It's Clyde," he called over Bonnie's shoulder toward the bedroom. And then, more quietly, he announced himself to Bonnie alone. "Clyde Barrow."

CHAPTER 13

She hadn't even said "come in" before he entered, sure anyone'd be happy to welcome Clyde Barrow.

"What's cookin'?"

"Red beans and rice," she answered, before she realized he hadn't meant it literally.

He was looking for Barbara's brother, but Bonnie and Barbara were the kind of girls who were quick to offer dinner to the kind of boy he was, even though all they could produce was a feminine portion and the two of them had to fill up on crackers and jelly after he'd gone. When he said he liked the food, Bonnie knew he was saying something else. She wasn't much of a cook.

He asked, could she make biscuits and gravy tomorrow, and then, doubting he would show, she feared she'd been a fool, but at eight he was at the door, smelling of soap.

"I believe you mixed your flour with your milk before you cooked this, am I right?" He held up a little gravy on the tines of his fork.

"That's the way my grandma taught me."

"That's the way I do, too," Barbara said.

"And there ain't nothing wrong with it. Tomorrow I'll show you how I do, though. Fry up the flour first. We'll see which you like better."

Clyde's gravy, which tasted more brown than white, was better. One night he made scrapple and greens, another night, ham hocks and red-eye gravy. He'd learned to cook in the country, he said, when he'd gone to live with his uncle.

"We wountna had nothin' to eat but salt pork and dry beans, if I hadn't learnt myself to cook by thinking what my mama done back on the farm. My mama can make a good dinner out of two stones, if she has to."

He strummed a guitar, while Barbara and Bonnie sang:

> *I hear a train comin' down the track,*
> *Gonna carry me away,*
> *But it ain't gonna bring me back.*

"My sister Nell's husband plays with a band. He might be able to get us some gigs, if we practice," he said.

"I doubt we'll make money that way," Barbara laughed.

"Who cares about any old money?" Bonnie said. "Let's do it. Let's do *something!*"

He started to come by in the middle of the day; he seemed to have nothing to do but court her.

"I see you don't have a job," she said.

"I see you don't, either."

"I would if I could get one."

"Not me."

He'd had plenty. He'd worked on the line at Brown's Cracker and Candy Company; he'd made thirty cents an hour at Procter & Gamble; he'd cut glass.

"I can do anything I set my mind to," he bragged.

He'd been sitting back, picking his teeth with a matchbook cover, but now he sat up straight. "But it don't matter how quick you are or how many ideas you have. It's all 'yes, sir; sorry, sir; right away, sir' all day long and after all that trouble back you go to the Bog with a little bit of pay packet. I can't live that way."

"How're you going to live, then?"

"I get by all right."

He drove her over to White Rock Lake in a Pontiac coupe, and they parked where they could see the big, bone-white moon over the water, although they didn't look at it much.

"Who's this?" He traced the black letters inside the heart inked on her thigh, *R-O-Y.*

She watched his fingers, more interested in them and in the ripple of current they were sending up her leg than in the question, as she was meant to be. "Just some boy who got under my skin."

She raised her hips toward him, but when he pushed his hand between her legs, she grabbed his arm.

"All these names!" she said, planting little teasing kisses inside his elbow. "You're like a book." With a pink nail, she underscored an ornate *EBW*, set over a heart with a dagger stabbed through it. "Who's *this*?"

"Just some old girl."

"Emily?"

"Eleanor."

"Who is Anne?" She pulled her nail through the waves of blue letters. "And Grace?" Her outrage was mock, but she couldn't deny that all those names were an affront to a girl who wanted to believe she was special.

"I don't even know where they are now."

"*USN*? Ursula? Eunice?" She figured he couldn't spell.

"That's the US Navy."

"You were in the Navy?"

"Naw. I tried to join up, but they wouldn't let me in. Bad chest, they said. Could be my heart."

"I don't believe there's anything wrong with your heart." She lightly scratched a Valentine on his chest.

"Want me to put 'Bonnie' there?"

"No. And I do not intend to get 'Clyde' inked on my other thigh."

Tattoos were puerile tokens. Scratching a name into flesh was hardly different from the schoolgirl's game of writing "Mrs. Clyde Barrow," "Bonnie Barrow," "Mr. and Mrs. Clyde Barrow" in the margins of a notebook. She was ready to put away childish things.

"I'll show you where Bonnie ought to be." Supple and strong as a cat, she overbalanced him and pinned him to the seat, her hands on his shoulders, her thighs around his hips.

CHAPTER 14

"Clyde! Come meet my mama!"

Emma had stopped by Barbara's after work.

"Come on in, Mama. Clyde!"

He stepped out of the kitchen, a pink apron tied around his waist, the sleeves of his shirt rolled up, a wire whisk in one hand and the other cupped under it to catch the drips. Bonnie hurried back to him and took his arm, as if he needed an escort to move across the few feet of space.

"Mama, this is Clyde." She looked up into his face, proud as if she'd created him.

He was taller than she was, although not by a whole lot. Emma was struck by how well they fit together; two well-formed people built on a small scale. Bonnie seemed to have attracted a dark-eyed, dark-haired, male version of herself.

"Pleased to meet you, Mrs. Parker." He nodded, his hand still under the whisk. "Can I get you some hot chocolate?"

Emma didn't have much of a sweet tooth. She sipped a little of her drink, while Clyde gulped at his. Bonnie, she noticed, hardly touched her cup.

He had a confidence about him that made him appear relaxed, even though Emma could see that he was exquisitely alert. His hair was combed and his shirt was pressed; he even wore a tie—Emma approved of good grooming. And his eyes were ardent when he looked at her daughter.

"You like him, don't you, Mama?" Bonnie's voice was a whisper. He'd gone back into the kitchen to pop some corn, but the house was very small.

"Well, he looks darn cute in an apron."

"Mama! I'm not fooling! He's . . . well, he's just the man for me. That's all."

◆

He courted her energetically for some weeks in the usual ways—car rides and picture shows, chilly walks around Fair Park where they posed for photos in Edwardian togs and cowboy gear. Love made all of these outings exhilarating—the harsh wind through the open car window invigorated Bonnie; the grubby costumes made her laugh so hard she staggered; the stilted, often silly, dramas she watched with her head on his shoulder transported her—the hero with his dark, soul-baring eyes was always so like Clyde. Clyde told her he was going places, and she believed him. She understood his desire to be special, because it matched her own. But while she only wished and dreamed, he went out and did things. And if those things weren't strictly what he ought to be doing, well, it was her job to improve her errant boy.

"Lazy bastards think I done practically every crime in Dallas. How can I be robbing a garage in Denton and a dry goods store clear over in Mesquite the same night? What do they think I am? Some kind of Slim Jim?" He shook his head, but she could tell he was proud. "I wish I pulled half the things they say I done." When he grinned, she frowned back at him, playing her part.

"You know I don't think that's funny. You got to use your smarts for something better, Clyde." They were entwined on the davenport at her mother's. Barbara's cast had come off a week or so ago, and Bonnie had moved back home.

"Like what, sugar? You tell me what I oughta do."

"You could fix cars at your daddy's service station. Make it into one of those clean places like over in Dallas, with an awning and flower boxes and one of those bells that dings when you run over the cord. Or you could play in the clubs with a little practice. Bring your girl along to sing. Or why not another job in Dallas? You said you never once got fired. You're a good worker. You just got to settle down to something, that's all."

"Tell you what. When you're a famous singer, I'll be your driver, take you round to all your gigs, make sure you get paid what they owe you. How about that?"

"I'm serious, Clyde. What if you get caught?"

"They ain't going to catch me. Them laws don't know the first thing about how to catch a fellow moves around the way I do."

◆

That was why he had to go away for awhile, he explained a couple weeks later. He was standing at the Parkers' door. She could see that he didn't want to come into her house with news like that, and she loved him for his gentlemanly scruples.

"Can't you come in?" She reached for his arm, slid her fingers down until they held his. "You don't have to go right this minute, do you?"

It didn't take too long for her to lace him to her with her arms and legs, as they sat in the front room. "But where are you fixing to go?" She'd asked this twice already, but there wasn't much else to say.

"I told you. Nowhere special. I just gotta go away." He traced the rim of her ear with his nose. "I'll be back."

"When?"

"When they find someone else to bother and forget about me, I guess. I don't know. A couple of weeks. A month."

"A month!"

"C'mon, Blue-eyes, don't be blue."

Mrs. Parker tried to ward off her daughter's unhappiness for as long as she could. "It's so late now. Why don't you stay over? Sleep on the davenport tonight." She nodded at the couch. "Then we can all get to bed," she added, a touch of dryness in her tone.

"Yes, Clyde! Stay here! You don't want to go out now in the dark and cold." Bonnie pressed on him with all her weight, holding him against the cushions, and though he could have extricated himself, he would have had to use a firmness he didn't feel.

"I suppose one more night in Dallas won't hurt."

Bonnie hurried to find a blanket and took the pillow off her own bed. "You comfy?" She knelt beside him to kiss his forehead in the dark room. Her mother had given him a pair of Buster's pajamas and the shirt gapped loosely around his slight chest. "I better get to bed. Mama won't like me being out here when you got your pants off." She giggled.

He smiled at her, a little boy tucked in the covers.

"Good night." As she rose to her feet, she kissed her two longest fingers and held them out to him, as if proffering an invisible cigarette.

He answered with his own chaste fingertip kisses. "Good night."

◆

Bonnie dreamed of a dragon whose wings banged against the sky, which turned out to be the laws pounding on the door. By the time Bonnie and Emma reached the front room, two officers were standing over Clyde, watching him exchange Buster's pajama shirt for his own dress shirt.

"What are you doing?" Bonnie shrieked.

"I got caught," Clyde said.

"Why don't you run like a rabbit?" one of the officers sneered. "Why don't you run the way your brother Marvin did?"

Clyde squinted up at him and pulled one hand through his sleep-mussed hair. "Buddy, I'd hop it, if I could."

He reached for his tie, but the other cop batted his hand away. "You ain't gonna need that."

Clyde only shrugged, but Bonnie gave her emotions full sway. "Don't take him!" She dropped to her knees and raised her clasped hands. She blocked their path to the door.

"Step aside, miss."

"Don't fret, honey." His hands were cuffed behind his back, so the best he could do was dip his head in her direction. "I'll be out in a couple of hours. They got nothing."

The cop who'd taunted him laughed. "If you believe that, you ain't as smart as you look, cookie. Denton wants him; Waco wants him; and I don't even know where else. We're picking up the trash for the rest of Texas."

"What do you want to be rude for?" Emma scolded. "You gotta take him, then take him. You don't have to be rude and scare my daughter."

"Get her out of the way, then," the other cop said.

"Bonnie, you gotta let them by." Emma tugged her daughter's arm.

Bonnie's steadfastness accomplished nothing. The laws finally just stepped around her with Clyde in handcuffs between them.

While Bonnie slammed her palms on the floor in protest, one cop pushed Clyde outside and the second closed the door behind them.

CHAPTER 15

Emma believed Clyde had spent the night in her law-abiding household because he'd thought he'd be safe there, but Bonnie was convinced he'd been caught because he hadn't wanted to leave her—like Cinderella at the ball. Less than an hour after they'd hurried him off, her eyes swollen nearly shut, she'd dressed to take the streetcar to the jail. Her mother said she wasn't fit to go out, but Bonnie was proud to show her grief.

When she'd worked at Marco's, she'd admired the Dallas County Criminal Courts Building, which was practically around the corner. It was not so dramatic as the Old Courthouse, but with its arched windows and stone trim, it resembled one of the better hotels, like the Athletic Club. Now, however, its grandeur cowed her.

The jail was on the fifth floor, visitation on the fourth. The staircase, wide and bright between the sheriff's offices on the first floor and the courtrooms on the second, narrowed and darkened as it climbed to the jury rooms on the third. Visitors going beyond that point were directed by a curt, grim-lettered sign to proceed to the rear of the building, where the windows were barred and the railing was unpainted iron.

At the top of those stairs, a policeman blocked her way.

"He's barely been booked," he said, scornfully, when she gave him Clyde's name.

She nodded, comprehending that some degree of penance had to be suffered before relief of any kind could be allowed.

But later that afternoon, the law continued to refuse to let her in, and the next day he hardly glanced at her before shaking his head, although she'd gone to a lot of trouble to fix her hair and make up her eyes.

"Not unless you're kin," he said, turning the pages of a newspaper at a pace that revealed he was too bored to read them.

"Well, when *can* I see him?"

"I wouldn't know," the man said. "Depends on how busy we are."

There was nothing much going on at that old jail that she could see. Finally, she understood that he had all the power, and she had none.

CHAPTER 16

Although Bonnie couldn't get into the jail, she hoped that her letters could. Every evening, she played the blues and other melancholy selections on the radio and luxuriated in the emotions her words evoked.

> *Mr. Clyde Barrow*
> *Care of The Bar Hotel*
> *Dallas, Texas*

(Not much in the way of wit, but the best she could muster under the circumstances. Her confidence that he would appreciate the joke made her love him all the more.)

> *My Sweet Sugar:*
> *How's my baby tonight? I truly hope you don't miss me as much as I miss you, because I couldn't bear to think of my sugar so blue.*
> *I tried again to see you today but because I'm not your wife, they don't have to let me in unless they durn well please. I guess they don't know I love you until death do us part. You better know that however long this takes, I'll be waiting for you.*

Other boys came over—apparently, it wasn't any more clear to them than it was to the laws that she was now essentially Mrs. Clyde Barrow—but she did not encourage them.

That fool Walter Crump presented her with a heart-shaped box of chocolates. "I brung you a Valentine," he announced, in a way that said he expected a kiss or some such favor in return.

"Well, how sweet. Thank you very much," was all she gave him.

Pointedly, she didn't open the box, but set the garish thing—its shiny, cartoonish shape an affront to the complex, desperate emotions she experienced at the thought of Clyde—on the little table beside the door that served to collect keys and coins, sticks of gum and single gloves and bills from the electric company that no one wanted to open.

She nodded politely at his story about a girl they both knew who'd gotten into a fight with her fellow—"Say, you could hear them barking and howling clear across the river, I'll bet," he said—but she didn't ask questions or tell any stories of her own.

"Ain't you going to open that candy?"

"Not just now. Did you want a piece?"

He sighed. "I guess not."

Pretty soon he got the hint. "I can see you're tired tonight. You sure you don't want to go out and get some air?"

"No, I'd rather stay at home, thank you." She took pleasure in saying it. She smoothed her skirt over her thigh. Its dark gray color pleased her, too. If Clyde had to stay in prison, maybe she'd become a nun.

"Well, you enjoy that candy, then," Walter said from the doorway.

They both looked at the unopened box on the table, he with regret and she with satisfaction.

◆

Well, since I couldn't get in there to see you, I ran over to West Dallas and met your mother.

West Dallas was Bonnie's polite way of referring to the "Bog," the campground across the Trinity that grew like a fungus from the tree trunk that was Dallas proper. There those who'd escaped from farms that could not sustain them, finding themselves barred from a city that prohibited the poor, squatted in a welter of filthy, collapsing tents, until they could keep hold of enough cash to rent four walls. Among them, the Barrows alone had erected a permanent structure, either because that family had been more resourceful than others or because they'd inhabited the Bog so long that they'd despaired of moving away from it. Clyde had told Bonnie how his mama had saved pennies to buy wood and shingles and nails, back when they'd had to sleep under their wagon for lack of even a tent, and how his daddy, in his dogged way, had pieced together bit by bit a shack about the size of a wagon bed.

◆

"You sellin' Maybelline? I ain't interested in none of that junk."

The scuffed, wooden door had hardly opened and already it was shutting.

"I'm here about Clyde," Bonnie'd said quickly. But she didn't know what his people were like. Maybe they'd want nothing to do with a boy in jail.

As she'd hoped, the door opened up again. The woman in the dim space looked like a grandmother, with her gray hair cinched in a severe bun, as if it were more nuisance than glory, a sack-like dress, and a mouth straight and thin as a needle. Like almost all the cropper women that Bonnie had encountered, Cumie Barrow had been worn down to a tough nub. "What about Clyde?"

"Mrs. Barrow? I'm Bonnie Parker."

A girl, maybe ten years old, with cheeks soft and round as dinner rolls, appeared suddenly from the far side of the house, a battered tin plate dangling from one hand. Behind her strutted a bedraggled rooster, its comb ripped nearly in two. "You Bud's new girl?" As if to second the question, the rooster tipped its head to level a black beady eye at Bonnie and then scratched its long, forked claws at the hard-packed dirt.

"I'm Clyde's girl," Bonnie said. "Is that what y'all call him? Bud?"

The girl nodded. She had Clyde's warm brown eyes and the sprightly expression he had when he was happy.

"You must be Marie. Clyde told me how pretty you've been getting."

Mrs. Barrow frowned and her eyes narrowed. Lines bristled around her lips like porcupine quills. "So you're what he's been running around with anymore, trying to impress."

Bonnie had made a mistake, obviously, doing herself up. The very embellishments that made most people—men especially, but women, too—approve of her looks—her fluffy, bobbed hair; her brightened lips; and, yes, her Maybellined eyelashes—made this woman sneer. Almost unconsciously, Bonnie curled her fingers into fists to hide her polished nails. But then she opened her hands and squared her slight shoulders;

after all, Clyde loved the way she looked. "Yes, ma'am," she said. "I suppose I am."

The woman sighed. "Well, you might as well come in and we can worry about him together, then."

Inside the Barrows' house, surrounded by walls papered with the *Dallas Morning News*, they were protected from the chill wind and the rooster, but the room had the airless cold of a freezer. In the places where the newspaper had peeled off, the backside of the exterior boards was visible. Two wooden chairs and a couch-like piece of furniture that looked like it may once have formed the back seat of a car stood with no relation to one another on the wooden floor and crowded the dim space. A shelf jutting out from the wall, supported by two legs, held mismatched bowls and plates and a few odd-sized glass jars. On a small bureau with holes where drawer handles had once been stood a framed photo of a mother and her children, the woman—her hair upswept in a way that made her resemble the rooster and her eyes wide and bright—was recognizable as Cumie only by the somber set of her fleshless lips.

Bonnie seized the picture. "Oh, how darling! Which is Clyde?"

"You can sit down," Mrs. Barrow said, taking the photo from Bonnie's hands, and scooping a cat off the grimy pillow that served as a cushion on one of the chairs.

"I don't know what it is about Buck and Bud," Cumie said, settling herself on the car seat with the cat on her lap. "Elvin ain't like them two. Neither is L.C. And all my girls is good girls. Marie here goes to school pret' near every day."

"Clyde says she's real smart." He hadn't said that exactly, but Bonnie supposed the sentiment would please the girl and maybe the mother, too.

"Clyde give me a bicycle," Marie bragged.

Cumie frowned. "Oftentimes I wish we never came to this city. In the country a body don't get in the habit of wanting. There's nothing to want. No fancy clothes, no guitars, no movie houses, like you got here." She looked accusingly at Bonnie, as if Bonnie had personally sponsored these temptations.

"Nothing to eat in the country, neither." A young woman stood in the doorway, her brown hair in the stiff frizz the cheap beauty parlors turned out.

"Bud's latest," Cumie said, nodding in Bonnie's direction.

"Nell!" Marie exclaimed, brightening at the sight of this older sister.

"Why don't you tell her about the time you had us scrape the paper off the wall, so you could cook up the old paste, Ma?" Nell said. "Now there's a nice story about country living."

Mrs. Barrow snorted. "I ain't sayin' we're goin' back!"

Bonnie stood and offered Nell her rose-tipped fingers. If no one was going to introduce her, she would do it herself. She knew that Nell was for Clyde what Dutchie had been for her—playmate and protector. She'd also been second mother when their first didn't have time even to let her eyes settle on her children's faces and sent various combinations of them to live with this uncle or that. Bonnie wanted Nell, especially, to like her.

"So *you're* Bonnie," Nell said.

He *had* talked about her, then. Bonnie resisted an urge to smile triumphantly at Cumie Barrow.

"He'll get off, won't he?" Bonnie said. "He says they try to grab him up every time someone pinches a dollar in Dallas. He says he'd be a millionaire, if he'd done a quarter what they try to pin on him."

"Oh, to hear him tell it, Bud don't do nothing wrong—so long as he don't get caught," Nell said. "I sort of hope he don't get off. That boy always was one for squirming away rather than taking his medicine, and it's done him no good to get off easy."

"I don't want my boys in jail."

"Well, of course, you don't, Ma. But it's his own fault he's in there, and he's got to take some responsibility for keeping himself out."

"If he gets in, maybe I can go to the governor. Get him a pardon, like I'm fixing to do for Buck."

"If he can get out," Bonnie said, "I know he won't do anything to get himself back in there."

"Well, I hope you're right," Nell said, "but he's got to learn to say no to his own self, and he's a hard one to say no to."

"If he could get himself a good job . . ." Bonnie began.

"Oh, he's had himself plenty of good jobs. But he plays hooky like a job's no different from school and grown-up life's no different from being a kid. He just can't stand to trudge along every day like the rest of us."

"But he has me now," Bonnie said.

"Well, let's hope he gets out, then," Cumie said dryly.

"I heard Frenchy Clause got twenty years," Nell said.

"Clyde isn't anything like Frenchy Clause!" Bonnie exclaimed.

For nearly an hour longer, the women worried the issue—the likelihood of Clyde's release, how he might avoid further trouble—pulling it this way and that, as if they were manipulating a snarl of yarn, looking for the knot they could pick out to straighten the whole mess and roll it into a neat ball. There was nothing to be done, however, except show up at the trial.

"I want Clyde to know I'm going to wait for him," Bonnie said. "As long as it takes."

"There's no call for it," Cumie said. "You ain't married to him, are you? Seems to me just about a month ago, he was going to marry that Eleanor over in Florida."

Bonnie raised her chin. "We may not have known each other long, Mrs. Barrow, but we are in love, and I'm not going to abandon him in his hour of need, no more than you are."

Marie, who'd seated herself close to Bonnie, seemed unable to keep her eyes from Bonnie's bright hair and mascaraed lashes and the pink blush on her fingernails. "Can I sleep over to your house tonight, Bonnie? I got me a nightie."

"If it's all right with your mama."

Cumie granted permission with a shrug. "Whereabouts is it you live?"

"Oh, we live over in Dallas," Bonnie said casually, well aware of the prestige this would convey to a woman stuck in the Bog. Bonnie might have started out in Cement City, but her people—who had the wherewithal to rent a house—were the sort Dallas let in. "I live with my mother."

And this, Bonnie thought, would tell the woman everything she needed to know about Bonnie Parker. Whatever Cumie Barrow thought of her makeup and her open disposition, the truth was that she was a loving daughter, a good girl, just like Nell and Marie.

◆

Emma rose even earlier than usual the next morning, the bed she shared with Bonnie being uncomfortably crowded with the addition of that Barrow girl, and noticed that the envelope Bonnie had carelessly left among the litter of splayed movie magazines and scrapbook clippings on the table was not yet sealed. She slid the letter out and glanced at it furtively. It mooned for some lines about the prodigiousness of Bonnie's love and protested helplessness against the power of such emotion. (As if, Emma thought, her daughter would ever choose not to abandon herself to love.) It strayed into complaints of loneliness before rallying with a paragraph of cheerleading and future plans in which Bonnie declared that she knew better than all the world, better, in fact, than Clyde himself, how "good and sweet" Clyde really was.

In that this mixture of drama, impatience, generosity, and self-pity revealed a Bonnie her mother knew intimately, the letter was reassuring. Nevertheless, Emma felt mildly troubled as she slipped the thin pages back into the envelope. The handwriting itself caused her disquiet. Neat and buoyantly rounded, Bonnie's was still the hand of a callow schoolgirl.

CHAPTER 17

Bonnie dreamed that she was talking to Clyde through the bars of a jail cell, but when he turned and walked away with a casual wave, she realized in that abrupt, unreasonable way of dreams that she was in and he was out. Forty-five minutes later, Dutchie, from whom Bonnie was borrowing a car, was also discouraging.

"You already got a husband in prison," she said, scrabbling in a drawer for the key with one hand, while she slipped bobby pins from her hair with the other. "Maybe you want to wait and see if this boy gets out before you love him."

"That wouldn't be love," Bonnie said.

After she dropped Marie at school, she drove to the Criminal Courts Building and parked near the jail, making sure the car was well out of the road and its wheels were straight. She used the rearview mirror to apply a third coat of mascara, the wand trembling slightly in her fingers. "I'd like to see Clyde Barrow," she whispered to herself, practicing. She would make them let her in. She drew her lipstick around her mouth and watched the bright ring form her demands back at her: "I want to see Clyde Barrow. You let me see Clyde Barrow." She was not going to ask, this time; she was going to announce her intentions. They'd better let her in or it was going to be jam up for someone.

"Clyde Barrow, please," was what she actually managed when she got to the desk. But it seemed she'd hit the right note at last, because the policeman dragged the big record book on the desk toward him and began tracing his finger down the middle of the page.

She was going to get in. What should she say to him? Should she kiss him or wait for him to kiss her? Would there be bars between them?

She rocked from heel to toe and boosted the ends of her hair with her palms.

"No Clyde Barrow here."

"Clyde Chestnut Barrow. He was here yesterday."

"Well, he ain't here today," he said with satisfaction. "I guess he went and saw some other doll when he got out."

"He ain't out. Show me where it says he's out."

He tipped his head to peer around her, as if she were no more than an inconveniently placed architectural feature. "Next."

"Please."

He sighed and turned a page impatiently. Then his lip curled. "Looks like your boy's a two-time loser and Denton's got first dibs. He stole a safe over there about a month ago."

Clyde might have taken a joyride or diverted a few turkeys, but to accuse him of stealing a safe was ridiculous. That the law presumed his guilt made Bonnie want to spit, and her indignation propelled her down the five flights of stairs and into the street.

◆

A week later, well before nine a.m., when Clyde was scheduled to appear, Bonnie, Cumie, Nell, and Clyde's father, Henry, arrived in Denton by bus. Denton was hardly a city compared with Dallas, but its ivory-stoned and blue-cupolaed courthouse, standing in the center of its own square, was just as imposing as Dallas's red one. Inside the doors, Bonnie stood with Cumie and Henry—three dry leaves swept into a corner—while Nell found the courtroom in which Clyde's case was to be heard. Bonnie sat between Cumie and Nell on the wooden bench, using their bones to prop herself up. The judge, with flowing white hair and gold-rimmed reading glasses, looked like God in *The Children's Book of Bible Tales*. Please, God, Bonnie found herself praying; she could tell Cumie was praying, too, and she felt ashamed, knowing that Cumie's prayers were focused on a higher judge.

Cumie knew she'd let the boys get away from her. They'd been sweet babies, the both of them. Well, at least Buck had been easy. When she needed to, she could still recall the easeful content of a Sunday night back in those days, the baby a warm, sweet sack on her lap; Elvin and Artie, her oldest two, rolling a spool on the bare wooden floor to amuse little Nell. Henry in the armchair, his eyes closed, satisfied like a baby himself with what she'd fed him for his supper, asleep probably—he was nearly always asleep if he wasn't standing up, except when he was on top of her. Clyde was just becoming heavy within her then.

And then the spool had rolled close to the stove, and Nell, crawling to retrieve it, had burned herself, and her wailing made the others cry and Henry swear.

She couldn't remember any easy times after Clyde was born. Of course, she wouldn't say that was his fault, although he was a troublesome baby, quick to cry and hard to settle. Almost as soon as he could walk, he squirmed and ran away when she tried to dress him, and while she would have chased him had he been her first, or even her fourth, she let him go. If he wanted to go naked, let him. It wouldn't kill him. If his feet and hands and face were filthy when he went to bed, what difference did it make? The bare mattress he slept on had long been too dirty to get clean.

In them years they couldn't get no money for cotton, so she had to be out all day long with Henry, turning another quarter acre, and even still they had to send the ones who were too little to work—Nell, Buck, and Bud—to her brothers, because they had to eat, didn't they? Them were the years she finally learned to understand her husband, who was often sick and couldn't spare even the energy it took to smile. It was plod or die, and believe you me, many a day she would just as soon died, but her body went on.

Eventually, they'd had to give up and live under the wagon all them years in the Bog, but things were better now that Elvin and Artie had got some money out of the man that had kilt Henry's horse, and they had the Model T truck for the junk. Even more important, Buck had sent them a letter another prisoner had wrote for him at the Walls, swearing that if God gave him another chance, he would renounce the crooked ways that had so pained his mother and father. She'd resolved to get him that pardon from the governor. But she had to concentrate on Bud now. Cumie sat tall and stern-faced on the hard bench, hoping that the judge could see that Bud had a mother who'd set him right.

They had to sit through three other cases in which the prisoner was found guilty with discouraging speed and a startling rap of the judge's gavel, before Clyde, looking like a child scrubbed for church with his hair slicked back behind his prominent ears and his body overwhelmed by an oversized denim shirt, was led in. The guard beside him was taller by more than a head. When Clyde scanned the room and his mouth turned up in a way that wasn't a smile—because who could smile in this situation?—Bonnie knew it was a sign of gratitude especially for her, and she straightened her back to give him support.

She hated the lawyer who was against them from the moment he stood up next to his table, hated him for the sure way he buttoned his coat, and for keeping his eyes on the paper from which he read, not deigning to look at Clyde. "The prosecution will show that Clyde Champion Barrow," he droned—not even getting Clyde's name right!—"along with his brother Marvin Ivan Barrow and one Francis Clause, both currently serving time at Huntsville"—in a wash of panic at the mention of Huntsville, she neglected to follow the thread of his words for a moment—"and removed a safe. That they carried said safe in the back of a truck, which they had also stolen, to 34 Remson Road, Dallas, where they attempted to open it. Failing in this purpose, they abandoned said safe in a field on Route 26, just north of Grapevine, thus demonstrating that they are not merely thieves but also incompetents." A titter rippled through the room, and the hateful lawyer finally looked up from his papers and smirked.

"He has no call to be rude," Bonnie whispered to Nell.

"Let him," Nell said. "If he's calling names, maybe he doesn't have much else."

He didn't have anything, it turned out, beyond the fact that Clyde and his brother and Frank Clause were known associates, and someone had seen a third man, slight with brown hair, in the back of the truck that had driven away too fast from a certain house in Denton.

The judge looked over his gold-rimmed spectacles at Clyde for a long time and pulled absently at a few of the hairs in his bushy eyebrows. "I have no doubt," he said finally, "that if you weren't in on this, you were in on something else, but in this matter, the law is clear. There's not enough evidence to convict."

Cumie lifted her hands and tilted her face to the ceiling. The face

Clyde turned to his family was on the verge of tears, so Bonnie knew how afraid he'd been.

It was done! She had to press her bottom to the bench to keep from leaping off and running to him. But the judge, who had been studying his papers, was speaking again. "You're a popular young man. Waco's waiting for you."

◆

Mrs. Parker decided love had carried Bonnie far enough. "You can't run all over Texas after that boy."

"I'll stay with Mary." Bonnie's cousin Mary was also nineteen, but she'd been married to a truck-driving Waco boy for two years. Emma often referred to Mary's life with an irritating note of wistfulness.

"How're you getting down there? You're not taking that old car. What if it breaks down again? You can't walk back from Waco."

"I'm taking the interurban with Mrs. Barrow."

Emma shook her head. She'd followed Bonnie into the bedroom and sat on the bed, while Bonnie stood in the door of their shared closet, choosing dresses. "Gallivanting all over the state after a jailbird. I don't understand how any daughter of mine grew up to think being attached to a boy in prison was part of the normal course of life. First Roy and now you've got another one to treat you like a dishrag. What would your daddy say? He was a decent man, Bonnie. He had a trade. He built things. He didn't go around stealing what other people worked hard to earn."

Bonnie's recollection of her father amounted to a few indistinct images, heavily influenced by the photograph her mother kept beside her bed. Speculation as to his opinions had no bearing on her decisions. She turned to face her mother, holding a dress under her chin.

Emma shook her head. "Not that one. The almanac says it's going to stay chilly."

Bonnie chose another with long sleeves and a short, matching jacket. "I thought you liked Clyde!"

"He's got charm, that I grant you, and I don't wish him ill, but that don't mean I want him for my daughter!" Emma smoothed the sleeves of the dress Bonnie had laid beside her and folded them over the bodice.

"A boy who brings the police banging into my house at all hours! A boy who's wanted in three different towns! No, that is not the kind of boy I want for you, Bonnie Elizabeth."

"The laws are just lazy. They can't be bothered to find the right person when someone is handy who's got a little bit of a record for something he did way back when." Bonnie held up a knit with a bold stripe.

"That'll travel well. You can't tell me they picked him at random. He may not have done everything they say, but you know as well as I do, if they know who he is, he's done plenty. I wish your daddy hadn't died, then you'd know what a good man was and you wouldn't have anything to do with a boy like Clyde Barrow."

"Times are different now, Mama. A man can't work like Daddy did, because there ain't no work." Bonnie wanted to slam the drawer from which she was selecting underthings, but she kept her hands moving calmly. Only her lapse in grammar revealed her inner agitation.

"You told me yourself, Clyde never was fired. Don't tell me he's stealing to survive." Emma, sensing her advantage, pushed forward. "Bog trash like them Barrows, there's something wrong with them. They just don't care to raise theirselves up. As long as they've got enough drink, they're happy."

With this declaration, Emma, who had indeed been making inroads with her daughter, who, after all, couldn't help but recognize that her feelings did not entirely square with her sense, stumbled.

"Oh, Mama!" Bonnie sat on the bed beside Emma and enclosed her mother's callused fingers in her own soft ones. "I don't believe Cumie Barrow's ever had a sip of alcohol in her life, and that's more than I can say for you. Anyway, Clyde wants better. He'll make good. I know he will, because I'm going to help him." Bonnie had rarely given a thought to the Baptist training that had filled the Sundays of her childhood, but one of those early lessons pushed into her mind now. "I'll be a help-meet for him, Ma," she said, and was herself amazed at how true and right the Bible was. What she'd long perceived as a chronicle of strange desert people and hectoring authority turned out to have been written expressly for her. She felt as if God had cupped a giant palm against her back and had given her a nudge. She had been created, she suddenly understood, to help Clyde.

Her mother, however, was oblivious to God's plan. "Clyde wants too much," she said, shaking her head. "I blame the pictures. Decent living isn't good enough for him."

"Oh!" Bonnie dropped her mother's hands. "You argue one way, you argue the other!" She stood up, nearly crying now with frustration.

"I know, honey." Emma stood, too, and put her arms around her daughter. She wasn't one to argue with love.

◆

The Texas Electric Railway Company cars dawdled and swayed from town to town—Duncanville, Red Oak, Midlothian, Waxahachie—stopping dead at each cluster of plain brick and wooden boxes, the backs of the main streets' false fronts. Had she been traveling with her own mother, Bonnie would have chattered. Plenty of people worthy of comment got in and out of the car, and the anticipation of seeing Mary would have spawned myriad reports of those connected with her branch of the family. Cumie Barrow, however, sat with her hands folded on the Bible in her lap, undistracted by the journey. Bonnie wondered if she was again praying.

"If they send him to the Walls, maybe it won't be so bad with Buck there," Cumie said, finally. "Maybe they can look after each other."

Bonnie nodded, refraining from reminding Cumie that Buck had been the one who'd led Clyde into trouble in the first place. "Who's looking after Marie?"

"Well, she's got her daddy, but Blanche is there." Buck's girl had recently squeezed into the Barrows' shack, intending to stay until Buck was released from Huntsville. "You know Blanche is a preacher's daughter," Cumie went on. "She knows right from wrong and Buck'll listen to her. When he gets out, she'll get him on the right way."

Bonnie had expected the Waco hearing to be like the Denton one, but, whereas in Denton, Clyde had appeared to be an innocent boy nabbed because of his unfortunate association with a scofflaw brother, in Waco, it was obvious that he was a scheming thief who'd assumed a raft of names to cover his tracks—Roy Bailey, Jack Hale, Eldin Williams, Elvin Williams. As she listened, Cumie's sharp face wilted along the edges, like a lettuce leaf in the sun. That lawyer in Denton who'd painted Clyde as a fool was, in fact, the idiot. Clyde had gotten away with money and cars for months and had left the laws stumbling over their own feet. Bonnie's fingers trembled for want of oxygen when the judge announced the sentence: two years for each of the seven indictments.

CHAPTER 18

March 1930

"It's only a .32," Clyde wheedles, as if this meaningless number ought to reassure her. "I drawed you a map of Willy's place, so you can find it."

Bonnie has been holding the hand he's extended through the bars of the bullpen in both of her own. Now, with his other hand, he's forcing the sharp edge of a folded paper between her fingers. He goes on making words—key, mother, sister, hiding place—but she can't spare any attention for them.

"But what do you need it for?" she whispers.

"The One-Way Wagon might come tonight. You got to bring it this afternoon, before I get took to the Walls."

The fourteen-year sentence has been reduced to two, because Clyde, technically a first-time offender, is allowed to serve all seven terms simultaneously. Bonnie, who has stayed on with Mary while Clyde waits to be transported to Huntsville, runs errands for him and some of the other inmates and is happier than she'd expected. Relaying requests to mothers for fresh clothes and molasses cookies, delivering cigarettes and chewing gum, she feels stimulated and appreciated and not inclined to dwell on the months that stretch ahead.

"But they won't let me back in. Only one visit a day."

"If you hadn't of brought your damn cousin yesterday, I could of told you then, but I couldn't in front of her, could I?"

"Well, how was I to know?"

"Let's not argue." Gently, he rearranges their hands, so that his are now doing the holding. "We don't want to wait no two years to be together, do we?"

"Oh, Clyde, let's not risk it. Let's wait and see. You may get a pardon and be out early. Then we can forget all about this and go somewhere and be happy. I'm glad to wait, if that's what I'm waiting for."

He twists his head right and then left, as if unwilling to face what she's telling him. Then, he brings his eyes back to meet hers and renews his suit. "Baby, listen. This jail ain't so bad, but the Walls is a prison and we don't know what might happen to me there." His tightened grip seems to be squeezing tears from her eyes. "Baby, you know once I'm out, we're going to have to git anyway. They're never going to leave me alone, whether I done my time or not. So why not go away now? We can go to Arkansas or Oklahoma. Or how about Louisiana, where they got them pretty pine trees? We can find us a little house there to have babies in."

He adjusts his argument as smoothly as he shifts the gears of a V-8. "Louisiana?"

"You ever been?"

She shakes her head.

"They got moss hanging from the trees like a pack of ghosts. Don't you want to see that?"

"If we go there, you won't ever do anything to get in trouble again, will you? Because I couldn't bear that, honey. I couldn't bear that at all, but especially not if we were so far from Dallas."

"You know I never will. I'll be good, because I'll be with you. That's what the both of us want, ain't it? To be together? Honey, let's get started being happy now, as quick as we can, because who knows . . ."

"Time!"

She contracts her hand into a fist around the folded paper.

◆

Bonnie walks a good portion of the distance home in a jittery state, the hand still clamped around the paper that's jammed deep in her coat pocket. Her shoes clack and scrape on the sidewalk, sounding in her ears as if they belong to a stranger behind her, eerily keeping pace. The cold wind that was at her back, urging her on, when she was hurrying toward the jail, is now blowing in her face. She keeps her eyes down, unable to focus on anything but what rattles and bangs inside her head like a farm truck on a rough track.

She can say the gun wasn't where Willy said. If she can't find it, he can't fault her for not bringing it. Then they can go on as they were.

But the way he shifted his gaze when he didn't like her answer makes her uneasy, as if he might just as soon find someone else who would do what he asks. She tells herself that she ought to appreciate that he isn't treating her like some girl who has to be shielded from danger.

The paper has been torn from a Big Chief tablet, the kind with the lines spaced wide apart that children labor over when they learn to make their letters. Clyde has written an address in East Waco at the top, neglecting to put the *a* in "east." He's filled most of the page with a crude floor plan and drawn a large *X* along the inside wall of one of the two back rooms, probably a bedroom closet. The diagram is hardly necessary, the house being small and simply laid out. But at the bottom of the page, he's included a message that induces her to do whatever he asks: "You are the swetest baby in the world to me. I love you."

It has been well established that Mary's car cannot be borrowed, and before Mary will drive Bonnie to East Waco, they have to wait for the washing machine to finish slapping away at the sheets. And when the machine gives its final sigh, Mary delivers the obvious in her stolid, exasperating way: "Now we gotta wrench 'em." Bonnie tries to get the hanging done quickly, but Mary removes and realigns every piece that Bonnie has crookedly pinned.

"You may say 'how high' every time that boy tells you to jump," Mary says as sternly as is possible with a clothespin in her mouth, "but I don't see why I should."

CHAPTER 19

The house in which Clyde's new friend Willy had lived with his mother and sister is just like all the other houses in the neighborhood, just like Mary's for that matter, and like Emma's back in Dallas; the façade a small wooden square with a triangle on top.

"Why don't you wait in the car?" Bonnie says, feigning casualness. Near the front door, a potted red geranium has grown lopsided, reaching for the sun. Bonnie tips the pot to retrieve the key and then gives it a quarter turn to help the plant correct itself.

The small room at the back retains a mannish smell—a hint of sweat and gasoline—although it has been recently cleaned. A worn pink and green quilt is pulled tightly over the narrow bed and the bleached white case on the pillow is stiff with freshness. The room has no closet, only hooks screwed into the wall. The mark that Clyde has drawn against the back wall denotes a trunk with a pair of broken-down boots on top. Inside is a hodgepodge of men's things. Bonnie removes each item slowly, holding her breath in anticipation of the moment when her fingers will encounter the cold, slippery metal. An oilcan and a rubber mallet; trousers and a jacket in the pockets of which a pistol could be burrowing; smutty magazines she touches only with a finger and thumb, averting her eyes; a leather pouch of marbles and a slingshot—evidence of the former boy; an olive-green sweater, inexpertly knitted—evidence of some woman's interest.

She hasn't opened the curtains and the day is gray, the light dim. Nevertheless, she can see that nothing is left in the trunk. She sweeps her hand along the bottom, not wanting to get off easily, now that she knows she is saved.

She won't have to refuse him and yet she'll run no risk. She ought to thank the Lord. But instead of the relief she might have expected, she feels only frustration. Screwing up her courage to jump recklessly over the abyss has made the prospect of trudging on as before unendurably tedious.

Also, he will be disappointed. He won't gaze at her with gratitude and approbation but will turn away and stare at the floor and hunker into himself. He's put his faith in her, and she's failed. He'll think that she isn't much good. Not a helpmeet for him. He may even disdain her waiting.

She strikes the side of the trunk with her palm. This Willy Turner is an idiot, who doesn't know where he's hidden his own gun. Maybe it's somewhere else in the house. She'll do her best to find it, before she goes to Clyde and admits that she isn't the girl he thought she was.

She's putting the items back into the trunk, shaking the trousers and jacket one last time, although it's obvious from their lightness that they're empty, when she hears Mary's voice at the front door.

"Bonnie?"

"Back here."

"What are you doing?" Mary's head is in the door now. There's hardly space for both of them to stand in that little room.

"Looking for something." The bottom of the trunk isn't quite flush with the floor. Bonnie pushes her fingers under it.

"Well, what is it?" Bending to peer under the bed, Mary knocks against Bonnie.

"If you must know," Bonnie says with both impatience and self-importance, "it's a gun."

Mary rears, as if she's spotted a snake. "What for?"

"Oh, for pity's sake." Bonnie is twisted uncomfortably. The trunk's lid presses against her cheek, while the bottom corner cuts into the flesh of her upper arm. "So Clyde can get himself out of there."

"No!" The bed squeaks in alarm, as Mary sits down hard on it. "No, no, no. I'm not having anything to do with this and you ain't either, Miss Bonnie Elizabeth Parker!"

"I never said you had to have anything to do with it! Go back and sit in the car, why don't you?"

In the next room a wooden cross with a palm leaf tucked behind it stands watch over a bed covered in a white candlewick, darned in several places. Half a dozen women's dresses and a man's black suit hang in the wardrobe. With the press of time beginning to panic her, Bonnie shoves them this way and that along the rod, as if they are flimsy witnesses capable of choking up secrets. She searches between slips and stockings and in the toes of T-straps. She empties a window seat of an afghan, a Parcheesi board, a cylinder of Lincoln Logs, and a Brownie camera and leaves them in a jumble on the floor. She knocks the flowered seat cushions off the chairs and pulls papers out of a small desk.

"Bonnie!" Mary has followed her from room to room, contributing to the search by glancing under each piece of furniture. "You're messing up the house!"

"Better they find a mess than us."

Mary gasps and hurries into the kitchen, where she yanks the drawers from the cabinet and dumps their contents onto the wooden table. Bonnie stirs the flour in the bin, paws through the sugar canister, and removes the bread from the breadbox. She even peers into the icebox.

"Let's stop now, Bonnie. We've looked every place a gun could be. And, honestly, I'm glad we didn't find it. I've never touched a gun and I don't want to!"

"Wait a minute." Bonnie, her head between the borax and the bleach in the curtained space under the sink, remembers Krause and gets to her feet.

She nearly screams when the pistol isn't under Willy's pillow, and she goes to check the other beds without much hope. She's angry with Clyde now for expecting her to do an impossible job, for suggesting with his cute, childish map that she ought to regard this grievous matter as a game of treasure hunt. She hesitates in what is surely the mother's room, sobered by the white expanse of respectability and the stark warning of the watchful cross. Delicately, she peels the spread from the pillow and folds it neatly over itself.

It had been so awkward to lift the pillow cleanly from the bed when she was a child too short to stand over it. Pinching the edges of the pillowcase now, she aches with tension.

This gun is smaller than her grandfather's, barely larger than her fist, but she recoils just the same, as she had as a child, when Krause's pistol had threatened to swallow her with its dark, empty eye. Recalling how Dutchie had lifted it, she does likewise, sliding her palms beneath it, transferring it to the night table beside a bottle of medicine and a Bible.

"Mary!" When her cousin appears, Bonnie nods at the head of the bed. "Help me make this nice, would you? My hands won't quit shaking."

CHAPTER 20

On the way back to the house, Bonnie and Mary keep their eyes on the road. The little gun rides between them, concealed by a fold of Bonnie's skirt and, over that, Bonnie's hand. As if the weapon is emitting a signal, people on the street seem to look at them as they drive by.

At home, they test various places of concealment. Her coat pocket? Too likely to be searched. In a boot borrowed from Mary's husband? Even in their anxious state or perhaps because of it, they can't stop laughing when she pulls the oversized galoshes on.

"How about here?" Bonnie tucks the piece into her brassiere. When the cold metal touches her breast, her chest caves and her shoulders curl inward.

Mary giggles. "Yours aren't big enough to hide it."

Finally, Bonnie uses the belt from one dress to hold the gun in place at her waist and wears a dress with a wider belt over it.

She rehearses in front of the mirror, hunching to create a deep opening at the neck, surreptitiously unbuttoning another two buttons. Quickly, using one shoulder as a screen, she snakes her hand into the *V* of fabric between her breasts and hooks the butt of the gun with two fingers. When she draws it out, she spreads her fingers to hide the piece behind them.

She practices, too, the look she'll give Clyde, as she produces the weapon. "Here you go, baby," she whispers. Or should she say nothing and just look deeply into his eyes? In a movie the very idea of inserting a pistol under her dress would have sex appeal, but in real life, it does not. The hard knot of the gun feels like an insult, a metal fist in the gut, frightening, mean, and grossly out of place. She can't wait to get it off of her body.

"You're gonna get caught." Mary has been watching Bonnie's performance with a sick look on her face. Although the cousins are the same age, Mary often feels like a timid, following little sister when she is with Bonnie, but now she sees that Bonnie is the child, who doesn't know enough to stop at sensible boundaries. It is one thing to have a man in jail—goodness knows, plenty of women do—but they get on with their lives and go about their lawful business on the outside. They don't get stuck in jail, too. The kind of women who go to jail—well, they're drunk or crazy mostly. Or whores. "Bonnie!" Mary bursts out, rushing to her cousin and shaking her by the shoulders, as if to wake her from a nightmare. "Don't do it. You're not that kind of person. Think what could happen."

Bonnie notes that throughout the shaking, the gun stays still, firmly attached to her flesh. "What if it were Buzz in there? You'd be with him, right or wrong, wouldn't you? That's love, isn't it?"

Mary frowned doubtfully.

"I've got to get over to the jail while they're still letting people in. Borrow me your car, Mary. Please."

Mary shakes her head. "You tell him he's got to pay for his mistakes. That's the right thing. That's the only way you and him are going to be happy someday."

"I'll be too late if I walk all that way again. Why doesn't this damn town have a streetcar?"

Mary sighs. "I'll drive you. But I'm not going in."

◆

Bonnie has to sit very straight on the car seat to keep the barrel from poking into her breastbone. Once she's up there with Clyde, he'll guide her, but she has to get in on her own. She hopes the red-haired policeman who likes her is on duty.

Despite her declaration, Mary comes into the lobby, frowning and gnawing at her thumbnail. There she stands, fingering the temperance pamphlets, obviously agonized.

"Siddown, why don't you?" Bonnie hisses. It doesn't help a bit for Mary to look like she's about to shit a fishhook.

The top of Bonnie's head and, in fact, all of her skin tingles, as if she's slightly electrified.

"You been in already." The turnkey, not the redhead, is the one who'd been on duty that morning. "Prisoner's allowed only one visit per day."

"Please, I got to go back to Dallas tomorrow. Let me see him for just a minute and I promise I won't bother you again."

He lets her stand another few seconds, working his tongue at something stuck between his teeth.

"I want to tell him goodbye." She steadies her gaze on the guard's eyes—which are a pretty, pale green—and tries not to look at the distasteful bulge of his tongue and the patches of brutal stubble on his jaw. "I'm going to let him know that I need a man, not a thug. I got better things to do than wait around for him to do his time."

"He ain't gonna like that." The guard lifts his brows.

She shrugs, but takes care to keep the gesture small, so as not to shift her belts or even tighten the fabric bloused at her waist.

He turns the visitor's log so she can sign in her neat, schoolgirl penmanship. "I'll let you up to his cell long enough to give him what for. But mind you make it quick. We don't go in for torture here in McLennan County." He grins, baring yellow teeth.

She doesn't dare even to glance at Mary and she's mindful, as the guard moves past her to open the door, of leaving extra space between his body and hers, so he doesn't accidentally touch the knot of steel. She follows him up the black linoleum stairs that lead to the cells, her legs as weak as new grass. At the top, he unlocks a second door.

This is not the visitor hall and the bullpen that she's grown used to, but the corridor between the cells themselves, the prisoners' own territory. In response to an assault of shouts and catcalls, the guard bangs his stick against the bars of several cells.

"Hey, Bonnie," calls a young man to whom she'd delivered molasses cookies.

"Hey, yourself, Jimmy."

Two men who stand beside Clyde at the bars fade back as she approaches.

"I'm going back to Dallas," she announces loudly, pressing her hand to her solar plexus. "Thanks to you, my heart is so heavy, it might as well be lead."

"One last kiss?"

His eyes are on her torso. Fear fizzes painfully in her veins. She lifts her hand to her mouth to stifle a gasp or a giggle and glances at the guard, who stands only four feet away, waiting for a show. Clyde's lips form the words, "C'mere, baby," but her ears are buzzing so loudly, she can't hear them.

As she leans into the kiss, she twists and presses her shoulder to the bars, as a shield against the guard's eager eyes. With her lips on Clyde's, she inserts her hand furtively into her dress and draws the small gun out, splaying her fingers to cover it, just as she'd practiced. Even after all that time under her clothes, it's still cold.

Their fingers meet, forming a warm cradle around the cool metal.

"Be careful," she whispers.

"It's the laws that gotta be careful now." He gives her a wink.

The guard shifts. "That's enough."

She turns obediently from the cell.

"Time's up," the guard says, but though Bonnie steps back, he doesn't lead her out but moves to stand in front of Clyde's cell.

He's seen it. He'll grab it and then her. Maybe he'll shoot her with it. She tries to run, but her muscles and bones are soft as custard and can barely hold her upright.

"She's wants a man, not a thug," the guard says to Clyde. "She tell you that?"

Clyde makes no answer.

"Guess you're a loser," the guard says. "Too bad. Pretty girl."

CHAPTER 21

Back at the house, Bonnie and Mary lock the door.

"Might just as well put our hands over our eyes," Bonnie says, as they go from room to room, cocooning themselves behind Mary's paper shades.

They perch formally to wait, Mary in the rocker, Bonnie on the davenport. The afternoon sun makes gold rectangles of the shades, and Mary's rocking squeaks in time with the tock of the clock.

Feet scrape the road, and Mary stills, but it's only two neighbor women, their careless voices leaping and dipping like birdsong.

"You think they'll wait until dark?" Mary asks, setting her rocker to squeaking again.

"I don't know."

"I'm sure glad Buzz ain't here," Mary says. "I couldn't act natural to save my life."

"No."

"I think they'll wait until dark, don't you?"

Bonnie had developed a habit of picking at her cuticles when Clyde was in jail in Dallas. She's let her fingers alone since she got to Waco, but now she starts in on them, pressing one thumbnail into the skin at the base of the other.

"I'm sure glad Buzz ain't here."

Whenever an engine flutters and tires purr on the road outside, the women look at one another and stop breathing, but every car goes on past.

"Funny how you hardly hear that clock most days and now it's like an ax in a woodpile," Mary says.

The golden rectangles turn brilliant copper and, finally, blue. It's already night at the back of the house where the kitchen is. Mary presses on the light and for about an hour they're ordinary girls on an ordinary evening, frying eggs and bacon, buttering slices of bread. But after they've washed and dried the dishes, they sink again, this time at the cramped kitchen table, clinging to that bright, familiar space.

"I wonder when they're going to try it," Mary says.

Bonnie pictures the short barrel of the little gun pressed to the neck of the guard who'd mocked Clyde. But that guard would be home by now, eating his own supper.

"If they catch him, he'll get the chair, sure," Mary says.

"Mary!"

"Well, it's a fact."

"You don't need to say it."

The single-minded urgency that has driven Bonnie through the day has leached away. "What if I shouldn't have done it?"

"Bonnie!"

"Maybe I should have told him to do his time, pay for his mistakes. What's two years in exchange for a happy life?"

"Well, I told you . . ." Mary begins.

"What if he doesn't know what he's doing? I hate this waiting!"

Mary yawns.

"Go on to bed, why don't you? Sitting up's not going to do any of us any good."

"Let's both go to bed, Bonnie. It'll make the night go faster."

"No, I can't, but you go."

When Mary wakes with her cheek on the table, Bonnie is standing at the front room window, peeking out through the crack along the edge of the shade.

CHAPTER 22

The escape of Clyde "Schoolboy" Barrow, William Turner, and Emery Abernathy from the McLennan County Jail by means of a smuggled gun dominates the front page of the *Waco Tribune-Herald*, topping news of an accidental, fatal gunshot wound; the arrest of a radio singer; an update on a murder trial; a counterfeiting case; the discovery of four charred infant bodies; and a car wreck. A trail of stolen cars suggests that the cons are heading west. No speculation is offered as to how the gun might have found its way into the prison.

On page six, the paper also runs a paragraph about the mysterious ransacking of a house in East Waco. No connection is drawn between the occupants, a Mrs. and a Miss Turner, and the Turner on the lam, and there is no mention of the recently swiveled geranium pot or the missing gun.

"Must have been raccoons," Mary giggles.

◆

They keep the shades drawn all the next day and by six o'clock the gloom coupled with the sleepless night causes Mary's chin to fall onto her chest. They lie together on Mary's bed, where Mary closes her eyes, but Bonnie overflows with anticipation and plans. She smokes continually, lighting a new cigarette with the butt of the one she's just finished, and spews words meant to shape her future along with the smoke.

"He isn't a bad boy. He just hasn't had a chance."

"He'll never be able to come back to Texas," Mary murmurs.

"That's all right. I don't mind going far away, as long as we're together. I'm going to divorce Roy, so Clyde and I can get married, and

I'll help him start over. Maybe we'll even change his name. His middle name is Chestnut. He could use that."

Mary laughs.

"What's wrong with it?"

"Well, for one thing, it's a nut."

"All right, Chester, then. We can use my name, too. We'll be Chester and Bonnie Parker. Mr. and Mrs. Parker, just like my mama and daddy. Clyde's good at getting work. He's never been fired," she assures Mary.

But her cousin is asleep.

He just can't stand to be dull, Bonnie thinks, that's why he quits his jobs and gets into trouble, but he won't be dull with her, so he'll never do another thing to get the laws after him. She imagines a house with walls of colored stones and a shiny tin roof, where she writes poetry, while he sells cars. He knows all about cars and loves them sincerely. They might not give him that kind of job in Dallas, but in some small town out west they'd give a fellow a chance. She repeats Clyde's promises again and again to herself, papering over the image of him turning away when she'd balked at getting the gun.

◆

At 9:30 p.m., knocking jerks them awake. "Yeah, this is right," a man's voice says, and then the knocking sounds again.

Breathing shallowly, the women squeeze each other's hands.

The knocks become pounds, and the answering wallop of Bonnie's heart threatens to toss her off the bed.

Outside, feet scratch and shuffle; footsteps recede but then stop. When the women can no longer stand to lie still, Bonnie slides off the bed and crawls on her hands and knees to the front. Across the street, two red dots—lit cigarettes—hover above the curb. She crawls back to the bedroom, where Mary sits with her back against the headboard, chewing on her fingers. "They're still there."

"I don't want to go to jail!"

"Oh, shush. Nothing's going to happen to you. You don't know anything about it."

"But I do! I know all about it!"

Later, the pounding is rough and impatient, produced by the side of a fist instead of knuckles, more a message of frustration than a summons.

Mary pulls the covers over her head. "Maybe we ought to try to sneak out the back window?"

"Maybe they got men in the yard," Bonnie counters.

"Do you think they do?"

"I don't know. We just got to sit here, Mary. Sit here until they give up on us."

When the men finally leave, long after midnight, Bonnie pulls her cardboard case out from under Mary's chest of drawers. She remembers how they cornered Clyde in her mother's house early in the morning. She'd meant to take the interurban, but the police might be staking out the stations. Her fear of being spotted and nabbed makes her feel close to Clyde, who must be fearing the same.

At 4:00 a.m., the street is quiet, and a dense constellation of white cigarette butts along the opposite curb stands out starkly under the streetlight. Mary's car engine growls like an alarm, but no one runs out of his house to investigate. The only other vehicle on the streets as they drive through Waco is a milk truck. They pass the courthouse, haughty on its hill with its fluted pillars and its winged statues and its crowning dome. Bonnie despises it and is glad, so glad, that he's flouted all it stood for, its arrogant crushing of insignificant lives like theirs.

When the streetlights end, grasslands and fields stretch out gray to meet the dark sky, against which a few trees, darker still, mass.

"Here, Mary. This is good enough."

"You sure? Maybe I oughta drive you on up to Dallas." Mary's low on gasoline and no filling station will be open yet. Besides, she doesn't have much money in her purse. Also, the idea of driving all that way back home alone makes her nervous. But it seems unkind, dangerous even, to dump her cousin on this empty road. Tentatively, she slows the car, waiting for Bonnie's answer.

"I'll be all right. You better get on back. Buzz'll be home today, won't he?"

Mary remembers that she has to get her hair done and make her husband the red-eye gravy he likes. She has to think over what she ought to talk about with him, because she certainly isn't going to tell him what she's done that she shouldn't have and what she should have but didn't, neither of which Mary is precisely sure of. Really, Bonnie got you not knowing which way was up.

Bonnie opens the door and the chilly air swoops in.

"Want me to stay, Bonnie? Sit here in the car and wait 'til someone picks you up?"

"No one's gonna stop if I've got a car already sitting by me. You go on." Before Bonnie closes the door, she adds, "Thank you very much for having me. I had a lovely time."

Mary has to drive on a little farther to find a place to turn around. On her way back to Waco, she waves when she passes Bonnie, but the dawn is still deeply gray, and Bonnie looks up blindly, her small face gaunt in the glare of the headlights. Mary's final view of her cousin, through the rearview mirror, is of a girl so slight the wind generated by a passing car might push her into the ditch. Her head is down and her shoulders slump; her case is beating against her knees. But she walks with a steadiness that suggests she will slog all the way to Dallas.

◆

When the knocking begins again at Mary's door the next day around noon, she hesitantly opens it. She doesn't know where Bonnie is—that's what she intends to say and that is the truth. But the two boys who stand on her front porch, one smoking a cigarette, the other with his hands in his pockets, are obviously not the law.

"We're looking for Bonnie Parker," the boy with the cigarette says. "Her mother sent us down to pick her up."

"Say," the other fellow puts in, "that must have been some party y'all were at last night. We pret' near froze ourselves out here waiting the whole damn night for you to get home."

CHAPTER 23

The road stretches long.
My only song
Is the clump of my feet in the dirt.
He runs free.
But what about me?
I'm just the girl he left hurt.

An egg truck pulled over, and the driver swept greasy papers and ash from the seat for her. Climbing in, her cheeks freezing, her fingers in their light cotton gloves stiff around the handle of her case, and her underarms clammy with sweat, Bonnie was acutely conscious of the difference between the person she was now and the girl who'd ridden down on the train beside Cumie Barrow, with her case tucked behind the heels of her clean shoes and her gloved hands folded in her lap. She'd been on Clyde's side then, too, of course, but she'd also been on the side of the law. She'd been proof, along with Cumie and her Bible—to Clyde and to the court, too—of how tightly he was bound to the upright and the obedient. He may have drifted, but two determined women were reaching to pull him back.

She'd let him drag her in instead, and now where was he? She'd sworn to Mary that he'd come for her, but she already suspected that she—like the laws—had been duped and outrun.

◆

"Sit down, why don't you? You're wearing a rut in the floor," her mother said, when Bonnie had gone for the dozenth time to the window Friday afternoon. "He's not going to show up here. You said yourself he can't come back to Dallas."

By Saturday, her anxiety had overwhelmed her pride, and she went to the campground to find out whether Clyde had contacted his mother.

"Ain't heard nothing from Bud," Cumie said, "but who do you think stuck his head in that there door last week with a grin like I'd caught him ducking out of Sunday school?"

Buck, incarcerated at the Walls, had been on work duty, peeling potatoes, when he'd noticed a guard's car parked and empty outside the kitchen.

"He was on the lookout for Blanche," Cumie went on. "He really loves that girl. Her daddy's a preacher, you know."

Bonnie acknowledged that she'd been made aware of that advantage.

"The two of 'em went off and holed up someplace. You ain't heard nothing from Bud, neither?"

"I'm sure I will," Bonnie said. "I'm sure Clyde's fixing to get back here. He's just got to figure out how to do it without getting caught."

"Well, Buck, he just drove straight on up, pretty as you please. Just stuck his head in the door and said, 'howdy, Mama.' "

Bonnie tried delicately to suggest that Clyde was less impulsive than Buck, more apt to plan and act with caution, which would explain his failing to make a beeline to his love, but she didn't convince even herself.

Back home her own mother was scornful and sympathetic by turns. "The Walls don't sound so rough, if someone as simple as Buck Barrow can just walk right out. What're you hoping for anyway?" she demanded. "Are you fixin' to find a hole someplace in Arkansas for the two of you to crawl into?"

Emma softened later, as she always did when Bonnie cried, and tried to transfer her daughter's tears to her own hardened fingers. "He's done you a favor going off. Maybe he loves you enough to let you have a life with a future."

A telegram from Nokomis, Illinois, suggested otherwise: "Al wel. Be in toch sun."

With this primitive promise, the distance Bonnie had been feeling between herself and Clyde closed with a snap, like the clasp of a bracelet. Buoyed, she spun around Dallas, trying to convince the owners of the few cafés still open that a girl with her charm and energy would bring in regular business, so she could start a nest egg.

But at the end of the week, she received an envelope from Mary containing a clipping from the *Waco Times-Herald*. The escapees had been captured in Ohio when they accidentally looped back past the train station they'd robbed, just as the crime was being investigated. "Boobs," the newspaper called them. "Dummies." The youngest, Clyde, was the "Baby Dumbbell," although he was given credit for being slippery enough to make the cops work for hours to chase him down.

Pep Schulz, the manager who'd hired her, a serious young man who supported his mother and two sisters and their families with the café's lagging take, sympathized. How much could Bonnie mean to Clyde, Pep asked, probing her with his patient blue eyes, if he'd thrown away happiness with her in favor of a few quick jobs with a couple of thugs?

So she didn't run right down to Waco, as everyone expected her to. She dithered, irritated by the irony when Clyde wrote that he'd changed his middle name from "Chestnut" to "Champion"; at once touched and offended when he informed her that he'd claimed her as his wife, so they could freely exchange letters.

She wrote pages full of underscored phrases and exclamation points, wiping her eyes on the heel of her hand, so that the ink smudged and the paper tore. She ripped up these missives and balled the pieces and smashed the balls against the table. But, one morning, faced with the prospect of another day of aching legs, plates stuck together with congealed yolk, and Pep's yearning glances, she called in sick.

On the table between Bonnie and Clyde, elongated triangles of darkened wood marked the spots where those who'd sat there before had stretched out their arms, but Bonnie kept her hands in her lap. She felt half-ashamed for showing up; she would not do more.

"Been busy?" His sneer confused her.

She'd expected buttery blandishments, which she could resist to restore her dignity. She'd planned to hold out until he produced a measure of solid regret. That, she would readily swallow.

But he pointed an accusing finger. "You think I don't know what you been up to? I got eyes in West Dallas. They tell me you're running around."

She recoiled, sucking in air that ignited in her head and chest. "Your talking eyes need glasses," she spit back. "I ain't the one didn't do what he promised. Ohio? That's your idea of together? Robbing train stations? That's your idea of being good? You *are* a dumbbell!"

"Better a dumbbell than a filthy little whore!"

If one of the guards had not stepped forward, she would have scratched him until he bled.

The apology she'd anticipated arrived two days later in a letter. "Just be a good little girl and always love me," he begged.

Throughout the summer and into the fall, while he was shuttled around Texas to slough off various charges, she received fulsome musings about people and places he remembered and fantasies about the fun they would someday enjoy, peppered with references to her sweetness and blue eyes. She kept them in a packet tied with a red ribbon in her underwear drawer, but she did not often send a reply. And when she did, she was careful to express no desire for future happiness with him. To do so would have been ridiculous and degrading, when he had so casually shoved any possibility of such out of reach. He may have been able to view his incarceration as fate rather than consequence, but she would not, and, in any case, fourteen years was far too long to live through letters. She went out with other men, although thus far they merely confirmed the sentence to which she, indulging her propensity for moping, condemned herself in dramatic diary entries: "life without love."

◆

Somewhat reflexively, Bonnie maintained her connection with the Barrows.

"He didn't get the Walls," Cumie said bitterly in October. "They sent him to that terrible Eastham."

"At the Walls, they learn you shoe mending," Marie explained. "The work out in them cotton fields is so bad at the Bloody 'Ham, we hear cons chop off their own fingers to get shut of it."

In July, Buck, still on the lam, married Blanche, but acceding to the wishes of his wife and his mother, agreed to surrender himself to Huntsville to finish his sentence. Bonnie ignored the sympathetic look that Blanche gave her as this information was revealed, a look that conveyed that she, Blanche, had a husband who loved her and would do what she and Texas required, so that they could live a happy life together, while Bonnie did not. Cumie, not content with meaningful glances, crowed about the workings of God. Bonnie, Cumie insisted, should not trouble herself with thoughts of Clyde, because she could do nothing for him.

Cumie and Henry had finally established a foothold in West Dallas, a couple of lots on the dirt thoroughfare that was Eagle Ford Road to which Henry had hauled the shack. He'd added two gas pumps and a room up front from which he sold oil, tire patch kits, soda pop, pretzels, moonshine, water, and telephone calls.

Meanwhile, Cumie had found her calling as a suppliant, and with gnat-like persistence petitioned the governor to give Clyde a pardon. On February 2, 1932, about a year and a half after Clyde had gone to Eastham, she revealed a mother's power.

"I'm gettin' him out," she said, when Bonnie came by with candy.

"What?"

"There's too many new ones comin' in, I guess. What with the way things are nowadays. They got to let the old ones out to make room."

"But that's wonderful!" Bonnie managed to spit out, although her feelings were far more confused that this expression suggested.

Cumie shrugged. "I know you've got some other fellow now."

◆

In mid-February, Bonnie heard, the way people did in West Dallas, that Clyde was back in town. Restless, distracted, and down, she resisted the urge to crawl over to Eagle Ford Road. On a Friday night, she was at home with her "other fellow," wishing Andy would go on home, so she could brood over her diary, but at the same time wanting him to stay all evening, so she could pretend she didn't care. Poor Andy; she felt sorry for him, trying to jimmy himself between her and her mood. She turned on the radio, so they could quit trying to talk. That was why she didn't hear the knock.

Billie finally opened the door. "Clyde!"

The name detonated an explosion in Bonnie's chest and without a thought she was off the divan and across the room. He was leaning on crutches, and, as he put his arms around her, one crutch banged to the floor, while the other jammed against her ribs.

The other fellow picked his hat off the table and went out the open door. Whether he was angry or sorry, she didn't know and didn't care.

"What happened? Are you all right?" Bending to pick up the fallen crutch, she saw that his foot was wrapped in a grimy bandage.

"Your poor foot! C'mere, c'mere, c'mere." As his presence unclotted her feelings, she clung to him and pulled him along toward the divan.

Emma stood frowning in the opposite doorway.

"Mama, look! Clyde's hurt."

"I see. That happen in the pen?"

"We don't want to talk about that now, Mama. Clyde's back. He came back to me."

"Like a bad penny," Clyde said.

When Bonnie laughed, Emma smiled, because what mother isn't happy to see her child happy? She allowed herself to hope that after nearly two years in prison, Clyde might have changed.

CHAPTER 24

Clyde had changed. He was dolled up like a gangster, for one thing, in a new charcoal-gray suit, kid gloves, and a silk shirt. He was still slight—even skinnier, actually, than when she'd last seen him— nevertheless, he was somehow weightier. His face had aged into a man's, the bones and flesh solidifying. Pressed tightly against him on the sofa, Bonnie tucked her head against his chest and rubbed her cheek against the silk.

But Clyde was glowering and sulky. "Who was that pasty fellow?"

"He's no one. Not now that you're back."

"Where's he live? I'd like to have a word with him."

"Stop it! What's the matter with you? You come here to see me and all you talk about is some boy who has nothing to do with you."

"I don't like the idea of that horn toad taking advantage."

"He didn't take advantage. He's gone now anyway."

"You mean you asked him for it?"

"What are you talking about?"

He reached under her dress. "Little show-off. You asked him for it, didn't you?"

"Not here," she hissed. "Not like this."

But he wasn't the boy who'd slept chastely on that couch two years before. He pushed at her too hard and too fast, her mama and Billie right in the next room. She yelped, but his crutch crashed again to the floor, masking her cry.

She sobbed quietly, but the radio was playing "Night and Day," and that made her feel better, because, after all, he was the one.

Over the next few days, she worked on this new, hardened Clyde, who wouldn't hold her gaze but glanced away whenever their eyes met for too long. She kept touching him, trying to tease away the carapace under which the boy she remembered must be hiding, the one who preferred hot chocolate with plenty of sugar to the stuff his father sold in Mason jars.

They made plans on the stoop of the oil room on Eagle Ford Road, or rather he pronounced and she buttressed. The weak, spring sun wasn't warm, but it seemed to gild the scraps of clouds overhead, and a fresh wind stirred the stale winter air.

Clyde was going to help his daddy expand the service station into a repair shop. He and his little brother, L.C., could make any tin can run, he boasted, and when Buck got out, they could bring him in, too. They would be the Barrow Brothers and people wouldn't bother taking their machines no place else. "We can get some old junkers, fix 'em up and sell 'em, too."

It was a sure thing, she agreed, a way to make a good life from his natural-born talent. For them both, she added, squeezing his arm. The gesture or the words snagged some other, submerged Clyde. His eyes filled with tears.

"I was scared you wouldn't want me no more," he choked. "After I been in that dirty place so long."

"I don't care where you been," she said, tracing his eyebrows and letting her fingertips slide over his cheekbones and onto his lips. Love hadn't abandoned her after all. It had just gone dormant without him to spark it on. "I'll always want you."

In the oil room, Henry wiped a screwdriver fastidiously on his trousers before using it to stir a jelly glass full of the merchandise he kept hidden behind the oilcans. "Thanks for sticking by Bud," he said formally, stepping outside and offering the glass to Bonnie. "I put a touch of Dr Pepper in, so's it'll taste good."

It did not taste good, but it had other qualities, and she sipped it greedily, enjoying the way it melted her insides. "It's warming," she promised, handing the glass to Clyde.

He gulped half of it down at a go and then pulled her roughly onto his lap. "You're what I want to warm me." Then his cheek was slick against hers and his breath smelled thick. "I'm never going back," he sobbed.

Awkwardly, reaching around her body, he leaned to pull off his sock and unwrapped the bandage around his toes, or rather the grotesque, swollen, red lump where his first two toes had been.

She made herself touch it. "Oh, poor little piggies!"

"I told you," he said, "plenty others done worse. A whole foot. Or a hand. You want to know? You want to know what it was like?"

She did not. She wanted to go back to the day before the laws had taken him from her mother's house and pretend it was yesterday. But with his raw, sloppily stitched wound exposed, she could not deny that her boy had been altered and diminished.

"When the tilling started again, I knew I was likely to be one of them that got outta there in a box. You remember my heart? How the Navy wouldn't let me in on account of it?"

She nodded and put her hand to his chest, protecting that delicate organ.

"It wasn't working right. I couldn't get my wind. And when you ain't puttin' your back into it, that's when they beat you the hardest."

An ax was easy to come by. He just went over by the chopping blocks one day. No one tried to stop him.

"It was harder than you'd think to swing it just right."

"Stop! Please, stop!" She covered her face with her hands.

Clyde kept on, however, as if, once begun, he had to spew out the rest of the incident that had obviously continued to churn in his mind. "I didn't want to get more than two, but I had to do those clean. If you don't see it through and leave a toe or a finger hanging, they just wrap it up and send you back out. Then, when the blood starts comin' through the bandage, they gather everyone round to see what a mess some dolt has made of hisself. I don't know that two toes would have been enough, now that I think on it. They would probably have sent me back by now, if it hadn't been for my ma's begging."

He seemed to see the loss of his toes as a necessary sacrifice, even though, if he'd waited a single week, he would have enjoyed his freedom whole. She knew the laugh the paper would have had, if they'd paid attention: "Dumbbell Cuts Off Toes to Spite His Fate."

"I hate those damn guards," she said. "I wish you could show them. But you're done with that now. You're never going back."

"No." He was talking more to himself than to her now. "I promise I'll die before I go back."

◆

For a few weeks, her wounded baby stayed close to home, chastened and belligerent by turns, nursing his toes and his grudges. Plenty of young men with nothing much to do stopped by, and Clyde held court. They filled each other in on who was doing what time for what crime, dissected the finer points of various models of automobiles, and robustly expressed their support for Dallas's plan to send all unemployed coloreds back to the farms to live on the surplus wheat no one was buying. On one occasion Nell happened to be there and convinced them otherwise—she was married to a musician and had different views—but the next day they went back to their old way of thinking.

Cumie gave only a cold nod to the boys that hung around; she hadn't worked so hard for that pardon, she said, so Bud could stir up new trouble with that trash. Bonnie assured her—and anyone else who would listen—that Clyde wasn't going to slide back into that old groove, because he was good inside. Nell, however, didn't trust her brother's insides. At the end of February, when he could limp without a cane, she announced that she was sending him to Massachusetts, where she'd arranged a job for him with a construction crew.

"You can't send him away!" Bonnie protested. "He just got back."

"You want him to start over, don't you?" Nell said. "They're never going to let him do that here. You know they'll be hauling him in every time a dime gets stole in Dallas, and pretty soon he'll figure he might as well be stealing them dimes. You got to take the long view."

"You're going to go all the way to Massachusetts," Bonnie whined to Clyde, "and leave me here?"

"It's Nell's idea." He was sullen as a child.

"But what about fixing cars? You and L.C. and your daddy."

"They say we ain't got money for the parts."

"You do this job Nell's got for you," Henry said, "and you can save it up."

"Slow and steady?" Clyde sneered.

"That's right. Like I done."

"Your slow and steady got you a pile of scrap," Clyde said. "The service station was pure luck."

"At least I got me in a position to be ready to catch me some luck, when it came my way."

Clyde shook his head, a gesture that seemed to negate all the Barrows and Bonnie, too.

"I'll come with you," she said. But no one took her seriously, not even herself.

◆

It was his last chance to be good, but to take it, he had to stand on his own in an unfamiliar place and he wasn't up to it. He didn't have Nell's focus or Henry's stoicism or Cumie's faith. Bonnie knew she ought to have hoped for him to stay in Massachusetts. She should have rooted for him to establish a new life and to send for her, if, having made his way, he found he couldn't do without her, but she was overjoyed when, less than two weeks later, he'd quit and come back to Dallas. The long view, she'd found, was as gray and flat as the horizon, and she was sick of it.

PART 2

CHAPTER 25

April 1932

Telling Emma she's found some scraping sort of job in Houston, Bonnie packs her cardboard case and practically skips down the street, too excited to hide her exuberance. The purpose of the errand on which she is about to embark doesn't trouble her. The end—the humiliation of the institution that tortured Clyde—justifies the means. And, after all, she won't actually be stealing cars; she's only along for the ride.

When the blue Model A pulls over, she knows he's been waiting for her. He reaches across the seat to pop the door and grins wide enough to perk his elfin ears. "Hey, baby, wanna ride?"

She only has one foot on the running board when he grabs her hand and yanks her in, as he picks up speed. She tumbles into the seat, as if she's mounting a ride at an amusement park, instead of traveling down an ordinary Dallas street, and her exultant kiss matches her mood.

"Watch the road!" Ralph Fults says from the back.

Their plans have expanded since yesterday. After they get the cars in Tyler, they're going to stop in Kaufman where Ralph has spotted a good selection of rifles and shotguns in a hardware store.

"I don't like guns," Bonnie says coquettishly, producing a little shudder.

"Aw, baby, we won't be but five minutes," Clyde says. "You'll just wait in the car."

"You can lay on the horn if you spot the laws," Ralph says.

Clyde frowns. "Little place like that, there won't be no laws. Don't worry, sugar. Daddy's not going to get his baby into trouble."

"I'm not worried." She strokes his silk sleeve. She's decided that Clyde looks natural in silk.

He turns his palm up, so that her hand fits into it.

"I like that you want me along," she says.

"How about me?" Ralph says. Among the members of Clyde's newly formed Lake Dallas Gang, Ralph is Bonnie's favorite.

"Oh, we want you along, Ralph," she says. She turns to grace him with a puckish expression that she knows suits her little face. "Someone's got to hold the flashlight."

In Tyler, Clyde uses the screwdriver he always carries to start a Chrysler 60 parked in front of the train station. They leave the Ford and cruise around in the Chrysler, admiring its wide seats with their plush upholstery and its powerful engine, until they spot a Buick Master 6 for Ralph. Conveniently, the owner has left the keys in the ignition.

◆

The fast cars and the guns that they're now speeding to collect in Kaufman are for a raid on the Eastham Prison Farm, plans for which have preoccupied Clyde since he returned from Massachusetts. In preparation, Bonnie, Clyde, and Ralph had driven some weeks before into the enormous, empty space between Dallas and Houston, where the spring haze of pale green lay like mold on the crust of the dark brown fields and a few budding trees stood like sentinels.

Bonnie, playing messenger, drove alone the final stretch to the cluster of prison buildings. Her hands trembled on the wheel when she spotted the men in black and white, bunched in the fields like exotic herds, their mounted keepers balancing rifles crosswise on the pommels of their saddles. She passed a plot of slender headstones, arranged in rows, residue of lost men.

"First time?"

She delivered her lie: she was visiting her cousin. Their grandmother had taken ill; he'd want to know. She'd not intended for her voice to tremble, but it served to elicit sympathy. The guard wished the old lady well.

Aubrey Scalley, a trusty privileged to meet visitors unsupervised, turned out to be so slight that his striped trousers gathered in folds around his waist. His thin hair had receded well back from his delicate forehead, and his narrow jaw had crowded his front teeth into a mess of overlapping angles. Despite his physical disadvantages, he carried himself with an easy, open confidence. His gaze was neither pushing nor ducking but purely patient as he waited for whatever she'd brought him.

"Bud sent me," she said. Clyde had told her that Aubrey would know that name.

"Yer his sweetheart?"

She nodded, the old-fashioned term rendering her shy. "He's planning a party. Probably next month."

Aubrey shook his head. "He ain't be needing to trouble himself for me. It ain't hurt me none to get that one-way ticket chalked to my account."

Nonplussed, but embarrassed to admit she was unaware of a context he assumed a sweetheart would know, she said, "It's no trouble." As if the scheme were, indeed, only a party. "He wants to do it."

Scalley nodded sagely. "I know. He wants to scorch this place. When I got your boy that pipe, I told him, I'll take the rap, but you got to do it yourself, or you won't be shut of it. Well, I guess even that weren't enough. An evil like that tends to get inside a man, and he's got to wait for it to worm its way out. I heard of some kilt theirselves. Or done worse even, trying to get rid of it. We don't want that for young Bud, do we?"

"No," she agreed. She still had no idea what he was talking about, but the answer was obvious.

"Old Aubrey don't need nothin'. You tell Bud never mind about that party."

"Well, I don't know," she managed. "I suppose he knows best what he wants."

A guard opened the door, and Aubrey rose obediently. "He may want," he said, his eyes still gentle and steady. "But has he sat down and counted the cost, whether he has sufficient to finish it?"

She was well-versed enough in the Bible to recognize its cadence, but what he meant by the quotation she could not guess and hardly bothered to wonder. She'd played her part and escaped to tell about it. She drove away from the prison fast enough to spit gravel and was relieved to find Clyde and Ralph waiting where she'd left them.

◆

"They won't know what hit 'em."

Clyde's tone startles her. Bonnie's been enjoying the ride to Kaufman, relaxing on the Chrysler's wool seat, letting the cool air engorged with imminent rain flow in a refreshing stream through the open window. She glances at his face and sees that it has narrowed and stiffened the way it always does when he talks about the prison. From where she sits, his eyes, focused steadily forward, appear to be empty sockets.

"Can we go faster, sugar?" She puts a hand on his thigh to give him comfort and encouragement, and he responds with a sly smile. The muscles in his leg flex under her fingers as he forces the accelerator toward the floor and draws even with Ralph in the Buick.

Driving soothes and steadies Clyde's nerves like whiskey. Pushing as much gas as possible into the engine and keeping the rocking car on the uneven, dirt road consumes the whole of his concentration, leaving no room for worry or anger.

The two cars rush headlong at the darkness, their headlights illuminating the next few feet of dust and gravel. First one, then the other, strains ahead a foot or two, then falls back. Bonnie, pressed against the seat, digs her nails into the upholstery. The wind whips around her head and the ends of her hair scratch her eyes. She closes them, exalting in the speed, savoring the unfamiliar flutter in her gut whenever the road dips. After a few minutes of speed, however, her senses adjust, and fast feels as dull as any old driving.

"Faster, sugar," she murmurs. "Let's go faster."

But they are going to have to slow down because yellow headlights appear in the darkness ahead. Bonnie braces herself for the abrupt slackening that will come the second Clyde eases up on the pedal and lets the car fall behind Ralph's. Instead, he leans forward, trying to squeeze more speed from the Chrysler.

"Honey. Clyde."

The oncoming truck is now so close that Bonnie can make out its black bulk. Its lights waver, but only slightly—there is nowhere to turn except over in the ditch. The truck's horn blasts.

Panic balloons in her chest, stuffing her throat. She closes her eyes and turns away from the imminent crash of metal and explosion of gasoline in which she will die.

Then—so suddenly that she falls against the door—Clyde swerves. The truck roars by, its horn filling the night and then growing fainter. Clyde toots back and glances over his shoulder, grinning at Ralph's car behind them.

"Now this is an engine a man can trust," he says, turning his attention back to the road. "I oughta write to Chrysler."

CHAPTER 26

When they park the two big cars behind the Kaufman hardware store after midnight, they expect an easy job. "Five minutes," Clyde mouths, as he and Ralph leave Bonnie with the door open and the engine running. From the car, she watches their flashlights wink in the store windows and wills them to hurry. Around her, the tender leaves fidget and whisper, anticipating a storm.

The sharp, grotesquely loud crack turns her bones and muscles to gravy, and she slides off the seat and presses herself against the floorboards in the space meant only for feet. Not thunder, but a watchman with a gun.

Clyde's driving even before he slams the car door shut. They speed through the startled town that clangs with alarms and is checkered with yellow houselights, Ralph in the Buick behind them. A woman in curlers shouts at them from her stoop, her mouth a dark hole in a lopsided, yeasty doughnut face.

"We've got to get off this road," Clyde says. "They'll have called ahead."

They turn hard off the main road onto a farm track and burrow into the darkness, but now the thunder finds them and a fierce rain pummels them, pounding on the metal roof, sluicing over the windshield, and making mud that grabs at the tires. The wheels fight, skid, slop, and spin, and the heavy Chrysler sinks into the mire, halting so abruptly that Bonnie's face nearly slams into the windshield.

Clyde jumps out and runs around the front of the car, so that for an instant he appears in the beam of the headlights, his head bowed under the force of the rain. She can't think why he would get out of the car in the middle of a storm, until he wrenches her door open and grabs her wrist. "C'mon! Run!"

Ralph slams his door and splashes toward them. "What do we do?"

"We gotta run!" Clyde says. "Ain't nothing else!"

Bonnie sets a tentative foot on the running board.

"No, *run!*" He yanks on her wrist again.

The wavering twin yellow lights are so small in the distance that they might as well be fireflies, but they're coming on. Another pair appears behind them, and another still.

The hem of her skirt is caught under the seat. He tears the fabric, and they throw themselves over the banked mud that forms the shoulder of the road into the mud that is the field on the other side. Ten steps and her shoes stick so fast that her feet come out of them. They're her best, caramel-colored Mary Janes with a two-inch heel. She bends to tug them free, but he still has her wrist and won't stop, so she has to leave them.

At a farmhouse, Clyde and Ralph point their guns but the farmer shrugs. He has no car, only a pair of mules, on which they plod through the remaining hours of the wet night in no particular direction, until the meager light of dawn reveals the outskirts of a town and an Oldsmobile parked in a driveway.

"That's for us," Clyde says. He falls awkwardly off the mule, pulling Bonnie with him, and staggers for a few seconds, his legs unsteady. Then he fishes the screwdriver from his pocket.

Bonnie and Ralph can hardly walk; they're so stiff and numb. Now that they're home free, though, they can laugh quietly at each other's halting steps and muddy faces. Ralph gives his mule a little pat on the behind, and both animals turn and start of their own accord back the way they've come.

"Keys are in it!" Clyde announces, and instantly the engine rumbles.

As they roll backward out of the driveway, a man, hoisting suspender straps over his shoulders, runs out of the front door.

Bonnie lets her head fall back against the seat and imagines lowering herself into a tub of hot water. Maybe she'll ask Clyde to stop at a drugstore for some bubble bath. She's thinking about how she'll make that request and when she ought to do it—sometimes he gets real mad about the littlest things—when the car begins to lose momentum.

"Don't slow down now, baby." They can't be more than a mile out of town.

"Damn idiot has no gas in the tank."

The car lurches forward on its last drops and then the engine sputters and dies. They get out and Ralph kicks a fender, while Bonnie begins to cry, but Clyde plunges straight into the ditch that runs between the road and yet another muddy field. "Keep your gun handy," he says to Ralph.

Bonnie stands stubbornly beside the disabled car as Ralph splashes into the ditch after Clyde, who is already scrambling up the far side. "Let's just go on back to that town and take another car," she begs, wrapping her arms around herself. After being in the car, the air feels colder than ever. "I'm soaking wet and my feet are frostbitten."

"You want to get us caught?" Clyde's face is masked with dirt except for white patches that encircle his red eyes. "Those bumpkins'll be coming after us from both towns now, toting pitchforks and shotguns. They got us trapped like rats."

"Then I'm getting back in the car." She opens the door. "I may as well sit down while I wait to get myself shot."

"No one's getting shot," Ralph says.

"No," Clyde agrees, "and we're not caught yet. If we can hide until dark, we'll have another chance at a car. Baby, you want I should carry you? I know your feet are awful cold and beat up."

She clings like a possum to his back as they slog to a network of gullies lined with thickets near an intersecting road. Lying flat on the cold mud, they squirm under a sharp tangle of twigs. Clyde slides a little pillow of grass under Bonnie's cheek.

The brush pins their arms; he can move his hand only far enough to cover her fingers with his own. They can hear the men already, one hawking, another cursing a twisted ankle. Her heart pounds hard enough to hurt. She concentrates on melding into the land, forcing down the panic that threatens to flush her out and send her flying into the open field.

The men search doggedly, poking the barrels of their shotguns into the stands of brush and shuffling through the gullies. Several times, they seem to move on, only to circle back and check again. Still, hours go by, and although she's shivering so hard that her jaw aches, she be-gins to hope that they might indeed make it until dark, when surely the posse will give up or, at the very least, she and Clyde and Ralph can creep away without being seen.

"Sit tight," Clyde hisses. "Just because we can't see or hear them, don't mean they ain't close."

CHAPTER 27

About ten minutes later, however, he's the one who moves, tentatively raising his head at the sound of a car turning off the main road. The engine stops and the door slams.

"It's across the road," he whispers. "C'mon!"

"No!" She tightens her grip on his fingers. "We've gotta wait until dark."

"We may not get another chance. I'm taking it," Clyde insists, and Ralph nods.

So she gathers herself into a crouch and follows him, breaking from the brush and running down the hill.

"There they are!"

The shout sends a painful spear of adrenaline through her veins, and her legs move almost without her willing them. But Ralph turns and raises his .45.

"What are you doing?" she screams. "Don't shoot!"

"I have to keep them back! I'm firing high!"

He shoots again, while Clyde fumbles at the ignition with his screwdriver. Clyde's fingers are inflexible as sticks, and he can barely hold on to the tool, let alone work it into the mechanism. With a crack and a thud, a bullet pierces the car's metal body, and Bonnie instinctively drops onto her heels beside the door. Another crack and another, and Ralph screams and drops his gun. He clutches his arm, as his sleeve becomes wet and red. Blood wells out between his fingers.

"I can't do it," Clyde wails. "Let's go!"

They run full out, directly in the path of more bullets, until the ground drops away six feet or so down to a stream. At the bottom, they crouch in the ooze.

"This looks like where we get ours, honey," Clyde says, his mouth against Bonnie's ear, but his voice ripples with excitement; there is no despair in it.

The posse—fifteen or twenty men—approaches with stamps and shouts. Ralph, who somehow had retrieved his gun before they bolted, suddenly stands and shoots. Bullets hit the opposite bank in return, but the footsteps cease.

"They ain't going to rush us," Ralph says, grinning.

While Ralph goes one way, sending up a shot every thirty seconds or so, Clyde drags Bonnie in the opposite direction, duck-walking along the streambed toward a church about half a mile away.

"Stay here, baby," he says, pushing her inside. "I'll come back for you."

Alone, she looks for a place to hide and chooses the tight space under the altar, where she sits for a good while, listening to the occasional cracks of the guns. When nearly an hour goes by and the posse has not broken through the door, she begins to feel as if she's in a womb, present, but safely removed from the hunt outside. Finally, the noises from the creek fade, and she hears in their place the scratch of claws and teeth inside the wooden walls.

Her muscles ache. She's thirsty and hungry. Whenever she shifts, cobwebs brush her neck and eyelids, and occasionally a bat rushes through the church, its fleshy wings beating the air, its alien, high-pitched chirps reverberating in every corner. She can endure the creepiness, but when she allows herself to imagine that Clyde's been caught or possibly shot, doubt gnaws at her.

At last, she unfolds herself and creeps into a chill and dripping twilight. Arms hugging her chest, she makes her numb-footed way along the overgrown dirt drive from the church to the highway. As soon as she reaches the main road, she regrets leaving the church and is about to dart back when she sees, glowing in the distance, the warm eyes of an automobile. She unclasps her arms and waves.

She will say she's had an accident. But then, where is her car? A fight with her husband. He'd put her out on the road, told her to walk. She will say she wants to scare him a little, let him know he can't treat her like that. She'll say she could sure use a ride to a telephone.

And when she gets to the telephone, she'll call the police. She'll ask flat out and get it over with: Is Clyde Barrow going back to jail or is he killed?

The car slows. She quits waving and passes a primping hand over her dirt-encrusted hair. "Hello, mister," is on her tongue, but before she can utter the first syllable, the long barrel of a rifle pokes out the window.

Ralph's been caught, too. When they shove her into the calaboose, a tiny, one-room brick building, he's sitting on the dirt floor, his arm flopping at his side, a fearsome, bloody mess.

"This boy needs a doctor!" she shouts at the people who are peering between the bars that block the single window, trying to get a look at her and Ralph, as if they're captured animals. "You'd better get him a doctor right now!"

There is some shuffling outside and the faces disappear.

A new one takes their place. "I'm a doctor."

"You'd better fix this boy's arm," she demands. "He didn't try to hit any of you, but you shot him anyway."

"You know what you get when you steal a man's car?" the doctor answers coldly. "You sure as hell don't get his help."

"We didn't drive your damn machine hardly a mile. You got it back, didn't you?"

But the doctor has gone.

"At least give him some aspirin!"

Outside, they laugh at her desperation.

"You can say you were kidnapped," Ralph offers with a gallantry that makes her teary. "I'll put it all on me," he assures her. "They don't have to know nothing about Clyde. And don't worry. He'll get us out."

◆

The next day, they're both taken to Kaufman and then Ralph is transported someplace else. Clyde, as it turns out, has gotten away scot-free, while she, who was just along for the ride, is stuck in jail and may end up in some horrible place like Eastham, where she'll have to cut off her toes.

◆

"Jesus? Is that you, Jesus? I hear you, Jesus!"

Inside her cell in the Kaufman County Jail, Bonnie leaned against the wall and pulled the writing paper the sheriff's wife had given her into her lap. She was working on a collection of poems she called "Poetry from Life's Other Side," about good girls gone wrong and sweet love soured, featuring tenacious but doomed heroines. The alienation she meant her title to express was undercut by the scallops with which she'd decorated her looping letters and the tiny rings with which she dotted her *i*'s.

"Wait! Is you the devil? You don't fool me, Devil. I see you."

She reread a ballad about a "jilted gangster gal" who'd served five years at Alcatraz while her man got away to enjoy the money they'd stolen. She was satisfied with the rhythm and the rhyme—those aspects always came pretty easily to her—but she was experimenting with the moll's vocabulary and that made the composition tricky. It felt somewhat unnatural to use phrases like "bump 'em" and "hotsquat" and "sub-gun," so she buffered them with quotation marks; they were Suicide Sal's words, not hers.

"Devil, wait! I want to talk to you! Devil, don't go!"

And how did "Sal" feel about the perfidious "Jack"? Bonnie summoned Clyde's mud-caked face as it had appeared in the dim light of the church, when he'd promised to return for her. The recollection made her want to howl like the crazy Negro woman next door, and she pressed so hard with her pencil that she tore a hole three sheets deep in the cheap paper.

CHAPTER 28

June 1932

"This here dress is Marie's," Cumie said, setting a brown paper sack on the table, "but Blanche and me thought it'd suit you. Clyde brung us one to give you, but we knowed you wouldn't want it, considering how he come by it."

Bonnie agreed that Marie's day dress was perfect for the grand jury. A sober slate fabric with a frill in the cap sleeve and a floppy bow at the neck, it telegraphed sincerity and hinted at girlish charm.

Mrs. Adams, the sheriff's wife, washed Bonnie's hair in her kitchen sink and set it in pin curls so it would fluff. She was confident that Bonnie would be released.

"When you get home, you'll have to do something about these bugs." She pinched a few away from Bonnie's part. "Happens to everyone in this place."

Bonnie knew just how to act in front of the jury. With wide eyes and a trembling lower lip, she described the evening on which she'd left her mother's house to catch a bus to Houston, where she'd heard of a job.

"I hated to leave home," she said, "but you know how it is anymore. You have to keep looking."

Every juror nodded.

"They had a big car," she said.

"Was it a Chrysler 60?" the prosecutor prompted.

"Oh!" She shook her head, causing the ends of her hair to tremble prettily. "I wouldn't know. I can't tell one automobile from another. It was big and green, that's all I remember. Scary looking, I guess, now that I think about it. I wish I'd thought so then," she added.

She told how the young men had offered her a ride, and how she'd decided to accept. They'd seemed like nice boys and saving carfare would allow her to buy a meal when she got to Houston. She wouldn't have to start work the next day on an empty stomach, which would help her to do her best.

When the prosecutor pressed her to specify where she'd been planning to stay in Houston, she claimed she'd intended to find a room when she arrived.

"But I never did get there," she said, turning the question to her advantage, making the jury feel the helpless position in which she'd found herself, sitting in that car, one man pointing a gun at her head while the other broke into the hardware store, driving faster than she'd known a car could go through that frightening storm, being shot at by the very police who ought to have been saving her, and being dragged through mud, even after she'd lost her shoes—shoes she'd just bought so she'd have something decent to wear in Houston.

"But if you didn't help them to steal the guns or drive the car, if your presence didn't even dissuade the police from shooting at them, why did they want you along?"

With that, the prosecutor proved himself a fool. When she answered, "I couldn't tell you what was in those gangsters' minds," the members of the jury understood that they all would have wanted this girl along, useful or not.

◆

The day after Bonnie came home, Emma regarded her sorry household through a scrim of cigarette smoke. Buster, at least, had a productive adult life underway. He'd been a sober, practical child and had become a sober, practical husband and father. Not so Billie's husband, Fred, who'd been arrested for burglary two weeks after Bonnie'd been caught. No point trying to convince a judge that *he'd* been kidnapped. Emma let out a small snort at the thought.

And here little Buddy was sick again. Emma stubbed out her cigarette and used the hem of her apron to wipe away the trail of snot that ran from his nose over his upper lip. Dallas wasn't healthy for kids. Lighting a fresh Chesterfield, she mused, as she so often did, about what might have been if Charlie hadn't died. Billie Jean, at least, would have been happy in Rowena, married to some farmer or railroad man, playing cards with her girlfriends, going out dancing on a Saturday night. Billie went the way the wind blew; she'd be all right, if she could get out of Dallas's bad air.

"You can quit giving me the look, Mama," Bonnie said. "It's over."

Emma hadn't realized she'd been frowning at her elder daughter, who sat like a Madonna, a blue towel wrapped around her mayonnaise-coated hair, Billie's baby, Mitzy, asleep on her lap.

"You can lie her down, you know," Billie said. "You don't have to hold her all day."

"I want to hold her." Bonnie stroked the baby's fine hair. "From now on, this is all I want. I'm going to help you take care of these two darlings. They love their Auntie Bonnie, don't they?" She wiggled her fingers at Buddy, who laughed, ran to her, and gave his baby sister a squeeze that made her emit a little sound.

"You'll wake her," Billie warned. "Then you'll be sorry."

"Clyde." Emma made her contempt clear with her pronunciation. She'd stuffed down her worry and outrage all those weeks that Bonnie had been in jail, because the humiliation of that cell was punishment enough, but now that she had her daughter home again, those feelings rose into her throat like acid. "He'll ruin you. Drag you down. Can't you see that's just how it is?"

"He's got nothing to do with me," Bonnie said.

She spoke so coolly, Emma was startled. It was unlike Bonnie not to spit and snap. But the light, bright girl, who had mooned over movie stars and written with such fervor in her diary, who blushed when she laughed, who would twirl spontaneously to feel the hem of her dress rise around her knees, who'd lied to her mother without an iota of compunction, had been replaced by a pale-cheeked, stern woman in a terrycloth wimple.

"He's nothing but a hood, and sooner or later he's going to end up back in the pen," Emma pressed on. "You're not going to see him. Ever again. You hear me? You've got to start using your head for a change and quit letting your heart push you around."

In one corner of her mind, Bonnie played with the rhyme—"he swore they wouldn't pinch him again; but he ended up back in the pen."

He'd never visited her in Kaufman. He hadn't even bothered to let her know where he was.

"Mother," she said formally, "I told you. I'm not going to have anything more to do with him." She stood up and, with as much dignity as a woman can muster with a towel around her head and a baby in her arms, stalked from the room.

Emma frowned at the empty doorway.

"Well, she's crying now," Billie said.

"Good," Emma said. "She ought to cry. She'll feel better when she gets him out of her system. We all will."

◆

When Bonnie returned Marie's dress to the Barrows, she couldn't help but express her bitterness over Clyde's neglect.

"Of course, he didn't visit you in Kaufman," Nell said. "How could you have claimed not to have known him?"

In fact, none of them knew where he was. He was hiding, because he was wanted for a murder in Hillsboro.

"He didn't do it!" Nell exclaimed, seeing the look on Bonnie's face.

"Of course, he didn't do it," Cumie repeated impatiently.

"He wasn't in the store when it happened," Nell explained. "He was outside in the car. Clyde's friend Ray Hamilton is wanted, too, and he wasn't even in the county. That's the way the law works in this town."

"They have it in for my boys," Cumie said. "That's the trouble."

"Ma," Nell said, "the trouble is that Bud goes around with crooks who carry guns. It was bound to happen. Even the judge said so."

"I know he shountna done none of this burglaring," Cumie was saying. "But taking somebody's money that like as not was took from somebody else in the first place isn't the worst a body can do. These storekeeps feed off of people who got nothing. 'We got to have three dollars, Miz Barrow,'" she said derisively. "'Can't give you no flour, no sugar, no bones without them three dollars.'"

"The Buchers weren't rich, Mama," Nell said. "You remember Madora Bucher from over at the camp."

"He has to tell them he didn't do it," Bonnie broke in. But even as the words came out, she saw how foolish they were.

◆

When Clyde finally showed up, they sat in the car, while Emma twitched the front curtain open and closed, as if she were sending smoke signals.

"What do you want?"

"Aw, baby, don't be like that."

"You mean don't let it bother me that I had to rot in jail? When I didn't have a thing to do with it except ride along in your car? You promised you'd come back."

"I came back. You're the one gave up waiting for me."

Clyde told her what had happened up at Hillsboro. "I was with two boys—you don't know them. Just a couple of boys I met around. I went in the store and asked about a guitar string. I really did need one, you know. I wanted to see did they have a safe, but I wasn't lying about needing that string." He looked at her earnestly, holding her gaze to be sure she was giving him credit for this thin slice of sincerity.

The proprietress turned out to be the mother of a boy Clyde had run with in the Bog, and she obviously recognized him. So he went back out to wait in the machine and sent the others in to get what they could.

"Who woulda thought they'd use a gun with a couple of white hairs like that?"

"What happened?"

"Damned if I know. I heard the popping and I beat it out of there. I don't know how they got away and I don't care. Dumb eggs. I got to do everything myself from now on."

The sound of a car engine swelled suddenly behind them, and Clyde's head swiveled.

"They won't be looking for you here."

"Course, they will. You're my girl. Everyone knows that, don't they?"

"I'm not your girl," she lied.

CHAPTER 29

July 1932

They gave up promises—her demanding them and his making and breaking them—for a fresh courtship. He pursued, coaxing her into the car to pet, staying away until she itched. She lured him on, luxuriating in her powers of attraction, the tingle of the tease. But as the dewy June settled into the thickness of July, the chase dulled. Clyde proposed a change.

"I got a little house up in Wichita Falls. How about you come on up and stay with me awhile?"

Telling her mother would mean having to listen to her go on. So Bonnie lied again, announcing another job out of town, as she repacked her cardboard case.

From the street, the dingy love nest near the railroad tracks was identical to her mother's house—parlor and best bedroom in front, kitchen and second bedroom in back.

"It's darling." She locked her arms around his neck. "Carry me in."

He did, or tried to, anyway. He swung her off her feet and supported her in his arms. But the door stuck. Giggling, she loosened her grip on his neck and leaned to turn the knob, while he battered the wood with his hip. "I'll get you in this here house, baby, if it kills us!"

The door opened with a jerk that sent Clyde stumbling, so that he dumped Bonnie on the floor.

"What the fuck you making all this racket for?"

Bonnie knew Raymond Hamilton only slightly. In school, his brother Floyd had been in her grade, and Raymond had come up a couple of years behind. He was the other man who, just like Clyde, hadn't been in the Bucher store when the gun went off but was wanted for murder, just the same.

Shotguns were propped against both arms of the settee and a pistol lay on the end table. Observing her take them in, Raymond began to whistle languidly, almost lewdly, "Pop Goes the Weasel."

Still it was not her mother's house in Dallas, where the days sagged as limply as the pages of her magazines.

◆

Clyde and Raymond had decided to unlatch a safe at a packing company.

"No more baby stuff," Raymond said. "No reason we can't be like Pretty Boy."

While Raymond paced impatiently, Clyde chewed on the end of his pencil and composed a plan.

"Road like a street has an *a* in it," Bonnie said, glancing at one of Clyde's pages. "Drill has two *l*'s."

"What the fuck does it matter?" Raymond said.

"I guess it doesn't," Bonnie said, "if people like you are reading it."

"Let's just do it," Raymond said. "I'm sick of talking about it."

"We got to think this through," Clyde insisted. He held the paper and pencil out to Bonnie. "You write it." So she was drawn into arguments over who would drive the getaway car and how the timetable should be arranged. Between the guard who would certainly have a gun and the police who would be after them in half an hour, they would have very little time to work.

"Think she can sit out and watch?" Raymond indicated Bonnie with a jerk of his head.

"Why don't *you* sit out and watch?" she said. "I'll go in with Clyde."

"You ain't going near this thing," Clyde said. "It's too risky."

They talked the job over so many times that she began to assume that the plans were as fantastical as the letter she was inventing for her mother about the good-looking cook and the persnickety owner at the café where she was pretending to work. But, remembering Kaufman, Bonnie waited until Raymond went for cigarettes and then slid her arms around Clyde's neck, the way Carole Lombard had slipped hers around Clark Gable's in *No Man of Her Own*. She used her most wheedling voice: "Honey, I've only just got you back. Why don't you skip this one and stay with me?" Instead of picking her up and carrying her into the bedroom, as Gable had done with Lombard, he shrugged her off. "Don't do that."

When her eyes filled, he softened. "It's just that I can't afford no doubts, sugar. You tell me I shouldn't and it gets me worried and then I can't concentrate. When I'm thinking about how maybe I shouldn't be doing something, that's when I'll get caught."

"What good is it for me to know your stupid plans, if you don't want me to tell you what I think? If you want someone who'll sit quiet like a sack of potatoes, you got the wrong girl."

"Oh, Clyde," he mocked. "I'm worried. It's dangerous."

She raised her hand to slap him, but he caught her wrist. He thrust his face into hers, so that his saliva sprayed her as he spoke. "I can't do nothing no more that ain't dangerous, get it? I stick my head out the door, I'm liable to get snatched. If you can't stand that, you got the wrong man."

"You oughta keep your head down, then," she said, raising her other hand.

When he caught that wrist, too, she drove forward with the whole of her body, backing him against the wall. He let her, and, when she had him pinned, he hooked his leg around hers and covered her mouth with his own.

◆

On the first of August Clyde drove Bonnie into Dallas and dropped her on Eagle Ford Road. He didn't bother to get out of the machine.

"Switch on the radio, honey," he said before she closed the car door. "See if we get away."

"Don't, Clyde! You'll jinx it!" The idea that he was going to do something grand enough to be broadcast over the whole city made her lift her chin with pride.

"Why didn't you do nothing to stop him?" Cumie whined, her fingers alternately balling and smoothing the apron in her lap, as "Aunt Sammy" chirped relentlessly from the radio about the importance of sterilizing jars.

"You think I didn't beg him? I'm sure you told him plenty of times not to do the things he's done."

"I never got no chance," Cumie complained. "He never told me nothing."

"If I told him not to do it and he got caught, it'd be my fault. It would make him worry, and then he wouldn't be concentrating on the job." Bonnie paused. The logic that had taken her in when Clyde had delivered it sounded silly when she repeated it.

Cumie nodded. "I guess Bud's not a one to change. He'll tell you whatever you want to hear and then he'll go off and do what he was going to do in the first place. He told me pret' near every day for a year that he was having a dandy time at school and he weren't there maybe but once a week. Nothing I could do, short of dragging him there myself and tying him to his seat with a rope."

A siren sounded and they both started, recognizing WRR's familiar introduction to a police bulletin:

This just in. The Neuhoff Packing Company was held up by bandits at approximately twelve thirty this afternoon. Two men escaped west on Industrial Boulevard in a black Ford V-8. These men are armed and dangerous. One reported stocky. One slight with a limp. Both wearing dark suits and tan fedoras. Repeat, these men are armed and dangerous. Anyone observing them should contact the Dallas police.

"That's them! That's Clyde! They got away!" Bonnie had been unprepared for the flush of pride that made her jump to her feet.

The car rolled between the gas pumps with a crunch of gravel and a light tap on the horn. He hadn't left her behind.

"They want me," Bonnie said. "So long."

She let the screen bang behind her.

CHAPTER 30

They drove west on Eagle Ford Road, past the colossal gray towers of Cement City, past Chalk Hill Road, past the road to the house where she'd lived with her grandparents.

"Aren't we going back to Wichita Falls?" Bonnie asked, when it became clear that they weren't turning north.

"We can't go back there," Clyde said. "It's way too hot." This seemed to delight him. "We just stole four hundred and forty dollars. Didn't you hear it on the radio?"

"I just heard you got away."

Clyde frowned. "They ought to have said about the money. That's a real piece of money. That's not small potatoes."

"You should have told me. I left my case."

"I didn't know, did I, until we seen what was there. They don't publish their account books in the paper."

"But I need my clothes."

"We'll buy new ones. With four hundred and forty dollars, we can buy whatever we want."

"Two-twenty," Raymond said.

"Fuck you, Raymond," Clyde said, but his tone was playful. "I ain't trying to steal your money. I'm just saying, we've got plenty."

In her mind, Bonnie saw the green case Mrs. Jancek had given her when they'd left Rowena, its edges worn and its top and bottom scratched. She'd left it propped open, its soft innards—her folded clothes—exposed, faithfully awaiting her return. She tried to concentrate on the road that ran flat and straight ahead of them. The green suitcase belonged to the old Bonnie; she wasn't that girl anymore.

A ways out from Grand Prairie, Clyde turned onto a grass track that led to a house with a sagging foundation and a tin roof that dipped on one side, as though the structure were cringing from a blow from the sky. The inside smelled of rotting wood, and dead flies coated the windowsills. The rooms were receptacles for objects too heavy—a wood-burning oven—or too insignificant to be carried off. Traces of other people's lives—broken crockery, an empty lard can, a wadded baby's dress of indeterminate color, a saucepan without a handle, a cobalt-blue bottle that retained the odor of its sticky cure, a single black shoe with the sole tearing away from the upper—had collected in the corners. In the bedroom that Clyde claimed by dropping a blanket and pillow on the floor, a family of clothespin dolls huddled in a rag, abandoned by some other Bonnie.

"You thirsty?"

She wasn't, but to reward his solicitousness, she cupped her hands in the flow while he vigorously worked the pump, and she drank the water acrid with iron.

◆

Raymond stayed a night and a day, sucking on Lucky Strikes, whistling disconnected phrases, and bragging about the jobs he intended to pull. Then he said he was sick of sitting around and Clyde said he was sick of listening to Raymond complain about sitting around, so Clyde and Bonnie drove Raymond back into Dallas. Returning to Grand Prairie without him, Bonnie felt elated to be getting away from Dallas with its straight streets and square front yards, its shuttered shops and closed cafés. She pressed against Clyde, tucking her shoulder into the hollow of his armpit, laying her head on his shoulder. With his arm around her, he strummed her thigh as if it were his guitar, and they flew through gentle hills of scruffy grass, past lonely clusters of compact trees, along the beckoning road.

For two days, they slept late, curled in a blanket nest, and then moved outside to lie in the sun. They coupled when they chose, drank Coca-Cola, ate baloney and bread, and washed in the iron-steeped water. She was pliable and warm as the grass on which they lay, but what made her fully flower was the reading. Clyde had packed along three dime novels—*Jesse James: Knight Errant, Jesse James' Terrible Raid,* and *Jesse James' Last Chance*—their pages so swollen with humidity and frequent turning that they had burst from their cheap bindings. When he left one lying on the blanket, she began to read it aloud. At first, she meant her performance to be a joke. The novel was pulp, after all, the boy's version of the movie magazines that she'd realized long ago depicted lives no more real than the pictures their subjects starred in. She made fun of the earnest diction, employing her elocution training to the utmost, until she detected the tentativeness in his laugh. He could scoff at the bangs and pings and thuds; he could appreciate the ridiculous formality of words like "mollification" and "altercation" and "braggadocio"; but he believed in the character.

On the third day, the sky was brown and dusty; the Coca-Cola was cloying; the baloney was gone; and the few remaining slices of bread were dry. Clyde stood the bottles they'd emptied on a rock and blasted them one by one. Trying to escape the unrelenting explosions of gunpowder and glass, Bonnie walked across the rough, abandoned fields, knotted with black-eyed Susans and bristling with thistles. With the house out of sight behind the undulating hills, she frightened herself, imagining that everything she knew on earth had vanished. By the time she'd run back, Clyde had pulled the guns apart for cleaning and spread the pieces across their blanket-bed.

"You'd better take me home," she said. "I need to see my mother."

CHAPTER 31

August 4, 1932

"Maybe I oughta stay with you." Bonnie's hand was on the door handle, but she'd not yet twisted it to let herself out of the car at the Barrows'.

"But you want to see your mama." Clyde frowned. "What did we come into Dallas for?"

"I do want to see my mama! I just . . . well, what're you going to do while I'm at home?"

He shrugged. "I'll be all right."

"Promise you won't go down to Eastham."

"We ain't ready for that. I'll just lie low, I guess. But I can't sit here. You git out and I'll come find you in a couple days."

"You promise?"

"For Pete's sake, honey. Go see your mama and give this to mine." He handed her a grubby envelope, thick with bills. "I'll be back."

She wanted to run after his car, but when the door opened behind her, she turned to Cumie with a smile. "He'll be back, Miz Barrow. He's just getting a little rest, nice and safe out in the country, where it's not so hot."

Cumie didn't smile, but she opened the door wider to invite Bonnie in with one hand, while she slid the envelope into her apron pocket with the other.

◆

An hour or so later, Bonnie found her own mother in her usual spot, three machines over and four up among the grid of sewers. Her ears full of the constant whir, her head bent low over the furiously punching needle, Emma started when her daughter placed a hand on her shoulder, and her line of stitches veered off the course.

"You got time off already?" Emma reached for a stitch ripper, conscious of the circling foreman.

"I traded with a girl," Bonnie said. "So I could have a good long visit."

"That's no way to keep a job." Emma flicked the ripper stitch by stitch through the ruined seam. Her count would be low now. "You got to make them depend on you, not be skipping off."

"Ain't you happy to see me?"

"Course, I am." Emma struggled to pinch the fabric in the right spot with the foot. It was nearly impossible to get the interrupted seam to line up properly. She ought to rip the whole thing and start again, but she couldn't afford to be so conscientious.

"You don't look happy."

Emma shook her head. "I'm working. Go on home. I'll be there soon."

"Can I borrow your suitcase? I want to take some things back with me, and I didn't think to bring mine."

"Go ahead. I'm not going anywhere."

◆

Billie disappointed Bonnie, too. Not understanding that Bonnie had come from what might just as well have been the moon, she had no sense of the momentousness of her visit.

Bonnie amused herself with the babies that evening and listened to talk about a neighbor with a growth the size of a melon on his hip. Whenever she heard a car, she was tempted to look out the window, but it couldn't yet be Clyde.

The following night, she refused Billie's invitation to join her out dancing, because it wasn't too soon to start waiting. Besides, she no longer craved that kind of thrill, which, when all was said and done, was only play. When Buddy and Mitzy had finally settled into a damp sleep, Bonnie and Emma sat outside in the dark, beaten into passivity by the thick, hot air and the steady shrill of the crickets.

A car turned the corner onto their street, and the engine growled as it built speed. Bonnie squinted, trying make out the face behind the headlights, but the car passed.

"Does Clyde ever come there?" Emma asked.

"Where?"

"To Wichita Falls. Or," Emma added drily, "wherever it is you're at."

Bonnie longed to say "yes;" her mouth, her mind, her chest, even her arms and fingers—every part of her felt full to bursting with the idea of Clyde.

"I told you, Mama," she said, cloaking her lie with petulance, "I wouldn't let him come anywhere near me. Not after that mess down in Kaufman."

"Don't be throwing your life away," Emma warned.

Bonnie thought of her mother, curled like a snail around a sewing machine, afraid even to turn her head for longer than the foreman might allow. "I don't aim to."

◆

Emma was conveniently at church when Clyde knocked the next morning. He stepped inside, but he watched the windows nervously, his hand tucked in his jacket.

Bonnie, who'd answered with a baby on each hip, shifted the children into her sister's arms. "Aren't you going to say hello to Billie Jean?"

"Hey, Billie," he said. "We got to go, baby. It's worse."

CHAPTER 32

Clyde made Bonnie wait until they got to his mother's; he didn't want to tell it twice. He drove to Eagle Ford Road fast, his eyes focused ahead and his fingers tight around the wheel.

They'd gone up to Oklahoma, he and Raymond and a fellow named Tom Dyer.

"Don't I know the Dyers from over to the campground?" Cumie interrupted.

"This ain't them Dyers."

Bonnie could see that Clyde was eager to puke up the whole story, as if his mama could soothe him.

"We was driving on back to Dallas, and we come up on one of them dances scraped up from a string of lanterns under some shed and a band wearing overalls. Well, Raymond, having no more sense than a stump, says he's got to stop. Says he ain't had no fun since before he went to the county. And Dyer spots a flask, so it's two against one."

Knowing Raymond, Bonnie was sure the three of them had had plenty of moonshine already, but she forbore mentioning this in front of Cumie.

"I said to myself, let Raymond and Tom have their dances. Kiss some girls. Get it out of their systems. To be honest, I couldn't take them two whining at me the whole way back to Dallas."

Cumie had heard on the radio about the shooting in Stringtown, Oklahoma, but she'd known Bud couldn't have had a thing to do with that. When Henry'd looked at her, she'd scoffed. What would Bud be doing at some country dance in Oklahoma?

She remembered how the report had described Eugene Moore: brave, hardworking, cruelly taken from a wife and two small children.

"Why'd you have to go and kill a man that had babies?" Cumie exclaimed.

"I told you, Ma. I didn't kill him. It was Raymond. Or maybe it was Tom. They were shooting at us pretty bad, and there was lots of bullets zipping around. But I never aimed one shot at none of 'em."

Clyde waited until they'd left his mother's house to tell Bonnie that it was too bad that Eugene Moore had had babies, but worse was that he was a law. If they caught Clyde now, he'd for sure get the chair.

◆

On the way back to the Grand Prairie house, the story settled around Bonnie's neck, and she tugged at it. Had Eugene Moore been dancing innocently with his wife or had he been surveying the crowd, looking for trouble? Had Clyde been dancing with some other girl? Had Moore said anything? Had he been angry? Where had the bullet hit? Had he died instantly or bled?

Clyde was damned if he knew anything about the man other than that he'd been among those blasting when their car had turned over and they'd had to shoot like hell.

"Your car turned over?"

But he refused to piece events together for her. She let her mind slip to the children, washing their teeth and saying their prayers in that limbo before a man would come to the door to tell their mother.

Grand Prairie wasn't far enough for a man who'd killed a law—or even for a man who'd been with a man who'd killed a law—but Clyde turned in at the grass-covered drive. When he shut off the engine, he turned to her, his skin shiny with sweat, his eyes large and darting. "Can you make me different?"

She thought he was begging her to reform his character, but from under the seat, he produced a bottle of hair dye. "Do you know how to use this?"

◆

Clyde's head emerged from under the pump as bright orange as a bottle of Crush. Against that hair, his skin turned sallow and his eyes dulled, so that he looked like the kind of man who could have shot a man dead just for approaching his car.

Bonnie vomited under a pecan tree until her muscles cramped and then, spent, lay on her back, gasping, staring up at the lint gray of the flat, indifferent sky. She waited for him to find her, but, in the end, she had to go after him. She found him inside, sitting with his back against the wall, listlessly pushing his fingers through his wet hair. Beneath the waxy skin and behind the hard eyes, she saw the boy the laws had caught on her mother's davenport, afraid and uncertain. He'd finished the two things he'd instinctively thought to do—collect Bonnie and confess to his mother—and now he was lost.

CHAPTER 33

"Let's start over," she urges. "Let's get in the car and drive to where the laws don't know you from Adam."

She chooses Carlsbad, New Mexico, which, with its pink sky and jewel-like flowers, she knows is nothing like Texas. The state's very name suggests rebirth. She tucks the clothespin family inside Emma's suitcase and is ready, but he melts, sliding along the wall until he's lying full-length on the bare floor.

"Tomorrow," he murmurs, as his eyes close.

◆

The delay is costly, at least from Bonnie's point of view, because Raymond appears just after dawn, laughs at Clyde's hair, and, unfortunately, approves of Bonnie's plan. When they start west, he's stretched out across their back seat.

Nevertheless, on the far side of Fort Worth, Bonnie and Clyde begin to relax. Clyde takes off his shoes, so he can "feel the car," and pushes the new V-8 to eighty. The hot wind funneling through the open windows scours them clean, and brown dust veils the road behind them. They have 475 miles of packed dirt to travel, most of it in Texas, and Bonnie lets the monotony of the brown and red earth lull her to sleep. When she awakens in New Mexico, the sky, intensely blue and dolloped with white clouds, suggests heaven, even though Carlsbad itself, which they reach by late afternoon, does not appear very different from the towns of East Texas.

◆

In Millie Stamps's airless kitchen, Bonnie remembers her aunt's fondness for pretty, fragile things. At least a dozen flowered teacups dangle from hooks below the cabinet; whimsical pairs of salt and pepper shakers—a hen and a rooster, a white sheep and a black sheep, a turnip and a beet, a squaw and a brave—line the back of the counter; cut glass creamers and sugar bowls of various hues cover an open shelf.

"I gotta study what I can make for y'all." Millie picks a shred of tobacco off her tongue as she gazes vaguely around the room. "We weren't expecting no company. Not that we ain't thrilled to see y'all." She frowns slightly, pulling on her cigarette. "I recall you was married to a fellow named Roy. This ain't that fellow, I suppose."

Bonnie feels herself blushing, as she shakes her head, aware that Millie may see her as half of a damaged set, a salt that has carelessly come detached from her pepper. Millie is balancing her cigarette on the edge of a pink glass ashtray, when gunfire explodes in the back yard, followed by triumphant hoots. Bonnie, quick and clever, explains to her startled aunt that "Jimmy" and "Jack" must be practicing for the hunting they plan to do up in the mountains.

"My tomaters!" Millie bleats, as more fat fruits burst in her garden.

"I'll tell them to quit." Bonnie starts for the door.

"You tell them boys to run into town for some ice," Millie calls after her. "Dink, get out the churn. I bet you kids'll love you some ice cream, Bonnie Elizabeth."

Ray goes for the ice, while Clyde cleans the guns. He wants to bring them into the house, but Bonnie won't allow it. "Don't you have any idea how decent folk live? Put them in the car when Raymond gets back." Stopping at the Stamps' has been a mistake. The problem is not that they haven't gone far enough, but that they've brought themselves along.

❖

At dinner, Bonnie, Millie, and Dink try to conduct a normal conversation, but Clyde makes the whole table jittery, turning his chair askew so he can see out the window and glancing up the drive every time he puts a forkful into his mouth. However, after the meal, when Bonnie, Clyde, and Raymond are sitting in their car with the doors open, sharing a drink from a jar, Bonnie doesn't care if her aunt and uncle are shaking their heads inside the house. They're like her mother, encased in cooking oil and cigarette smoke and the fussy anxieties of those who want to avoid notice. The enormous, spangled sky only reminds them that they ought to be asleep in their beds. She tips her liquor-laced head out the window, so that there's nothing between her and the stars, and exults in the western air, which has sharpened the insects' throb to a twang and smoothed her sticky skin.

"We'll leave early," she promises the boys. She wants to see the caverns when the light is fresh. Millie doesn't remember sending the postcard and hasn't been to the tourist attraction since they first moved to the state, but she's written detailed directions in her swirling script. They'll go from the caverns to Albuquerque—a city with a beautiful name that Bonnie alone can spell—and by the time they reach Santa Fe, their connection to some random Saturday-night dance in Oklahoma and a couple of children whose father would never come home will have stretched so thin that it will snap in the dry New Mexican ether.

CHAPTER 34

The knocking awakens them at nine. Clyde instantly rolls off the bed and onto the floor, pulling on his pants.

"The old man must have a gun," Clyde says to Raymond, who's crowded into the bedroom. "Check the closets. I'll look under their bed. You answer," he orders Bonnie. "Tell him you'll have to wake us. Act like nothing's wrong."

"But what *is* wrong?" Bonnie wails. "We didn't do anything."

The man wearing the deputy's star looks more fatherly than frightening, but she crosses her arms and can't keep the tightness from her voice. "Yes?"

"Sorry to bother you, miss. Would you tell me who that automobile belongs to?" He nods toward the V-8.

"Oh." She feels his authority compelling an answer. She tries to speak casually, but her heart is thudding so loudly that she can't tell whether she's whispering or shouting. "That's my husband's. I'll get him." She turns toward the bedroom, leaving the front door yawning, and then remembers Clyde's instructions and turns back. "He's still sleeping, so it may take a few minutes. You'd best wait out here." She closes the door and quietly slips the bolt.

She's aghast at her lousy performance but has only seconds to chastise herself. Clyde and Ray have found the shotgun Dink keeps to scare crows and have slipped out the back. Too late, the deputy reaches for his piece and, when Clyde sends a blast of birdshot over his head, the pistol slides from his fingers.

"Bonnie Elizabeth!"

Through the back window, Bonnie sees her aunt, stumbling through the rows of string beans, the vines catching at her ankles.

"Baby, c'mon!" Clyde commands from the front.

◆

Beside the car, Clyde and Raymond are arguing.

"Shoot him," Raymond says.

"The hell I will."

"Bonnie!" Aunt Millie has reached the front door. Her voice is high and weak for want of breath.

"Get in! Get in!" When the deputy doesn't move, Clyde takes a step toward him, his rifle raised. "Get him in!" he orders Raymond, who shoves the man into the back seat and throws himself in afterward.

They can't stay in New Mexico with a New Mexican hostage, so they drive back to Texas, last night's certain escape eradicated. Soon after they cross the Texas line, a radio report informs them that near El Paso two truck drivers have found the headless body of a man police assume is Joe Johns, sheriff's deputy of Eddy County, New Mexico, abducted earlier that morning by two men and a woman in a Ford V-8 with Texas plates.

"It's not fair," Bonnie says to Johns. "They're coming after us for killing you, when here you are, safe and sound."

"Get out the map," Clyde says. "We got to get away from Odessa."

The map flutters on Bonnie's trembling legs. She slides her index finger over the maze of roads, unable to orient herself, and Clyde pulls impatiently at the paper. "Do I gotta do everything?"

"Let me drive," Raymond says. "You think I don't know how to drive a car?" He lunges over the seat, reaching for the wheel.

"Get off me! You're supposed to be watching the law!"

"You think I'm going to jump out of a machine going eighty miles an hour?" Johns puts in.

"I heard you were dead," Clyde says. "Why're you talking?"

"You already got at least twenty years for transporting me over state lines," the officer says stoutly. "You kill me, you'll get the chair."

"He ain't going to kill you!" Bonnie exclaims.

But at the same time, Raymond says, "He's already getting the chair."

"So I might as well kill you," Clyde says.

"He's not serious." Bonnie frowns at Clyde. "We had to take you, that's all. So you wouldn't turn us in."

"Well, as long as that's all."

Johns isn't much like the laws who wouldn't let her into the jail to visit Clyde or those who mocked Clyde in her mother's house. Bonnie is surprised to find that she almost likes him.

Sometime after midnight, about a mile north of San Antonio, Clyde finally pulls off the road. "All right, you can get out here."

Johns creeps hesitantly from the car, like a rabbit newly sprung from a hutch.

"You sure have caused us a lot of trouble," Clyde says. "We didn't do nothing to you, you know. We didn't even do nothing in your town. In your whole state. I think you oughta give us an hour before you call us in."

As they drive off, Bonnie presses her face to the window, but the lawman has already been folded into the darkness behind them. "Is it true what he said about the twenty years?"

Raymond laughs. "Probably."

Later, after the sun is up and they've nosed into a copse out of sight of the highway, the reports begin to issue from the radio. "Bonnie Parker of Dallas." All of Texas can hear her name. ". . . and a woman, Bonnie Parker of Dallas." ". . . a blond, petite female, Bonnie Parker of Dallas." People who live near the border in Arkansas, Oklahoma, Louisiana, and New Mexico can probably hear it, too.

"Clyde." She whispers in his ear, so she won't wake Raymond who's sprawled across the back. "Baby, I want you."

But he's dead asleep, too, his breathing heavy and slow.

CHAPTER 35

They shed Raymond at last by driving him to his father's house in Michigan. On September 3, when they dropped him at a wood frame bungalow in Bay City, fall was already insinuating itself into that part of the country. The summer blur had been wrung out of the sky, leaving behind a distilled, melancholy blue, and here and there a crown of yellow or orange betrayed the shock a tree had experienced at the advent of the cooling nights.

Invigorated, Bonnie unfolded the Marathon map she'd found in the glove compartment of their current car and traced the red and blue veins through the hand of Michigan to Chicago, where, contrary to the shadowed scenes they'd been led to expect by *The Public Enemy* and *Little Caesar*, the sun burst off the lake and spangled in a thousand windows. Dazzled by a city that made Dallas look like a country crossroads, Bonnie sent postcards crammed with skyscrapers and crowded beaches and streets so jammed with automobiles they were being stacked twelve high. "Look where we got to," she wrote.

Chicago suited her style, but it made Clyde jumpy. Bonnie wanted to walk the streets, as if she and Clyde belonged among the purposeful pedestrians, but he was forever stutter-stepping, attempting to avoid contact and therefore always meeting it with a bump that made him recoil and scowl.

So in a couple of days they were driving south and west again, their tires sizzling over freshly rolled asphalt. With every mile, the buildings became squatter and plainer and the space between them grew longer, but Bonnie kept the metropolis fizzing inside her with an elixir she sipped from a flat, brown bottle. They'd bought a boxful in the city, where a quizzical glance and a few bills were all it took to unlock a back room. The pictures had been right about that.

They breezed through towns like Manteno and Bourbonnais, snags of mundane, dusty shops. In the evenings, Clyde parked near creeks, and they bathed in water rusty with decomposing leaves, the bronzed air above its surface effervescent with tiny insects. She made him thrash the weeds with a stick to scare off reptiles and amphibians, so he yelled "snake" when she was settling down, and in turn she shrieked to please him. Too late in the year for mosquitoes, too early for snow, they pulled the back seat from the car and lounged on it as if it were an outdoor divan. While she read aloud from *True Detective*, they drank from their brown bottles and fed each other sardines on crackers and Vienna sausages they dug out of the can with their fingers. When the sun was thoroughly extinguished and the titanic darkness blacked out all the earth except the ring around their restless, flickering fire, he played his guitar and sang "My Blue-Eyed Jane."

"C'mon, little show-off," he said, when he'd had enough from the bottle, and she responded extravagantly, sure of her audience. When he was liquored up just right, he touched her with the appreciation he would have lavished on a 16-cylinder Cadillac that he was running on a clear stretch of highway, trying to coax out all she'd got.

During the day, however, any time he wasn't driving, his hands were on his Browning Automatic Rifles, part of a stash of weapons they'd stolen before they'd left Texas simply by raking the padlock on an unassuming National Guard Armory outside Fort Worth.

"These them army boys keep for theirselves," Clyde said, shouldering a BAR. The telltale lethal cartridge extended from its underside, like the member of a stallion or a bull. "They're too much for the laws."

With a hacksaw he cut one rifle short and attached it to a sling of rubber he'd sliced from an old tire. He sacrificed the pocket of his coat to what he called his "scattergun," because the weapon would make the laws scat like scaredy-cats, cutting the seam so that he could reach right through and grab the piece hidden under the fabric. Practicing, he fingered the gun, stroked the gun, pulled it out and held it up, stiff and ready, over and over. Inspired, he determined that they would borrow an alias from Jesse James and call themselves Mr. and Mrs. Howard.

Bonnie was flattered by the care with which he chose a gun for her, a rifle with the back and front ends cut off. He called it a "whipit," because, as he explained, it was supposed to be easy to whip out. But the thing was heavier and more unwieldy than it looked; the front end sagged when she held the back. He positioned her, lowering her akimbo elbows, drawing forward the chin she'd pulled back like a turtle. She felt stiff as a dummy when he was through, and her index finger trembled weakly against the trigger. When she finally managed to squeeze it, the metal pinched her skin; the bang was a slap to the head; the kick, a rebuke so sharp that she dropped the gun.

"I don't like it."

He laughed. "You'll get used to it. You just gotta practice."

She shook her head. "I'll aim and make them think I'm going to use it, but I don't want to shoot no one."

"You think I do? It made me feel sick when that law crumpled up back in Stringtown. I thought I was going to black out, I got so dizzy."

"But it wasn't you that killed him."

He shrugged. "Mighta been. Hard to know for sure. You don't have to pull the trigger, sugar," he said. "I don't want you getting that sick feeling. But it'd be handy, if I learned you to load."

◆

While Clyde fooled with his guns, Bonnie played with a poem, attempting to put their most recent fresh start into words. As they drove through rain in Arkansas, she changed the title from "Fall Starts," which sounded too much like "false starts," to "The Start of the Fall," which sounded ominous, and settled finally on "Starting Out in Fall."

"*Fall was their spring*," she wrote, the letters jagged as each bump unseated her pen.

> *The starting of their road.*
> *Under smoky skies they drove;*
> *A car was their abode.*
> *Where they would wander,*

What distance they would go,
Was hidden in the clouds.
Only God could surely know.

Sometimes, if they came upon a likely looking farmhouse, they would stop and pay for a night in a bed. In the hills outside Fayetteville, they pulled in at such a place, and a passel of children darted and swooped around the car like insects around a light bulb.

"You can touch it," Clyde offered, and their fingertips left spots in the dust.

"Who wants a ride?" asked Lady Bountiful.

Of course, they couldn't let anyone inside—there were too many guns under the blankets on the back seat—but Bonnie showed them how they could stand on the running board, a few at a time, and hold on through the open window. The children shrieked as Clyde drove them around the dirt yard, while their parents and an old man shyly waited their turn.

Slender Mr. and Mrs. Howard squeezed onto the ends of the benches on either side of the table for a supper of squirrel and dumplings, which made Bonnie unexpectedly homesick for Krause. In exchange for the hospitality, Bonnie entertained with her impressions of Chicago.

"You tell quite a story," her host said, holding one hand in front of his mouth to hide his twisted teeth.

As a token of her veracity, she took out a cigarette case she'd purchased at Marshall Fields. "Clyde, run out and get me my lighter, would you?"

Instead, he stood up abruptly and laid two bills on the table. "We're going."

Back in the car, she argued. Those people could not possibly have heard of a stray thief named Clyde Barrow, and even if they had, they'd have no desire to turn in the man who let them ride on his car and the woman who'd made them laugh and stare, and even if they did, they had no means to do so other than a mule, and it was his sudden leave-taking that would make them suspicious, not her use of his first name. And why was he always the one to say where they could stop and how long they ought to stay and what they could say?

For miles he answered only with his driving, which was too fast for the curving, hilly, dusky road. At first, the reckless speed matched her mood, and she didn't complain, but when their tires caught on the soft shoulder and threatened to drag them into the trees, she screamed at him to slow down. When he finally braked to execute a turn onto a side track her fingers were stiff from clutching the door handle and the edge of her seat, and her calves were sore from her cramping muscles.

The track narrowed gradually until their car could no longer pass between the trees, and he had to stop. "How could you be so dumb?"

She leapt on him, pinning his shoulders to the car door behind him. "The dumbest thing I ever did was go with you."

He clamped his fingers around her wrists and pinned her left leg with his right. Her upper arm collided with the steering wheel; his chin banged against her lip. Twisting free, she slithered over the seat into the back, but he followed. Afterward, he rolled down the clouded windows, and she lay with her head in the hollow of his shoulder, so she could look up at the stars.

"From now on, when we're with people, I'm Bud and you're Sis."

"I'll be Anita."

He shook his head. "No, Anita's a name people would notice. Don't you understand? We gotta be no one special."

To apologize for his temper, he stole a typewriter for her in Little Rock. It was set up in the window of the stationery store with a fresh ribbon and a sheet of white paper rolled into the carriage. Before the clerk was even aware that someone had entered the store, Clyde snapped the varnished lid over the machine, paper and all, and carried it out to the car.

From then on, Bonnie spent some hours each day in her office—the back seat—composing, as well as copying all the handwritten lines in her notebooks. No matter how unsteady her desk, the keys struck the ribbon cleanly. The official-looking type seemed to change her work from girlish, personal whims into truth.

CHAPTER 36

By Halloween, Clyde decided they'd given Dallas plenty of time to cool, but to be on the safe side, he didn't stop at the service station but only slowed long enough for Bonnie to heave at the door a Coca-Cola bottle with a note rolled up inside it that read "red beens and rice," the signal that their families were to meet them on Chalk Hill.

"It says here you done another murder," Cumie said that night, pulling a folded page of newsprint from an envelope and shaking it open. "What's wrong with you?"

"Lessee that." Clyde plucked the article from her hand.

Authorities are offering a $200 reward for the capture of Clyde Champion Barrow, who is wanted for the brutal murder of Alfred Brown, a grocery clerk in Akron, Ohio, on October 11. Witnesses heard shots coming from the grocery around 4 pm, just before a slender, dark-haired man ran with a definite limp from the grocery and got into a waiting car, driven by a woman in a black hat. Barrow is known to travel with Bonnie Parker, 22, of Dallas, Texas. The pair is also wanted for the murder of two sheriffs' deputies and for armed robbery of several banks in Texas and Oklahoma. They are thoroughly dangerous and will not hesitate to kill.

Clyde whistled. "Thoroughly dangerous! I like that!"

"Bud!"

"That's not us." Bonnie, with Mitzy on her hip, crowded close to study the page. "I don't even own a black hat."

"I told you so," Cumie said to Henry. "I knew them kids wouldn't be mixed up in something like this."

"I bet there never even was a woman in that car," Bonnie said. "They like to say there's a woman, but there usually isn't. I'm pret' near the only one."

Emma, who hadn't seen Bonnie since August, found she couldn't release her daughter's hand.

"You got my postcards, Mama? From Chicago?"

"I couldn't believe it when Millie telephoned me," Emma said. "I told her that's not possible. That's not Bonnie. And now you done all this?" She gestured at Cumie's pile of clippings.

Bonnie examined the articles. "It's not the way they make it sound."

There were two accounts of the kidnapping of Deputy Johns, one of the Hillsboro murder, three of the Stringtown fiasco. Two stories included mug shots of Clyde—one a boy with a wistful expression on his finely wrought features, slicked hair neatly parted in the center, and an open collar that revealed a delicate neck; the other a man with thick, wavy hair and a tie cinched below a solidified jaw, who looked as if he knew what he was doing. There were also reports of bank robberies in Texas, Oklahoma, Kansas, and Missouri.

They had not been nearly as successful as those stories suggested. One afternoon, for instance, Clyde and a couple of accomplices were laughed out of a bank that had happened to fail the afternoon before they attempted to rob it. After that, they'd tried using Bonnie as a scout. When she entered the Farmers and Miners Bank of Oronogo, Missouri, dressed in what she considered appropriate banking clothes—a gray flannel suit, pearl gray gloves, and a maroon cloche, Bonnie realized that the browsing she'd envisioned, as one might in a dress shop or department store, wouldn't be possible. What did one do in a bank, if one had no actual business there? She studied a portrait of a man from the last century on one wall and then the calendar beside it, decorated with a river scene. She thumbed a pad of deposit slips.

A man in overalls turned away from the teller in his narrow cage, folding a handful of bills, so she knew there was money in the place.

"May I help you, miss?" A young man was suddenly at her side.

Having no experience with banks, she had no idea how odd she looked, an unfamiliar woman, without a male escort to speak for her, but she was quick enough with a satisfactory answer. "My husband was supposed to meet me. He's looking for a place to put some money. He's in oil," she added. "We're up from Texas."

"I see. Won't you have a seat while you wait?" He indicated a chair on the near side of a wide, wooden desk.

She should have accepted, she realized later. She should have sat there, smoked a cigarette, asked impatiently for the time once or twice, and then stalked out in a mild fit of pique. That's how a Texas oilman's wife would have behaved. But, instead, she lost her nerve, declined the offer, and with that suspicious behavior tipped off the teller, who was ready with his own pistol and a quick finger on the alarm when Clyde came in the next day. Accomplices tended to drift away after such failures.

They tried to spring their old friend Ralph Fults from the McKinney Jail, but before they could do more than have Bonnie deliver a pack of Lucky Strikes and the message that Clyde was waiting with a car outside, the One-Way Wagon snatched Ralph out of reach. In desperation, they might have gone back to Michigan for Raymond had he not been plucked off an ice rink and returned to Texas to stand trial for the murder of Madora Bucher, as well as for two major bank robberies. It galled Bonnie to see a man she knew to be no more than a reckless braggart enjoy that kind of success, when Clyde, for all his careful plans, had not scored so well in nearly a year.

"Probably they're lying about what he done, the same way they lie about us," Clyde said.

Certainly, the authorities were wrong about Raymond's involvement in the Bucher murder.

"I'm not saying I like the thief," Clyde told Bonnie, "but I'm not going to let him get the chair for something I know he ain't done."

CHAPTER 37

Emma Parker lifted the edge of her window curtain so she could see the man who was knocking before she opened her door. A strange man on her stoop made her uneasy at any time of day, especially if he wasn't carrying a sales case, and now, being so close to Christmas, it had been fully dark for at least an hour.

"Mrs. Parker?" He must have sensed the curtain's movement, because he turned toward the window. His eyes drooped a little at the corners, like a hound's. "Can I talk to you about Bonnie?" He removed a badge from his jacket pocket and held it up, so she could see it.

Emma unlocked the door and opened it a few inches. "She in jail?"

"No. No, she's not. But I know she's in trouble, and I'd like to help her. Would you let me come in?"

Emma snorted. "Help her? You want to catch her."

"I'd like to persuade her to turn herself in, yes. I knew her back at Marco's, you see. She's a friend of mine."

Emma opened the door. "I didn't know Bonnie was a friend of any law."

"I was at the post office then," the man said, removing his hat and stepping inside. "Ted Hinton." The hand he extended was warm, although he hadn't been wearing gloves. "Two Sugars is what she called me."

Sitting with him on the divan, listening to him talk about how he'd always imagined seeing Bonnie onstage someday, singing songs that came out of that poetry she used to write—"I believe she's still writing poetry," Emma put in—or maybe even in the pictures, Emma could not help but feel that it was a shame this man had not put himself forward as a beau, back before it was too late.

"If she turns herself in, I doubt she'd get more than two years for the kidnapping," he said.

Reminded that it was too late, Emma drew hard on her cigarette.

"We know it wasn't her idea," he went on, "and Mr. Johns made clear that she never handled a gun."

"Anyone knows anything about Bonnie could tell you she's always been scared to death of guns," Emma snapped.

"I believe that," Mr. Hinton said. "She's not the kind of girl who should be mixed up in something like this."

Emma felt again the welling of confusion and panic she'd experienced when her sister Millie had telephoned long-distance from New Mexico. "I'm not sure anymore what kind of girl she is."

"The kind that will think of her mother on Christmas, I believe."

Carefully, Emma made no response.

"Can you get a message to her?"

"I don't know. I might could."

"If you speak to her," he said, leaning to stub out his cigarette, "will you tell her Two Sugars wants to help her?"

What a gentle-looking face he had, Emma thought. He'd a small cut just below his ear, no doubt from his razor. She almost cried to think how vulnerable they were, all of these young people with their tender feelings and hopes.

CHAPTER 38

December 1932

On Christmas Eve, Clyde and Bonnie parked on the shoulder of Eagle Ford Road and waited in the drizzle for L.C. to come riding by. Staying still was nervous business—a stopped car tended to make a cop curious—and Bonnie, curled into her coat with her feet tucked under her, alternating sips from a flask with flecks of lemon peel, couldn't quit shaking with tension heightened by the cold. She'd prayed to have a baby growing inside her by this night, but instead the hateful blood was oozing out, cooling as it pooled between her legs.

"There he is." Clyde tapped the horn.

The Model T pulled over and snuffed its lights. Two doors slammed, and then L.C.'s face, carrying with it the sweet-sour scent of home brew, appeared in Clyde's open window. He smiled big enough to crack his head in two, but his eyes had a wobbly, uncertain look. Clyde often evoked a combination of joy and worry, Bonnie noted.

"Heard you been in," Clyde said.

"Yep."

"I don't want you pulling shit, hear me?"

"Hell, they drug me in just for walkin' down the street. Half the time, they figure I'm you. Half the time, they figure I'm fixin' to pull a job with you. Half the time, they just figure I musta done it. I'm a Barrow, ain't I?"

Bonnie laughed. "That's three halves, L.C."

"What?" He stuck his head in farther. "How you doin', Bonnie? You got any Baby Ruths on you?"

As she leaned over Clyde with a candy bar that she'd tied with a red ribbon, she glimpsed a second boy, dark and bashful, lurking behind

L.C. He had a cigar sticking out of one side of his mouth and was chewing on it in an obvious attempt to look older. It had the opposite effect. "Who's your friend?"

"This here's W.D." L.C. stepped back to make room for the other to come up.

"You know me, Clyde," the boy said, dipping his head in a sort of bow. "I'm Deacon. Tookie Jones's boy."

"Well, what do you know?" Clyde said. "It's Little Deacon Jones!"

"That's right," the boy said, nodding like a hen at its corn. "Most call me W.D. now."

"You want to ride around with us for a bit, Dub? You want to be our lookout for a couple, two, three days?"

"What about me?" L.C. protested.

"I told you," Clyde said. "You ain't gettin' into this. Besides, Deac's experienced." He gave the boy an exaggerated wink that made him blush, even in the freezing air. "C'mon in here." He tilted his head to indicate the back seat. "Shove that stuff over and sit with us while L.C. fetches our people."

W.D. squeezed himself onto the corner of the seat and sat crammed against the door, not daring to displace any part of the mess of blankets and papers and the couple of brightly wrapped packages. William Daniel "Deacon" Jones had admired Clyde, since the days when the Joneses and the Barrows had both camped under the viaduct, along with the rest of the flotsam that had come loose from its tenuous sharecropper moorings and washed up on the wrong side of the Trinity. Even then, W.D. had known that he could never possess the older boy's ease and power of asserting himself. Clyde was always first in line at the round steak truck, and W.D. had seen him swipe extra baloney many times when the driver's back was turned. He would give those slices away to the little ones at the back, more than once to W.D. himself.

Some years later, when the Joneses had left the campground, Clyde paid W.D. a nickel to keep watch while he called on Dorothy Jean Lennert, who rented a room in Tookie's house. Dorothy Jean sometimes gave W.D. a stick of gum out of her purse, and she told him what songs he ought to like, if he ever went to a dance. W.D. had sat on the step for awhile, wishing he were Clyde and hating him at the same time.

Finally, he couldn't stand it no more and went and threw the nickel in the river.

"The trouble is," Clyde was saying, "that me and Bonnie are dog tired. I wonder if you might be so kind as to keep watch later on tonight, while her and me get some sleep."

"Would you do that for us, W.D.?" Bonnie didn't like a lot of the men that Clyde was friendly with. They were too loutish to appreciate her particular charms and always trying to prove how tough they were, either sneering at her or ogling her when Clyde wasn't looking and constantly shoving at each other with their words. But a boy like this—bashful and earnest, like a worshipful kid brother—was someone she could play to, dazzle even. "We'll get you right back to Dallas first thing tomorrow."

"I told you I don't know about that," Clyde said. "Us driving up to your mama's house on Christmas morning. That's just what the laws'll be expecting."

"He thinks he's that important," she said. "Don't you know the laws got better things to do on Christmas than to bother with us, Daddy."

Clyde didn't answer.

"Baby, you promised." She rubbed her cheek against his shoulder. "We see your mama tonight; mine tomorrow. I gotta give out my presents."

"I told you they should meet us out here tonight."

"And I told you that they're not bringing those babies out in the cold."

In the darkness ahead, headlights jittered. Bonnie touched Clyde's arm.

"Relax," he said. "That's my daddy's car."

The lights swerved as the car pulled onto the shoulder. When the Model T's flimsy doors flapped open, Clyde, Bonnie, and W.D. got out to meet the Barrows on the other side of the damp dirt road. In a moment, Cumie and Clyde, with Marie clamped on his back, were interlocked, rocking together from foot to foot. W.D. and L.C. had drifted off, so Bonnie and Mr. Barrow, unshaven, as always, were left standing awkwardly together.

Mr. Barrow pushed two jars at her. "Merry Christmas."

◆

Clyde, refreshed by the visit, was magnanimous as they drove away. "We'll run you back here tomorrow morning," he assured W.D. "You'll be home in plenty of time to get the coal out of your stocking."

"I'm sure W.D. has been a good boy."

"Have you been a good boy, Deacon?" Clyde asked.

"I been all right, I guess."

Bonnie laughed. "Don't worry. We're not going to get you into any trouble. We're just going to find someplace safe to sleep and then get right back to Dallas, because I've got the best presents for my babies. Do you want to see?"

"He don't want to see no toys."

"I bet he does too."

Clyde sighed. "W.D., you want to see some baby toys?"

"Don't force him to take sides, Clyde. W.D., you don't have to say whether you want to see my babies' presents. They're all wrapped up back there anyway." Bonnie made a little waving motion with her hand. "I'm sorry we don't have a gift for you."

"That's OK. I ain't never had no Christmas present."

"That's the sorriest thing I ever heard. Clyde, slow down! You want the laws after us for speeding?"

"I ain't speeding."

"Yes you are. You're so used to driving too fast that you don't feel it no more."

CHAPTER 39

Their three bodies and the guns seemed hardly to fit into the shabby room in the tourist court, which was already crowded by its chair, night table, and double bed, under which Bonnie pushed the wrapped gifts she'd brought inside for safekeeping. It was around 3 a.m., nearly Christmas morning, by the time they were sitting on the bed eating light bread and sardines, using the thin bathroom towels as plates and drinking Mr. Barrow's moonshine from the tooth glass.

After dinner, Bonnie was last to use the tiny bathroom, because a woman's upkeep was time-consuming. Being low on cash meant she had to do without Kotex. While her rag soaked, she dabbed nail polish on the end of a run and scrubbed her makeup and powder off. Then she made a few suds with the slim tablet of soap and washed her stockings.

By the time she emerged, Clyde was already asleep. W.D., the lookout, had fit the chair into the few feet between the bed and the window and settled into it. She appreciated the way he kept his head turned away, his gaze on the narrow strip of glass between the curtains. Probably she was reflected in it, but she didn't mind a boy like W.D. getting an eyeful of her in her slip.

She wasn't as good at sleeping as Clyde was, because riding didn't wear a person out the way driving did. She wrote for awhile in her notebook, and then flicked off the light and tried to pretend, as she always did, that this room was their own bedroom in their own house, not just a place they were squatting in for a few hours. But W.D.'s shadow hunkered by the window inhibited the dream. "Are you really going to sit up all night?"

"I guess so. Clyde said for me to watch."

"Well, don't wake me unless you see Santa Claus."

She curled herself tightly, careful to keep to the edge of the bed so as not to touch Clyde while he slept, because he couldn't abide the feel of someone "on him," as he put it, in the dark, when he didn't know what was what. She dreamed she was trying to run, but her feet wouldn't move, and she awoke with a weight on her ankles. W.D. had slumped over the end of the bed, and his shoulders were pinning her feet to the mattress. Clyde was kneeling beside the bed with his head bowed over his clasped hands. His habitual fevered four a.m. prayers had initially alarmed and then charmed her, but she'd come to resent being awakened to witness a communion that excluded her. Gingerly, she freed her feet and turned her face to the wall.

◆

"Christmas gift!" Clyde demanded, pouncing on her the next morning.

She'd revised a poem for him that she'd composed in the Kaufman jail:

I'll Stay

I'll cling to you and love you,
and you'll never be alone.

Just like the stars in heaven,
fling round the moon at night.

I'll stay with you forever,
whether you are wrong or right.

Just like the perfume lingers,
on a rose until it dies,

I'll stay with you and guide you,
with the love light in my eyes . . .

She'd rolled the page into a scroll and tied it with a ribbon like she had L.C.'s Baby Ruth bar. She didn't expect Clyde to notice the rhyme of "fling" and "cling," since the words weren't at the ends of lines, nor would he see the way she'd linked love to stars with the word "light," but she knew he'd appreciate the theme of loyalty, the quality he most valued.

"I got one for you, too," she said to W.D.

"You wrote me a poem?"

"Last night. It's not too good. I didn't have much time." She tore the page from the notebook. "Sorry, it's not typed."

"You'd best read it to me," he said. "I ain't got much schooling."

"Wait 'til you hear her," Clyde said, giving Bonnie an affectionate tap with his scroll. "She's won prizes."

Bonnie pushed her shoulders back to allow for the free flow of air and read:

> He'd never a present for Christmas.
> Not a top or a bat or a ball.
> He'd never a present from Santa,
> Though good as Adam 'fore "the fall."
> His mother'd no money for candy.
> His father lay cold in the ground.
> His sister was off with her dandy.
> His brothers were hardly around.
>
> He'd never a present for Christmas,
> Though he hadn't done a wrong.
> Santa'd overlooked him,
> Thought he wasn't worth a "song."
> But this year will be different.
> He'll find a gift under the tree.
> It's this poem written just for him,
> A present for him from me.

"Kind of dumb, huh? I messed up on some of the rhythm."

"It's not one of your best," Clyde agreed. "For instance, there ain't no tree."

But W.D. made her read it over several times slowly, while he moved his lips, memorizing.

Finally, Clyde interrupted. "All right, you'll get plenty of time to work on that in the car. Blue, go get us some food. W.D., you change the back tires."

"It's awful cold out there," Bonnie said.

Clyde frowned. "Them tires need changing. We're lucky they didn't blow last night."

"I guess you're right."

W.D. had gone into the bathroom and the heavy stream of his pee was audible through the door.

"I know I'm right. I don't know why you got to question me all the time."

"I wasn't questioning you. I just didn't know if you were considering how cold it was, when you decided to send that boy out to change the tires."

"What difference does it make how cold it is? It's got to be done."

"I don't mind," W.D. said. He'd wet his hair and combed it back with his fingers. He picked his coat off the floor and shrugged himself into it.

"Where are your gloves?" Bonnie said.

"Ain't got gloves," he said, pushing his hands deep into his pockets.

"Clyde, whyn't you lend him your gloves?"

"I don't want grease on them."

"But it's cold."

"Clyde's right," W.D. said. "I'd ruin his gloves. I'll be OK."

"Let's get going," Clyde said, swinging his feet off the bed. "We can't stay here all day."

Bonnie, with her head wrapped in a wool scarf, squinted against the glare of the sun on the tissue of snow that brightened the gray drive and the brown grass. "You hurry up," she said, leaving W.D. at the car. "I don't want you freezing your fingers off."

As she walked toward the café, she heard the trunk open and then slam shut again. She hadn't told him about the extra guns and neither had Clyde, she guessed. She looked back at W.D. and the consternation on his face was almost comical. "Of course, you know better than to take anything but tires out of there."

CHAPTER 40

She'd been dreading Christmas Eve, knowing that, on that night when everyone else was putting the extra leaf in the table and gathering in their glowing houses to eat ham and red-eye gravy, she and Clyde would be like lost puppies on an empty, winter road. But having W.D. along had made her feel part of a little family; even sardines on the bed had been festive with that boy to show off for. And now they'd have a big Christmas breakfast and go on into Dallas and wouldn't they all be so happy to see and love her, Lady Bountiful with her gifts? They'd know she was bestowing her very self for that hour in which she was risking her freedom to be with them.

But the café attached to the tourist court was closed. Bonnie looked through the window of the locked door at the empty counter, festooned with dusty paper bells. They should have known it would be closed on Christmas Day.

By the time W.D. had finished changing the tires and they'd loaded the guns back into the car, the sun had expended its full measure of winter brightness. The light through which they drove had a blue cast, like skimmed milk. They'd been on the road half an hour when she remembered the gifts she'd stored under the bed.

"Goddammit!" Clyde spun the car in a U-turn. "I told you to leave 'em in the car!"

"Doesn't seem right," he grumbled, when she'd collected them and they were driving again, "you bringing presents to your sister's kids when I didn't give nothing to my mama."

"Guess you should have thought of that before."

"We barely have enough money to get us some baloney sandwiches."

"We *had* money. That's when you should have thought of it. Now it's too late."

"Maybe not," he said grimly, turning the car around again.

"What are you doing?"

"Going to get my mama a present at that drugstore back in Temple."

He parked the car around the corner from the main street and twisted in his seat to shove the handle of a revolver toward W.D. in the back. "Come with me. Bonnie'll stick with the car."

"What?"

"C'mon, Dub. Nothing's gonna happen. No one's going to put up a fight on Christmas Day."

Reluctantly, the boy accepted the gun and opened the car door.

"Hold on! Put it in your coat, for God's sake. This ain't the Wild West."

"Better let him stay with me, Clyde. You don't want to get him into trouble."

"I told you to quit questioning me. There ain't going to be no trouble. Now let the boy be a man."

Clyde let the engine run, and Bonnie moved into the driver's seat and rolled the window down, so that, if there were shots, she would hear them and drive to the rescue.

"Get some crackers or something," she called.

She'd hardly had time to turn her collar up against the cold when Clyde stalked back, W.D. hurrying nervously beside him.

"The idiot wouldn't do a thing."

"You said I'd be home this morning," W.D. said. "I want to go home now."

"All I wanted him to do was hold the goddamn gun. It's not like I was going to make him shoot it. I doubt that old .41 could even get a bullet off anyway."

Bonnie laughed. "Even I can hold a gun, W.D."

"You said you'd take me home this morning. You said I was supposed to be a lookout. You didn't say nothing about no robbery."

They were taking a circuitous route out of Temple to throw off anyone who might have guessed what Clyde had intended when he'd hovered near the clerk, whispering angrily at his sidekick.

"I want to go home," W.D. repeated, folding his arms and pouting like a child.

Suddenly, Clyde jerked the wheel and stopped the car along the curb. "All right. Go on home. Take that there car and drive yourself." He thrust his chin in the direction of a Model A parked about half a block away.

"Look at those cute window boxes, shaped like ducks!" Bonnie pointed to the house to which the Model A obviously belonged.

W.D. shook his head. "I ain't gonna."

"Jesus Christ!" Clyde exploded. "Can't you even steal a fucking car? Get out there!"

W.D. obeyed. His first few steps were slow, but then he began to jog, his footprints marring the thin layer of snow. When he reached the car, he turned and made a twisting motion in the air with his fingers. The keys were in it.

Bonnie could see his tan hat bent over the wheel. She waited, expecting to see the machine shake as the engine turned over and then slide smoothly away from the curb. But the car remained still.

"What the fuck is he doing?"

"You've said plenty of times Model As ain't worth stealing. What're you making him take that car for? We don't want that old car."

"Fuck it!" He flung himself out and slammed the door behind him.

CHAPTER 41

Bonnie can't help but think how elegant Clyde looks in his soft wool coat and flannel hat. Like a gentleman, he raps on the Model A's window with one gloved knuckle, until W.D. folds it down. She can't hear what Clyde says, but the boy slides quickly over, and Clyde pulls the door open and gets in.

She feels sorry for W.D. She knows that it's hard to think straight when Clyde is angry, that his explosions can make your fingers shake and your eyes blur. Plus, Model As are hard to start; Clyde has told her this more than once. She wills the engine to turn over. They're lucky that, because it's Christmas, no one's on the street, but even so, they shouldn't be fooling with it this long.

Bonnie focuses so intensely on the car and the two men in it that she doesn't see the movement at the house with the duck-shaped window boxes until the front porch is already full of people. Three men and a woman spill down the few steps and rush across the yard toward the street. None of them wears a coat. The man in front is running in his socks. Their steps pock the white yard behind them with black prints.

"Clyde," she whispers, as she slides into the driver's seat. She knows better than to shout his name.

It's too late to yell anyway. The man in socks is already on the running board, reaching with both arms through the open window. His head is inside the car; his arm is around Clyde's neck, as if they are lovers, but his voice is ferocious. "Get out of my car!"

The woman, who's hung back on the lawn, makes a high-pitched, breathless sound. "Get . . . get out of there!"

Finally, the car shakes to life, but the one man is still clamped around

Clyde, and the other two are pounding with their palms on the Model A, so that the metal rings. "Get out of the car!"

"Don't let him take it, Doyle!" Another woman, dark haired, stands in the open doorway of the house. She holds a wooden spoon near her ear, as if it's a hatchet she's poised to throw, and "The First Noel" seeps out around her.

The two harsh cracking sounds don't make sense on this side street in Temple among the faint notes of Christmas music. As if he can't stand the noise, the man in socks throws his head back violently. His shoulders heave and his arms slip out of the window, limp as empty sleeves. He tips backward, away from the car, which begins to roll forward.

"Doyle!" a woman cries, more reproachful than anguished.

Bonnie's hands are shaking so violently that she can scarcely grip the wheel. She puts too much pressure on the accelerator and pops the clutch, so that the car lurches forward after the Model A that's going fast now, getting too far ahead. As she drives by, all the people who've come from the house are huddled over a dark lump on the ground from which protrudes a pair of legs, akimbo like a rag doll's, that end in two narrow feet in black socks.

A few blocks ahead, the Model A waits against the curb. Bonnie pulls over and slides into the passenger seat. Clyde and W.D. hurl themselves into the V-8.

"That guy was choking me. I couldn't breathe and all the time this idiot just sits there."

"What happened?"

"I said I couldn't breathe! It's because he couldn't start the fucking car."

"Did you shoot him?" She doesn't mean to sound so stupid, but her mind can't yet make sense of the legs and the socks.

"I couldn't breathe! Was I supposed to let him kill me? Is that what you want?" Clyde *is* gasping for breath. Although he keeps his hands on the wheel and pushes the V-8 to go faster as they shoot past the last of Temple's houses, he's writhing in his seat, as if still trying to escape someone's hold.

"I want to go back." W.D.'s eyes are liquid and his face is a frantic red. "Take me back to Dallas. Or you can just let me out here. Some-one'll give me a ride. I have to go back."

W.D.'s distress calms Clyde. He frowns and shakes his head. "You can't go back. If they catch you, they'll try you for murder."

"But I didn't shoot no one."

"Are you sure?" Clyde says. "You had a gun. Anyway, it don't matter who pulled the trigger. You gotta run with us now. We ain't going back to Dallas 'til this cools down."

"But what about my mama?" Bonnie says. "What about my presents for the babies?"

"I don't want to hear another word about them fucking toys. Don't be stupid."

"Stupid! You're the stupid one, making this boy steal a car you don't even want."

"Shut up."

"You never wanted to go today and now you made it so we can't. Didn't you? Didn't you?" She swats at his face with her left hand.

"Don't be crazy."

"You're telling me not to be crazy? You're the one just shot a man in his socks for no reason, no reason at all!"

"I told you he was choking me!"

She draws her legs up and turns, so that she's kneeling on the seat, hanging her head and shoulders into the back, but she can't reach what she wants. "Hand me those presents, W.D.!"

Shaking, he passes her the packages. She's carried them in and out of various motel rooms for weeks, and the paper, patterned with red Scottie dogs and silver lettering, is rubbed and worn along the edges. One box holds a black truck with red wheels and a bed that can be tilted to dump its cargo. The other contains a soft pink elephant. Bonnie rolls down her window and heaves the packages out. They bounce along the road behind them.

"Fuck! What're you doing?" Clyde brakes, and they're all thrown forward.

"I'm throwing the fucking toys away!" she shrieks. "That's what you want, isn't it? Just throw everything away. His life, my life, your own life. And that man back there! You shot him, and he was only wearing socks!" She does feel crazy now. They're speeding backward, careening slightly. The cold wind pours through the open window, whipping up the tornado inside her.

Clyde's mouth and eyes are set in hard, angry lines. He steers expertly with one hand, the other arm thrown over the back of the seat, so he can look out the back window, straight toward the forlorn, cheery packages.

Bonnie is poised, waiting for him to stop to gather the boxes up. She'll fling them out again the minute he brings them in; her arms are tingling, ready.

But he doesn't stop. The car *thunks* over the boxes, shimmying as the tires hit the smooth paper. When he's flattened both going backward, he shifts into first and rolls over them again.

The destruction subdues them all. The toys pulverized so deliberately and thoroughly are a simpler fact than the man in the road in his socks.

◆

When they turned in at another tourist court, he told W.D. to get them some food and take his time about it.

She expected him to be rough, but the driving had drained that out of him. He turned the light on and caressed her, as if she were some kind of flower or soft fruit, easily bruised. When they were finished, he pressed his eyes against her shoulder, and she knew he was trying to black out the memory of the afternoon.

"Maybe it *was* W.D. that got him," she suggested, smoothing his hair behind his ear with her fingertips, as if he were a child.

"That old gun I gave him was jammed. It was me. Makes me feel sick."

"Maybe he isn't dead."

"He shountna held on like that," Clyde said. "What'd he want that old car so bad for?"

◆

On December 27, as Bonnie waited at a lunch counter for sandwiches, she saw the house with the duck-shaped window boxes on the front page of the *Houston Chronicle*.

Twenty-seven-year-old Doyle Johnson of 606 South 13th Street, Temple, died of a gunshot wound to the neck, received while he was attempting to keep two men from making off with his motorcar. Mr. Doyle's sister-in-law, Theresa Krause, reports that the killer was wearing a tan hat. Mr. Doyle is survived by his wife, Tilda Krause Johnson, and their infant son.

Bonnie felt her gorge rise at the sight of the words crawling like insects on the page, but she forced herself to read on, searching for a reference to Clyde or W.D. No details other than the hat identified the killer. The V-8 was not mentioned. Still, God knew who had done it, and that the women shared Bonnie's mother's maiden name showed that He blamed Bonnie as much as the boys.

"Horrible, ain't it?" said the woman behind the counter. "Nice Christmas gift for that baby."

Bonnie emitted a sound that was part grunt and part hum. She turned the paper facedown and started for the door on jellied legs.

"Your sandwiches!" the woman called after her.

CHAPTER 42

They wove through eastern Texas like flies, occasionally lighting in tourist cabins to wash and sleep. Bonnie felt as if a brick were stuck somewhere between her chest and throat, pressing against her windpipe. She took long, steamy showers in dim bathrooms, which loosened tears that streamed down her cheeks with the hot water, but nothing softened the brick except sips from the flask.

Clyde, however, had put the killing aside. A few days after the new year, the *Chronicle* reported that Theresa and Tilda Krause had chosen some other men as Johnson's killers, so he felt safe swinging through Dallas to do what he could for Raymond Hamilton, who was awaiting trial in the Hillsboro jail. Raymond's sister would get a radio with a couple of hacksaw blades hidden inside its case, and Bonnie would get her visit with her mother.

◆

On January 6, under a heavy gray sky that made the time of day uncertain, the V-8 turned down Lamar Street in Dallas, where the carcasses of discarded Christmas trees littered the yards.

"Hey." Clyde leaned across the seat, as Bonnie got out of the car. "You want to leave that." He reached for the flask from which she'd been tippling.

When she bent to smile at him, she had to put a hand against the doorframe to steady herself. "I'll keep it right here." She patted her purse. On her way up the walk, she put a scrap of lemon rind between her teeth.

"Fifteen minutes," he called.

Ten minutes later, having cooed over her babies, Bonnie sat on the divan with her mother, waiting. The room was gloomy, but both of them thought it was safer not to switch on the lamp. Emma stroked the back of Bonnie's hand with her thumb. "You hadn't ought to stay much longer. Lamar's a busy street. The laws are always running up and down here."

"We're just setting, Mama. There's no law against setting on the divan."

"We was hoping to see you on Christmas. Cumie said you was over by Eagle Ford Road. I don't know why you would stop over there and not let me know."

"I know, Mama. I'd intended to."

"Well, your sister was upset. You know she don't have much for them kids since Fred's been gone, and she promised them you'd visit." Emma had promised herself that she would not be querulous, but she had to release her emotions in some way and complaining seemed least likely to lead to an eruption of anger and tears from which neither mother nor daughter might recover.

"Mama, they're too little to care about a thing like that."

"Well, I don't know."

"Well, I do."

Bonnie went to the window. Chances were he wouldn't park directly in the front of the house but would tuck their car behind another somewhere along the street.

"I didn't like thinking of you out there all alone on Christmas," Emma said.

"I wasn't alone."

"You know what I mean. You're out there somewhere; I don't know where." Emma motioned vaguely with one hand. "Maybe you're in trouble."

The wobble in Emma's voice caused the brick in Bonnie's chest to slide upward so that it tore at the delicate lining of her throat. "I wanted to come so bad, Mama. I had a truck for Buddy and the sweetest little elephant for Mitzy. I wanted this to be a *nice* Christmas!"

"Why didn't you come, then, honey? We would have been glad to see you."

Bonnie saw again the head snapping back, the arms following, the black socks making the narrow feet look so vulnerable. "I just couldn't, Mama. Something happened, and I just couldn't."

"I don't think it's right that he makes you stay away from your family on Christmas."

"He didn't mean to! I told you—something happened."

"I've been thinking." Emma hesitated. She began smoothing the cushion on which Bonnie had been sitting, and then stopped herself, sorry to have been erasing the evidence of her daughter's presence.

"What is it, Mama?"

"Well, a man came by, little bit before Christmas. Said you used to know him back when you was working at Marco's. 'Two Sugars,' he said to tell you."

"Ted Hinton?" With embarrassment, Bonnie remembered how seriously he'd entertained her intention to become a singer or a poet.

"That's right. Apparently, he's a deputy now. Said he was working for Sheriff Schmid."

"You didn't tell him anything!"

"What do I know to tell? I don't know your whereabouts. Not even on Christmas Day."

"Seems to me Clyde was right to keep us away from here."

"Ted Hinton wants to help you, Bonnie!"

"He wants me to turn on Clyde. That's what he wants."

"Oh, I don't think anyone would expect that."

Bonnie laughed scornfully. "Mama, you don't know a thing about the laws."

Emma sniffed. "I might not know about the laws, having no reason to, but, honey, that man you've tied your life to is going to get caught or worse, and I know all about worse. You can't blame me for trying to save my own daughter."

"Mama, you don't understand how good Clyde is underneath. Right now, he's getting ready to help Raymond Hamilton, who he don't even like, because he doesn't want a man who's been wrongly blamed to have to suffer the way he did in that terrible Eastham." She squared her shoulders and tipped her chin back a little, as Miss Gleason had taught her.

"You've been drinking," Emma observed.

"Why shouldn't I?"

◆

Bonnie is still drinking at noon, when they give the radio to Raymond's sister, and at eleven p.m., when they circle back to find out whether it's been delivered to Raymond. As they make a first, experimental pass in front of the sister's single-story side-by-side, Bonnie glimpses a red warning light in one of the back rooms.

"It looked like the room was on fire," she says anxiously, leaning forward and then back, trying to spot the window again.

"On fire?" Clyde scoffs, as they cruise by a second time. "You're just jumpy." He's cut the headlights, just in case, but this time the light in the back room is ordinary yellow. "You oughta lay off the sauce."

Leaving the car door open behind him, Clyde moves stealthily across the shallow yard, his hand inside his coat closed around the scattergun in its rubber sling.

The front porch is a slab of concrete, nearly flush with the ground. Clyde sets a foot on it, and, as if he's sprung a trap, from inside a woman screams: "Don't shoot! Think of my babies!"

A blast shatters the front window. Doubling over, Clyde runs toward the corner of the house. Feet pound the earth; the scattergun stutters; Bonnie hears a grunt and a thud. From the back of the car, W.D.'s gun answers, the blasts deafening Bonnie's right ear.

"Quit shooting!" Bonnie shrieks. "You might hit someone!"

As if Clyde has sent a telepathic message, she envisions a dark form running through the center of the block, and she slides behind the wheel and drives. But around the first corner, the vision fades, and by the time she reaches the second corner, she knows Clyde must be searching for her on the street she's abandoned. For several teetering seconds, the car rolls forward on its own, while Bonnie demands that W.D., who knows less than she, tell her what to do. At last Clyde darts out from between two houses.

The way he tells it, gulping air and driving fast, it was a lucky thing he'd had the scattergun ready, because they were shooting at him from every window, and the man coming around the corner of the house would've killed him sure, if Clyde hadn't shot into the dark toward the sound of the footsteps.

"Why are you looking at me like that?" he demanded. "Would you rather I be the one dead?"

◆

The ambush hadn't been meant for them. Apparently, Clyde Barrow didn't rate that level of police effort.

"Odell Chambless! What's he got to do with it?" Clyde threw the *Dallas Morning News* on the carpet.

"You oughta be happy you got that Sheriff Schmid fooled. You already got one law's life on your hands. You don't want another."

"But Odell Chambless! He ain't in my league."

When, the following week, Chambless proved he'd been in jail in Los Angeles that night, the laws claimed Pretty Boy Floyd was the shooter. "Who next? Jesse James?" the *Daily Morning News* wanted to know. The only thing Clyde got credit for was popping some bullets from the car.

"As if I'd ever be the one sitting in the car," Clyde said with disgust, which Bonnie could see hurt W.D.'s feelings.

Bonnie, however, got an honorable mention. According to the sheriff, a girl had been "riding with the hunted slayers," "a tough, two-gun girl."

At first this description affronted her. "Why would they say that?" she whined, reading it for the fifth or sixth time. "I hate guns. All I did was drive the car. And what does that mean 'as tough as the back end of a shooting gallery'? I don't appreciate being compared to the back end of anything."

"I keep telling you," Clyde said. "They see what they want to see. You oughta be happy they think you're tough."

"I don't want to be tough." But as she reread the passage again, she began to value its admiring tone. A man with a gun was a dime a dozen, but a "two-gun girl" was extraordinary. More extraordinary even than an actress, singer, or poet.

CHAPTER 43

So they returned to circling Texas, driving muddy back roads under ash-gray skies, holding up grocery stores for baloney and light bread and Bonnie's Chesterfields, pharmacies for pints of whiskey, and filling stations for gasoline. They took any cash there was, of course, but no one had much, so it only amounted to enough to pay for cabins or to give to people who let them spend the night in a spare room. Once in awhile, Clyde promised to return the money they stole, and when a feed store unexpectedly yielded more than a hundred dollars, they did indeed loop back and repay several of those they'd robbed. As W.D. observed, it made a person feel like a million bucks to hand some poor slob a wad of bills and watch his face go all slack and silly.

Mostly, though, they felt like two cents. While no one chased them on the roads during the day, they were all three hunted in their dreams. Nights in tourist court cabins or strangers' houses passed in patches of shifting and rearranging, sewn together with a frayed thread of sleep. They drank themselves into unconsciousness, Clyde and Bonnie on the bed, W.D. on the floor, because a separate room for W.D. was too expensive, and, besides, the one time they'd splurged, he'd shown up at their door in the middle of the night—Clyde nearly shot him—confessing in that straightforward W.D. way that he was scared to sleep by himself. He wasn't used to it, he explained, having never slept in a room alone in his life.

But the floor was uncomfortable, so around two o'clock, W.D., smelling of sweat and cigars and sardines, would climb into the bed beside Bonnie. An hour or so later, Clyde, on her other side, would slide out to kneel and pray in frantic whispers, until, by stroking his bent head, she coaxed him back under the blanket. It was noon at least, by the time they slogged out of the damp and twisted sheets, depressed in the knowledge that losing half a day made no difference because they had nothing to do with themselves.

Outside Kansas City, Bonnie tried to talk Clyde into finding them some morphine. But Clyde refused. The drink was one thing; he might be slow with the drink in him, but he could still drive and shoot. Besides, he despised hopheads; he wanted to live a real life, not some shit dream. You mean a shit real life, she said. She'd begged, he pointed out. He'd promised, she answered. Their argument would go on, like a car rolling down a mountain, until she was screaming that the hell of the chair would be preferable to this one and he was screaming that if she wanted to know what hell was she might want to try some time in a real prison and she was threatening to go home to her mother and he was threatening to take her there.

These fights were vicious and exhausting, but they were blown up entirely with air that, once pumped out, left them essentially unchanged. The fight that involved W.D., however, was different.

◆

One of W.D.'s main responsibilities was to steal license plates to disguise the cars they stole. Proud of his collection, he often played with the plates on the grass when they camped, arranging them in various patterns according to color and state and number.

One morning in a tourist court lot, he spotted a plate he'd never seen before, bloodred with white numbers and the letters C-o-n-n across the bottom. He waited until they'd pushed their way into an Arkansas woods for the night, before leading Bonnie and Clyde to the back of the car for a surprise. "You ever seen one like this?"

Clyde snorted, poking the metal with the barrel of his rifle. "When you put this on?"

"This afternoon. When you told me to change the plates."

"I guess I oughta know better than to rely on a moron."

"What the hell? What's that shit?"

W.D. sounded tough, but Bonnie could see he was hurt. "Don't be so nasty, Clyde."

"Better not call me Clyde. This idiot's likely to slip up and blab it in front of the next law we come across. Make him suspicion us."

"Suspect us," Bonnie corrected.

"What'd I do?" W.D. said.

"Conn?" Clyde sneered. "What the hell is Conn?"

"It's Connecticut," Bonnie said.

"Where's that?" W.D. asked.

"The point is, it ain't in Arkansas. Don't you know anything, you dumb cluck?" He dropped his rifle in the grass and began unscrewing the plate.

"Don't call me that."

"I'll call you whatever the fuck I want, you dumb fuck." With a sharp thrust, Clyde elbowed W.D., so that the boy stumbled back.

Bonnie didn't intend to pick up the rifle, but she found it in her hands, as she'd found the scrap of metal she'd held at little Noel's neck after school.

"What the hell—?!" Clyde jumped, lost his balance, and sprawled on his back. "Be careful with that."

"*You* be careful," Bonnie said. "The last time you bullied W.D., a man ended up dead. This time that man might be you."

"You ain't gonna shoot me!"

"You ain't gonna be mean to W.D.!" She spoke forcefully, through gritted teeth, but already she felt the limpness that always followed when fury overwhelmed her. "I'm sick and tired of it, and I'm sick and tired of you!" she said in a final burst of disgust before the gun, suddenly heavy, wobbled in her hands.

As soon as she let the barrel dip, he was up unscrewing the plate again, and when he got it off the car, he bent it back and forth fiercely until the metal snapped in two. He threw the pieces into the woods.

"You should have let him keep it," Bonnie said, "for his collection."

"Fuck his collection and fuck you, too. I'm the one who's sick and tired. I'm the one who drives all day and night, who gits us money so we can eat, who keeps us away from the laws. What do you do?"

"What do I do?" she said with contempt. "What do I do? I love you. That's what I do. And you are mistaken if you think that's easy."

◆

The next morning, she awoke shivering in the thin light. W.D. was still asleep, rolled in a blanket beside what remained of their fire, like an enormous caterpillar. The bedding beside her, in which Clyde had turned his back to her the night before, was limp and empty. The V-8 was gone.

She'd flown off the handle, and he'd left her stuck, like the hatchet head in the wall of the outhouse. First she was afraid, then tearful. Then she nearly kicked the smugly sleeping W.D. But she roasted two extra wieners over the breakfast fire and set them aside.

In an hour or two, they heard an engine and the slap and scratch of twigs against metal. Clyde had returned with a gift for W.D., a camera that had been carelessly left on the back seat of a V-8 coach.

He'd also swapped their car for the coach. It didn't have a trunk, like the coupe they'd been driving, but the seats had more room to stretch out in.

◆

"You with that gun," Clyde said.

They were jouncing over weedy hummocks, making their way back to the highway, so he had to hold tight to the wheel to steady the car, but she could tell he wanted his hands on her, and she wriggled in response. In the back seat, W.D. contentedly fooled with the camera, folding back the cover of the slim, black case so that the lens stretched forward on its accordion sleeve and then squeezing it back together, until it was hardly bigger than a package of cigarettes. The sun grew stronger; the new car smelled fresh; the haze that had for the last few days been furring the fields and the tips of the trees had become overnight a definite green.

In the hours he'd spent on his own that morning, Clyde had come up with a couple of refinements for their gang. "It'll be a like a code, see? We'll each have a tune that means just us. Say I've got to call to you, but I don't want to give out my location. I'll make a sound like this." He pursed his lips and blew three notes. "Then you'll know it's me and I want you."

W.D. imitated the three notes.

"That one's mine. You got to have your own."

"I'll have Dixie," Bonnie said and whistled the first line.

"You can't have no song. It's gotta be like a bird or a creaky fence, something natural."

"I'll be a creaky fence," W.D. said. Whistling on the inhale, he produced a wheezy sound.

"You sound like an old man walking up a hill!" Bonnie laughed.

"This is serious. Y'all act like we're on a picnic."

They were not to use their real names again, even in private, so they wouldn't slip up in public.

When they stopped for lunch, they bought a roll of film, and later they parked the car on a newly made road, a narrow canyon between brown-scabbed banks of wounded earth. Against a grim background of gray sky and brittle, leafless trees, they played for the camera, using the car as a prop and swapping hats.

"Let's see you hold that gun on me again," Clyde said. "Make like you're grabbing for mine." He pulled his jacket back, exposing the hard ivory handle of his favorite pistol in the holster at his belt. Crooking her right arm, she leveled the Remington whipit and stretched her left hand in a gesture, consciously graceful—like Clara Bow would do—toward the pistol. For the first time in weeks, Clyde pushed his hat back on his forehead, allowing the light to bathe his face. He looked at Bonnie as if she were a new V-8.

"Got it," W.D. said.

"Let's do one of Blue and the car with a gun," Clyde said.

Her pose was extravagant: an elbow propped imperiously on the round headlight, fingers loose to display her bloodred nails, a foot on the fender, so her knees spread open like a man's, the .45 hanging casually off her fiercely jutting, feminine hip.

"Look mean," Clyde said, but though her eyes were narrowed against the sun, she couldn't keep from smiling.

W.D. took his cigar from his mouth, wiped it on his trousers, and held it out to her. "Chew on this. It'll make you look tough."

It was disgusting, a smelly, wet rod, but she took it between her teeth and scowled at the camera, playing the part.

PART 3

CHAPTER 44

March 1933

Clyde, Bonnie, and W.D. drove with the windows open, so the car could suck in the night air. It was cool but soft and plump with moisture, promising spring. Fifteen miles south of Dallas, their headlights revealed the entrance to the farm they'd been aiming for, where Blanche had taken Buck upon his release from Huntsville to stay with her mother and stepfather. Out in the country—"away from temptation and frustration," as Cumie put it—Buck and Blanche were going to figure out how to live straight.

Clyde had to knock hard on the glass window of the front door four times before an old man, one side of his face pressed into folds by sleep, answered. Without a word, he jerked his thumb toward the narrow staircase on the right, before shuffling back into the room from which he'd emerged.

"Buck!" The stairs were pinched between two walls, and the sound of Clyde's voice boomed back at them.

"*Shhh . . .*"

Clyde frowned at Bonnie over his shoulder. "Quit shushing me. We're waking 'em when we get up there anyways. Buck!"

A small white dog with disordered fur barked at them from the landing.

Bonnie's toe caught the edge of a step, and she stumbled and grabbed at Clyde to catch herself. The silk of his shirt was slick as Crisco between her fingers. He stopped to steady her but freed himself in a hurry. His impatience made her so mad. When he had plans, he behaved like nothing else mattered. "I might as well get back in the car, for all you care!"

"Boy!" Clyde hissed. "Can't you help her?"

"Boy's happy to help his Sis, ain't you, sugar?" she slurred, letting her arms be transferred to W.D's neck.

She couldn't remember whose house this was. She'd thought he'd said Blanche's mother lived here, but the old man wasn't Blanche's father, she knew that much. Blanche's father lived in Oklahoma, and they were definitely still in Texas. She was sure of that, not because she kept close track of the states they drove in and out of, but because she was always aware when they were in Texas, close to her mama, even if they couldn't manage a visit.

Buck, his hair sticking straight up in back, was letting Clyde into a room at the top of the stairs. Bonnie had never met Marvin Ivan Barrow, who'd been in the Walls or on the lam pretty much all the time she'd known Clyde, and she was predisposed to hate him, knowing that some caper of his had been the cause of Clyde's being nabbed off her mama's davenport in the first place. But she forgave him when she saw the way he grabbed Clyde and held on, as if reunited with half of himself.

The brothers hadn't seen each other since the night of that joyride more than two years ago, when Buck had been shot in the leg and caught, and Clyde had escaped—for a few weeks, at least—by hiding under a house. If anyone had predicted then which brother would be in more trouble with the laws now, it would have been Buck, who, as Nell once said fondly, had nothing on a possum when it came to quick thinking. But as of three days ago, Buck was free to go wherever he liked, using his real name. Cumie never stopped talking about how Blanche had convinced him, after he'd escaped Huntsville, to turn himself in and serve out his time.

The preacher's daughter was reclining on the bed that took up most of the little slope-ceilinged room. The white dog gave up barking and retreated to a position against her flank. Blanche pulled the sheet and blankets decorously over her breasts, even though she was wearing a man's rumpled shirt over her nightgown. That was Blanche all over, Bonnie thought, making out like they'd violated the royal bedchamber.

But when Blanche saw Bonnie, she relaxed and patted the space beside her. Bonnie cast herself off from W.D., pushed past Clyde and Buck, and fell onto the bed. "You don't know how good it is to see another woman!" She leaned to stroke Blanche's hair back from her face. "You oughtn't to let it hang forward like that. You ought to show your pretty eyes."

"I was sleeping! My eyes were closed!" Blanche protested. "And you're drunk." But she tugged the blankets from under Bonnie and held them open. "Take off your shoes and come on in here. You look like you could use a little sleep."

"You got a lemon? I like to chew a little bit of the peel. No one knows you been drinking, you chew a little lemon peel."

"You need more than a lemon, honey. Now come on in here."

"I'll have plenty of time to sleep when I'm dead. Right now I have me a girl to talk to. Oh, Blanche, you must be so happy."

"I am happy," Blanche agreed. "I've got my daddy back. Look here." She unhooked a tooled leather purse from the bedpost and drew from it three papers, which she unfolded and flattened with her palm. "We're all legal." The certificate documenting the marriage of Marvin Ivan Barrow and Iva Bennie Blanche Caldwell was nearly transparent where it had been folded. The other two papers were Buck's pardon from the governor of Texas and the title to their car.

"Are you going to keep on at the Cinderella?"

"Oh, no." Blanche replaced the documents in her purse as she spoke. "Buck wasn't at all pleased that the Barrows made me work outside the home. That was never what he wanted for me. I know Clyde feels the same."

"He does," Bonnie said solemnly, as if she were in a position to refuse a job setting hair at a beauty parlor. Then, overwhelmed with envy for Blanche and sorrow for herself, Bonnie pressed the edge of the blanket to her eyes. "You are so lucky."

Typical of Bonnie, Blanche thought, not to recognize that this state of affairs had been deliberately arranged. "Clyde ought to have gone straight."

"You know he tried. They wouldn't let him alone." Just like a preacher's daughter to be so holier-than-thou, Bonnie thought. Sure, Buck had done what Blanche wanted. From what Bonnie had heard, she judged him a born follower, easily swayed. Bonnie told herself that she would rather have a man with backbone, even if that meant he didn't bend the way she wanted him to.

"C'mere, baby." Bonnie fit her hands under the little dog's forelegs and dragged him into her lap. "Who's this little fella?"

"That's my Snowball. My mama's been keeping him for us."

"I wish we could have us a soft little sweetheart like this." Bonnie pressed her cheek against the dog's head. "It's funny," Bonnie said, her words slurred from the drink, "you'd think me and Clyde were the ones who could go wherever we want, live however we want. But it turns out we can't do hardly a thing but run and hide. And you and Buck were the ones who bowed down and buckled under, but now you're free."

"Buck never bowed down," Blanche said. "He just paid for what he done."

"There's no payment for what Bud's done, except the chair. I don't guess we'll be offering that."

"We can't hardly live in Dallas no more, thanks to Clyde," Blanche complained. "Just the day before we left, Buck and L.C. were drug down to the station. I had to drive myself after them and the greasy wheel in Buck's old car ruint a brand-new pair of white gloves."

"I got a sweet yellow pair down in the car," Bonnie said. "I want you to have 'em."

Blanche noticed that W.D. had not stepped away from the window. If he was worried about the laws showing up way out here, Clyde must be plenty hot. She didn't like the uncertain look on Buck's face or the way Clyde kept touching his brother's arm. "What're you two talking about?"

"I'm just asking Buck to take you on a little drive," Clyde said, with that innocent smile he could turn on like a goddamned light bulb. "Here, let me show you."

He took a map from his jacket and spread it on the quilt.

Blanche frowned. "What do you want with Eastham?"

"We got a nice piece of money the other week. Gonna use it to break Raymond out."

"He's going to get even with those guards down there," Bonnie said. "Break out as many as he can."

"Buck and me can't have nothing to do with a breakout."

"Of course not," Clyde said. "I wount put you and Buck in any danger. You oughta know that," he added, in a tone tinged with outrage and hurt.

"What I know is that W.D. is standing in that window watching for the half a dozen police who're going to come blasting into my mama's house," Blanche said.

"The laws don't want you," Clyde said.

"They do, baby," Bonnie said, quietly. From the bed, she reached for him and drew her fingers down his arm suggestively. "They want anyone who has anything to do with Clyde Barrow."

The booze had made her miscalculate her charms and his mood; he moved impatiently out of her reach.

"You just need to tell Ray when we're coming and where we'll be hiding the guns. All you're doing is visiting a con, Blanche. You ain't going to get into any trouble."

"Where you going to hide them?" Buck asked.

"Buck!" Blanche turned on her husband. "I'm not fixing to lose you again."

Clyde spoke directly to his brother, as if Blanche weren't sitting right there. "I can give you some money to get you started living straight. You can buy into a secondhand car lot like you wanted and get you and Blanche a little house. It's what you need to help you live straight."

Buck looked at Blanche. "Baby . . ."

"I don't want money that's come by the way you get it. That's living crooked from the get-go. Besides, Daddy, they ain't just going to let us waltz into Eastham. We can't drive two miles without the laws stopping us. I'm sorry, Clyde, but we're not going to help you. If you want my advice, you wouldn't do this thing yourself. You're liable to get yourself killed and Raymond, too."

"If I don't get him out, he's better off dead," Clyde said.

"You don't do this, Blanche," Bonnie burst out, "if you don't want to."

Clyde refolded his map. "I ain't going to force it. It's a free country."

He went to the door. "C'mon, Buck, let's let these girls sleep and you and me'll sit in the car awhile." He leaned to kiss Bonnie and let her put her arms around his neck.

"Don't go, baby," she said. "C'mon in here and get warm. You said we could stay until dawn."

"I'm not going anywhere, just downstairs. You're wore out, Blue. You get you some sleep."

"All right. I'll stay here with Blanche." Bonnie shut her eyes obediently.

When the three men had left the room, though, she rolled over and opened her eyes. "Let's us talk, Blanche. I don't get anything but 'this gun shoots farther and this gun shoots truer and this car runs faster' day and night."

◆

They were still talking at 4:15, when the men came back up the stairs, each deliberate footstep audible on the squeaky wooden stairs.

"We got us a new plan," Buck said.

Bonnie could smell the bottle she'd left in the car on his breath.

"We're going up to Joplin and renting us a place for awhile! All of us!" Clyde broke in, like a kid who couldn't keep from tearing the wrapping off his Christmas present.

"We're not hiding out with you," Blanche said.

"We wouldn't be hiding out," Clyde said. "I mean, we got plenty of money, so we wouldn't have to pull any jobs."

"We'll just be living there?" The pathetic eagerness in Bonnie's voice made Blanche want to cry. "Like normal people?"

"Sure," Clyde said.

"We'll be keeping Bud out of trouble, Baby," Buck said. "That's the Christian thing to do, isn't it?"

"We'll be getting us into trouble," Blanche said grimly.

"No we won't," Buck insisted. "Bud says he won't do anything that would make the place hot."

"Won't need to," Clyde said. "Like I said, we got plenty of money. You and Bonnie could buy whatever you want, fix the place up, and then when you and Buck get ready to come on back to Dallas, you could take the fixins with you."

"Wouldn't we have fun, Blanche?" Bonnie said.

"What we all need is a little vacation," Clyde said. "Enjoy each other's company."

"Oh, Blanche!" Bonnie said. "Please."

"I don't like all them guns around," Blanche said.

"We won't keep but one or two in the house," Buck said.

"No, Buck," Clyde said reprovingly. "We won't keep *no* guns in the house. It'll be like Blanche wants. The guns can stay in the cars."

Blanche looked silently down at the dingy quilt. Finally, she sighed. "Why Joplin?"

"It's a nice town, ain't it? Not so small that people notice you, not so big you don't know where you are. Close to Oklahoma and Kansas, so we can run over the border, if we have to pull a little job sometime."

"You said we wouldn't be pulling jobs," Bonnie interrupted. "We got plenty of money!"

"I know, and we won't. But let's just *say*," Clyde insisted. "Well, then, we do it in another state, and we take all the guns with us. If the law gets after us, Blanche, you and Buck will just be rocking in your rocking chairs, knitting your afghans, like the good citizens you are."

"Knitting!" Blanche had to laugh at this.

"I'll get you a mess of wool, and Buck can wrap up his hands, the way they do."

Blanche laughed again. "Well, I can't knit, but I suppose I could crochet."

Bonnie clamped both her hands around Blanche's arm, which was smooth as a china cup. "We could make such a cozy little nest. It's awful to ride around in the car all day, Blanche, day after day. You'd think it would be all right, just riding, but it wears you down somehow."

Bonnie's fingers felt oddly rough. Blanche turned her hand over and saw that the skin was peeled away in tiny shreds. "How did this happen?"

"I bite at my fingers once in awhile. It doesn't hurt."

Blanche rubbed her thumb gently over the corrugated flesh. "I don't know. Buck and me'll have to talk about it."

"If we stick around," Buck said, "maybe I can talk Bud into turning himself in, the way you did me."

"Daddy, Clyde's killed people. I'm not saying he wasn't in a position where he didn't have to, but the laws don't want to put him in the pen. They want to kill him."

"What do you want to say things like that for, Blanche?" Bonnie threw off the covers and went to the window, but she could see only her own reflection in the glass.

"I don't *want* to say it, but I got to look out for Buck."

"Just a week, Blanche," Buck said. "Nothing's going to happen in a week."

"We're losing the dark," Bonnie said.

No one who welcomed the daylight would call it anywhere close to morning, but the blackness was indeed thinning.

"We best get going," Clyde said. He slung the cut-down Browning on its strap over his shoulder as casually as if he were sliding into a pair of suspenders, tucked his pistol into his belt, and put his coat on over both. "C'mon, Blue."

Buck followed them down, and the brothers stood beside the car for several long minutes after Bonnie and W.D. got in, Clyde talking and Buck nodding. W.D. fidgeted with the Remington in his lap and kept his eyes on the drive. Once the dawn began in earnest, the sky's brightening would be after them like a bloodhound.

Finally, Bonnie opened her door. "C'mon, baby, we've got to go."

Through the murky morning, Bonnie, Clyde, and W.D. slid like ghosts. Bonnie thought about Blanche putting on smooth, fresh clothes when she got up, not standing beside a car, trying to shake the wrinkles from a crumpled dress that stank of French fry oil. Blanche would eat hot food off plates she took from a cupboard. She could look out a window and know where she was. Once Bonnie had despised such steadiness as the dull lot of those who had no ambition, but now she craved it. Perhaps those who stayed put weren't going anywhere, but, as it turned out, constantly going didn't amount to going anywhere, either.

"Did you mean it about Joplin?" she asked.

"I'd just as soon raid Eastham, but there's time for that. I think we need a rest."

"Blanche won't do it."

"Buck's a wheedler. He'll wear her down. And where else they got to go, honestly? Buck never can think what to do with hisself."

CHAPTER 45

Four days later, Bonnie and Blanche were inspecting a bright, airy apartment above a two-bay garage in a decidedly middle-class Joplin neighborhood, better than any place Bonnie's mother could afford and far better than any the Barrows could hope to set foot in. Its creamy yellow paint was hardly scuffed and the bathroom fixtures looked practically new. Big windows on all four sides afforded a long view of the street in front and the yards behind, which Clyde would certainly approve of.

"Does it come fully furnished?" Bonnie asked, admiring the way one of the radios—there were two radios!—had been tucked into a little alcove in the cunning kitchenette.

"It's furnished, yes." The landlord didn't bother to hide his impatience. Obviously, he thought the place was beyond their means. "It's twenty-one dollars a month, you know. Plus, a dollar for the night watchman."

Bonnie flushed. "My husband said not to take any place that was less than thirty. But he'll be glad to hear about the watchman." She opened her purse and counted out the rent deliberately, so as to reveal that several bills remained.

Blanche looked away. She liked the place and the money wasn't her concern, but Bonnie's referring to Clyde as her husband always rankled. She and Cumie agreed that it wasn't any of their business, but it certainly was a strange way for a Christian woman to conduct her life, staying married to a man she didn't have anything more to do with, so she couldn't marry the fellow she was running around with.

"You gave him twenty-two dollars," Blanche said, when they were back in the car.

"That's what he asked for, wasn't it?"

"But we're staying a week not a month."

Bonnie shrugged. "He's renting by the month. Asking for a week would make us look like we aren't solid people. Besides, who knows how long we'll stay?"

She started the car but gazed through the windshield for a few moments at the building constructed of irregularly shaped stones, glued together like a crazy quilt. It was like her house back in Rowena, a place that could be a home.

◆

Like so many things, the apartment turned out to be not quite the treasure Bonnie had anticipated. The backyard was weedier than Bonnie and Blanche had remembered, and the furnishings had been reduced considerably. The beds remained but had been stripped down to thin, hard mattresses; the dishes and flatware had been removed from the kitchen, and the radios were gone.

"Guess we're April fools," Bonnie said.

"It doesn't matter," Clyde said. "We can buy whatever we want."

He had several rifles stacked in his arms like kindling, and Blanche stopped him at the top of the stairs. "You said you weren't bringing those in."

"I didn't know you girls was going to be getting something on the second floor. What if we need them? How're we going to get to them, if they're down below?"

"You said you wouldn't need them."

"I don't expect we will, but we got to keep 'em cleaned and oiled up. We can't be tramping up and down the stairs all night, fetching them in and bringing them back."

"Clyde's just trying to keep us all safe, Baby," Buck said. He and W.D. were pulling the curtains closed over every window.

Bonnie had forgotten that no matter how much light and air a space might potentially admit, they couldn't enjoy it unless the place was moving at eighty miles an hour.

Clyde and Buck clomped down the stairs, and under the living room floor, a garage door creaked open. Bonnie leaned out the window to shout: "Don't forget the radio!"

From the back stoop of the house next door, a man in a plaid jacket stared at their car as it pulled out of the garage nose first, gangster-style. The blue DeSoto parked in the other half of their garage belonged to him. It was prettier than a Ford V-8, Clyde admitted, but not as fast.

Bonnie waved. We're delightful, her gesture said. We're not the kind of people who have to hide behind shades.

The man raised his hand but held it still; an acknowledgment, not a greeting. Bonnie knew he thought they were the type that came to Joplin for its speakeasies and dance halls. But he was in for a surprise. They were going to be good neighbors. They were going to live like normal people.

Resolved to keep order in the new apartment, Bonnie supervised W.D. as he stacked the guns in the front room closet. On the hangers the former tenant had left behind, she hung her dresses and Clyde's jackets and trousers, making sure the creases lined up properly. She set W.D.'s camera safely on the dresser. He'd agreed to let her use the remainder of the roll to take pictures of the cute apartment, so she could show them to her mother the next time they got down to Dallas.

In a couple of hours, an engine slowed outside, and the garage door creaked open again. Clyde and Buck had bought pillows and feather beds, three quilts in a peach and pink pattern, and dishes decorated with a bunch of wheat tied in a blue ribbon. They weren't to Bonnie's taste, but she appreciated that the men, in fulfilling their own notions of what the women would like, had done their best, so although they'd forgotten the radio, she bit her tongue.

CHAPTER 46

In the middle of the living room rug at two in the afternoon, Bonnie knelt before her typewriter in her nightie.

> *She pieced herself together*
> *In a jigsaw house*
>
> *At peace in the pieces of a jigsaw house*
>
> *A piece of peace*

Now that she could sit still and think, ideas seemed to bubble up into her head like coffee in the top of a percolator. Sometimes they came so fast, they made her scalp itch. Although that might have been her latest dye job. She'd decided that a new dwelling warranted a new color and had tried a deep, almost cherry red.

Blanche made no secret of her opinion. "It's not a bad color, it just don't suit your complexion."

If Blanche had been someone else—Bonnie's mama or Billie or Dutchie or Nell, or any number of Bonnie's friends for that matter—Bonnie would've welcomed the comment. It was just the sort of subject she liked to examine: Could she use a touch more gold or a little more chocolate? Shorter bangs?

Blanche's criticism, however, cut deep. In everything she did, Blanche made clear that she was Bonnie's superior, always adjusting the ring Buck had given her; refusing beer when the rest, including Bonnie, were vying to get the most down quickest; loudly snapping out a game of solitaire when the others, including Bonnie, were playing poker, as if Blanche had decided what it meant to be a woman and had relegated Bonnie to one of the boys.

Blanche was prettier than Bonnie. Bonnie wasn't bad to look at, but most of her attraction came from somewhere behind her features and shone through them, the way the sun lit up the blood under her skin when she held her hand against the window. On the surface, Bonnie was cute, but Blanche's cheekbones seemed smoothed out of marble, and her brown curls enriched her dark, dramatic eyes. On the other hand, Blanche could be sour. Bonnie liked to think she had more charm.

Blanche banged the carpet sweeper back into the closet and, clanking glass, began to collect the beer bottles that had sprouted like mushrooms around the chair legs overnight. Beer had been legalized in Missouri the very week they'd moved in, and for the boys it seemed almost an obligation to work their way through a case each night, while they wrenched the metal pieces of their guns apart, wiped and oiled them, and then smacked them back together in a racket of snapping and cracking that certainly carried at least some distance beyond their closed and shaded windows. When they'd finished cleaning and turned to poker, they left the weapons wherever they were, as if a pistol on a couch were no different from a splayed book, or a rifle propped against a wall might as well have been a broom. Obviously, delivery boys could not be allowed in.

As a further precaution against what Clyde called "nose trouble," Buck had gone that afternoon to get some Kansas plates for the Marmon, while Clyde and W.D. were off having "a look around."

Sighs issued from the kitchen. Silverware clinked and clanked resentfully into its drawer. A cupboard door closed with a sullen *thunk*.

Blanche kept the bedroom she shared with Buck neat and didn't leave her stockings and underthings hanging in the bathroom so much as an hour past the time when they were dry. She also picked items of Bonnie's and Clyde's clothing off the floor and dropped them at their bedroom door. Bonnie scooped them up, but she generally left them in a heap on the chair to be put away another time that never came. Now she pecked at a few keys to prove that she was occupied. Blanche didn't understand that an idea had to be grabbed when it offered itself.

Finally, Blanche stalked out of the kitchenette. "Aren't you going to get dressed? The store's going to close before we get there!" She tapped smartly on the glass face of her wristwatch with a pointed fingernail.

"You're not dressed, either," Bonnie said.

Blanche had turned a blue crepe evening gown into a housedress with a hem that just covered her knees. The shoulders were lace, the back low-cut. Some might have thought it tacky, but Bonnie approved of both Blanche's attempt at elegance and her economy. She wished her mother had taught her how to sew.

"I'll be ready in a jiffy," Blanche said. "You take longer."

Bonnie did often need time to experiment with her costume. It might take her a good five minutes to decide whether to cinch a jacket with its own belt or to use a colorful scarf or one of Clyde's neckties.

They would be safe together, two women, taking the bus into town, but the prospect gave Blanche another excuse to find fault with Bonnie's newly dyed hair. People noticed redheads.

"I hope they do," Bonnie said, pushing her fingers against her scalp to give the style a little fluff and her head a surreptitious scratch. "We're not going to be doing anything we don't want people to see, remember? While we're in Joplin, we're living ordinary, happy lives.

CHAPTER 47

"Hi, Miss Betsy! Hi, Miss Blanche!" Liza was sitting on her back steps when they came out. "Where's Snowball?"

Blanche stiffened. Liza was only seven or eight years old, but Blanche knew that children were more observant than most people gave them credit for, and this particular child was attached to the neighbor Clyde had nicknamed "The Nose." The Nose seemed to linger in the garage underneath their apartment, and he stood disturbingly often at his back door, staring up at their shaded windows.

"We left him upstairs, honey. Why aren't you in school?" Bonnie hurried over to the girl and, reluctantly, Blanche followed. Bonnie couldn't help herself when it came to children.

"I'm sick."

"Well, that's a shame. Want some Doublemint?" Bonnie pushed her fingers into her small cloth bag. "Sometimes a stick of chewing gum'll perk you right up when you're feeling poorly."

"I threw up three times last night," the girl said, accepting the gum. "Did you hear me?"

Bonnie laughed. "We must have slept right on through that."

"But your lights were on. Daddy says you don't sleep at night. Like skunks."

"Who're you calling a skunk?" Bonnie teased.

Blanche frowned. She'd warned the others that this was going to happen.

"Nocturny. That's the word for people who stay up all night. We don't get many of those around here." The father's worldly observation sounded cute in the little girl's high voice and Bonnie laughed again.

"Do you ever get scared of the dark, Liza?"

The girl nodded.

"Me, too," Bonnie said. "But when you're a grown-up, you can stay up all night, just like it was daytime. Then it's not scary anymore."

"Do you wear your boots at night?"

"My boots?"

"Daddy says you got bootlegs, but I ain't seen you in boots."

Bonnie laughed. "Your daddy's barking up the wrong tree, if he thinks we're bootleggers. You can tell him we've had nothing but beer and that's strictly legal, as of last week."

If Blanche hadn't nudged Bonnie on with another couple of taps on the face of her wristwatch, Bonnie might have talked with the girl for half an hour. She'd lost the habit of being aware of the time.

◆

Joplin's S. H. Kress & Co. was on a smaller scale than the Kress store in Dallas but equally dolled up with ornamental stonework and brass lettering. Bonnie and Blanche twittered over milk-glass ashtrays, faceted drinking glasses, pearl-encrusted picture frames, embroidered guest towels, engraved compacts, beaded coin purses, leatherette scrapbooks, and a red kimono decorated with roses made from folded red ribbon. Cut-glass rings and earrings were only twenty cents apiece, but they looked like real gems. Bonnie and Blanche loaded their fingers and splayed them, tipping their hands to catch and release the light.

After an hour they'd filled three baskets, and Blanche attempted to edit their loot.

"Oh, let's just buy everything!" Bonnie said, replacing the dish towel that Blanche had removed. It was decorated with a cross-stitched dog—"Snowball's black brother, Eight Ball," Bonnie had said when she'd first picked it up, which had made them laugh so hard, they had to lean against each other in the aisle. "And we need more jigsaw puzzles."

At the bus stop, a baby stared over his mother's shoulder, and while Blanche sorted through the bags, organizing their purchases by rooms, Bonnie contorted her face for his amusement. Leaning over his mother's restraining arm, he reached a soft, knuckleless paw toward her.

"I want one of those so bad, Blanche."

Blanche was studying a picture frame set with pastel-colored sea-shells. "You got one just like it. Yours maybe has a little more blue."

"I wish I had a baby. Don't you want one? I wish I could have six or seven."

"I can't have children," Blanche said, folding the paper back around the frame. "Calloway done something to me down there, I guess."

Calloway was the man Blanche's mother had forced her to marry when she was seventeen.

"Doesn't it hurt?"

"No, I don't feel a thing. I wouldn't know it, if a doctor hadn't told me."

"No, I mean doesn't it hurt here." Bonnie pressed her hand against her chest.

Blanche slid the mirror carefully back into the bag before she spoke. "Once in awhile." Then she looked at Bonnie in her superior way. "But I got Buck. Buck is my man and my baby, my everything. Buck is more than enough for me."

Buck had left his two previous wives not long after their babies were born, so if Blanche was so devoted to Buck, maybe it was for the best that she wouldn't have children. Bonnie wished that Clyde were all she wanted, but loving a baby was different from loving a man. It would never be wrong to love a baby too much.

CHAPTER 48

"Watch this." Blanche stood at the top of the stairs, a slice of hot dog pinched between index finger and thumb. Snowball sat at her feet, head cocked toward the disk of meat. "To the car," Blanche said. She closed her hand around the slice and thrust her chin encouragingly toward the staircase that led into the garage below. "To the car."

The dog *tick-tock*ed brightly down several stairs, then turned, scampered back up, and fixed an unwavering brown eye on Blanche's closed hand.

"I said 'car.' "

"How is he supposed to go to the car when there is no car?" Bonnie said.

Blanche sighed and allowed Snowball to pluck the meat from her fingers. "How am I supposed to train him, if they keep going off like this?"

It was the eleventh day, four days beyond the period Blanche and Buck had agreed to. Bonnie had done her best to prolong an atmosphere of vacation, teasing Clyde in the evenings until he quit his obnoxious gun cleaning and took up his guitar instead. She sang with Buck, picked out the puzzle pieces that made up the sky for Blanche and W.D., and persuaded Blanche, who hated poker, to join them at the table as Buck's lucky charm.

At night, when their shades weren't the only ones in the neighborhood pulled low, they might have been any happy people. Bonnie, her head purring with beer, studied the faces of the men, each warm and soft in the yellowish lamplight, and loved them as husband and brothers, and when Blanche fell asleep with her head on Buck's thigh, Bonnie took her sister's feet into her lap. Since they'd been in Joplin, the red leatherette scrapbook into which she pasted newspaper articles about

Clyde and herself had remained buried under dirty socks and shirts on the bedroom floor.

◆

At breakfast on the afternoon of the twelfth day, Clyde announced that he and W.D. would not be home for supper. "You wanna go with us, Buck?" He looked sideways at his brother, as he wrapped his lips around the peas balanced on his knife. It was more command than question.

"You can't pull any jobs," Blanche said quickly.

Buck patted her hand. "I ain't going to pull any jobs, Baby. I promise."

"I trust *you*, Buck."

"Even if Boy and me decide we gotta pull something," Clyde said, "we won't let Buck have anything to do with it. I just want him to come along with us. I want to see my brother as much as I can. We ain't going to be here forever and who knows how much time I got?"

"We going to see some pretty birds again?" W.D. asked. "Last time we rode around," he told Bonnie, "I got a picture of a black and white one with red on its front. Looked just like a suit and tie."

◆

Blanche had given up complaining about the gloom, although occasionally she lifted a corner of some shade and looked up and down the road. At dinner, because it was just her and Bonnie, she sliced up the last pork chop, and they ate it cold with mayonnaise between slices of bread. Around eleven, she pushed the bed against the window that looked out over the street, raised the shade halfway, and sat cross-legged in the dark, staring out, her tooled leather purse on one knee, Snowball curled against the other, snoring softly.

Bonnie hardly bothered to knock before coming in. "You look like you're waiting for your date to show up," she said, sprawling across the bed and propping her chin in her hands, so that she, too, could gaze at the empty street.

"We been here too long," Blanche said. "They're pulling some job. I know it."

"We gotta have money, don't we? I don't see y'all making a contribution."

"You know Buck hasn't had a chance to find any work."

"You seen the papers anymore? There's no such thing as work."

"Clyde had a chance to work. I wish to God he'd stayed in Massachusetts."

"No you don't, Blanche. You wouldn't want him all alone up there, away from his family and everybody he loves."

"Why didn't you go up there? That's what I would have done. It doesn't matter to Buck and me where we are, so long as we've got each other." Blanche cupped a hand over the clasp of her purse, protecting its official contents.

◆

Finally, a car slowed in the street below and turned its headlights away. Bonnie and Blanche, with Snowball darting between their feet, were down the garage's internal staircase before the boys had finished backing in.

"Wait 'til you see what we got!" Clyde crowed from the driver's seat.

"*Shhh!* At least wait until Boy gets the garage shut."

Across the back seat, three Browning Automatic Rifles balanced butt to barrel atop a thicket of lesser rifles, pistols, magazines, boxes of bullets, and ammo belts.

"There's a bunch more in the trunk," Clyde said.

The quantity was a shock. "What'd you do? Rob a gun factory?"

"Better than that. This here's more United States issue. W.D. and I found another armory the other day. We got plenty for the breakout and then some. And look at this little dealie." Clyde held up a pronged bit of metal. "This here will hold a gun steady. I'm gonna bolt it on the dash, so any one of us can get at it and blast away. The laws oughta hire me to outfit their vehicles. They'd be a lot better against guys like me, if they kept up-to-date with their weapons."

Buck had only gotten halfway out of the car before Blanche attacked him. Now she was pounding on his chest with the sides of her fists and crying. Playing a girl, Bonnie thought.

"Jesus, let the man out," Clyde said. "We've got to get this shit upstairs before Mr. Nose decides to go for a drive."

Wailing, Blanche covered her face with her hands and ran upstairs.

It took the rest of them several trips to move everything into the apartment, where they deposited the weapons and their accessories higgledy-piggledy on W.D.'s divan and the floor around it. No point trying to fit all of that into the closet.

Blanche was still crying and shaking her head at Buck. "You promised."

"Blanche," Clyde said patiently, as if he were reasoning with a child, "what are you going on about?"

"You shut up, Clyde Barrow!" Blanche was practically choking with the effort to utter quietly words that she wanted to scream. "You said you weren't going to take him on a job. You said you just wanted to spend time with your brother. You don't care about your brother! You don't care if you get him kilt!"

"Now, Blanche," Buck said, "no one's gettin' kilt." He tried to put his arms around his wife, but she wrenched her shoulders free.

A bottle of beer emitted a sigh as Clyde opened it. "I know how you feel, Blanche," he said, his voice smooth as cream cheese, "because I feel just like you do about Buck. And that's why, while W.D. and me did all the dirty work out there, Buck was off yonder, just keeping the car seat toasty. He didn't have a thing to do with this."

"And I picked these up for you," Clyde said, bowing his head so he could slip over it the strap from which a pair of US Army issue binoculars hung. "So you can keep an eye on our young Buck."

Bonnie felt sorry for Blanche, but she also felt slightly—meanly—triumphant. Now Blanche must see that it wasn't as easy to get her way as she'd made out. Not if she wasn't prepared to give up what she loved most. Blanche was sewn to Buck and Buck was sewn to Clyde, and Blanche and Buck both might tug and squeal, but unless they tore those stitches out of their flesh, they had to go whichever way Clyde decided.

But Blanche quit crying. "We're leaving tomorrow," she said.

CHAPTER 49

In the end, Blanche agreed to stay until Friday, which would give her time to organize and pack the housewares they'd collected and Buck time to make some repairs to the Marmon. The following afternoon, Bonnie lay in bed long after she'd awakened, trying to sponge through her pores the stillness that remained. She could reach the window shade, but she needn't look out to picture the tidy scene in which she nestled, the rows of paint-box red tulips glowing against the clean yellow boards of the house behind, the neatly coiled garden hose, the white rectangular sheets and dish towels drying in the neighbor's yard. If she'd had a child with Roy, she would be old enough now to go to school. She might be walking home now with Liza from next door, her yellow hair escaping from the braids Bonnie would have tied it in that morning.

Slowly, so as not to disturb her vision, she slid her legs out from under the sheets and stepped into the living room, which Blanche was already restoring to its original state. The guns had disappeared, as had the empty beer bottles. On the coffee table, the Perfect Picture Puzzle had progressed. Bonnie began searching for the bits of pink that would form the tongue of a reproachful cocker spaniel in the bath.

"Good," Blanche said, when she and Snowball came in from their walk. "I want to get that finished up and put away. Only three more days."

Around eight o'clock, the men stumbled up the stairs, having spent the afternoon shattering beer bottles and tree limbs, as they tested the weapons they'd taken from the armory.

"One of 'em wouldn't quit!" W.D., so excited he could not contain his saliva, wiped the escaping drip from the corner of his mouth with the back of his hand. "And it wasn't one of them BARs, either. It was just a riot gun. Clyde was popping off at some bottles and all of a sudden *pow, pow, pow, pow!*" W.D. gestured wildly around the room with one finger, like a little boy playing cowboys and Indians.

"I thought he was acting all crazy on purpose," Buck said, "so I'm yelling at him to quit fucking around. I had to pull W.D. down. We messed up our shirts good."

"And Clyde's yelling, 'I ain't doin' it! She's firing on her own!' " W.D. said.

Clyde smiled. While shooting wound the others up, it seemed to calm him. "I finally thought to chuck her in the creek."

"I bet it took out a dozen fish!" W.D. said. "That fucker was hopped up!"

◆

Blanche had been right; the guns made it impossible to sustain the illusion that they were normal people. The following afternoon, one of the BARs went off while Clyde was cleaning it in the garage and sprayed seven or eight bullets around the room.

"You might have killed someone!" Blanche scolded.

"What are you doing cleaning that thing in the middle of the garage, where anyone can walk in anytime?" Bonnie said.

Luckily, none of their neighbors seemed to have heard the barrage. At least no one came out of any of the houses to investigate.

"Probably thought it was some automobile engine acting up," Clyde said scornfully. "These people wouldn't recognize a BAR if it bit 'em. Anyway, what does it matter if they get suspicious now? We're getting out of here, ain't we?"

◆

After midnight W.D. parked a V-8 roadster with Oklahoma plates next to the sedan.

"What the hell are you doing?" Bonnie said, meeting him at the top of the stairs. "That's Nose's spot."

In the living room, Clyde looked up from the whipit he was cleaning. "The Nose is going to park on the curb for a couple of days, while we use the garage. He don't mind." He'd disassembled the gun on top of the jigsaw dog, which by this time was embodied down to the bottom of his darling wooden bathtub. The oily parts were making a mess of the Perfect Picture.

"He don't mind?" Bonnie opened her eyes wide to dramatize her disbelief. "You're crazy, you know that? Crazy to bring that car here when we're trying to hide. Someone's going to call the law on us."

Clyde shook his head, turning back to the whipit. "It'll just be one night. We're going to use it to pull a job tomorrow, and then we'll ditch it. No one's going to see it. It's in the garage, remember."

"You promised Buck and Blanche that you would keep this place from getting hot, and now you've gone and lit us on fire!" Bonnie, flouncing toward the bedroom, turned in the doorway for a final jab. "And it's *doesn't*—he *doesn't* mind. Except you can bet he does!" She slammed the door behind her.

Though a rush of breath and blood filled her ears, she could hear the thud of the table overturning and his feet pounding across the floor. She gripped the knob, but it slid under her fingers when he turned it. She pressed her shoulder against the door and absorbed the impact of his body, as he slammed against the thin slab of wood. The final jolt catapulted her into the room, until she hit the mattress and spilled face first over the sloppy folds of pink and peach and the rumpled feather bed. He grabbed her wrist, yanked her up, and flung her, so that she smashed into the wall. The swift motion, over which she had no control, and the pain that instantly commanded her attention were a relief and a release. Angry words gushed over her tongue.

"You know you're going to die, and you want other people to die with you!" She charged and overbalanced him, so that he tipped sideways onto the mattress. She threw herself on top of him and locked her hands around his throat. "You want us all to go down together."

In an instant, he flipped her, but she kneed him in the stomach and slipped out of his grasp. He caught her again, around the waist, and threw her back onto the bed. And then his lips were on her neck and he was hard against her groin and she arched her back, offering her breasts to his mouth.

Afterward, they lay, spent and damp. This was the sweet time she could count on, Clyde nestling his cheek in the softness between her shoulder and collarbone, letting her hold him.

His eyes were glassy with tears, his voice uneven. "I wouldn't hurt my brother for anything."

"I know that."

"Or you. Especially you."

CHAPTER 50

On Thursday morning, Clyde and Bonnie are still treating each other tenderly. He tries not to wake her as he slides out of bed, but she reaches her arms around his neck and pulls him back in.

"I've got to get us some money, so we're ready to go tomorrow."

"Wait," she murmurs, her face half-muffled by the pillow. "I'll come with you."

"There ain't nothing for you to do but sleep."

She does love sleep, which blunts the fear that prods her whenever she's conscious. But when he closes the door behind him, a dark, sad space yawns in her chest and behind her eyes, and she wishes she hadn't let him leave without her. She concentrates on the sounds Blanche is making as she cleans, her kid pumps *tick-tock*ing over the floor, Snowball's toenails clicking after her. The wheels of the carpet sweeper roll over the rug, provoking Snowball's bark; the chair legs scrape; water rushes into the bathroom sink. Bonnie considers removing the smeared plates and encrusted flatware from the floor and dresser top to the kitchen.

Her shoulder is sore where Clyde has wrenched it, and her hip black-and-blue where it collided with the wall. She manipulates these areas gently, deriving pleasure from the twinges of pain, proof of Clyde's love. Emotionally, too, she feels bruised and delicate. Shrugging her limp red kimono over her nightgown, she makes her way gingerly into the kitchen.

"Blanche, honey, I don't feel so good. Would you boil me an egg?"

Blanche sighs. She wants to say that the kitchen is closed, or that Bonnie can boil her own egg, for Pete's sake. But she's aware that when they part the next day, she and Buck will be free to begin their lives, while Bonnie will have to go back to living like a hunted animal. "Of course, sugar. You just sit down, and I'll bring it to you."

Bonnie drifts into the living room and sinks to the floor in front of her typewriter, where she's left the start of a clean copy of "Suicide Sal," one of the poems she'd composed in the Kaufman County Jail, rolled into the carriage. She pecks at it listlessly.

"Your egg is on." Snowball follows Blanche from the kitchen—*click, click, click*. "He's nervous. He can tell something's up. He doesn't want to be left behind." Blanche picks up a deck of cards and begins to lay them out for solitaire.

Bonnie reaches to scratch behind the little dog's ears. "I know what it's like, Snowball."

Outside, an engine slows to an idle and beneath them, the garage door creaks open.

"Damn it!" Bonnie jumps up. "I knew I should have gone with them. Something's gone wrong."

All three men are in the garage when Bonnie and Blanche get downstairs. Buck, who'd been tuning up the Marmon out on the curb, now has his head and shoulders under the hood of the roadster.

"Forget it," Clyde says. "Damned motor's burned out. We'll have to take the sedan. Boy can drive this damn thing out of town and ditch it."

Now Bonnie can go with them after all. She runs upstairs to change, while Clyde and W.D. transfer the guns to the sedan. Blanche follows Bonnie up to the apartment, where she goes to the kitchen to rescue the egg, which has boiled too hard already.

"Are you going to eat this?" she calls toward the bedroom, but there's no answer.

Every step Blanche takes, the dog follows. "For heaven's sake, don't worry, Snowball," she says, as she sits again at her solitaire. "We'll be going soon."

Blanche can't wait until she and Buck and Snowball are packed into the Marmon and driving south. She's had enough of the inconsistent hours and the relentless, almost aggressive untidiness. The men's excitement over the guns has appalled her as much as the weapons themselves, and she hates the way Buck hangs on Clyde's pronouncements, as if Clyde were his king.

A muffled sound of gunshots penetrates the apartment.

"Damn those guns." Blanche carries the cards she hasn't yet been able to play, shuffling them absently as she goes to the window. Why Clyde can't be bothered to be more careful is beyond her.

Then, from the garage below, Clyde shouts. "Oh, Lordy, let's get started!"

Feet pound up the stairs, and Buck shoots through the door. "Let's go! It's the cops!"

Blanche, unable to process this outrageous command, balks. She squeezes her playing cards until the deck bursts from her hand in a paper explosion. "We haven't done anything!"

"We got to go!"

Buck disappears down the stairs again, but in a moment comes thumping back up with a shotgun in his hands. W.D. staggers through the door behind him, his shirt darkly, redly wet.

Bonnie, who's managed only to remove her red kimono, pushes past Buck and W.D. in the doorway and runs down the stairs in her nightgown. "Clyde!"

Buck and Blanche follow, supporting W.D. between them. Snowball slips down with them, nearly tangling their feet.

Downstairs, Clyde peers out of the closed garage through a crack where the door meets the wall. Then he slides the door open to reveal a police car, studded with bullet holes, a front fender collapsed over a shredded tire, blocking their escape. Directly in front of the car, a man slumps like a pile of gory laundry. His head is misshapen, and his arm is barely attached to his shoulder.

"Help me!" Clyde shouts.

W.D., despite his bloody wound, darts forward, and he and Clyde plant their shoulders against the crippled car and shove, while Buck grabs the dead man by the ankles and starts dragging. The severed arm threatens to detach altogether, and what remains of the head tips back to open the mouth in grotesque, silent anguish.

"Don't, Buck!" Bonnie gasps.

"We ain't going to run him over," Buck grunts.

With a crack, another bullet slices the air and bores through the metal skin of the police car. Clyde and W.D. run back to the garage,

Clyde twisting to squeeze off a couple of shots over his shoulder. Buck drops the feet and runs, too.

"Get in the car!"

Clyde's command loosens Bonnie's limbs, and she hurls herself into the front seat of the sedan. Through the windshield, she has a clear view of the ragged lake of blood between them and the street. And then she sees the long white V and blue lace of Blanche's back.

"Blanche, come back!" Bonnie screams.

But Blanche, who's made it to the street and is starting down the hill, keeps running.

The sedan rocks as the three men throw themselves into it and slam the doors. Clyde revs forward and slams into the police car, shoving it out of their way. They back up and are free, speeding down the hill after Blanche, who's slowed to a trot, her head thrown back and her arms lifted to heaven. As they pull alongside her, Buck throws open the door, hooks his arm around her waist, and drags her in.

"Snowball," she gasps, and then shrieks. "Snowball!"

Aside from her screams, the neighborhood is as quiet as ever. No gunshots, no sirens, no shouts follow them.

Bonnie squints, scouring the verge ahead for a flash of white, but Snowball might be anywhere. "We'll come back later. We'll find him."

Everyone knows this is a lie.

Blanche, who has been draped over Buck's lap, sobbing, recovers her breath and lifts herself, so that she's sitting straight in the seat. She's amazed to find a few playing cards still in her hand. Everything has happened too fast; she's not been able to think and make the proper decisions. She reviews the items left undone: she's not wearing hose; her underthings are tangled in a pan of gray water in the kitchen sink; the hard-boiled egg is still in the saucepan; the wristwatch that her father gave her for her graduation is ticking away in the kitchen cabinet, where she'd placed it for safekeeping. The car speeds her faster and faster away from all of this unfinished business. "We have to go back."

No one responds. If anything, Clyde pushes the car even faster.

"No, listen to me. We have to back! Buck, we haven't done anything! Let us out, Clyde. We have to go back and explain that we were just visiting. We're not Bonnie and Clyde! We haven't done anything!"

Buck pats her awkwardly. "*Shhh*, Baby. It's all right."

His useless motions and empty words sicken Bonnie. "Oh, let her be! It's not all right."

"I wish I was dead!" Blanche wails. She paws at the door and rolls her head and kicks her feet in their kid pumps against the floorboards.

"No you don't!" W.D. says. "Don't say that!" Blood seeps between the fingers he's pressed to his stomach.

"Baby," Buck says, "I'm as sorry about this mess as you are."

His words only make Blanche more desolate. He doesn't understand how this has ruined everything forever, because he hasn't shared her anxieties or her dreams. He's never longed, like she did, for a life in which they could just walk in and out of their front door without worrying about who might see them. He never thinks about the future. He's like a dog. Oh, Snowball!

"Blanche, kin you look at my gut?" W.D. slides his hands apart, exposing a soaked and brilliantly red patch of shirt. "Is the bullet in there?"

The fear in his shaky voice interrupts Blanche's free fall. Although she gags as she leans over Buck to examine the hole from which W.D.'s blood leaks, this new experience of terror and revulsion relieves the panic that's been overwhelming her.

"Am I going to die?"

Blanche's fingers shake so much, she can't unbutton his shirt, so she grabs two handfuls of material and yanks them apart. The buttons make a soft, popping noise as they fly off.

"I guess this shirt was pretty much done for anyway," W.D. says.

Clyde shakes his head. "I don't feel so good. Less stop a minute. We've gone far enough."

He lets the car roll to a stop in a patch of weeds, not yet tall, but already thick and green. The trees have fulfilled their promise of two weeks before and reached full flower, the gray limbs shucking off all restraint and parading exuberant white masses before the brilliant blue sky.

Clyde gets out of the car, breaks off one of the flowering twigs, and strips the blossoms off the wood with one hand. "Blue, get me a cloth."

Except for a wool blanket that Clyde and W.D. have been using to hide the guns, the only fabric in the car is that of the clothes they're wearing. Bonnie bites the stitches loose along the hem of her night-gown and tears off a strip, which Clyde wraps around his stick and soaks in whiskey from a bottle in the glove compartment.

"Yer a lucky bastard again, Boy," he says, as he pokes the implement into W.D.'s wound. Groaning, W.D. grips Bonnie's hand almost hard enough to break her fingers. "Bullet went clean through." Clyde tugs the gory stick out through the exit wound. "You ain't gonna die."

They examine each other, taking inventory of less severe wounds. Clyde has been hit with a ricochet in the temple and has a large bruise, but now that he's quit driving, he doesn't feel faint anymore. Buck has a red mark fast turning purple on his chest.

"That happened when I was going for the stairs to get you girls," he says. "Felt like it'd gone right into my heart, but I heard somewhere that if you got shot in the heart, you could stay alive if you held your breath. Long enough to say a few words, anyway. So I held my breath all the way up the stairs, so I could tell you goodbye, Baby." He looks sorrowfully at Blanche, and she presses against him and cries loud and long, until she feels as cleaned out as W.D.'s wound.

"Why did this happen?" Bonnie asks. "Why did the laws come?"

No one has an answer. As they drive on, they are beset by their usual woes. The temperature drops and rain begins; a tire goes flat. Most worrisome, however, is W.D., who despite Clyde's assurances and a packet of aspirin Clyde buys at a service station, seems likely to die. He lies with his head in Bonnie's lap, shivering violently under the wool blanket, barely able to open his eyes. Once in awhile, he utters incomprehensible, slurred syllables.

They drive toward Texas—because that's the way Clyde always goes when they're in trouble—and cover about four hundred and fifty miles that night, reviewing twenty times over what, along with Snow-ball, they've lost: most of the guns, Clyde's guitar, Bonnie's typewriter and the copies of her poems, Blanche's purse containing the papers that make Buck and her legitimate—and identify them. At one point, W.D. rouses himself to bemoan a stash of cigars, which makes Bonnie remember the camera, still loaded with undeveloped film. They've left their clothes and all the pretty things Bonnie and Blanche bought at Kress's. They do, however, have the stolen field glasses.

"Of all things," Blanche says with disgust, when Buck triumphantly pulls them out from under the seat.

"But think," Bonnie says, "of the look on Nosey's face, when he finds out who he's been sharing a garage with."

They're somewhere in the panhandle just before dawn, when they decide to hide in a tourist court. The room, which has no running water, is filthy with nests of dust and hair along the baseboards and a blanket dotted with cigarette burns, but its stove warms them. They fill a pan, its bottom blackly encrusted, with liquid from a rusty pump and drink, which revives them all somewhat, and then they clean W.D.'s wound as well as they can with another strip torn from Bonnie's nightgown.

They discover that Clyde has also been hit in the chest, although his shirt button must have deflected the slug, because it has burrowed only a little ways under his skin. Bonnie digs it out with a hairpin she finds on the floor, dipped in alcohol.

In the morning, although it's cold and Blanche is wearing nothing but a sleeveless bit of lace-trimmed, bloodstained crepe, she's more presentable than Bonnie in her torn nightgown, so she's selected to walk to the grocery about twenty yards farther on down the road. While she waits for the clerk to wrap some baloney, she pages quickly through two newspapers and is relieved to find nothing on Joplin. Still, that they aren't yet reporting the incident in Texas doesn't mean that a manhunt isn't underway. She's no longer hysterical, but back in the dirty room the tears won't quit forming and spilling. She raises her sandwich to her eyes and sponges at the tears with the bread.

"Clyde," Bonnie says, "why can't we tell the laws that Blanche and Buck didn't do anything? It's the truth."

"That's an idea."

Blanche can tell by the relief in Clyde's voice that he really is sorry for the mess he's gotten her and Buck into and that makes her feel a little better.

"I could write a letter," he says, "and say y'all were just visiting with us. You ain't got nothing to do with our crimes. And it was me that shot that law. Buck didn't even have hold of a rifle."

"That's right," Blanche says eagerly. "That's nothing but the plain truth."

But Buck is shaking his head, reminding Blanche of a stubborn hound dog. "It won't work, Baby. You don't understand the laws. They don't care about the truth. They just want to get someone. I was with Clyde when that man went down; I'm going to get the chair."

"I'm so sorry, Blanche." Bonnie wraps her arms around her sister-in-law, and the two of them rock together, because there is no other comfort.

In a few hours, W.D. lies flat out on the bed beside the women, and Buck sits on the floor, his elbows hooked around his knees and his head drooping, but Clyde is restless. He can't stop twitching the curtain open to check the parking lot and the road.

"Look at all them cars," he says once or twice. And then, finally: "I don't like the look of all them cars. Less git agoing."

CHAPTER 51

Stories began to appear in the newspapers around the time they reached Great Bend. Wes Harryman, who'd left a wife and five children, and Harry McGinnis, who'd been only three weeks away from his wedding, had come to the Joplin apartment to investigate suspected bootlegging.

"I guess you must have hit that other fellow, too," W.D. said.

"Wes Harryman," Blanche said. "Harry McGinnis."

"Blanche, don't," Bonnie said, as the names swelled the list in her mind. Which one belonged to the man with the severed arm, whom she saw whenever she closed her eyes? "I wonder which one of 'em shot you, Boy," she said. It wasn't right the way the paper used the word "vicious," as if Clyde had set out on purpose to kill those men. If W.D. had ended up dead, would the papers call the laws vicious?

They applied some salve from a stolen doctor's bag to the divot in Clyde's chest and the hole through W.D.'s middle. It hurried the healing of the skin, but W.D. seemed to have lost something besides flesh and blood. He fingered his wound while staring out the window in a way that looked more like studying his reflection than keeping a sharp eye out for the law.

"Leave it alone, Boy." Bonnie lightly slapped his hand. "You have to let it scab over."

He took his hand away, but she could tell he wasn't listening.

"You don't want a big scar to mess up that pretty belly."

"It's not going to be like it was," he said. "I been shot through. I coulda died like them other fellas did."

◆

They'd cut through Nebraska and were driving east into Iowa when the photos that Bonnie, Clyde, and W.D. had taken back in February appeared. The papers drooled over the one in which Bonnie glowered with a pistol on her hip and a cigar between her teeth. "Cigar-smoking, quick-shooting accomplice" the caption read. Bonnie recoiled at the thought that her mother—or anyone else for that matter—would believe that she'd become so coarse as to smoke cigars. By the time they reached Illinois, the papers were publishing the poem she'd been retyping on the apartment floor. She read it aloud as they drove south, and if she'd believed the typed version was an improvement over the handwritten one, that was nothing compared to the authority with which the rat-a-tat rhythm and the tough slang, which she'd learned more extensively from the pictures than from riding with Clyde, came across on the printed page. However, while the poem might have been about the woman with the cigar, as the papers claimed, she wasn't Bonnie.

CHAPTER 52

April 1933

"This is the one." Clyde nods as they drive by the State Bank and Trust Company in Ruston, Louisiana, which he reasons is big enough to be full of cash but small enough to employ only one guard.

"We're going to rob that?" W.D.'s fingers creep to the sore spot under his shirt.

Its stone-block façade is imposing, the front door deep in the walls of a two-story arch flanked by columns and capped with an elaborately ornamented pediment. The bank is a temple to money, and they are unlikely worshippers.

They're still wearing the clothes they bought two days after leaving Joplin. The dribs and drabs they've stolen don't amount to enough to buy new ones, and they haven't dared stay anywhere long enough to get what they do own cleaned. In fact, they haven't stopped at a tourist court more than three times since they've left Joplin, so most of their bathing has consisted of a splash of creek water. Their hair clumps in greasy hanks, dust rings their wrists and gathers in the creases of their elbows and knees and in the corners of their eyes. They exude a sharp, cheesy odor.

But living conditions never get Clyde down, and he's regained his confidence. "First, we need a new getaway car. This heap'll get us nabbed before we go two blocks."

Although the sedan was practically new when they'd started, they've been driving it hard for two weeks. The engine labors when Clyde pushes it past sixty; the front axle is cracked, and a loop of wire holds one of the back doors shut.

As they cruise a leafy residential neighborhood, Bonnie ignores potential cars and tries instead to peek inside the grand houses they pass, which hint at rooms to let with telltale cards in front windows and too many slat-seat chairs lined up along front porches.

"How about that one?" Clyde says, spotting a black V-8 sedan, almost identical to the one they're driving but much cleaner, in the driveway of a large, white house. "You want to grab it, Boy?"

When W.D. doesn't answer promptly, Bonnie feels queasy. The driveway is short; the car close to the house. She can see again the man running in his socks, his warm feet melting a dark trail in the thin snow. "Clyde . . ." she begins.

But Clyde is already braking, and his voice runs over hers. "C'mon, get out! What you waiting for? Christmas?"

W.D. opens the door, jumps out while their car is still moving, and runs the four steps up the driveway to the parked sedan. Clyde hovers in case W.D. has to rabbit. In neutral, they slowly roll past the drive, and Bonnie twists in her seat, so that she can watch W.D. open the shiny black door and then turn with a smile and a thumb in the air, before sliding in.

"It's got keys," she reports, relieved, and Clyde puts the car in gear and picks up speed.

About a mile out of town, they turn onto a side road and slow, so W.D. can catch up.

"Shouldn't he be here by now?" Bonnie looks as far as she can along the road behind them. "Move your head, Buck. I can't see."

A black car flies like a crow's shadow across the mouth of the road behind them.

"Was that him?" Bonnie says.

"Goddammit! That boy don't never pay attention!" Clyde grinds the gears, and the exhausted car growls its objections. Bonnie, Blanche, and Buck sway back and forward and back again, as Clyde executes an awkward, angry about-face on the narrow road.

Another black car shoots through the intersection before they reach it. "Maybe that's him," Blanche says.

"Naw, that's a coupe," Buck says.

They race behind the coupe that's chasing the sedan along the dappled, undulating, twisting roads. At intervals they glimpse the coupe, but W.D. is so far ahead that even when they crest a hill and the road lies open before them, they don't see the sedan.

"That moron in the coupe is making us lose Deacon," Clyde says.

On the far side of town, they spot arcs in the dirt where the cars have changed direction.

"He ain't taking the right road," Clyde says. "He'll have only hisself to blame if he runs smack into a police station."

Apparently, however, W.D. has not run into anything. He is gone.

"Hell, I don't know what to do," Clyde says.

The coupe is coming slowly toward them now. A woman drives; a man rides in the passenger seat.

Clyde reaches his arm out the window and holds his palm up, politely asking it to stop. "Hey," he calls to the man, who gets out, "you seen a black Ford coach out this aways?"

Approaching their car, the man nods eagerly.

"Why were you following it?" Clyde's voice stiffens.

The man's expression tightens in response. "It's my car."

Like a jack-in-the-box, Clyde opens the door and springs from the seat in one motion. He swings his .45 by the barrel sharply but with restraint, so that the butt strikes the man in the head just hard enough to make him stumble. "It ain't yer car no more."

Bonnie is almost as quick as Clyde. She dashes toward the coupe, furious. W.D. is lost, and these two are to blame. The driver, cringing, fumbles with the ignition, but Bonnie locks both hands around her arm, soiling her crisp white sleeve. "Goddammit, get out of there."

The woman obeys, stumbling beside Bonnie back to the old sedan. Clyde has pushed the man into the front seat beside him, and Bonnie does the same with the woman. The four of them are a tight fit, but the scared captives make themselves as small and still as possible.

Before long, Clyde has built up their speed again. His tires churn the mud, and clumps knock disconcertingly against the chassis.

"When was the last place you seen that shit hunk of metal? Did it turn here?" Clyde jams the brakes suddenly, and they all bang against the dash. Just before the car stalls out, he accelerates, and they're thrown against the seat back, their heads jerking on their necks.

"I . . . I don't know." The man's voice quavers.

"How can you not know? Shit! You were following him. You got to know which way he went."

"What he means," the woman hurries to explain, "is that the car was so far ahead of us, we couldn't see whether it turned or not. The last we saw, it was headed north. It might have turned, but it might have kept going. We just couldn't tell. That's why we gave up and came back. My automobile can't reach those speeds and, frankly, I wouldn't drive that fast, even if it did. Speeding is dangerous."

They hit a bump that sends them briefly into the air and come down hard, which causes the door to the glove compartment to drop open. Several heavy metal blocks fall onto the woman's feet.

Clyde leans over the man's lap, which puts his eyes well below the dashboard.

"Oh, God, watch where you're going!" the woman screams.

Clyde ducks down another two or three times to tease the woman, who's nearly in tears with fright. Finally, he gathers the ammunition clips off the floor and drops them in her lap. "Hold these."

◆

They seem to have traveled every road in northwestern Louisiana, but they still can't find W.D.

"I oughta kill the both of you," Clyde says, when they've turned and turned again. "What the hell are we driving around with you fuckers for?"

The man lets out a little squeak.

"Why would you do that?" the woman cries.

"Why don't you, Bud?" Buck puts in from the back. "Why don't you just kill 'em?"

"We ain't never gonna find him or that car," Clyde says.

"Please," the man says. "I don't care about the car. Please don't kill us."

"Please," the woman says.

"You'll be all right if you don't try any fucking funny business," Clyde says.

Bonnie can see that these people aren't thinking of trying anything. The woman keeps glancing at the magazines of bullets in her lap, obviously afraid to touch them but at the same time afraid that they might fall again to the floor.

"They won't hurt you," Bonnie says.

"I didn't say that," Clyde says.

"I mean the clips. She's scared they're going to explode."

Clyde laughs. "Them clips are the least dangerous thing in this car."

Bonnie leans forward to address the man who's rubbing the back of his head where Clyde struck him. "What do you do, mister?"

Startled, the man says, "I didn't do nothing except try and get my own car back."

"No," the woman says. "She's asking, what's your line."

"Oh." The man straightens himself a little in the seat. "I'm a mortician."

Clyde snorts. "An undertaker! Are you serious?"

The man frowns. "Of course, I'm serious."

"No need to take offense," Clyde says. "It's just funny, that's all. Do you know who we are?"

The two shake their heads.

Clyde looks so crestfallen that Bonnie laughs. "Don't you read the goddamned paper?" She leans down and, with the barrel of the whipit she's been holding loosely in her lap, taps the newspapers at her feet, several of which are open to the page with her cigar-smoking picture on it.

"You're Bonnie Parker?"

The woman sounds so incredulous that Bonnie can't help but put a hand to her matted hair. During the hot, tense drive, the woman's powdered nose had moistened and her crisp, white shirt had grown limp, but the fabric gave off a clean, starchy scent that made Bonnie conscious of her own filth and decay.

"I'm Buck Barrow." Buck leans forward. "And this here's my wife, Blanche. We was in Joplin, too."

"Be quiet, Daddy," Blanche says. "We got nothing to do with this. They don't need to know who we are."

"Maybe you'll be the one to fix us up after the laws get us," Clyde says. "Would you like that?"

"Oh, no." The man shakes his head. "I wouldn't like that at all. You ought to live a long, long time. That's what I hope."

Even Blanche laughs at this.

"Now, y'all got to tell us your names," Bonnie says.

Surprisingly, it turns out that Dillard Darby and Sophia Stone are not formally acquainted, although Mr. Darby confesses to having observed Miss Stone in downtown Ruston on various occasions.

"*DD* and *SS*, stung by a swarm of *B*s," Bonnie says.

"What in hell does that mean?" Buck says.

"They both got double letters. I like that."

"I do, too," Darby says. "Dillard's really my middle name."

"I'd like to get those names into a poem," Bonnie says.

"A poem?" Miss Stone's tone is incredulous again.

"One of hers was in the papers," Clyde says.

They ride for a few minutes in silence, before Miss Stone says, "My name's really Sophronia. It's from a poem, I believe."

"It's very pretty," Bonnie says.

"I had to make it snappier for the radio."

"You're on the radio?" Only a year or so ago, Bonnie would have wanted to know how she, too, could be on the radio.

"It's part of my work as a home demonstration agent," Miss Stone says. "I tell people how they can plan their meals to stretch their budget. I provide recipes and tips, that sort of thing. It's an essential service, times being what they are."

"You talk like you're on the radio," Buck says.

"Let's hear one of those recipes," Bonnie says.

"Well, we did make something very nice over at the high school this morning. It's called a macaroni papoose. It's a ham and macaroni dish. You roll the ham around the pasta. That's the papoose. It's something a little different."

"Tell it like you would on the radio," Bonnie says.

Miss Stone begins haltingly, but Bonnie draws her out with questions about the proportions of horseradish and cheese and nudges her on to describe a side of lima beans in tomato sauce. "You can add some bacon, but then you might as well go ahead and serve it as the main course. You can turn it into a succotash, if you've got some corn and some okra. The idea is to develop a few good, basic dishes and then vary those, depending on what you've got handy. You learn a good boiled dressing, and you can use it to make a nice composed salad out of cabbage, potatoes, beans, brussels sprouts, or what have you. And if you don't have any meat, why you can make a perfectly delicious cutlet with some potatoes and onions and any sort of root vegetables, dip it in a little beaten egg and some cracker crumbs, and fry it up."

"Don't you got nothin' for dessert?" Clyde asks.

"I saw something in the paper the other day I've been meaning to try. Have you ever had popcorn custard?"

They get her to talk through at least half a dozen more dishes until they're over the border into Arkansas, and Clyde turns onto a side road about six miles from the last town they've driven through.

The road, its bed made of pale dirt and grayed pine needles, is too narrow for two cars to pass, but they don't expect to meet anyone way out here. The tall pines standing straight as bars on either side line a ne-glected passage too far from town or railroad tracks even for tramps. As usual, Clyde drives faster than the road or the car can comfortably bear. They bounce and jangle, wincing as trees fly at them and then fall away.

"Why are we going down here?" Darby asks.

"Time to get rid of you," Buck says.

"Shut your goddamned mouth, Buck," Bonnie says. "We're trying to enjoy the ride up here."

Privately, she, too, takes some pleasure in scaring these respectable people. Back in Ruston, they have everything, but out here they're at her mercy. She can turn Sophia Stone into nothing more than torn flesh and sticky blood, no different from one of those pieces of meat she likes to cook. Frightened by her own thoughts, Bonnie loosens her grip around the slick wooden handle of the gun in her lap.

Clyde stops the car. "You got any money?" he asks Darby.

Darby raises his hips to dig into his pocket, extracts a coin, and holds it out to Clyde. "I'm afraid this is all."

Clyde shakes his head. "You can put that away. I'm sorry for hitting you back there. I hope I didn't hurt you too bad."

"Thank you for the food," Bonnie says as Darby and Stone slide awkwardly out the door she holds open for them. "I hope we catch your program one of these days."

"Now turn around and don't be watching after us," Clyde warns. As soon as Bonnie is back inside, he pushes the accelerator. The tires spit rocks as the car shoots backward.

"Clyde, wait!" she says. "How're they going to get back home on twenty-five cents?"

"You're right."

He speeds forward again. Dillard Darby turns his head and closes his eyes, while Sophia Stone steps to one side, readying herself to run into the trees.

Bonnie thrusts her hand out the window, flapping a five-dollar bill. "In case you need to wire or something."

When neither Darby nor Stone approaches, she releases the money. It flutters to the ground, a gift from Lady Bountiful.

CHAPTER 53

"But it's Mother's Day!" Bonnie stomped her foot, driving her heel into the red Oklahoma soil.

"We can't risk it," Clyde said. He and Buck were sitting on a blanket, shotguns, rifles, and pistols between them, a variety of clips and shells within easy reach. Clyde, focused on a sawed-off lever-action Winchester, didn't bother even to glance at Bonnie as he made his pronouncement. "We'll stop by Eagle Ford Road quick, like we did the last time, and see if Boy's showed up, but we can't be driving anywhere outside of West Dallas." He swept aside a box of cardboard shells. "I hate this paper shit." Having selected a handful of brass cylinders, he inserted them one by one into the Winchester's magazine and snapped the lever into place.

◆

Their luck had not improved since they'd lost W.D. in April, when Sophia Stone had told the Shreveport *Times* that Bonnie Parker swore and stank and whacked her in the head with a sawed-off shotgun. Bonnie had tossed the disgusting rag out the window, where it *whoosh*ed up in the car's draft and then tumbled into the ditch behind them like a shot bird.

"We should have killed them." She'd meant it as a joke, but no one had laughed.

They'd gone right to Dallas, expecting to find W.D. waiting for them there, but he was not.

"It ain't good for him to be driving around with that hole in his stomach," Clyde said.

"I guess he wanted to get away," Buck said.

"Course he wanted to get away. Those idiots were after him," Clyde said.

"I mean from you."

"From us?" Bonnie had whirled to stare at Buck over the back of the seat. "You've said a lot of bonehead things, Buck Barrow, but that's the dumbest."

Like a hookworm, however, the distressing notion corkscrewed its way into her bloodstream. Obviously, from the start, they'd involved Boy in things he wanted to run from—the images welled up in her (the helpless feet, the rip of bullets, the thud of a body against the earth, the mangled meat of the lifeless arm, the blood seeping between his fingers)—but she'd thought the attachment binding him to her and Clyde had been stronger than any fear or horror, the way her love for Clyde rushed her past her own doubts.

Without Boy to boss between them, Clyde and Buck had argued all the way north to Minnesota—where they'd had to cling to the outside of the car to make a getaway when a man they tried to kidnap sent a load of shot into one of Buck's legs—and then east to Indiana—where, trapped after another botched bank robbery, Bonnie had squeezed the trigger on a BAR, releasing a spray of bullets, one of which had found its way into a bedroom and grazed the arm of a woman as she sat at her dressing table brushing her hair.

◆

But Clyde and Buck were easy with each other now, united in cleaning and loading their weapons. The repeated clicks and cracks of metal on metal made Bonnie want to scream. "Why is it you who always decides what we can risk?" With the heel of her hand, she shoved Clyde's shoulder.

He swayed and turned to look at her, which gave her some satisfaction, but he spoke with contempt. "You're like a cow in a chute when it comes to your mother. You just want to go straight ahead, no looking right, no looking left, no idea what's coming up behind you. They get a whiff of us anywhere near Dallas, where's the first place the laws gonna go? Emma Parker's house." He placed the loaded shotgun on the blanket with an emphatic thrust of his arm, as if it marked her mother's house on a map of the city.

"*You're* going to see *your* mama."

"Because she'll know where W.D.'s at. We have to get this gang back together." He shrugged and picked up a Colt pistol. "Besides, West Dallas is different."

"I can't never see my mama again, because she don't live in the Bog?"

"I never said never. I said not this trip."

"Not last trip. Not this trip. You talk as if there's plenty of trips. What if this is the last chance?"

"I'm just trying to keep me and Buck out of the chair."

"And I'm just trying to see my mama." As she spoke, she lunged for the Winchester. It was heavier than it looked, but she knew it would be. She needed a substantial weapon through which she could explode and blow a hole in his bossy head. With her left hand, she supported the stubby barrel so that the mouth opened toward Clyde's right ear.

Instantly, Buck was off the blanket, wrapping his long fingers around the barrel to tug it out of her grasp. "Now, c'mon, Sis. You don't want to do that."

"I could go into Dallas," Blanche said. She'd been sitting a little away from the rest of them, observing a pair of nesting birds through the field glasses.

"What do you mean?" Buck said sharply.

"They're looking for you and Clyde and the cigar-smoking gun moll, right?" she said. "Course, they know I'm with you, but they're not on the lookout for me by myself. I bet they wouldn't even know me if I sat down next to 'em. I could go into Dallas, round everybody up, and bring them someplace out in the country."

CHAPTER 54

Emma, on the sprung back seat of a Model A touring car beside Marie Barrow, listened over the sounds of the engine coughing and the wind leaking through the crooked doors and windows to Blanche complaining to Cumie in the front.

"L.C. can have this old motorcar when we're done with it." L.C., who was driving, sat up straighter. "One hundred dollars it cost me, because Nell said she was too busy to drive us. She wouldn't even go get me these boots."

Cumie shook her head but didn't comment. Emma suspected that Cumie, like Emma herself, approved of Nell's behavior. Nell obviously understood that guilt rubbed off like soot on the innocent. Only the mothers were desperate enough and the young ones foolish enough to keep running these punishing errands. Even Henry Barrow hadn't come.

As far as Emma could see, one piece of dirt was just like another out here, but at a certain smudge Blanche said stop, so they pulled off and waited a good while.

"You sure you got the right place?" Emma asked.

Blanche, absorbed in examining the leather of her new knee-high boots, shrugged. "It's where Clyde said. You can't count on them being dead on time, you know. They gotta sneak their way."

Emma was relieved finally to see the roadster and, as they followed it along the thread of a dirt road to a creek, the familiar happy anticipation at the thought of reunion with her daughter fizzed up in her. When Bonnie, Clyde, and Buck dragged themselves out of their car, however, Emma had to make an effort not to frown and press her lips together. They'd obviously been drinking; their clothes had been slept in, and Bonnie's breath smelled faintly of vomit. Although for Cumie's sake, Emma felt herself softening as she watched that mother hold her boys, she could not forget how vehemently she hated Clyde, and all the other Barrows to boot, when she lay sleepless in her bed.

Accepting $112 from Bonnie, Emma observed that Cumie got more—a few hundred, it looked like—but, of course, both her sons wanted to give her something. Blanche gave Cumie thirty dollars to deliver to Blanche's mother, and Clyde gave Marie a wad he instructed her to spend on bedroom furniture.

Bonnie behaved as if it were normal to have her mother snuck out to the back of some farm just to visit with her daughter. She might have been stopping by for a cup of coffee, given her conversation. She complimented Marie's outfit—a pale blue dress with a chic short-sleeved bolero jacket, too nice, Emma judged, for any Barrow to have purchased without Clyde's ill-gotten gains, and she asked so many mundane questions that Emma found herself in the absurd position of describing to her outlaw daughter the exact shade of green with which her new kitchen curtains were striped. Emma looked askance, too, at that Blanche, dressed in them riding britches like she was some Highland Park princess, going on like a body cared about her new boots.

L.C. gave the supple leather a playful slap. "How're you going to run from bullets in them?"

"You just try and catch me!" Laughing, Blanche and L.C. tore off into the long, wet grass of the meadow.

Everything about the way these people behaved was wrong. And wronger, still, was that Bonnie, who by nature was always in the thick of the horseplay, only watched L.C. and Blanche with eyes that seemed shadowed by their own sockets and took a long drag on her cigarette.

Someone who didn't know Bonnie might think she was just fine. She was young enough, after all, to appear fresh and pretty no matter what the circumstances. Anyway, Emma would be the first to argue that exposure to the sun and wind was far better for the complexion and posture than hunching in the linty, clattery atmosphere of a sewing factory. But Bonnie's eyes moved constantly, revealing her strain. When she talked to Emma, her glance kept slipping sideways over her mother's shoulder, as if, like an animal, she sensed hidden movement in the undergrowth. She'd coarsened, too. "Shit, you scared me," she'd said when Emma came up from behind and touched her sweet, bare neck. Emma bit her tongue. God would forgive her daughter's profanity. Her drinking, too. Emma wondered if Bonnie got hopped up. She knew that's what kids did.

Like Bonnie, Emma hungered for everyday details: what they were eating, where they were sleeping, how Clyde and Bonnie were getting along with Buck and Blanche. She had no desire to hear about any robberies or shootings, but she did believe it her duty not to shy away from the worst of her daughter's troubles. "What happened in Joplin," she ventured, "must have been awful."

Bonnie, however, shrank from allowing her mother a glimpse of that horror or any other. She shook her head, rejecting the invitation. "We were just playing around in those pictures," she offered instead. "I'll never smoke cigars, Mama."

"I know that," Emma soothed. "Come with me a minute."

Bonnie let her mother tuck an arm around her waist and lead her about twenty yards along the creek until they were out of earshot of the others.

"That nice Ted Hinton's been by two or three times," Emma began.

"Unless you're warning me to stay away, I don't want to hear about Ted Hinton."

"You got off in Kaufman, maybe you'd get off again. Or at least you wouldn't have to serve too much time. And then it would be over. You'd be free. It's not like you done any of these killings."

"How do you know?" Bonnie raised her chin defiantly. "I could've."

"No, you could not, Bonnie Elizabeth! I know you."

Bonnie closed her eyes. "If you knew me, Mama, you wouldn't love me anymore."

"Don't say that, Bonnie. It isn't true."

"Mama, why can't you understand that when Clyde dies, I want to be dead, too?"

Overwhelmed by the hopelessness of arguing with her daughter, Emma stroked Bonnie's dry, broken hair. "You're coloring this too much."

✦

After Dallas, Bonnie and Clyde and Blanche and Buck tried another vacation of sorts, driving to Florida and then meandering up the Georgia coast, stopping to play on the beaches. Until Buck smashed his hand while changing a tire, he and Clyde argued over who would drive. Bonnie and Clyde argued over which cabins to rent, and Blanche and Buck argued over how much Buck drank and how loudly he talked. When Buck was sober, he tormented Clyde by predicting that W.D. would do something stupid and get himself killed or get himself caught and squeal, to which Clyde invariably responded that W.D. was a helluva lot smarter than Buck, which made Blanche argue with Clyde, which made Bonnie argue with Blanche. Mostly, though, they enjoyed themselves.

They were halfway through North Carolina when Texas began to reel them back, and they turned west into Tennessee, then slid southwest through Alabama and Mississippi. In the evenings, through the insect blots on the windshield, Bonnie watched the road run straight and flat into the horizon until the orange hem of the sun had trailed away. In the blue-gray minutes between day and night, she pressed the vulnerable spot where her mother had embedded a splinter. She would never betray Clyde, but, despite what she'd told Emma, Bonnie did consider turning herself in to Ted Hinton. He'd cared nothing about poetry or music or acting himself, but he'd encouraged her aspirations, because of his affection for her. Now would he do what he could to save her, because he liked her? What if all she gave him was herself?

CHAPTER 55

June 1933

Boy is back! Clyde crows as he delivers the news after a phone call to Cumie from Yazoo City. He wants to drive to Dallas to collect W.D. that very night.

The following evening, sitting between Clyde and Boy, racing at eighty miles an hour up the Texas panhandle toward Oklahoma, where they'll be meeting Buck and Blanche again, Bonnie experiences the elation of a second chance. W.D.'s return renews her confidence, and, as the warm wind pours over her face, she glories in the sweep of purple and orange across the vast Western sky as an emblem of the life they've chosen.

They all feel the same—invigorated and relaxed—and the car's speed matches their mood. No one suggests they slow down when the rich sunset fades, giving way to the gloaming. No one notices the sign that says the bridge is out.

> *The rumble stopped; the engine screamed.*
> *And the never-ending bounce and the rattle-tattle jounce*
> *Of the ever-rolling road*
> *Vanished.*
> *Into air. Black air.*
>
> *Is this what it's like to fly?*
> *Is this what it's like to die?*

Bonnie doesn't remember any of the crash after the terrifying sensation of flying. Doesn't remember smashing through the wooden barrier or the black crack in the flat, bare earth into which they fell. Or the bangs of the car against the rocks at the bottom, harsher than thunder. She doesn't remember being flung against the door and the roof and the floor of the car, and then pinned under and pinched by searing metal that melts her flesh.

She doesn't lose consciousness right away. Later, W.D. will tell her that she screamed and screamed. Who could blame her, with, as he will put it, "the hide gone from your hip to your ankle," so he could see "the bone all white and wet"?

Clyde and W.D. are almost too beat up and dazed to walk, so some men who live nearby carry her up to a house. She doesn't remember this, either. In fact, W.D. will tell her that she'd passed out by then. "All droopy-like," he'll say, "with your head hanging back and your arms flopping down, like you was a rag doll."

When she comes to, she's panicked, not knowing where she is, a sharp pain in her chest when she inhales, stinging cuts on nearly every part of her body. Her leg feels numb, like she's slept on it funny. In some places it throbs, as if waves of fire are passing through it, but the pain is not unbearable. Not yet.

A kerosene lamp gives the room a dim glow, and she becomes aware that people move and murmur there, women and men she doesn't know. "Daddy?"

A dark shape turns from the window and hurries to her. "He'll be right back, Sis," W.D. says. "You ain't dead."

His face, smeared with blood, shows such relief, she has to smile. "Boy." She reaches a finger to touch his cheek. "You get shot?"

"Naw. Just glass. I'm all right."

A car engine turns over, and W.D. runs back to the window. "Shit! One of 'em's drove off. Let's go." He slides his arms under her and lifts her from the bed.

"She needs a doctor," a woman calls after them. "He's gone for the doctor."

They meet Clyde coming into the yard, two shotguns and the Browning across his arms like stovewood. "Is she . . . ?" he begins, and his loaded arms dip under the weight of his dread.

"Don't worry, Daddy. I'm all right." She wants to reach for his neck, to have him take her in his arms, but he has the guns.

"We got to get out of here. They must of seen all this."

"One of the fellas drove off," W.D. confesses.

"I heard."

"Boy was taking care of me," Bonnie says.

Clyde's eyes narrow with focus. "Get her behind that bush and then come back and take one of these. I'm fixing to get us a car."

The plant he's indicated isn't a bush, but the sort of brown, prickly scrub that seems to be the only vegetation that grows naturally in those flat, barren stretches of the panhandle. It's hardly a feature one can hide behind, but W.D. lays Bonnie down awkwardly yet gently on the hard earth, well out of the weak light that issues from the front door.

"Here they come," Clyde says.

◆

The officers—one stringy and one stocky—are casual and confident as they get out of their car. They have no notion of what is about to happen.

Clyde steps forward, his scattergun in one hand, a shotgun in the other. "Less have your weapons."

"What is this?"

"This is you doing what I say," Clyde says.

W.D. steps forward with a heavy tread to show them they can't escape. Cautiously, they slip their pistols from their holsters and drop them on the ground. W.D. bends to pick them up.

As he's straightening himself again, more slowly than normal for a teenage boy because he's so hurt and sore, something clicks near the front door of the house. Too jittery to distinguish the snick of a screen door latch from the cock of a gun, Bonnie gasps, which might be what causes W.D. to spin and swing his shotgun toward the house, pulling the trigger even as he turns. From inside, a woman screams.

"Let's go," Clyde says. "Get in the car." He motions with his scattergun.

"He might of hurt someone," the stocky law says. "Killed someone even."

"Then we got to go faster. Get in."

"Get in?"

"Don't play dumb. Get in your goddamned car." Clyde nudges at them with his shotgun, while keeping the scattergun trained on their chests.

When they're closed in the back, W.D. stands over them with the gun, while Clyde picks Bonnie up. She tucks herself into him.

"I think I might be hurt bad," she whispers, beginning to shake with shock.

They're speeding down the road when headlights appear.

"The doctor," one of the men says from the back, but they barrel past.

They've put her in front between Clyde and W.D., but she can't sit up. At every jounce, she tips over sideways or slides toward the floor. Blackness rushes at her, not from the night outside but from inside her head. "I have to stop. I have to get out. I'm going to be sick."

"Blue." Clyde takes one hand from the wheel and strokes her temple. "We got to keep going."

"I got to lie down."

He frowns, but pulls the car over, stopping gingerly, so there's no jolt.

"You two are going to hold her," he tells the men in back. "You're going to stay real still and make her comfortable."

The laws could grab her and Clyde both as he leans in to settle her on their laps, but one puts his arm under her, cradling her head against his shoulder, and the other adjusts his legs so they support hers, being careful not to touch or even hardly look at the side that is red and raw.

"You hold her easy," Clyde warns. "Don't make her hurt any more than she's got to."

"That feel all right?" the one at her head asks.

She nods. "Your shirt smells nice."

"My wife puts something in the wash."

"I'd like to get me some of that," Bonnie says. "Will you ask her what it is for me?"

"If your man there lets me go home, I sure will."

"You can write to me care of the road," she says. Pain has begun to pulse through her with every heartbeat.

"*Shh*," the man says, as if soothing a baby. "*Shh . . . shh*." He smooths the hair from her forehead, just as her mama would have. "You're going to be all right."

"She's out," she hears the other man say, but she's only closing her eyes, trying to cut off the darkness that's swelling up inside her again.

The car swerves slightly, and she groans.

Clyde's voice sifts into the back. "You holding her right?"

"We're doing our best," one of the men says.

She can't tell if it's Head or Legs. She concentrates on breathing shallowly, so her chest won't pinch so bad.

"You ever hear of the Barrow Gang?" Clyde says.

Legs shifts under her, and she groans again.

"Are you being careful?" Clyde says.

"I had to move a little, that's all," Legs says.

"Well, be careful."

"Barrett Gang?" asks Head.

"Barrow," she whispers. Or intends to whisper. In fact, no sound comes out.

"Not Barrett," W.D. says. "Barrow."

"Nope," Head says. "Never heard of it. You?"

He's playing with them, but Legs isn't as quick as Head. "Barrow Gang?" he repeats.

"You never heard of Clyde Barrow?" W.D. is outraged.

"I may have heard of a hood by the name of Buck Barrow," Head says slowly. "Any relation?"

Clyde laughs. "You're putting me on, ain't you?"

"So you're the infamous Clyde Barrow."

"That's right."

"And this here must be Bonnie Parker."

She thrills at this proof of her fame, before the blackness overwhelms her.

Bonnie regains consciousness when the car stops, and the laws shift her back into Clyde's arms. He carries her to a bed of clothes and blankets arranged on the seat of Buck and Blanche's car. Blanche, her expression shifting from the crazed, drunken look of someone suddenly woken from a deep sleep to fear and dismay, stares in at her.

"Am I going to die?"

Blanche shakes her head, but the movement is tentative and slight, conveying uncertainty.

"I tied 'em up good," Buck says. "I cut some barbed wire from a fence back there and twisted that around 'em."

"Why can't you ever do like I tell you? I said not to hurt 'em. I said to use their handcuffs. What do you got to be so mean for?" But Clyde is already behind the wheel. He leaves the laws who've cradled Bonnie pinned against a tree.

◆

They creep along back roads, crammed into the coupe. Blanche and W.D., who's also badly hurt, are stuffed in the rumble seat with the salvaged guns, while Bonnie lies with her head in Clyde's lap and her legs on Buck, whose own legs are on top of Blanche's new suitcase, an unyielding rectangle of beige linen trimmed with dark brown leather.

"Can't you do something to stop her screaming?" Blanche yells from the rumble seat. "I can't stand it no more."

Bonnie isn't aware that she's been screaming. The shrieks issue from her involuntarily, as if she's a bellows being squeezed. At first, her raw leg looked worse than it felt, but as the shock wears off and the burned nerve endings begin to regrow, the unremitting fire in her leg consumes her. Occasionally, she dozes, exhausted by the constant and fruitless mental effort to make the pain stop, but her torturer allows her only a minute or two, before it redoubles its rage and drags her awake.

In Kansas, Clyde steals a second V-8, so they have more space, and on the third night, when Bonnie screams that she has to stop, that she can't stand another minute of jouncing on the dirt roads when every movement adds a burst of pain, they risk a cabin in a tourist court, but only one, so that the owner won't suspect that there are five of them.

"Let me die," Bonnie moans as Blanche dabs salve onto the oozing, open wound.

Blanche is pretty sure that the salve and bandages are useless. "You going to let her die?" she asks Clyde in a whisper that might as well be a shout in that crowded little room. "Whyn't you do something for her? She needs a doctor."

Blanche expects Clyde to be angry, but he's only resigned. "I'm driving, ain't I?" he says. "I'll get her a doctor. But we got to get far enough first."

CHAPTER 56

Far enough turned out to be Fort Smith, Arkansas. Whenever she was alert enough to notice, Bonnie despised the room into which Clyde had moved her, although she knew she ought to be grateful, because without it she'd be shitting on the dirt, as she'd had to do often enough before. Or in some reeking outhouse with flies buzzing around her thighs. Although from now on, she thought bitterly, it would only be her thigh, because there wasn't much left of the second one. The shithole in this shithole was only two steps from the bed, but that was two more than she could manage. Clyde had to carry her—jimmy his hands around her ass in a way that would once have excited her but now made her grit her teeth and squinch her eyes against the pain. Luckily, she wasn't shitting much. The medicine took care of that.

Clyde had found a doctor and told him what he'd told the owners of the tourist court, that his wife had been burned when a camp stove exploded. Bonnie couldn't believe that lie would fool anyone. The idea of Bonnie Parker fiddling with a camp stove, the way Blanche fussed over the hot plate in the room, warming cans of greasy, yellow chicken soup, was laughable.

"You were raving," Blanche told her later. "Something about shitting chicken soup."

It felt like lightning was trapped inside her flesh, burning continually, unquenchable. If she could have removed her leg and thrown it out the window, she would have done so in an instant. When the doctor lifted the sheet, the air stung like alcohol, though it was as still and fetid as air could be.

The doctor said that she would probably die, that she had to go to a hospital, that at the very least she needed a nurse. He threw away the salve Blanche had been slathering over Bonnie's leg twice a day, explaining that it had prevented the wounds from scabbing over, dangerously increasing the risk of infection. At the time, Bonnie heard none of this, but Blanche told her every last detail later, some days after Bonnie had begun swallowing the cerulean pills that made the edges of the lightning melt into her blood where she did not mind them, where they were soothing even, a river of warm light.

"It was infection that was likely to kill you," Blanche said. "Not the blood or the pain. Infection gets in there and just eats up your body. I've seen it happen before with an injury not even close to as bad as this."

"Infection," Bonnie repeated. With one open eye, she followed the movements of the finger she'd raised, letting it trace the outline of the curtained window, before she remembered what she'd meant to do with it. She pointed at Blanche. "You're the infection. Can't get rid of you. You're going to kill me."

"I don't want to complain," Blanche said to Buck, as she fried sausages on the hot plate, "but when a person does like I do for her all day, it just isn't right. She's always whining about the cooking smells, but she's not the one who has to walk back and forth to the diner with all them plates."

"She don't know what she's saying," Buck soothed. "She's all hopped up on them pills."

"We'll never get away now," Blanche sighed.

◆

Clyde retrieved Billie to be with Bonnie in case she died, as the doctor kept predicting, but within two weeks they were riding through the Ozarks and around Oklahoma in their usual haphazard fashion, while Clyde railed at Buck and W.D. If they hadn't been such clucks as to steal a delivery truck—that was W.D.—and then have to return it, because, as Buck had pointed out at the time, the lettering would get them caught easy once the truck was reported stolen; and if, while driving back again, they hadn't attracted attention by going too fast and rear-ending another truck—that was Buck—then Bonnie would still be lying in a comfortable bed with her sister to help her.

"And W.D.'d have all his fingers," Billie, who was sweet on Boy, put in.

"As if," Bonnie said dryly, "every job you done, Clyde, went according to plan."

By the time they dropped into Texas, bought Billie a new dress, and put her on a bus to Dallas, they all agreed that it was best they hadn't stayed too long in Fort Smith anyway. Hadn't they learned their lesson in Joplin?

◆

In Enid, Oklahoma, Clyde made a lucky find in a hospital parking lot—a medical bag stocked with vials of Amytal. He doled out the drug to Bonnie cautiously, but she got enough to maintain what the blue pills had established, a calmness and distance, the sense that though her body might be experiencing something, her mind need not bother with it. She continued to study the maps stuffed into the glove compartments of the cars they stole, but made no attempt to relate the zigs and zags with the roads on which they traveled. Instead, she focused on the bigger picture, as if she were God looking down from far above. Clyde liked the county maps that delineated farm roads and even the ruts that tractor wheels had established between the back edges of fields and the tree lines that marked the beginnings of woods. Bonnie's favorite, however, was a map of North America, on which a meandering red squiggle ran from Mexico City to Edmonton. She let her finger wander through the white space in northern Alberta and up into the Northwest Territories. The blankness was interrupted by lakes and rivers but not a single road.

For a few weeks, cars, cash, and even enough guns to more than fill a cabin's bathtub came easily to them, and they felt relatively safe. When Blanche cried upon reading that $250 each was being offered for the two killers of Marshal Henry Humphrey of Alma, Arkansas, Clyde comforted her with the fact that no one knew who those killers were.

"We're famous," Bonnie reflected later that night, in one of the Amytal-induced hazes that seemed to make things so clear, "but no one ever knows it's us. That's why we're always lucky."

Blanche, on watch, was sitting cross-legged on top of the car, examining the moon and stars through her binoculars. "If you call this lucky," she said.

CHAPTER 57

July 1933

The Red Crown Tavern in Platte City, Missouri, had only two cabins, but they were the most darling pair, built of fancy brick with pointed roofs and little fake chimneys, like miniature versions of ritzy mansions. An internal door connected the garage to one of the cabins, which made moving the guns—and Bonnie—private. It was less convenient for Blanche and Buck, who had to exit the garage and enter their cabin through the front door, but all they had to carry was Blanche's suitcase.

Blanche, whose picture hadn't yet appeared in any paper and who was generally identified only as a "second woman," had to handle all of their public dealings.

"You wanna go get us dinners, Blanche?" Clyde said. "You still got that bag of money?"

"What are they going to think when I order five dinners? I checked us in as three."

"They'll think you eat like a horse," Clyde said. "Get me chicken, if they got it. I want baked. And some peas and mashed potatoes. I'm starving."

"You look in the bathroom, Blanche?" Bonnie said. "You seen the soap? It's shaped like a seashell."

Blanche sighed. "I hardly even got a chance to get in my cabin yet."

"And beer, Blanche," Clyde said. "Better get us some beer."

Reclining on the pink candlewick bedspread where Clyde had laid her, Bonnie pushed her fingernails into the healthy flesh along the inside of her ruined leg. The mild pain helped to distract her from the deeper pain that, even when she hid from it for awhile, always found her again. "I need my medicine."

Clyde opened the doctor's bag. "This is the last."

"There's no point saving it. I'm not going to need it any more later than I need it now."

She leaned back against the pillow as the drug melted the pain, and watched W.D. pin newspapers over the window shades, deepening the dimness and furring the walls with words. They hadn't had to run since Fort Smith, and they had money; they could afford to relax. "It's like we're in a fairy tale," she said, lighting a cigarette. "Two perfect cabins, waiting just for us."

Clyde had stripped to his undershirt and shorts and stretched out beside her. He balanced a glass ashtray on his stomach, so she could reach it. It was that kind of considerate gesture that made her love him, Bonnie thought, tapping her cigarette to cause the tobacco she'd burned through to collapse into a mound of velvety crumbs.

◆

The following morning, Blanche awoke at about what she guessed was ten o'clock, and, as she had nearly every morning since they'd run from Joplin, felt a dart of anger at the thought that her watch was gone forever. She was irritated, too, that the habits of her companions had so degraded her that it seemed natural to awaken so late. She flung the blanket off and washed and dressed as noisily as possible and, finally, snapped the latches on the suitcase shut, but Buck slept on. Finally, she shook him. "Shouldn't we be getting going?"

Buck rolled onto his back with a grunt. Comfortably asleep on an actual mattress, he was loath to emerge into another day of cramp and disquiet. "C'mere."

"Daddy, we stayed too long already. Let's get going."

Buck turned over. "Ain't up to me, Baby. You know that. Go on and talk to Clyde. See what he says."

She had to knock hard before W.D.'s voice came through. "Who is it?"

"Who do you think?"

W.D. opened the door, first half an inch, and then wide enough to let her into the darkened room. Clyde lowered his gun. Even Bonnie, sitting up in the bed, had been ready with her whipit.

"Dammit, don't point them things at me! I just come over to get y'all going. It's going on noon."

Clyde rummaged on the floor for the sack of coins. "Go on and pay for another day, Blanche. We like it here. Don't you like it?"

"I like it all right, but we liked it in Joplin."

"We're not staying weeks. Just one more night."

"I told you, I don't like the way that manager looked at me yesterday. Buck says that Jelly Nash thing is sure to have got everyone spooked around here," Blanche said.

The pain in Bonnie's leg poked its head up and looked around, wondering where to start gnawing first. Bonnie opened the aluminum tin that had recently been full of vials and stared at the useless syringe. "Leave us alone, Blanche. Clyde needs a rest. He keeps you two alive, and all you ever do is say black when he says white and generally throw sand in the gears. If anyone's going to do something stupid and get us caught, it's your husband. Look what happened in Fort Smith."

"We're hardly any distance from Leavenworth," Clyde said. "No one'll believe a crook could be stupid enough to stop here."

◆

"Busted your kid's piggy bank?" the manager asked, as Blanche laid four dollars in nickels and pennies on the counter.

She scowled, although it was Clyde she was angry with, not this fellow, who was closer to the truth than he realized with his stupid joke. The coins had come from a gumball machine; that was the kind of big-time crook Clyde was. "That's right," she said. "There's a depression on. Or haven't you heard?"

She'd counted it out ahead but wasn't surprised that he was the kind who had to check the count. She stood waiting, curling and uncurling her toes inside her boots, while he slid the pennies two at a time over the edge of the counter into his palm. "You don't have to pay until four o'clock, you know."

"That's all right. We want the rooms."

"Well, if you change your mind, I'll give you your money back. Long as it's before four."

◆

"It was like he was warning me not to stay," she reported to Clyde and Bonnie.

"I thought you said he was the type that'd report the least little suspicion to the laws," Bonnie argued. She had unfolded all of their maps on the bed, as if she were planning an emigration or a military campaign.

"He is."

"Well, why's he warning you, then?"

Blanche had to admit that her theories didn't make sense. But to her mind, the whole place was too busy, with cars constantly driving in and out of the lot. Holed up in their dark, sweltering room, Clyde and Bonnie had no idea how much traffic ran through here and how exposed they were. "It's a damn oven in here. And you're just advertising with that paper over the window. Who covers up their windows, besides people on the lam?"

"People who wanna sleep," Clyde said.

"When we get caught, don't say I didn't warn you."

"If we get caught, we'll be dead," Bonnie said. "So we won't have to listen to you say 'I told you so.'" Honestly, Bonnie thought, today she'd just as soon be caught and shot. Her leg felt like it was burning up all over again. "Clyde, you got to get me something."

"Blanche'll have to stay with you, then."

Blanche directed a sigh toward a papered window.

"Don't worry," Bonnie said, "I won't be talking to you. I've got to concentrate on not screaming."

Blanche understood that pain made Bonnie angry at whoever was closest, but she was sick of always being that person. "Just hurry up."

◆

The pain wasn't all that bothered Bonnie. In the car, she'd hardly noticed how her leg was bent, but now that she could stretch out on a bed, she found that she couldn't unfold it. As she had on and off all day, she tried again to push her knee straight, but her flesh felt stiff and clotted and the joint refused to open, as if the tendons under her coagulated skin had thickened and fused together. The effort made the burning worse and started an ache in her hip and back. She moaned. Blanche rolled her eyes.

"Why don't you just go?" Bonnie said.

"You heard Clyde. I gotta stay. In case you need anything."

"I mean you and Buck. Why don't you go off on your own? We're just making each other miserable."

"Buck's not going to leave his brother. Not when he's in trouble."

"You were going to leave us in Joplin. Seems to me the only difference is now you're in as much trouble as we are."

"Where do you suggest we go? Just drive around the countryside forever, like you and Clyde, except on different roads? What's the point of that?"

"I think you should go to Canada." From her blanket of maps, Bonnie shook North America free. "Look, Blanche, if you could get here, couldn't you lose yourselves?" With her index finger, she made loops around the vast white space, drawing an invisible sign of infinity. "No one would ever find you."

"But there's nothing there."

"That's what you want, Blanche. A clean page. A chance to start fresh."

Blanche scooted onto the bed beside Bonnie and leaned over the map, as if a scene might reveal itself if she concentrated hard enough. She smoothed a wrinkle near Hudson Bay. "I suppose Buck could hunt."

"And you could fish."

"Ugh. I'll leave that to Buck. I could plant me some vegetables, though. Tomatoes and such."

"You could have flowers."

Blanche nodded. The two women always worked well together on this sort of exercise, imagining scenarios in enough detail to make them feel real but not probing so hard as to puncture a delicate membrane.

"Maybe once we get us a little place," Blanche added, "we can help y'all get a start there, too."

But Bonnie shook her head. To pursue that line would be to admit that it was all a fiction. Weeding beans and scaling trout, holding still in some place where wind made the only sound, wasn't for her and

Clyde. They were doomed to circle the edges of civilization and snap up scraps, like feral dogs. She wiped her eyes impatiently, half-conscious that the medicine—or her need for more of it—was making her emotions deeper and darker than they might otherwise have been.

For a moment, Blanche pressed her shoulder against Bonnie's, but it was far too hot to stay that way for long; sweat formed instantly wherever their skin touched.

"I don't think we'd better leave you," Blanche said quietly. "What if Clyde gets killed?"

"If something happens to Clyde, I'm doing the Dutch act. Same for him, if something happens to me. We have a pact."

Blanche recoiled. "But God won't ever forgive suicide. I tell Buck he mustn't ever kill himself if something happens to me."

She looked so troubled that Bonnie stroked her arm tenderly but with authority. "God isn't going to forgive me and Clyde anyway, Blanche."

❖

Trying to keep cool that night, Blanche spread herself fully on the bed, so no stretch of her skin touched any other. Displayed like that, she knew she was an inducement to Buck, who'd spent the hour she'd been with Bonnie drinking beer, but she pushed his hands away. "Honey, you know I love you, but you got to wait until it cools down. I couldn't stand it right now."

So he occupied himself with her boots instead, applying polish with firm, circular strokes and then rubbing it away from instep to knee and back again, sweat sheening on his arms and face. He vowed he would indeed take Blanche to Canada and assured her of his ability to trap and skin any kind of animal that grew fur. Tomorrow, as soon as they got well out of Kansas City, he'd have his eye out for a good car that could take them up there.

"It didn't seem right to leave them when Bonnie was doing so poorly," he said, getting into bed beside her, "but she's better now. Better enough, anyway."

Blanche nodded. Bonnie still couldn't walk normally, but she could certainly ride around in the car as well as ever. "Besides, they got W.D.," she said.

"Oh, I expect he'll run out on them again. You can't blame him. He's just a kid. But this ain't no life for you, honey. I'm so sorry I got you into this."

He'd become maudlin, his voice nasal with the clot of mucus that had filled his nose, and Blanche was surprised to find that apologies that had once given her at least a modicum of satisfaction no longer moved her. Her husband's expressions of sorrow now struck her as no more meaningful than those of a baby crying itself to sleep.

"Quit being sorry and do something to get us out of this mess." She sat up abruptly and pushed her arms back into the sleeves of her blouse. "I need a shower. I'm going for more soap and towels."

◆

Outside, the crickets' vibrato assailed her. Generally, Blanche savored the chirp of crickets, which she liked to think of as the musical pulse of summer. In reminding her of the wealth of God's creatures, the sound reassured her of her own insignificance. For this same reason, she tried to lose herself in the stars during her night watches. Tonight, however, the chirping was oppressive. "Get out, get out, get out," the insects warned, as she threaded her way through the crowded parking lot.

The inside of the Red Crown Tavern was also humming and buzzing, as excited voices around crowded tables topped one another. But while Blanche stood at the counter, the boisterous sound seemed to fade. Had she grown accustomed to the noise or were people modulating their voices at the sight of her?

The manager that Blanche had paid earlier had been replaced by a girl who was talking on a telephone with her back turned to the room. When she hung up and turned to see Blanche waiting, she jumped. Was she merely surprised to find someone at the counter or was she alarmed by Blanche in particular?

"Uh, good evening," the girl stuttered. And then, recovering herself, added with exaggerated courtesy, "May I help you?"

"I'd like another bar of soap, please. And two fresh towels."

"Of course." The girl started off, then stopped. "I'll be right back." She started away and then stopped again. "You wait right here."

Blanche dropped a coin in the penny scale beside the counter. She was shocked to discover how much flesh she'd lost—at least twenty pounds since Joplin. This life was eating her up.

Behind her, a man who'd slunk over from one of the tables clucked his tongue and looked pointedly at the seat of her jodhpurs. "Ninety-one pounds! You ain't no bigger'n a minute. I wouldn't mind being your horse."

"You can't be my horse," Blanche said, stepping off the scale. "Because you're a jackass."

Conveniently, the girl returned then with the towels, so Blanche was able to collect them smartly and march out of the place.

"I don't like it," she told Buck. "There's too many people here. The girl behind the counter was acting funny. We should go while we can."

Buck barely lifted his head off the pillow. "You know it ain't my decision. Go tell Clyde."

Blanche gritted her teeth. "*You* go tell Clyde," she said to herself, as she crossed in front of the garage.

Clyde and Bonnie and W.D. were playing poker on the bed.

"We'll be all right overnight," Clyde said.

"You're just jumpy, Blanche," Bonnie said, her voice slurring. Clyde had not found any more of the drug, so she'd been drinking. "You gotta relax. If we ran every time we felt a little jumpy, we'd never sit still."

"All right," Blanche said. "I guess we're no safer driving than we are in this place. But I want to go first thing in the morning. My first thing, not your first thing." She paused at the door. "I'm going to do some wash. You want anything done, Bonnie?"

♦

Blanche showered and did her bit of laundry in the sink and then rolled Buck's shirt and her own and Bonnie's graying underthings in a dry towel. Buck had put a pillow over his head to block the bathroom light.

"I don't see how you can sleep," she said, twisting the towel with all her strength.

Clyde knocked as she was hanging the clothes over the shower curtain rod. "How about getting us some sandwiches, Blanche? That place across the way is open. And some beer."

"At this hour? I'm already in my pajamas. Get your own sandwiches."

From the window a few minutes later, she watched W.D. cross the road toward the crenellated walls of Slim's Castle and was reassured to see that many of the cars had left the lot and some of the lights had been turned off. The place was settling down.

"C'mon, Baby." Buck raised the corner of the sheet. "If something's going to happen, there's nothing we can do about it until it starts. We might as well sleep."

But nothing was going to happen. Blanche finally felt easy enough to enjoy the luxury of the good mattress and the smooth, clean sheets. She closed her eyes and let Buck's hands excite her skin. If they found a car in the morning, they could be in Minnesota by this time tomorrow, just her and Buck, charting their own course. As she pushed against him, she imagined a log cabin—not like the ones they sometimes passed that looked as if they'd been heaved up like fungi from a crevasse in some mountain but a clean place with straight and sturdy walls standing in a green meadow. She would keep a jug of yellow flowers on the table, and Buck would come in for coffee—there would be someplace to buy coffee—after a morning checking his traps. Doubts about where they would get the money to buy the traps and what they'd eat before her vegetables grew threatened to distract her, but Blanche concentrated, riding Buck into the open white space, where fear fell away and pleasure overtook them, and they could finally relax.

CHAPTER 58

The pounding on Buck and Blanche's door jerks the occupants of both cabins awake. Sated with chicken sandwiches and beer, Clyde, Bonnie, and W.D. had fallen asleep in the stifling room and failed to hear the car being positioned in front of the garage to block their escape and the police arraying themselves in front of the cabins. The officers hold metal shields before their bodies, like ancient Greeks ready for battle. The police have learned to be prepared when they suspect the Barrow Gang.

W.D., who's been sleeping on the floor, simultaneously draws his feet under him and a BAR into his arms and freezes in a crouch at the foot of the bed. Clyde pulls on his pants before joining him. Bright headlights penetrate the double layer of window shade and newspaper. They're trained on the door of Blanche and Buck's cabin.

After another burst of knocking, Blanche answers. "Who is it?"

Crazed with tension, Bonnie almost smiles at Blanche's rendition of the perfect innocent.

"This is the sheriff. Send the man out!"

"There's no man in here."

Clyde, also gripped by nerves, smirks. "Wonder what Buck thinks of that."

"Put them riding trousers on," the sheriff says, "and come out yourself, then."

Bonnie clicks her tongue against the roof of her mouth. She'd predicted that Blanche's shapely bottom in jodhpurs would draw attention. She longs to crawl between the bed and the wall, but stays still, waiting for Clyde's instructions.

"Get the keys," Clyde whispers, nodding at the jacket he's hung from the back of the straight chair.

Bonnie puts the jacket on over her nightgown, wraps her fingers around the keys in the pocket, and nods at Clyde. If the car is still in the garage, they'll be all right.

"Where are your men?" the sheriff asks Blanche.

"In the other cabin," Blanche answers loudly, so Clyde is sure to hear.

She's admitted to "men," when they've checked in as one man and two women, but shifting the sheriff's focus is a good move. Clyde and W.D. ready themselves for a rush at the door.

But the sheriff keeps talking to Blanche. "Come out yourself, then," he says again.

"I've got to get my clothes on, don't I?" she says, as if she's sniping at a husband who's rushing her toilette.

"Can you get to the car?" Clyde whispers.

Bonnie has hardly hopped as far as the bathroom by herself since the accident, and she's weak and shaky from the hot day in bed and the beer on top of whatever Amytal remains in her blood, but she nods and slides across the mattress.

Now the pounding is on their own door.

"Come out of there!" The sheriff's bawl issues from between the two cabins.

"Just a minute!" Clyde yells.

Instead of opening the door, however, he levels the BAR and squeezes the trigger. The window explodes and the bullets rip steadily through the wooden door. By now, Bonnie, in a nightgown, is standing on one bare foot in the garage. She opens the car door and shoves the key into the ignition. Behind her, W.D.'s bullets join Clyde's and then Buck's start up from the other cabin, like a three-part harmony. She lowers herself onto the seat and worms her way from the driver's side to the passenger's.

Clyde and W.D. appear in the garage, and Clyde dives into the car and starts the engine.

"Open the garage," he says over his shoulder to W.D., who hesitates, knowing the police must have heard the engine and will be expecting the door to swing up. Clyde, who would rather run into a barrage of bullets than be cornered, jumps back out of the car. He lifts the garage door with his left hand, while swinging the barrel of his scattergun up with his right. A black car, bulky with armor plates, blocks their way.

The car is made to withstand bullets, but Clyde hammers at it anyway. The horn bellows unceasingly, and then, as if succumbing to Clyde's will, the barrier moves forward, opening a path. In the dark, beyond the cars that illuminate the cabins with their headlights, the police stand still and quiet behind their shields, as if they've been turned to stone by the bursting gunfire and the continuous blare of the armored car's horn.

"Blanche! Buck! C'mon!" Bonnie yells from her window.

The door of the other cabin bursts open, and Buck and Blanche dash for the car. Buck fires a blast from a BAR blindly as he runs, while Blanche lugs her suitcase, leaning a little to one side to counterbalance its weight, as if she's merely hurrying to catch a train.

Rifles crack furiously from across the lot. Buck's head snaps sideways, and he drops his gun. Bonnie sees what appears to be a hunk of fruit fly through the air.

Buck's knees give out, and Blanche screams and turns back for him, dipping to hook her left elbow under his shoulder. She doesn't think to drop the suitcase, but drags it along in her other hand. While Clyde scoops up Buck's gun and fires in the direction of the shots, W.D. helps Buck and Blanche shamble, the three of them like some awkward, enormous insect, the few, final steps to the car.

"C'mon! C'mon!" Bonnie can't get out; she can't help; she can only urge their progress. "Get in! Get in!" W.D. and Blanche can hardly stuff Buck into the back seat, he's so heavy and limp. He collapses between them, unable to lift his legs or unfold his body.

A blast of gunfire causes a noxious cloud of smoke to swell around them. Before they can draw the tear gas into their lungs, Clyde throws himself behind the wheel again and drives through it. From behind them now, the laws discharge another barrage, and the back window explodes.

"My eyes!" Blanche screams.

Clyde wrenches the car off the road into a fallow field. He cuts the headlights but keeps up their speed, and they bounce over the rough earth into the darkness.

CHAPTER 59

But they could not get out of Platte City. At the far side of the field, they bumped up onto a farm road that stopped at the river. They drove up and down one road after another, searching for a bridge, but every route proved a dead end. Three of their tires were so flat they were no more than a layer of rubber on the rims. The fourth was pumped full of lead.

"What do you think?" Clyde demanded, every time a new road appeared. "Should we try this one?"

Bonnie guessed—yes, no, yes. Often it turned out the road wasn't a new one after all, but one they'd already tried.

"Christ almighty!" Clyde said. "Is that the place we passed ten minutes ago?"

"I can't see!" Blanche cried. "I can't see anything!"

Finally, the bottom of the car ground so hard against the crown of the rutted road that they had to stop.

"Boy, get out. We got to fix these tires. Blanche, get up there and watch for cars."

"I can't!" Blanche wailed.

"You got to! What's the matter with you?" Clyde says.

"I told you! I can't see!"

"What do you mean, you can't see?" Bonnie turned to look at Blanche.

The scene in the back of the car was gruesome. Buck was sitting up with his eyes open, but his head seemed to be squashed in. Blood ran glistening down the side of his head and neck and had soaked through his shirt and pants. Blanche's eyes were squeezed to slits, and she seemed to be crying gouts of blood. Her cheeks and forehead were smeared with blood she'd tried to wipe away, and blood ran down her neck into her blouse. Blood dripped from the hands she waved wildly in front of her eyes to test her sight.

"I mean I'm blind! I can't see nothing but black!"

"Jesus Christ!" Clyde said. "They get you, too?"

"I don't know. I guess so. I can't see. I told you that!"

"Lessee." He helped her turn, so that she faced outward from the car. He struck a match and bent toward her face. "Look over here at me."

"How can I look at you, if I can't see?"

Buck pushed at Blanche's back. "I got to get out! I can't breathe! Let me out!"

Blanche scrambled out and turned, grabbing blindly at her husband to help him out behind her.

"God almighty!" Buck screamed, tugging at his clothes. He'd managed to seat himself on the running board. "I'm soaking wet! Get this blood off of me."

"It's all blood back here!" Panic made W.D.'s voice high and quavery.

"Boy," Bonnie said firmly, "go in Blanche's suitcase and get her something dry to wipe her face."

Blanche's pajamas were neatly folded. Even as she shouted replies to the police, she must have been swiftly tucking the arms behind the back and matching the legs. Tentatively, almost formally, as if presenting an orb on a pillow to a queen, W.D. set a neat, blue rectangle of fabric on Blanche's gory palms.

Blanche's vision was a little better with some of the blood wiped away. She could see a blurred but bright star, so close she could almost catch it.

"Goddammit, get your hand down!" Clyde scolded. "You want to burn yourself, too? Dammit!"

The star went out.

"Well, best I can tell," he said, "your eyeballs ain't busted."

While Clyde was examining Blanche, Bonnie tried to look after Buck, reaching behind her seat to put her hand on his shoulder. "Does it hurt, Buck? Are you shot anyplace besides your head?"

"It don't hurt too bad. I'm just so thirsty."

"We'll get you some water," Clyde promised. "Soon as we can."

Buck sounded so plaintive, so like a little boy, that Blanche instinc-

tively bent to press her lips to his head. But the slick feel of the blood
in his hair, together with the smell of it, made her gorge rise, and she
vomited beside the car.

"Goddammit. A bunch of repair kits, but no goddamn pump and no
goddamn jack. What kind of an idiot drives without a goddamn pump
and a goddamn jack?" Clyde slammed the trunk. "Let's go, Boy."

"Get a flashlight!" Bonnie yelled after them.

"Get something for Buck's head," Blanche gasped.

◆

Bonnie rifled through the maps that remained in the glove compartment—sections of Oklahoma, Texas, Arkansas, a detailed map of a
single county in southwestern Kansas—no Kansas City, no Platte City,
certainly nothing that would make any sense of this maze of roads that
seemed to go nowhere but back to themselves again. Didn't the people
around here ever want to go no place?

"I said we'd been in an accident," Clyde explained, returning with
a bedsheet so worn it had been cut lengthwise and the edges sewn together to make a new middle, along with a twisted cheesecloth, stained
blackberry-purple.

"An accident!" Bonnie couldn't stop laughing.

She ripped the sheet into strips and wound the fabric around Buck's
head as firmly as she dared, while he pawed weakly at her hands and
told her to quit messing with it. She discovered that some of the blood
in the car was, in fact, hers; all the moving around she'd done had re-
opened the scabs on her leg. So she wrapped that as well, while Clyde
and W.D. pulled out the inner tubes, fished the bullets out of them,
and gently abraded the rubber so each finicky little patch would stick.
One tire was so shredded it couldn't be fixed, but three and a rim were
enough. Conscientiously, they left the pump and jack outside the door
of the dark house from which they'd borrowed them and then made a
few more stabs at finding a road that would lead them away from Platte
City, but when they ended up in the same place for the fourth time,
they gave up and drove the car into the undergrowth to hide until the
sky lightened.

CHAPTER 60

All of them longed to run home to Dallas, but the laws would expect that, so Clyde turned north. They watched the road behind them for black cars approaching fast and the road ahead for black cars blocking the way. When they drove by open fields, they felt as exposed as a beetle on a tabletop and shrank from the windows, but they were even more nervous when nearing a stand of trees, where the laws could be hiding. They feared bridges most of all. Bonnie held her breath when, finally, they crossed the Platte.

While they concentrated on getting away, they were also conscious of Buck's every breath, and they watched him, reassessing by the minute whether he was healing or dying. Much of the time he was asleep or passed out, the good side of his head on Blanche's shoulder or lap, the damaged side sodden with blood that continued to seep through the bandage. When they pulled into a service station for gas, they hid him under a blanket, but he awoke and began to vomit, so they had to speed away with an empty tank.

Blanche could see pretty well out of her right eye now, although the skin around it looked as if it had been used as a chopping block, and the sun made it water. Blinking her left eye was excruciating, so she kept it closed.

"Isn't there something we can do for him?" Blanche begged somewhere in Missouri, when they'd listened to Buck moan steadily for nearly an hour.

The road ran between cornfields, the stalks straight as soldiers, the leaves like arms raised in surrender.

"We can't stop here," Clyde said.

Earlier, they'd given Buck water, which he'd slurped sloppily, and then vomited up. Now Blanche kept offering him little sips of warm Orange Crush, but he turned his head away. As the sun burned higher and hotter, the blood began to stink. Buck twitched and then started to thrash, hitting out at W.D. and Blanche, who supported him on either side.

"Please!" Blanche pleaded. "We have to do something!"

"We can't stop here," Clyde said again.

"Well, when can we stop? We can't keep driving forever!"

"Let's get something to clean his wound," Bonnie suggested.

Except for gas, Clyde wouldn't stop until they'd crossed into Iowa, but then he pulled in at a drugstore. The items he handed Bonnie in a paper sack were pitiful, given the intensity of the injuries they were meant to treat: Mercurochrome ("for minor cuts and abrasions," the package read), aspirin, a pair of dark glasses, hydrogen peroxide, and a roll of bandages.

They drove on, putting distance between themselves and the clerk who could report a man with a limp buying bandages. Blanche looked better, at least, wearing the sunglasses. She coaxed Buck to swallow an aspirin.

Finally, on the far side of a little town, Clyde turned north again, and in a few miles, pulled off on a weedy drive that looked as if it hadn't seen traffic all summer. Bonnie soaked a wadded strip of bedsheet in hydrogen peroxide, but when they removed Buck's bandage, they agreed that dabbing seemed an ineffectual way to clean an actual hole in the head. Besides, none of them could bear to touch the wound. Instead, they helped Buck lie down on the seat, and Clyde poured the chemical into the hole directly from the bottle. It foamed madly and seemed to cause Buck no discomfort.

Encouraged, Bonnie applied Mercurochrome with the bottle's sponge applicator to the cuts that crisscrossed Blanche's face. Outlined in the pink of the mercury solution, the wounds looked more manageable.

No one, except Clyde, wanted to get back into the car. All over the floor and seats, bandages soaked with blood and vomit coiled like intestines. W.D. complained that the smell was making him sick.

"For God's sake!" Bonnie grabbed at the gore with her bare hands, throwing the used bandages along with the empty hydrogen peroxide bottle into the weeds. It was hard to stay clean and organized on the road, but disposing of garbage was never a problem. She and Clyde had chucked chicken bones, shampoo bottles, broken shoes, and laddered hose all over the countryside.

"We can't stay here. It's too close to the road." Clyde flicked the butt of his cigarette into the weeds, too. Someone was going to notice the bullet-pocked car, if not the bloody and bandaged crew inside it.

"I ain't getting back in," W.D. said.

"We gotta stay together, Boy," Bonnie said.

"I want to quit driving."

"Get in," Clyde said impatiently. "We're just going to head back in here a ways."

"Then we'll stop and everyone'll get out," Bonnie promised.

The tire nearest to where W.D. stood had collapsed down to the rim, so that the machine tilted in his direction, as if extending an invitation. He got back in.

The overgrown road seemed to run into a wood, but behind the first screen of trees the landscape opened into what had been in more prosperous times an extensive amusement park. They passed a huge concrete basin—an empty man-made lake—surrounded by a concrete deck. Beyond it, the setting sun bronzed an open-air dance floor, a motionless carousel, and an abandoned shooting gallery.

Two months ago, Dexfield Park might have been a private fairyland. Clyde and Buck and W.D. would have fooled around in the shooting gallery, aiming at the arrested line of yellow ducks and erecting pyramids of beer bottles, while Bonnie and Blanche would have mounted the stilled carousel horses. They all would have slid into the concrete basin to listen to their own voices echo off the sides and danced on the enormous wooden floor.

The road stopped, but Clyde bumped onto the grass and steered the car over a rise and through some trees, on the far side of which the land sloped down to a river. He stopped in a meadow on a fairly level plot. Through more trees and undergrowth, they could glimpse the water, slate-colored in the graying light.

The diminished gang threw open the doors and hobbled into the fresh air—Bonnie, who'd effectively lost a leg; Blanche, who was nearly missing an eye; W.D., whose fingers were foreshortened; and Buck, for whom Clyde was planning to dig a grave. For dinner, they drank water that W.D. carried up from the river in empty bean cans. They removed the back seat from the car and made Buck as comfortable as they could on it. They expected him to be dead by morning.

But in the damp, gray dawn, from her nest in the front seat, Bonnie could hear Buck still breathing. Worry over his condition ought to have distracted her from her own discomfort, Bonnie thought, but her body would not be shushed. Her leg bled and burned; mosquitoes had whined around her ears for most of the night; she was hungry.

Blanche, who had, at some point in the darkness, begged hysterically for someone to shoot her, so that she could go with Buck, had finally fallen asleep on the grass, her head on her husband's knee. Clyde slept slumped forward, his head cradled against his beloved steering wheel. He looked fragile and young, sandy-colored whiskers sprouting halfheartedly through the dirt and blood on his cheeks and chin.

He must have felt her looking at him, because he opened his eyes. "Blue?"

"Yes?"

"We forgot to pray."

He got out and knelt with his elbows on the seat, a position she was now incapable of assuming. She bowed her head and waited for him to finish.

When Buck awoke, he demanded fried chicken. His head had swollen to larger than its normal size, despite the missing piece. Clyde proposed going back to town to find some ice to bring the swelling down, so they pressed mud into the bullet holes in the vehicle and then smeared more mud over the whole thing, so it looked as if they were driving nothing worse than a filthy car.

"You ain't going to leave us," W.D. said anxiously, when Clyde and Bonnie got in.

"We can't all go into town," Clyde said. "You got to take care of Buck and Blanche."

"Don't worry, W.D.," Blanche said bitterly. "They're never going to leave us."

"Think he's going to die?" Clyde said, as they rolled past the empty lake.

Bonnie didn't see how Buck could keep living with that big hole in his head. But, aside from being weak from loss of blood and unsteady on his feet, he didn't seem sick. "Maybe not," she said. "Maybe we don't know what a person can do without."

In Dexter, Bonnie felt grossly conspicuous, sitting in the mud-dappled Ford in her tattered, filthy nightgown waiting for Clyde to emerge from a clothing store, but no one paid her any attention.

"Just my luck, he's a marshal," Clyde said, depositing a large parcel wrapped in brown paper on her lap.

"Who is?"

"The clerk. But I gave him a good story about how we were on our way to visit my mother-in-law, and my wife insisted we needed new duds. Making a big sale like this blew his wig."

At the other end of town, he parked in front of a restaurant. "Gimme one of them white shirts."

While he was inside, she examined his choices. He'd bought her a cream-colored satin nightgown, slinky and entirely unsuited to sleeping in the car or on an old blanket on the grass. She rubbed the luxurious fabric against her cheek. He'd also bought two dresses.

She held one up to her shoulders when he came back to the car. "What do you think?"

He was struggling with boxes and barely grunted. "I promised to bring the plates back," he said.

Waiting outside the drugstore next, she was ashamed for thinking about clothes and ashamed of Clyde for caring what his food was served on.

"We ought to get Buck home to your mama," she said, when Clyde got back in the car again.

Clyde nodded. "If he don't die today, I aim to try it. It's what I promised her. Don't know how 'til we find another car, though."

"Well, this is a nice town," she said. "There's bound to be one you'll like somewhere around here."

The next day, Clyde returned the plates and came back to the meadow with more dinners, a box of groceries, a case of soda pop, another block of ice, and a pair of tweezers with which he, Bonnie, and W.D. took turns trying without success to pick a sliver of glass out Blanche's left eye. The ice they chipped from the block with the tire iron, however, did seem to bring down Buck's swelling.

On the third day, Clyde and W.D. found a fresh machine, parked on a side street in Redfield with the keys in it, almost as if it had been delivered to them. Now that they could leave, W.D. couldn't relax.

"We ought to get going," he said, when he and Clyde returned from the woods, where they'd set the bloodstained back seat on fire. "This place don't feel safe. How do we know someone ain't up there, watching us?"

Bonnie looked back up the slope where the greens were deepening, becoming more lustrous in the soft evening light. Like Sleeping Beauty, their wounded family was protected by thickets of wild blackberry brambles and tangled, exuberant honeysuckle. It seemed impossible that anyone would wander into this place that humanity had so obviously forsaken.

"You ought to go on yourself, W.D.," Buck said.

"Yes, you could get away," Blanche said fervently, as if W.D.'s escape would bring her vicarious relief. "The laws don't even know who you are. You could just go someplace and start your life all over."

W.D. frowned. "Where could I go, though? I don't know no place but Dallas."

Blanche threw her arm out, sweeping the horizon. "Anywhere! Minnesota. Michigan. Montana. Go someplace where they never heard of the Barrow Gang."

"Any place gets a newspaper has heard of the Barrow Gang," Bonnie said. "I bet they know about us in New York City."

"Montana?" W.D. said doubtfully. "I don't know nobody in Montana."

"Boy means to stay with his people, don't you, Boy?" Clyde said. "He knows you ain't nobody if you ain't got no people."

"Better to have no people than certain people," Blanche said.

"If he goes off by himself, who'll take care of him, if he gets hurt?" Bonnie said. "Who'll take him back to Dallas, like we're fixing to take Buck?"

The fact that Buck would not need taking back to Dallas had he not been with them hummed like wind in electrical wires, but no one said it outright.

"Don't worry, Boy," Clyde said finally. "Platte City learned me. Never stay when you can go. We're leaving first thing."

W.D.'s anxiety had spooked them. In silence, except for Buck, who loudly described the dinner he intended to consume the following evening, they packed the new car and prepared early to sleep. With her red and purple eyes, Blanche, sitting up so Buck could stretch out across the back seat of the new car with his head in her lap, looked worse than her husband.

"You haven't slept two hours since we got here," Bonnie said.

"I'm afraid to sleep. What if Buck . . . ?" Blanche couldn't finish her sentence.

"I ain't going nowhere," Buck said. "You gotta sleep, Baby, or you won't be no help to me when we're driving tomorrow."

"I'll stay up with him," Bonnie said. "I'll wake you if he needs you. I can't sleep anyway, my leg's hurting so bad tonight."

Blanche, who indeed could hardly hold her head up, relented and got in the front seat, where she could lie down comfortably, and Bonnie took her place.

For some time, they were jumpy. They were used to scurryings and rustlings, but tonight, even the trembling bleat of the screech owl disturbed them, and a rabbit's scream made Clyde grab his gun. Finally, Blanche fell asleep, and then W.D. and Clyde slept as well. But Buck, who'd slept on and off a good deal of the day, remained awake.

"You won't leave him, will you?" Buck whispered.

"You know I won't." Bonnie was insulted by the question.

"I know." He sighed. "You and me are a lot alike."

With that, he, too, was asleep. Bonnie was sweating between and under her thighs and in the folds where her breasts lay against her ribs. She tried to lift her legs half an inch off the seat to allow a little air to circulate. But Buck's heavy head pinned her.

Trapped and wakeful amid the alien noises of the night, Bonnie sat in the spongy heat and mourned the loss of the light and music that must once have spilled over the hill. She was unaware that this place she perceived as abandoned and lonely was acreage the locals knew well and traveled through, observing discarded bandages and half-burned seat cushions—not so unusual in themselves, perhaps, because hobos dropped and burned all kinds of garbage. But so bloody! A farmhand picking blackberries might feel alarmed at such a sight, which might prompt him to report it to a marshal, who was also a clothing store clerk, who'd sold several items to a man whose shirt had been covered in brown stains that could easily have been blood.

CHAPTER 61

When the sky lightens to the pale blue of a girl's wash dress, laundered so many times that the color has leached away, and the sun is still only a narrow stripe of brilliance, Blanche wakens and rouses Bonnie. "How is he?"

"I'm fine." Buck speaks for himself. "Just dandy. C'mere, Baby. I got something for you."

The day is already so warm that Bonnie can't stand the thought of putting anything over her thin nightgown. Hopping on one foot, catching her balance with the toe of the other, she advances precariously toward the small fire where Clyde and W.D., their BARs well behind them, are roasting wieners on sticks.

"Morning, sunshine," she says.

Clyde smiles. "We can practically see through that nightie."

She shrugs. "W.D.'s seen about all there is to see by now."

W.D. keeps his eyes modestly averted.

"You gotta take it, Blanche. You're gonna need money." Buck and Blanche are on the far side of the car, but Buck seems to have lost the ability to modulate his voice. "Listen, it's all right. I stole it from one a them drunken soldiers. He'll never miss it."

"Put that wallet back in the car," Blanche says. "It's W.D.'s."

"It ain't. I got it from one a them soldiers lying around out there."

Bonnie, Clyde, and W.D. exchange looks; this is what they expect from a hole in the head. Then Clyde stiffens, like a rabbit scenting a dog.

At the top of the hill, the trees and bushes separate into hunters, twenty or maybe thirty of them, their rifles and shotguns tucked tight against their cheeks, ready.

Bonnie glances over her shoulder for the poor deer or fox or rabbit. She doesn't grasp that she's the prey.

"Look out!"

As if Clyde's shout were the signal, the guns produce a sudden storm of *cracks* and *bangs*, *thuds*, *rips*, *whizzes*, and *thunks*. Shot splatters like rain in the campfire. A hot dog explodes. When the BARs bark back, the hunters fall to the ground or dive behind trees.

"I'm shot," W.D. bawls. "I can't fight no more."

"Goddammit, you got to!" Clyde answers. "Get in the car!"

He supports Bonnie, half carrying and half dragging her, while she does her best to run on one leg. When they reach the car, he hurls her onto the broken glass that now litters the front seat. Blanche, glass mingled with her hair and strewn over her back, lies on top of Buck in the back seat, trying to shield his body and his broken head. The car zooms backward and jerks to a halt.

"Let's *go*!!" Bonnie urges.

But the car won't. Clyde has backed over a stump or a rock. He looks helplessly at the rest of them.

"Let's run, then!" Bonnie begins shoving at him. Clyde's paralysis scares her even more than the guns. "C'mon! We've got to go!"

"You can't run," he says dully. "Buck can't run."

"I can too." Bonnie says.

"I can run," Buck says. "But I need my shoes. Somebody get me my shoes."

The guns stay quiet. The only signs of the hunters are bulging tree trunks and a hat that has settled on a bush.

"Maybe we can make it to the other car," Clyde says.

While Blanche pours glass from her boots before shoving her feet in, Clyde slides out of the car and instantly catches a ricochet that snaps his head sideways. He staggers, blinks, and swings his scattergun in a wide arc, emitting a flurry of bullets. With his right hand, he continues to squeeze the trigger, while with his left he tries to tug Bonnie past the steering wheel. On her other side, W.D. shoves her bad leg, which makes her yelp.

"Where are my shoes?" Buck whines. "I got to have my shoes."

"I got 'em on you, Buck!" Blanche is sobbing. "I just got to tie 'em. Hold still."

"Leave the shoes be!" Bonnie yells.

"Come *on!*" Clyde booms between sprays of bullets.

Using W.D. as a crutch, Bonnie hobbles and hops as fast as she can toward the old bullet-tattered car.

Blanche, too, is finally out. Moaning "not again, not again, not again," she squats beside the car and maneuvers Buck's arms around her neck. She helps him up and out, and he tries to run, but his feet won't obey, so he hangs down her back, like a sack of cotton, and she hauls him forward.

"You got my shoes on the wrong feet!"

"Hit the car!" a deep voice shouts, and the air crackles and sings with bullets again. The old car squirms and rocks, while pieces of metal and shards of the windshield fly in all directions. Finally, the machine sinks to its knees, as its repaired tires rip open and release their air.

Clyde's BAR is spent; he tosses it to the ground and raises a rifle in its place. Blanche, nearly doubled over with Buck on her back, stands frozen; Bonnie and W.D., closer to the shredded car, turn back.

"Get across the river," Clyde yells.

Shooting judiciously, he manages to hold back for a surprisingly long time the passel of farmers and their half-grown sons who won't risk getting killed to catch some outlaws. Even after Clyde quits shooting and plunges down the hill himself, the posse hesitates, no one wanting to be the first to break from cover and become a target. But he's obviously been hit; his gait is jerky, as if his right leg can hardly bear weight, and this emboldens them. Encouraging each other with yells and whistles, they follow tentatively, as if he is a wounded bear that might abruptly turn on them and charge. When he reaches Bonnie, Clyde wraps his arm around her waist—the rifle in his hand burns against the underside of her breasts—and she dangles between him and W.D., until they pull her into a thicket along the edge of the river.

Blanche and Buck are still halfway up the slope, where Buck is slumped against a tree trunk. Blanche flits around him, tugging and prodding in vain. "Help me!" she screams. "I can't move him!"

Bonnie feels Clyde coiled beside her, and she wraps her fingers around his wrist, knowing it will do no good, that he will tear his hand away and charge back up the hill.

"Help!" Blanche screams again, her desperation sharp and gleaming as a razor blade.

W.D. looks at Clyde, waiting for an order. If Clyde wills it, he, too, will leave their cover to rescue Buck and Blanche.

Bullets thud into the earth around them as the posse shoots randomly at the undergrowth. Buckshot crackles through the sumac branches and the pellets sizzle as they penetrate Bonnie's chest. Across her nightgown a pattern of red polka dots rises and runs together, until the fabric is soaked in blood.

"C'mon out of there! Give yourselves up! C'mon now." Unlike Blanche's piercing screams, these commands, coming from men who are uncertain and nervous, who aim first in one direction, then another, are easy to resist.

"Stay here," Clyde whispers, pulling away from Bonnie at last. But instead of catapulting himself up the hill to Buck and Blanche, he slides feet first out of the thicket, slithers down the bank on his stomach, and disappears into the river.

"There's some of 'em over here!" The guns crack again, but this time the bullets come nowhere near Bonnie and W.D. They're aimed at Buck and Blanche.

Blanche has curled herself around Buck. "Don't shoot him!" she cries. "You killed him already! Don't shoot him no more."

Bonnie feels as if her deepest insides are being yanked up through her mouth with a hook. She gags and tastes an evil liquid on her tongue.

"That's it for them, I guess," W.D. says.

"Where's your gun?"

"I don't know."

"I want your gun!" She clutches at him. "Give me your gun!"

"Shut it, Sis! What's the matter with you?" He grabs her hands. "I dropped it someplace. I been shot, remember?" He lowers his chin to study the holes in his chest.

If only Blanche would be quiet, but she won't stop screaming. "Get away from me! Don't take him! You can't have him! Don't die, Daddy! Don't die!"

If only Bonnie had held Clyde fast. Blanche at least is holding Buck, but Bonnie, crouching like a helpless groundhog behind a bunch of sumac bushes, is going to die alone. "I need a gun."

"What for? You shoot from here, they'll know where we're at. You can't shoot enough to stop them."

"I don't want to shoot them! I want to shoot myself!"

From the far side of the river, three whistled notes repeat over and over, sounding like no bird that ever lived. While the men of the posse, arrayed in a ragged circle around Buck and Blanche, laugh and slap each other, W.D. lifts Bonnie in his arms. Just before the plunging riverbank blocks her view, she sees Blanche twisting like a cat between two men who hold her wrists.

"Look at them dark glasses on that she-devil," a man shouts. "Think you're a movie star?"

◆

On the other side, Clyde, who has to squint his eyes nearly shut against the blood that flows from his forehead, has found a young man with eyes as big as hubcaps and a milk pail that jangles on its handle in his shaking hand. Clumsily, Bonnie, in her wet and bloodied satin night-gown, is tumbled over the fence and transferred from W.D.'s arms into the boy's.

As they reach the farmyard, a woman rushes from the house, followed by a girl with her hair half-braided.

"Marnie's on the horn! She says the Barrow Gang's over to the park!" the woman shouts, before the screen door slams like a gunshot, and she pulls her breath in hard, as if trying to suck her words back.

"We ain't going to hurt you," Clyde says, smearing blood across his face with his arm. "We just need to borrow your car. The laws have shot the hell out of us."

The farmers are too poor to buy gas for the two cars—a Model T and a 1929 Plymouth—in their garage, but at least the Plymouth is still on its tires. Someone siphons a can of kerosene into the tank, while the young man settles Bonnie gently on the back seat. Clyde promises they'll leave the machine somewhere along the road, good as new, but, his left arm being useless, he loses control near Polk City and rams it into a telephone pole. They drive on with the front end smashed in, the

windshield shattered and the engine complaining until they comman-
deer a flathead Ford about twenty miles north.

"Can't be helped," Clyde says as they pull away from the wreck, and
Bonnie knows he means more than the car.

◆

The picture in the *Des Moines Tribune* covered the entire page above
the fold. In a tableau of light and shadow, Blanche was the focal point.
She writhed in the clutches of a fat man in a black suit, her mouth
contorted, her curling dark hair falling over her forehead. Her eyes,
covered by dark glasses, looked like holes in her face. Buck—to whom
the caption referred as Mr. Marvin Barrow—was invisible, his position
clear from the attitudes of a cluster of men bent low over the ground.
Studying the photo, Bonnie rubbed her own wrists.

The reports followed them through Nebraska, where Clyde kept
off the roads, driving along the edges of fields in which the corn and
wheat stood higher than the roof of the car, and into Colorado. The
young man with Clyde Barrow and Bonnie Parker was identified as Jack
Sherman, a sign, Clyde insisted with admiration, that Buck was alive
and doing his best to protect W.D., whom the laws still didn't know.

"Why didn't you go back for him?" W.D. asked. When he got no
answer, he pressed on. "It's stuck in my head, her screaming like that.
Why didn't you do nothing?"

"If Daddy had run back up that hill, Boy," Bonnie said angrily, "he'd
of been shot dead, and then where would you be, I'd like to know."

"Weren't you the one squealing—'I'm shot! I can't fight no more!'?"
Clyde said. "Up to you, you would have gived up the first minute. Then
we'd all be dead. I got you out of there."

"I wish I was dead," W.D. said.

"Soon enough," Clyde said.

◆

With Buck and Blanche, they'd been a whole community unto themselves, but now they were reduced to a scant family. Exiled and aimless,
they circled eastward again and drifted north. When they camped out
in the country, they felt like the only people left on earth, so Clyde

started the trick of cutting the engine and coasting onto some driveway in town late at night, which kept the laws from getting suspicious of a car stopped overnight along the street. It was a decent trick, but parking so close to the life they'd denied themselves also made them feel bereft. They were in Minnesota, eating a watermelon they'd bought off the back of a truck, when W.D. declared his desire to go home.

Clyde spit several seeds out slowly before he spoke. "Home? We're your home, Boy."

"I want to go back to Texas," W.D. repeated in the same stubborn tone he'd used that first Christmas.

"He's scared, Bud," Bonnie said. "We ought to take him home. Let him see his mama."

"What if they catch him?"

"He can say we made him, held him against his will. They don't know how long he's been with us."

"I ain't gonna get caught," W.D. said, sounding so much like his normal self that they all felt better.

They made their way steadily south, skirting Iowa and driving through Illinois, where they restocked at another armory, and then worked their way through Missouri and Arkansas to Texas. At ease for the first time since Platte City, as the thick, soft air billowed through the car and the night throbbed with humming, chirping, wing-beating insects, Bonnie knew she'd been right to persuade Clyde to bring W.D. back, right to insist they all come home.

"We gotta stop for a Coca-Cola." She was thinking ahead to the empty bottle tossed at the door of the Star that would be their signal to meet on Chalk Hill the next day.

"Pick you up in a coupla weeks," Bonnie said, as W.D. slid out of the car at a bus stop in Marshall.

W.D. looked older in the harsh light of the streetlamp. He did, indeed, feel he'd been held against his will, if only because what had happened in Dexfield Park had finally caused a will of his own to take a shape that he could recognize and follow. However, he nodded and waved, giving no sign that they'd repelled him.

PART 4

When Clyde tried to lower Bonnie onto the blanket he'd spread on Chalk Hill, his injured arm gave out and he dropped her the last few inches. She tucked her permanently bent leg under the good one, so only her unscarred ankle showed. When she straightened her back, her collarbone stood out like a yoke.

Emma shook her head. "You ain't eating enough." She pulled her daughter's body against her own, as if she meant to meld them, and her fingers registered the hard nubs of Bonnie's vertebrae. "And quit cryin'." Unwilling to unclasp her arms, Emma wiped her own tears with her shoulder. That Bonnie seemed to have no notion of her coarsened skin, her dulled hair, and yellowed teeth hurt Emma most of all. "You gotta take better care of yourself, honey."

Cumie and Henry talked only about Buck, marveling at the number of days he'd held on in the hospital. He'd become heroic merely by staying alive under the circumstances.

"Shot six times," Henry said proudly, "not counting the one in the head, and the doc said it weren't even that what got him but the pneumonia."

"He never told a word about what you and him done or where you and Bonnie was," Cumie put in.

"They had guards there night and day. They was sure you was going to bust him out." Henry spoke a little wistfully, as if he, too, had been expecting Clyde to swoop in and carry Buck away.

"Clyde was getting ready to bring Buck to Dallas, when we got shot up," Bonnie said. "He knew you'd want him back with you."

"Oh, I know he would have done it if he could," Cumie said.

"Folks around the Bog think Clyde's another Jesse James," Henry said. "Even when he's outnumbered, he manages to shoot his way out, and he saves Bonnie here, too. It's just too bad he couldn't save Buck. Buck never weren't so lucky as Bud."

"We brung him back," Cumie said. "He's right over there at the Heights." She gestured east.

"We didn't get no headstone, though," Henry said. "Figured we'd wait and get one for the both of you boys."

"What about Blanche?" Bonnie asked. She didn't want to talk about Clyde's headstone.

"They say Blanche'll only get ten years," Emma burst out. "If you was to turn yourself in, Bonnie, I bet that's all you'd get. I'm sorry," she added, turning to Cumie and Henry, "but I've got to think of my own child."

"You know me and Henry think Bonnie oughta give herself up," Cumie said.

"She can't do much anyway, can she, Bud?" Henry pointed out. "She can't even drive with that bum leg."

"Bonnie don't have to do nothing," Clyde said.

"I just meant if she turned herself in, it wouldn't make it any worse for you to . . . well, do what you do."

CHAPTER 63

Bonnie hadn't had a typewriter since Joplin, but Clyde regularly gave her pads of paper. Sitting on a lump of blankets in an abandoned farmhouse somewhere outside Dallas, she tried to make a poem about Dexfield Park, but when her memories of the morning butted up against her words, the lines seemed weightless and ineffectual.

> *The night before the posse came, the dark could not lie still;*
> *The leaves sighed; the owls cried, "There's lawmen on the hill."*
> *But those who hid there waiting for the cracking of the dawn,*
> *Heard not the words of those wise birds, and they slept on.*

The trouble was the literal cracking that had accompanied the dawn. She couldn't adequately convey the explosions of the guns, the sharp whistles of the bullets, the screaming, the experience of hurling themselves from crippled car to crippled car, let alone the desperation and loss.

She crushed her aborted attempts and pushed them beneath the blankets with the black socks and the severed arm, the burning metal against her flesh, the chunk of Buck's head breaking away, Blanche's screams.

"How do you know," she asked Clyde that night, "that the laws aren't out there now?"

"I know because there ain't no guns shooting at us. When they find us, they'll let us know."

But he went to the window, through which they could see only darkness, and pressed his forehead to the glass.

Clyde fancied himself a wolf, able to lead a pack, but Bonnie saw that he was more like a coyote, snatching at scraps. Or like a rabbit, poised to run even as it nibbled its blade of grass.

They were clinging as close to their families as they dared, circling Dallas and staying in a different abandoned farmhouse each night. During the day, Clyde hung around West Dallas, playing with L.C.'s motorcycle and signing copies of *True Crime* on the page where a version of their shootout in Joplin appeared. Bonnie, however, couldn't share in this idyll. She was more freak than celebrity among the women of West Dallas, who tolerated their scofflaw men but did not admire her. Besides, she was a sitting duck, unable to slide out the back door if a law knocked at the front. So Clyde left her wherever they'd passed the night, and she had nothing to do but lie on the floor and stare at the ceiling, observing how the yellow-brown water stains might have been a map of the dirty paths they'd taken around the fields and along the farm roads of all those states.

Twined with her in the dark, he whispered, "Mrs. Howard, I oughta take you to the laws myself and get you out of this mess. In ten years you'd be free. It ain't fair what I done to you."

She loved that he loved her too much to do right by her.

◆

Fearing they would come for her when she was waiting in the house alone, Bonnie kept a whipit beside her. She practiced holding it in her mouth, opening her jaws as wide as she could to keep it from knocking against her teeth and gagging at the bitter taste of the metal. Even more frightening was the likelihood that Clyde would be shot dead while he was away. No one would know where to find her.

◆

When Clyde promised a surprise to cheer her up, Bonnie expected a jar of pickled pigs' feet, but he delivered a pair of crutches and her mother, who'd brought Buddy, now four years old, and Mitzy, nearly two, and from then on, he fetched the children for her every day he went to Dallas.

Buddy, the little show-off, was always first out of the car, summoning her to see a bruised shin or a "letter" he'd scribbled with brown crayon on an old page of newspaper. If there was a front porch on the house in which Bonnie was staying, he climbed around it on the outside of the railing, securing himself with a hooked elbow. He hid behind internal doors and leapt out with a shriek when Bonnie swung by. Obligingly, she screamed and chased him, ignoring her sore shoulders and learning to maneuver around corners.

Mitzy, on the other hand, was quiet and deliberate. She studied the leaves Bonnie arranged for her in patterns on the floor, touching the colors with a careful finger. While Buddy snapped the stems of five dandelions in quick succession and scattered the seeds with an exuberant blast of air and saliva, Mitzy cupped the fluff of one flower tentatively with her palm. Like a kitten, she snuggled on Bonnie's lap, and let herself be rocked to sleep.

Bonnie ordered Clyde to buy them gifts; a wagon for Buddy, like the one Buster had had in Rowena; a baby doll for Mitzy, with a lifelike molded head and hands and a plump, cloth body zipped into a pink bunting.

One day in October, Clyde brought only Buddy and was in a sour mood. Billie hadn't been waiting at the place they'd arranged. Clyde had ridden past half a dozen times before, finally, furious at the risk, he'd scrawled "red beens" on a scrap of paper, stuffed it in a Coca-Cola bottle, and thrown it hard against the Parkers' front door to summon her.

"The kid's got a tummyache, so I've got to risk running into some trap?"

"If she's sick, I want to help." Bonnie was elated at the thought. "Take me home."

They argued, and she cried. She hit him with her crutch, and he knocked her down. Finally, comforting Buddy who'd been frightened by the scuffle, she admitted that the sheriff probably had someone watching the house. After all, her mother had told her plenty of times about Ted Hinton sniffing around.

"Them laws'll do anything," Clyde said. "I wouldn't put it past that sheriff to feed them kids a few green apples his own self, just to see if he could lure us in."

◆

The next morning, when neither child was brought to meet him, Clyde went straight to West Dallas and spent the day with L.C. He didn't feel like listening to Bonnie's demands, as unrelenting and infuriating as the whir of an engine that wouldn't turn over, or watching her tears that fell as copiously as rain. She could get along by herself for once.

It was dark when he finally drove up to the house where he'd left her. The door stuck when he tried to open it, and when he shoved it with his shoulder, some of the guns she'd heaped against it crashed and clanked against the wooden floor. She answered him finally from the dark of the farthest back bedroom, where she was hiding behind a bunker of full grocery bags.

She rose with the whipit in her hand, hopped one step toward him, and then tipped like a tree chopped in two, until her arms fastened around his neck. "I thought you'd been shot dead. I thought I'd never see you again!" She was crying—of course, she was crying, soaking his collar.

He removed the gun, which was uncomfortably cold and hard against his ear, from her hand. "Don't hold this thing so close. I wasted the whole day, trying to get them babies for you."

"Oh, Daddy, I've been so scared." She pushed her cheek, wet and sticky with tears, against his neck. "It got dark, and you didn't come, and I knew something awful had happened."

"Well, nothing happened." He unwrapped her arms. "Quit hanging on me, will ya? You're like a goddamn shackle around my neck."

When he released her wrists, she teetered, unbalanced and awkward. Then she reached for him again, but this time, she pushed her hand under his coat and closed her fingers around the stock of his scattergun. She yanked at it, but, attached by its rubber band, it remained close to his body. She had to bend herself to press the barrel to her forehead. "I wish I was dead."

He jerked back so violently that he stumbled and fell. Much later, when they were tender with one another again, they considered themselves lucky that the gun hadn't reacted to such rough treatment and killed them both.

"You kept me alive," he said, when they'd calmed down enough to pack the car and move on to a different house. "I would've given up back there in Iowa. I would have stood by Buck until I was shot full of holes. But I ain't gonna get myself killed, as long as I can save you."

The story sounded truthful enough to satisfy her. Their existence might be chaotic and dirty and sickeningly violent, but if they lived and died for that existence together it seemed, if not virtuous, at least significant and exceptional. She could still tell herself it was a love story.

CHAPTER 64

November 1933

Mitzy and Buddy were dead, killed by an egg custard tainted with salmonella. Bonnie had dyed her hair black and demanded to be taken to the funeral, until Clyde pointed out that her presence was likely to turn the sacred day of mourning into a shootout. For the last two weeks, she'd drunk as much as Clyde could deliver, and now, as she prepared for a secret birthday party for Cumie Barrow, her fingers shook, so that her Maybelline spattered in a sooty explosion around her eye.

Bonnie squinted critically at her nose and scraped with her nail at a stubborn, ugly little growth. When it had first appeared some months ago, she'd assumed it was only a pimple, but now it seemed to be permanent.

"Get a wiggle on," Clyde said. "It's already dark. I don't want to keep my mama waiting."

"What about my mama? It's all right if she waits?"

"None of 'em should wait," Clyde said patiently, picking her up and carrying her to the car.

The Barrows' Model T was parked on the shoulder at the designated stretch of road about three miles outside of Sowers. Clyde drove by without slowing to make sure it wasn't a trap.

"Some boy up front driving your mother," Bonnie observed.

"That'll be Marie's latest sheik."

Bonnie went directly for Billie, hung her arms around her sister's neck, and keened. "My poor babies!"

Billie stood stiffly and kept her face turned away. "Stop it."

They ate forkfuls of birthday cake out of the trunk and sang to

Cumie, their voices frail against the wind, and then they stood around in the dark, shivering.

Joe Bill Francis, Marie's beau, regarded Clyde skeptically. "Are you packing a heater?"

When Clyde obligingly opened his coat, the boy blinked.

Then Cumie and Emma began to tell how they'd put Sherriff Smoot Schmid, who'd tapped their phones, off the scent.

"I said, 'The Howards sure are hungry for some of them red beans, Emma,'" Cumie began.

"And then I said, 'Are they? I guess I better boil up a pot, then,'" Emma said.

Two yellow headlights, like eyes, appeared in the distance.

"Get behind the car," Clyde snapped.

The car already stood between them and the road, but the women obediently herded together and hunched themselves. Joe Bill, however, seemed inclined to step forward, until Clyde shoved him back.

The car slowed; the driver lowered the window and stopped. "Need a lift?"

This was generally Bonnie's cue to say something pretty, like, "No, thanks, mister. We're just meeting some friends."

But Clyde opened his coat again. "We don't need nothin'. Hook 'em."

Even Emma and Cumie laughed when the car spit stones in frantic acceleration.

"Ain't you got no present for your mama?" Joe Bill said.

"Oh, I don't need no present from Bud," Cumie protested. "Just to spend the time's all I want. Whatever time I can git." Her voice became tearful, and she put her arms around her son.

"I do have a present for you," Clyde said. "We just forgot to bring it."

"Well, never mind. It'll keep."

"Mama, you come back here tomorrow, and we'll do this party over."

"All right," she said. "We'll come back. But if it's just you and no present, I'll be just as happy."

"We'll be here at six o'clock," Joe Bill said, as he got behind the wheel. "I'll make sure of it."

"Who's he to be making sure of it?" Clyde said, when he and Bonnie were back in their car.

"Marie says they're getting married."

They rode in silence for a few minutes, before Bonnie said, "We shouldn't go there tomorrow."

"What are you talking about?"

"Never the same place twice. It's your rule."

"I gotta give my mama a present."

"You don't have a present."

"I'll get one. I said I'd get one and I will."

"If it's something you steal, she won't like it."

He slammed his hand against the wheel. "Well, what do you want me to do? You know we ain't got no money!"

"I want you to quit showing off. You shountna shown your gun back there, and you should not go up there tomorrow."

"Well, I'm going," he said, childishly. "And I'm getting her a present."

◆

Clyde got one of the boys for whom he'd signed a magazine to steal a pair of gloves from a shop in Dallas.

Trying the soft, cocoa-colored leather over her own fingers, Bonnie said, "You better tell her we had enough pennies."

"I'll tell her I didn't steal 'em. That's the truth."

At about 6:45 p.m., when their headlights illuminated a Model T, parked on the same stretch of road just beyond Sowers, Clyde slowed slightly but drove on, as he had the previous night. Ahead of them, a deep voice called out, "Halt!" or possibly, "Look out!" Three flames leapt toward them from the ditch and silhouettes rose behind brilliant orange daggers of exploding gunpowder. At once, the windshield and all four windows shattered, and a feathery, ghostlike thing brushed against Bonnie's ears and settled on her forehead. She screamed and waved her arms, batting back what turned out to be the material that lined the roof of the car. A tire blew out, and the car tilted and swerved, throwing Bonnie against the door.

Traveling at eighty-five miles an hour, they soon overtook another car and then stopped short in front of it, forcing it to veer off the road. Stunned, the two men inside only stared when Clyde came toward them, waving his scattergun.

"I said get out of there!"

He squeezed the trigger with the gun pressed against the driver's window and the blast peeled the metal roof off like a candy wrapper. The men scrambled out the far side, shouting and coughing.

"C'mon, Mrs. Howard. These fellows are letting us borrow their car."

From the passenger seat, Bonnie held the scattergun on the two men, while Clyde transferred armloads of guns from one car to the other. He laid two rifles and a BAR at Bonnie's feet, a sawed-off shotgun on the seat beside her, and the whipit in her lap.

Unfazed by the intricacies of starting an old 4-banger, Clyde turned the key, threw the spark, and started the gas. But the motor wouldn't catch.

"What the hell?" He tried again. "How do you start this damn machine?"

The driver shrugged.

"Want me to shoot him?" Bonnie asked. Watching the man scurry to the car and frantically jiggle the spark, she felt better than she had in weeks.

They zigzagged north toward Oklahoma on farm roads, railing against Smoot Schmid and Joe Bill, while freezing rain poured through the ripped-open roof onto their heads. They were so keyed up with adrenaline and outrage that they didn't realize that both of them had been shot through the knees, until Clyde's legs buckled as he tried to get out of the car to open a gate.

"Goddammit! What's the matter with me?" He struggled to lift himself off the wet, freezing ground and back into the car.

Leaning to help him in, Bonnie saw that the water around her feet was brilliant red.

In less than an hour, Bonnie, listless from blood loss and cold, let her head fall back against the seat. This death would float her through the open roof into the star-encrusted sky.

"Pretty Boy's people live in these hills," Clyde said. "Someone who used to run with him told me right where."

"You think they'll help us?"

"They'll be glad to. We'd sure help him, wouldn't we?"

In the dawn light, the iced tree branches shone as if they'd been dipped in butter. The mailbox marked "Floyd" appeared where Clyde had been told it would be, and Clyde managed to pull himself to his feet on the porch and stand, propped against the wall, before he knocked. The woman who answered admitted that she was indeed Floyd's sister-in-law. "She was just as sweet as pie," Bonnie would report back in Dallas in December, but, in fact, her mouth was set in a line as hard as the frozen branches. She shoved a dirty towel at Clyde and told him to try a certain doctor—"yonder in the hills"—who would keep his mouth shut.

The doctor, with a wide jaw and bulging eyes, resembled a toad. He laughed, emitting a blast of boozy breath, when Clyde asked after Pretty Boy. "Little fellas like you come sniffing around every other Thursday, thinking they're the Texas Floyd or the Tennessee Floyd. I'll give you some advice, though," the doctor added, as he helped them get back into their ruined car. "If you ever meet Floyd, don't call him Pretty Boy. He's liable to shoot you for it."

On Christmas they drove in a wide circle around Dallas. From time to time, the city lights appeared in the distance out of the early darkness like a mirage. Around five o'clock they found an empty house north of Fort Worth, where they roasted wieners over burning floorboards and drank.

A few days later, however, Clyde managed a good score at a grocery, so on December 29, they met their mothers again on the road to Wichita Falls to deliver baskets of fruit and nuts and candy.

Emma hardly glanced at her gift. Sitting beside Bonnie on the car seat, she smoothed her daughter's hair. Returned to its natural shade of ash blond, it softened Bonnie's face and made her look younger.

"I just hated Christmas this year," Emma said.

"I know," Bonnie said. "I cried about Mitzy and Buddy all day, too."

"All I did was worry about you, wondering where you were and what was happening to you." Emma paused. "What *will* happen to you?"

The orange flashes and the explosions that had erupted around them in Sowers had just been a big show, Bonnie thought, like a thunderstorm; she hadn't felt a thing when those bullets had gone into her legs. Her mother's rough palm fluttered around her face, like the fabric shredded and dangling from the roof of the car. Impatiently, Bonnie brushed it away.

"Oh, you shouldn't worry about us," she said. "We had a lovely Christmas. We had turkey dinners in Niles, and we bought a big bunch of fireworks—Roman candles, skyrockets, cherry salutes, lady crackers, every kind—and then we went out in the country and fired them all off."

CHAPTER 65

January 1934

That hophead Jimmy Mullen, released from Eastham, came home to Dallas with a message from Raymond Hamilton for his brother Floyd, who got in touch with L.C., who arranged a meeting with Clyde. They were finally going to spring prisoners from the Bloody 'Ham.

"Ray says they been cuttin' brush way out, where it's easy to get the drop on the guards." Floyd motioned with his arm to emphasize the distance.

He was earnest and excited, still the nice boy he'd been in the third grade, Bonnie thought, not sneaky and mean like Raymond.

"You stash a couple of gats under the bridge," Floyd was saying. "And then you park just beyond, at the edge of the fields. Raymond says you know the bridge. It'll be easy, Ray says."

"Ray says so, does he?" Clyde was talking to Floyd, but he was watching Jimmy Mullen, whose eyes flitted from one man to the other. "Listen, I ain't got no tommy guns, Floyd. And if I did, like shit I'd be stashing them for convicts."

"Well, whatever you got. Raymond says you're bound to have plenty."

"It ain't Raymond I doubt, but this one." He poked Mullen's shoulder. "I ain't doing it, unless he's the one goes in there and hides the weapons."

Mullen quivered like Jell-O. "I done enough. I ain't never goin' back there."

"I know better than to trust a stoolie that won't stick his neck out," Clyde said. "Floyd'll tell Raymond it's off, cuz you won't do it. Ray'll understand."

"Well, I'm not sayin' I won't do it. There's no need to be tellin' Raymond that I'm the cause of nothing. Tell you what—if Floyd here'll go along with me, I'll do it all right. But I won't go if he won't go."

"Jesus Christ," Clyde said when he and Bonnie were alone in the car, "they're like a bunch of kindergartners! And it's my goddamn plan that I fixed up with Ralph Fults, before we ran out of luck in Kaufman. The plan Raymond wouldn't be no part of, because back then he didn't care about no cons and no prison. He cares plenty now, don't he?"

She and Ralph had run out of luck in Kaufman, Bonnie thought, not Clyde. "I don't like your taking orders from Raymond."

"Raymond promised Mullen a thousand dollars to get this thing going. That hophead's got to do more for a grand than beat his gums at me."

"I don't think you ought to do it. Not for Raymond Hamilton."

"Raymond's serving for the Bucher murder."

"That's got nothing to do with you. You didn't do it."

"Still, they might have tried to pin it on me, if they hadn't had him."

"Even without the Bucher murder, he'd be in there for life. Didn't you say he got more than two hundred years for the other murders he done?"

"He's lucky he didn't get the chair."

"So, you're not doing it."

"Ain't no one deserves what they give you in there. And Raymond and me go back. We'd get Ralph, too."

She remembered how Ralph had done his best to save her before it was too late, advising her to claim she'd been kidnapped and promising to take the theft of the guns in Kaufman all on himself.

"And Aubrey," Clyde added. "I aimed to get Aubrey out back then, and I will get him now."

◆

They drive south on Sunday evening, with Floyd and Jimmy in the back seat. Jimmy has already found a fix and falls asleep before they get out of Dallas.

"Don't see how he deserves a thousand bucks for this," Floyd says. He's sitting forward on the seat, his chin practically in the front, and he turns the blown-out inner tube, into which they've stuffed two Colt .45s and some ammunition, round and round in his hands. The floppy ring of rubber is just the sort of detritus that might end up stuck under a bridge. No guard would pay it any mind, even if he spotted it.

"That's Raymond's business," Clyde says. "I expect he knew how much it would cost to get a guy that's just been sprung back within fifty miles of this place. Leave that tube alone. You want to blow your dick off?"

By the time they finally near the prison it has been dark for hours. Their headlights illuminate only brown stubble along the side of the road and an occasional dark trunk supporting a tangle of stiff, crooked limbs. Clyde sits tensely forward, gripping the wheel with both hands. "Raymond's got a big mouth. I wonder how many he's squeaked to about this."

"It's your plan," Bonnie reminds him. "But we don't have to do it."

"Makes me mad how Raymond wouldn't do this when I wanted him to, and now he's the one begging for it." He's quiet for a moment, his eyes staring steadily into the blackness ahead. "Buck shoulda come down here with me when I asked him to. If we done this, instead of going to Joplin, who knows what mighta happened?"

A year ago, that way of thinking might have snared her. If they hadn't done this or that; if they'd turned right instead of left; if they'd left an hour earlier. Now she understands that those details wouldn't change anything essential.

When Clyde stops the car, Floyd and Jimmy play for time, tying shoes and rechecking the weapon-filled inner tube.

"C'mon," Clyde says impatiently. "This is the easy part."

"I don't see no bridge." Floyd squints into the darkness beyond the barbed wire.

"You will. About fifty yards on. Careful you don't slip into the gully. I ain't comin' to retrieve you."

In about ten minutes, dogs begin to bark and bay in the distance. Clyde starts the engine and lets his foot play lightly over the accelerator. But the barking remains unfocused and gets no nearer, and, finally, the two stumble back out of the darkness, swearing continuously but quietly.

◆

Bonnie, Clyde, and the now jittery Mullen spend the following day in the car, while Floyd pays a visit to his brother to let him know the guns are in place. To pacify Mrs. Hamilton, who begged Floyd to keep away from the break—"What's the use," she said, "of getting one out, if I just turn around and get another one in?"—they've agreed that Floyd's job is now done. At night, Clyde and Bonnie take turns watching Mullen. When it's her turn to rest, Bonnie is lulled by the cadence of Clyde's prayers, which, for once, are not pleas and confessions but requests shot through with confidence and purpose. This time, he believes, God will be on his side.

◆

At six a.m., they park the black V-8 just beyond the bridge in a heavy fog. The bare trees hover vaguely, a denser gray in the thick, wet grayness. Clyde and Mullen, each with a BAR tucked close to his body, thread their way through the barbed wire and disappear.

Within the hour, the damp air carries the sounds of tramping feet and coughing, hawking, spitting, and grunting—the work crews approaching. From the car, Bonnie can distinguish the peremptory tones of the guards. A horse whinnies restlessly.

The shooting begins at seven o'clock. Behind the soft screen of the fog, the BARs erupt with their clacking, rapid fire and the Colts *bang-bang-bang*. Bonnie answers with the horn. *Here. Here. Here. Here.*

Clyde and Mullen appear first, then Raymond, then three others.

"Only Raymond and Joe," Mullen insists in his thin, nasal voice. "The rest of you, get out of here. This ain't your business."

Clyde frowns. "Everyone in," he snaps.

"Why'd you bring this machine? It's too small." Eastham hasn't changed Raymond.

"Where's Ralph?" Bonnie asks, sliding over to let Clyde get behind the wheel, and Mullen and another fellow cram in on her other side. The other three crowd into the rumble seat. They are full to overflowing, like a clown car at a circus.

"Where's Aubrey?" Clyde asks.

"Where's Ralph Fults?" Bonnie says again.

Raymond shrugs. Clyde looks back into the fog, but the dogs are baying purposefully now, and the sound is getting nearer. Bonnie's afraid until the car starts rolling; then she knows they're safe. When the sirens begin behind them, Clyde plunges into a field, and they piece together their own road, as they always do, out of tracks intended for tractors and sometimes directly over the winter-brown grass.

Clyde is angry about leaving Ralph. Raymond makes some excuse about the impossibility of Ralph's jumping his squad without raising suspicion, but Bonnie believes he's responsible, not wanting a man along who might displace him as Clyde's closest partner. Clyde's more circumspect about Aubrey Scalley, who, as a building tender, traveled the camp unsupervised, collected the guns from under the bridge, and delivered them to Raymond and Joe Palmer the previous evening.

"Aubrey's good at being in," Clyde says. "I guess he wouldn't hardly know what to do with himself out here."

They're lucky with cars and are able to change twice, although the tank in the second one is nearly empty. The attendant at the filling station can hardly contain himself. "Didja hear the news? There's been a big escape over at Eastham. Ten cons, I hear, or maybe a dozen, and Bonnie and Clyde's the ones that sprung 'em. Walked right in when they was having their breakfasts and let the bullets fly!"

Joe Palmer starts to cough. He's been coughing on and off all morning, spitting bright red spots on a handkerchief already rusty with blood.

"That's a bad cough, mister," the attendant says.

"We're going to get him some hot tea with honey," Bonnie says. "First chance we get."

CHAPTER 66

They shed Mullen in Corsicana with the promise that he'd have his thousand dollars within the month and exchanged the little coupe for a sedan. Free of Mullen, with three in front and three in back, they were no longer clowns but a gang of bank robbers, four of whom—Raymond Hamilton, Joe Palmer, Hilton Bybee, and young Henry Methvin—have been convicted of murder.

In Rembrandt, Iowa, while Bonnie waited in a fresh car at a crossroads outside of town, the gang staged its first job. With Clyde as driver and Henry Methvin as lookout, Raymond Hamilton and Hilton Bybee walked out of the First National Bank with a plaid suitcase full of money, as easily as if they'd had an appointment to take it. Joe Palmer was supposed to have gone inside, too, but his stomach ulcers had flared so badly, he'd been forced to stay curled on the floor in the back of the car, moaning and gasping.

"Thirty-eight hundred dollars!" Raymond gloated, counting the money, as they careened toward the Minnesota border. "What's that divided by four?"

A siren wailed weakly behind them, too distant to be taken seriously.

"Divided by six, you mean," Clyde said.

"How do you figure?"

"We're a gang," Clyde explained. "Whatever any of us gets, we divide equally."

"You a commie?"

Clyde gave the car more gas, as he steered it smoothly around a curve. "The way I see it," he said patiently, "a gang's like a family."

"And you're the daddy!" Bybee hooted.

"If you want to be in the Barrow Gang, that's how it works," Clyde said. "You'll thank me when you're the one sick or shot."

"What about Bonnie? What's she done?"

"You can't just park a car and expect it to be there when you want it," Bonnie said. "You need someone to sit with it and make sure no riffraff drives it off."

"Fine," Raymond said. "I'm sick of arguing. But we keep on like this, me and Hilton may form our own gang. You shoulda seen us in there. I said, 'Give us the money,' and this teller, he looks like he's about to shit his pants. He starts pullin' the bills out of the drawer one by one, and Hilton here, he just slides his hand in and clomps onto a big stack. 'When we say 'money,' he says, smooth as ice, 'we mean *all* the money.' And then that teller starts shoveling it like it's horseshit. He can't get it out of the fucking drawer fast enough."

Raymond re-counted the bills, lips and fingers moving steadily, and then, with an exaggerated sigh, divided them into six piles. Bonnie watched to be sure his count was accurate and his division fair.

As overbearing as he'd been that first morning back in Wichita Falls, Raymond seemed to need to ruffle those around him the way normal people needed to scratch an itch. On the way north, while the rest kept to themselves, mindful of the crowdedness of the car, he'd draped his arms over the back of Bonnie's seat and even unzipped her makeup case. She'd sworn and grabbed it from him and then wished she'd been cool, because he'd reacted only with his sneering smile.

"Sorry," he'd mocked.

Success, which soothed and reassured Clyde, only made Raymond more restless.

"Git your feet off me," Joe Palmer complained from the floor in back.

"Git off the floor, then," Raymond said. "Where am I supposed to put my feet?"

"You know I can't sit up. I got the ulcers."

"You got the ulcers. You got the TB. You got the azma. What ain't you got?"

"I ain't got a big mouth."

Raymond quit talking but began to play with his pistol, swinging the chamber out and flicking it with his finger so that it spun.

"That ain't good for the gun," Clyde said.

Raymond continued to spin the chamber, so a steady *click-click-click* ran under his words. "You're a decent driver—and we need a good driver—but I'm the one that's good at robbing banks. I'd like to see you try acting as slick as me and Hilton here, Clyde. We got authority. There's no call for shooting and screaming and having to face down the law. We don't plan for no week and then open a safe to get us thirty dollars. We just ask for the money, and they hand it over. You see, that's the way it's supposed to work. Why the fuck aren't I in charge of this gang, seeing as how the point isn't to drive all over Kingdom Come but to get us a piece of money?"

"Punk blabbermouth braggart," Palmer muttered. He pulled the blanket over his head.

Raymond smacked the chamber into place, straightened his arm, and pointed the pistol at Palmer's covered head. With one motion, Clyde swung away from the wheel and slapped Raymond across the face, and the car, going eighty miles an hour, flew off the road into the ditch and broke its axle.

CHAPTER 67

To Clyde's disappointment, the gang deteriorated quickly, as Bybee lit off as soon as they got back to Texas, and Palmer, after they'd driven him to San Antonio to visit his sister and then to Houston to murder an Eastham trusty he'd hated, asked to be dropped in Joplin because he decided all the driving around was making him sicker. That left Raymond and Henry, who Bonnie referred to as "the kid," because in his diffidence he reminded her of W.D. Self-conscious about his acne scars, he had a habit of covering his face with his fingers when he spoke, which gave the impression that he was half apologizing for his words. He had a dagger tattooed on his right forearm together with the word LOVE.

"Crib notes?" Bonnie teased.

Henry blushed. "What?"

She touched his arm. "Is that so you know what to do with it?"

"What to do with what?" His fingers rose to screen his chin and mouth.

"She means your prick," Clyde said. "She thinks she's funny." But he smiled.

Henry's story was that the guy who'd picked him up a year before on Highway 310, a little ways out of Henrietta, had pulled something he damn well shouldn't have. "Sure I tried to kill him. What was I supposed to do?"

The laws hadn't bought it because he'd kept the man's car. But, he argued to Bonnie, Clyde, and Raymond, he needed that car. After what had happened, did the laws expect him to risk asking some other pervert for a ride?

Raymond announced he would stick with the gang only if they robbed more banks and if his new baby from Amarillo could ride along.

He seemed almost like a girl when he talked about Mary O'Dare, bringing up every little thing Mary thought and said and liked and hated, and Bonnie had hopes that Mary would be a companion like Blanche had been until Raymond brought her to a family meeting on Chalk Hill.

Mary, who'd smeared her too-red lipstick beyond the limits of her lips in a crude attempt to fill out her narrow mouth and neglected to apply her thick coat of Pan-Cake beyond her chin, so that the makeup resembled the dirty border the tide left along the beach, was interested only in the men. She leaned into Clyde, brushing him with her breasts and drawing a finger along his thighbone. Bonnie was gratified when he got up and walked away, as if Mary were a cold draft.

L.C. had brought a newspaper article about a robbery in which the getaway car had been driven by a woman. She'd had a cigar stuck in her mouth, so, of course, the paper assumed that Bonnie and Clyde had committed the crime.

"You get credit for someone else's job," Bonnie complained to Clyde, "while I get slandered as a 'cigar-smoking gun-moll.'"

"C'mon, baby. You looked cute smoking that cigar."

"I was not smoking it! I was playacting. I don't want people thinking that's really me, all coarse and stinky, like a man."

"Nobody thinks you're a man, Blue."

"They don't think I'm really holding a gun on you. Why do they think I really smoke cigars?"

"You have held a gun on me."

"Well, I've never smoked a cigar, and you know it."

◆

Mary O'Dare, Bonnie thought, was the kind of woman who would smoke cigars, and even she preferred cigarettes.

"Lucky you got Raymond with y'all now," Mary said, snapping shut the compact with which she'd been examining her stained teeth.

The two women were sitting in a V-8 at the entrance to a farm road outside Dallas, waiting for Henry Methvin to deliver Clyde and Raymond along with whatever they'd managed to pry out of the R. P. Henry & Sons Bank.

"What're you talking about?"

"Well, Ray ain't afraid to heist a bank. You'll get you a real piece of money now."

"Clyde's robbed plenty of banks and got plenty of money."

Mary shrugged. "That's not what Raymond says. He says they quit running around together because all your man wanted to do was nickel-and-dime stuff. Ray says if you don't go for the big score, there's no point to it."

"The point might be to stay out of the Bloody 'Ham, which is where bank robberies got Raymond, if you recall. You seem to forget that the man you're calling scared had to prize Ray out of there."

"Raymond organized that."

"All Raymond did was remember that Clyde had a plan. Ray never came up with a thing like that himself."

Mary continued with her self-important ways when the boys drove up to exchange the getaway car for the Ford. She got in back with Raymond and lay down on the seat. When Henry tried to get in beside her, she shoved him with her foot. "You sit up front. I want to sleep."

"It's all right, Henry," Bonnie said, patting the seat beside her. "You c'mon up here."

"For shit's sake, hurry up," Clyde said, gunning the engine. "This ain't no picnic." But Bonnie could tell he was relaxed; he slipped his shoes off before they'd gone five miles and settled in to enjoy the drive across the panhandle to Oklahoma. "All we had to do was fucking ask for it," he marveled, shaking his head.

"It wasn't that simple," Raymond hooted. "When we told everyone to get down on the floor, this old fogey kept holding his money out to the teller." Ray was counting the take, and he held up a trembling handful to mock the old man's palsy. "Clyde kept saying—'Like this! Like this!' He got right down on the ground to show him! You shoulda seen it!"

Clyde grinned. "He's lucky that floor didn't mess up my new suit."

"And then Clyde decides to play Robbinghood and gives twenty-seven dollars to some grubby little loser," Raymond went on.

"What did you go and do that for?" Mary demanded.

"He worked for that money," Clyde said. "I guess you wouldn't know what that's like."

"This is a helluva lot better than work!" Henry put in.

"The pipsqueak had just cashed his paycheck, and his money was on the counter, so we scooped it in with the rest," Raymond said. "And then Clyde here has to say, 'How much was it?' And the little sniveler says, 'How much was what?'"

"He thought I was asking him for a count on the whole haul," Clyde explained.

"All I can say is this town's got the slowest bunch I ever met," Raymond said. "Finally, the penny drops and he says, 'Oh, twenty-six dollars and sixty-three cents,' and ol' Robbinghood here says, 'We don't want your money, just the bank's,' and counts out twenty-seven dollars, like he's got all the money and time in the world. You know, now that I think about it, I bet that fellow didn't have no twenty-six dollars and sixty-three cents in the first place. He weren't confused at all. I betcha he swindled us." Raymond spit out the window to underscore his disgust.

"You know what your trouble is, Raymond Hamilton?" Bonnie said.

"Yeah. You won't shut up and let me count."

"You think everyone's like you, always on the take, but your average person isn't a bit like that. Your average person just wants what he's entitled to, fair and square."

Raymond didn't answer. They could hear the whisper of his count and the rustle of the bills, as he separated and stacked them. It went on a long time, long enough for them all to become aware that they'd done even better than they'd anticipated.

"Maybe you're right that I'm not like your average person who wants only what I'm entitled to," Raymond said finally. "Because I can't say I'm entitled to . . ." He paused dramatically. "Four thousand one hundred and seventy-six dollars. Dammit, I wish we had that twenty-seven, make it an even forty-two hundred."

◆

In a little while, Bonnie heard the money rustling again. She turned to look into the back seat. "What're you doing?"

"Dividing it up."

"We ain't out of the state yet," Clyde said. "You oughta be watching for the law, not playing with the money."

"What's forty-two hundred divided by three?"

"I told you the last time, we ain't dividing by three," Clyde said. "It's me, you, Henry, and Bonnie who're getting this money."

"That's right." Raymond's tone was almost gleeful. "Your girl gets a share. So Mary gets a share, too."

The car swerved crazily, and Clyde had to work to bring it back under control.

"You want to split yours with her," Bonnie said, "you go ahead. She doesn't get her own."

"That's bullshit. How come you get a share and she don't?"

"I'm in the Barrow Gang," Bonnie said. "She's just your girl. We let her ride with us as a favor to you, but she's not one of us."

"Why do you get to make the rules?"

"She don't," Clyde said. "I do."

Bonnie was thrown hard against the dash and slipped onto the floor at Henry's feet as Clyde suddenly braked and swung off the road.

"Gimme that," he was yelling. "You think I can't see what you're doing?"

Through the rearview mirror, he'd seen Raymond stuffing a fistful of bills into Mary's waistband. Clyde dragged Raymond from the car, ostensibly to search for other hidden money, but it was obvious that what he really wanted was a fight. Bonnie, although she had to lean against the car to keep herself upright, longed for a fight, too.

The idea that Raymond's relationship with Mary could be compared to Clyde's with Bonnie gave Bonnie the bitter, poison taste a toad leaves in the palm that has held it too long. She wanted to spit. But it was Clyde she truly wanted to pummel, for his dismissive words.

Raymond let Clyde poke at him. He stood still and laughed, raising his arms to give Clyde access to his body. When Clyde found a wad of folded bills under Raymond's belt, he was incredulous. "You took it? You took the fucking money?"

Raymond shrugged. His lip curled in a smile of disdain that seemed to be meant for himself as much as for Clyde. "That's what we do, ain't it? Take money?"

"Not from each other. Don't you got no sense of what it means to be in a gang? We got to be able to trust each other."

Raymond narrowed his eyes. "You mean like I trusted you to say I weren't nowhere near that Bucher house?"

"I woulda," Clyde said. "Bonnie can tell you. If you woulda gone to the death house, I woulda."

"You went to Eastham for plenty more than Bucher," Bonnie said. "And Clyde got you out."

"Finally," Raymond pouted, like a neglected lover. "I had to send Mullen. Have to pay that hophead a thousand dollars."

"He woulda done it for a hundred." It was Clyde's turn to be scornful.

"Let's have Henry divide it," Bonnie suggested." He'll be fair."

Clyde looked at Henry. "Can we trust you, kid?"

"Sure," Henry said. "I can count."

◆

By the time they stopped to camp near the Kansas border, they had reviewed the robbery and the remarkable total several times, which restored them all to good spirits, except for Mary who complained that people with over four thousand dollars shouldn't have to eat franks and beans and sleep on the ground.

"You sleep like a king in a hotel, spending money so everyone can see it, you're going to get caught," Clyde said.

"If we can't eat nice in a restaurant and go dancing," she argued, "what's the point?"

"It's hard to dine and dance," Bonnie said, "with your head blown off."

It sickened her to hear Mary, who hadn't a thought in her head for anything but steak and whiskey and some fun with her daddy, say with scorn what Bonnie herself had often thought with despair. Obviously, they couldn't eat in a restaurant or go dancing—they hardly even dared to stay in tourist courts anymore—because they were big news again. The raid on Eastham had warranted huge headlines and articles, including photos of Clyde, on the front page and above the fold. By now the whole country must know that Clyde had a limp and Bonnie smoked cigars, and the more prominent the gun moll with the cigar clamped between her teeth became, the farther the real Bonnie had to withdraw. Her social life consisted of swapping swigs from a flask with a kid who hardly had two words to say for himself and sneering with Clyde at a washerwoman.

Clyde promised that when they got as far as Michigan or Ohio, they could eat in a restaurant, and they spent an enjoyable few hours discussing roast beef and baked chicken and tiny onions in cream sauce, but Mary remained unsatisfied and querulous all the way across Kansas the following day. She hadn't realized, she said sarcastically, that riding with the famous Clyde Barrow would mean spending days crammed in the back seat of a dirty car bouncing through dirty fields. Her back hurt. Her teeth hurt. She criticized Clyde for stopping in Peoria to buy new clothes, when they could have gotten much nicer things in Chicago. There were too many "dirty guns" in the back. Why couldn't Raymond drive and she sit up front for a change? This car stank. Why couldn't they get a new one?

CHAPTER 68

They did grab a new car outside Joplin, a dark green V-8, with two lit-tle dolls, connected by a string wrapped around their chests, dangling from the rearview mirror. While Clyde cared only about the condition and power of the machine, Bonnie was always excited to discover whatever treasures might be inside. Along with maps, they'd found cigarette cases, cigar holders, single gloves, pocketknives, and nail files, but also more personal items—shopping lists, baby rattles, letters to sweethearts, a Freemason's ring, and, in a heart-shaped candy box, a set of false teeth. Fingering these items made Bonnie feel more like a caretaker than a thief; they were only borrowing the cars, after all, and generally abandoned them with their contents intact. She liked to be-lieve she was somehow included in the lives into which these effects fit.

"Look how sweet!" She cupped the dolls' feet, at the tip of which little rubber toes were cunningly delineated. "What do you bet this car belongs to a family with twin girls?"

"More likely an old man who likes to look up little girls' skirts," Raymond said. "Look at the way he's got 'em hanging up there."

Bonnie, unknotting the string, frowned. "They aren't wearing skirts." Their outfits were painted-on bathing suits, the black-haired one in yellow and blue, the yellow-haired in pink and red. She nestled the dolls in her lap and concentrated on the view outside her window. Whenever they drove through Joplin, she hoped to spot a small, fluffy, white dog, happy in some front yard.

Outside a diner, where they next stopped for gas, two little girls in faded gingham dresses were amusing themselves by walking along a two-by-four. A dozen years ago, those girls with their scuffed shoes, windmilling arms, and raucous shrieks might have been Dutchie and

Bonnie herself. Bonnie struggled out of the car, intent on playing Lady Bountiful.

"Hey, there," she said, eyeing the board. Only a year ago, she would have walked it herself and shown them it could be done in heels.

The girls stopped their play and stood silently, staring at her. Bonnie held out the dolls with confidence; children always liked her. "These babies have been waiting for a couple of girls to take care of them. Would you be their mamas?"

The girls hung back, the younger glancing nervously at the older for guidance. Bonnie moved forward with one of her lurching steps. "Now who should have the brunette baby and who should have the blonde?"

The diner door opened, revealing a woman in a dress of pale, unbecoming pink and cheap shoes with deep cracks across the toes. "Bettina! Mildred Ann!" The girls quickly disappeared behind her.

The woman narrowed her eyes at Bonnie. "What do you want with my girls?"

Once Bonnie could have won this woman over with a smile. But Bonnie's smile was not what it had been. "I was just giving them these. They were setting on a picnic table a ways back." Bonnie tipped her head to indicate the road south. From the corner of her eye, she glimpsed her own nose and the witchy little growth at its tip. "Some little girls must've left them behind, and I figured they needed a new home." As she held the dolls out, she perceived how worn they'd become simply by riding in a car. The paint of their swimsuits and their wavy hair was flaking off where the sun had baked them through the windshield.

The woman leaned from the waist and stretched out her hand without moving her feet, so as to keep her distance and her place half inside the door. Bonnie was forced to take another step, bobbing to get the foot on her bad side to touch the ground, as if she were dropping a curtsy to a queen. The woman snatched the dolls in one hand and ducked back inside, letting the door slam shut behind her.

CHAPTER 69

That evening Clyde worked the car into a patch of woods near Terre
Haute, and Mary and Raymond barely got themselves and a blanket
behind a bush before they started rutting. Overhearing Mary's attempts
at coquettishness and her squealing expressions of pleasure was even
worse than listening to her carping. Henry announced his intention to
collect some wood and stalked off.

"I'm sick to death of that washerwoman," Bonnie said. "I don't see
why they have to ride with us." She spoke quietly, although it was obvious that Raymond and Mary were not listening.

"We're a gang," Clyde said. He dropped several guns on a blanket
and began taking one of them apart. "Raymond wants her. I got my
girl. He can have his."

Bonnie pushed her finger into the cigarette pack she'd started that
afternoon, hoping to find one stuck in the corner. "It's not the same.
I'm not the same."

"Course, you ain't, but that don't mean he can't have nobody."

"Well, let him have her. I don't know why we don't tell the both of
them to move on. Reach me another pack. I'm out."

"That was the last of 'em."

"It is not. L.C. brought us that whole bag. You just don't want to
get 'em for me."

"No, you ate 'em all. I saw that was the last one, when I gave it to
you this afternoon."

"Why didn't we get more in Peoria, then?"

He shrugged. "It was after Peoria I saw." He eased a long stick with
a bit of alcohol-soaked rag at the end into the barrel and worked it
around with a look of concentrated pleasure.

"You got what you need." Bonnie crossed her arms. "And you don't give a fuck what I need."

"You smoke too much anyway."

He wasn't even going to let her pick when to fight. "What else am I supposed to do? At least you get to drive. All I do is sit there and watch nothing go by."

"You want to go home? I'll take you home. I'll take you home, and you won't have to ride with me no more. Is that what you want?"

"What I want . . . ! What I want . . . !" She'd leaned forward, lifted one of the guns from the blanket, and waved it wildly, groping for some means by which she might be satisfied. "I want more goddamn cigarettes!" she said finally.

"Get 'em yourself!" He lunged, and she dodged, twisting her shoulders and throwing her arm back to keep the gun from him. They fought so loudly and wildly that they finally attracted the attention of the lovers, who came out from behind their bush and stood with their arms around each other, egging them on with crude comments. And although eventually they had to quit yelling, they jabbed at each other all through dinner that night, and in the morning Bonnie's eyes were swollen, her feelings still wounded, and her upper arm black and blue. She limped on her crutches, haughtily refusing Clyde's help, over uneven ground and matted weeds to the creek.

When Mary found her in the mud, unable to climb back up the steep bank, Bonnie was forced to cling to the other woman and had to press her cheek against Mary's sweaty neck.

"That man don't appreciate you the way he ought to," Mary said. "Here you stuck by him, when, with your looks, you could of found someone else easy. He ought to treat you like a queen."

"He makes me so mad saying it's all him," Bonnie said, relieved to make her case. "If it weren't for me, I'll bet you couldn't pay them papers to put his picture in."

"Well, honey, you just let me know when you've had enough," Mary went on. "I got some knockout drops. You pitch a couple of them in his Coca-Cola and you and Methvin come along with me and Ray. We'll take Clyde's money and leave him cooling his heels here. He sure deserves it, after what he done to you. Just think of him waking up without no car, no money, no girl, and no one to boss. That'd be something to see."

✦

If Mary had been more astute, she might have known from the warmth with which Bonnie and Clyde looked at one another and the way they let their bodies soften and touch that her scheme had backfired. They drove into the business district of Terre Haute, and Clyde pulled in front of a dirty Chevrolet among a smattering of parked cars in front of the shops. Then he turned suddenly in his seat, leveling his scattergun at Raymond and Mary, who were cuddling in the back. "Get the fuck out!"

"What the fuck?" Raymond and Mary instinctively slid to opposite corners of the car.

"You ain't my partner no more. If you don't know why, ask her." He gestured with the gun at Mary, who gasped and pressed herself tighter against the back of the seat.

"Raymond! Are you going to let him talk to me like that?"

Raymond was already opening his door. "Get out. Let's leave these losers to theirselves."

CHAPTER 70

They were driving to Gibsland, Louisiana, so that Henry Methvin could visit his people. Uniting to purge themselves of Raymond and Mary had elated Bonnie and Clyde, but Clyde's euphoria sank with the sun, and by the time they were bedded down beside the car somewhere in western Tennessee and had sipped the last drops in the flask, he was morose.

"I'll write a letter," he promised in a wild whisper, rubbing the purple blotch on her arm with an intensity that made her wince, as if by doing so he could erase it. "I'll tell them you never robbed nobody. I'll explain that the killings was all me. I got you into this, and you done nothing but ride along."

"*Shhh*. Whatever you did, I did. I'll follow you to hell," she whispered dramatically.

"But why don't no one else? I got plans. I got a reputation. I got a lot of success. Why don't no one want to follow me, the way they did Jesse? Everybody I get with, they think they know just as good or better than me."

"You got the kid."

They both looked toward Henry, who was sleeping with his back to them, curled in a ball.

◆

The Methvins turned out to be a weedy family whose sagging bungalows sprouted at the ends of underused and overgrown roads in the swamps and thick pine groves around Black Lake. If Ivy and Avie Methvin were more circumspect in their welcome than Bonnie and Clyde, who considered themselves to be Henry's saviors, might have expected, Bonnie was accustomed to the ambivalence of parents who were at once loving and disapproving, fearful and perversely proud.

"Yer gonna git my boy kilt," Avie said, pressing her sleeve to her eyes. She'd given them sweet tea in glass jars, but when she moved around the porch with the pitcher, she gave a wide berth to Clyde and the rifle he'd leaned barrel up against his chair.

"Now, Mother, it's no use . . ." Ivy began.

Clyde interrupted. "Don't you worry, ma'am. Them tommy guns the laws got can't make no headway with a new Ford like the one we're in. Your boy'll be all right."

Nevertheless, the Methvins insisted that Henry stay separately from Bonnie and Clyde while they were in town. "I got just the house for the two of you to hole up in," Ivy said. "The old Cole place, yonder by Cecil and Clemmie's," he explained to Henry. "Folks around here are so scart, they even left the beds and chairs and all be, but I doubt y'all will flinch at some old TB."

Bonnie should have known that an abandoned house in Louisiana would be no different from one in Texas. The place was, indeed, furnished, but the beds were full of dirty feed sacks, empty cans, and animal feces, and the floors were worse. The windows were glassless holes and the doors were too warped to close. Worst of all, from Clyde's point of view, was the house's situation at the end of a narrow dirt road hemmed in by pines.

"I know Ivy's trying to help," he said, "but he's too innocent-minded to see that this is a born trap."

They continued to live out of their car and spent most of the day driving. The spring, still so grudging in the north, here was fully committed to greening and blooming, and the land undulated in feminine curves. Here, they could disappear behind a protective screen of sweet-smelling pines, and even the ground on which they spread a blanket to sun themselves was sandy and soft. It invited roots, and Bonnie found herself susceptible to a fantasy she'd long since banished.

Bienville Parish wasn't far from Dallas, but it was outside of Texas, far beyond the reach and, presumably, even the interest of Sheriff Smoot Schmid. The Eastham raid—Clyde's preoccupation for so long— was finished; they had plenty of money from the bank jobs they'd pulled with Raymond. Why couldn't they buy one of these charming gingerbread-roofed houses on a sweet piece of land and start over?

When she'd embroidered the idea long enough to give it weight and texture, she presented it to Clyde. They were safe among the Methvins, who knew everyone—who *were* everyone. Clyde agreed that they could arrange some kind of secret purchase, and they spent several days playing at choosing property. They wanted to go to Dallas for Easter, but after that, Mr. and Mrs. Howard promised each other, they'd come back and settle down.

CHAPTER 71

April 1934

The rabbit is an Easter gift for Emma, but Bonnie, who plies him with lettuce and carrots, has had the joy of him for several days. Of course, he leaves his calling cards here and there on the mohair upholstery. The pellets are dry, easy to brush off, hardly worth mentioning.

"Does he have to do that?" Clyde says. "This is a nice car."

Bonnie gently draws her hairbrush through the rabbit's fur. "Doesn't he remind you of Snowball?"

"He reminds me of Boy," Clyde laughs. "The way he stares, all twitchy-like."

"How about we call him Sonny Boy?"

"Sonny Boy stinks." Henry's been bellyaching about not being with his family on Easter Sunday and has started pulling on the bottle early.

"*You* stink," Bonnie says, pressing her nose into the rabbit's downy fur. "Let's give him a bath in the river, Clyde. Make him pretty for my mama."

Sonny Boy despises baths. He writhes and beats at the water with his strong back legs, giving Clyde a long, deep scratch along the forearm, but Bonnie is able to rub a bar of soap into his pelt long enough to generate a few suds. He shrinks pitifully when they pull him out. His soaked fur sticks to his skin, making his tummy stand out round and vulnerable as an infant's.

At first, it's a pleasure to swaddle his trembling body in a towel and press him against her breast, but instead of calming, his shaking becomes more violent. "He's too cold!"

"Well, warm him up," Clyde says.

"I'm trying, but he's shaking like anything! *Shh, shh,*" she murmurs. She chafes at his matted fur with the sleeve of her coat. "C'mon, baby, you're all right. Oh, Clyde, he ain't . . . oh, God, he's passed out! I'm afraid he's going to die. I think we might have killed him! Stop! Please, Clyde! Stop!"

"What's the use of stopping?" Henry says.

"We can get a fire going," Bonnie says. "We have to warm him up."

"Oh, for fuck's sake!" Clyde says. "A fire in the middle of the day? To heat up a goddamn bunny?"

"Yum, yum. Roast rabbit." Henry rubs his palms together.

"That isn't funny!"

"Who said it was a joke?"

"Shut up the both of you and look for a good spot."

If Bonnie hadn't been so panicked, Clyde may have searched for a more out-of-the-way place, but as it is, he takes the first that presents itself, a stretch of grass beside the unpaved Dove Road on a rise above Highway 114. Every so often, a car floats past down below on the highway, distant enough to look and sound more like a machine in a picture show than a real automobile.

To Bonnie's relief, the rabbit responds to the warmth of the fire and is soon nibbling at the grass. She strokes him idly. It would be all right now to get back in the car and drive on, but they have nowhere to be until later, when they're going to meet her mother and Cumie, and maybe Marie and L.C. and Billie. Clyde has fallen asleep across the back seat, and she's inclined to let him be. They've continued their precaution of sleeping only in shifts at night, two hours at a stretch, so they're never adequately rested.

It's April 1, exactly a year since they moved into the apartment in Joplin, planning to live like ordinary, happy people for a week or two. She resists the urge to wallow in regret. Next year this time, maybe they'll have that place in Gibsland. For now, she'll be like darling Sonny Boy and savor the balm of the spring sun and the tender grass. She smooths the skirt of the new red dress Clyde's bought for her, as if stroking her own fur.

When she reaches for the bottle on the running board next to Henry, he flinches. "I just want a sip. What are you so goddamn jumpy for?"

He motions at the highway. "This place is too open. Anyone can see us."

She shrugs. "They're too far away and going too fast. To them, we're just any old car, two boys and a girl. No one special."

She helps herself to a few more swigs and then cuts herself a bit of lemon peel.

"Better get your bunny." Henry lifts his chin toward the rabbit, which has hopped to a point at which the hill begins to slope down precipitously.

W.D. would have collected Sonny Boy for her, Bonnie thinks, as she limps across the grass.

If they don't want to attract attention, maybe she shouldn't be wearing a red dress. Maybe they shouldn't be driving a car with wheels yellow as crocuses.

◆

On the highway below, three motorcycles appear, their drivers wearing the stiff navy jackets and flat-topped caps that announce they are the law. Bonnie stands over Sonny Boy and watches, waiting for them to pass on down the highway. One of them does. The other two exit onto Dove Road.

Despite her lurching gait, she can be quick. She scoops up the rabbit and hurries to the car.

"Clyde, get up! It's the laws!"

The rear car door is hinged at the back so, open, it can shield them from those who approach from behind. Only Bonnie, sitting on the front seat with the rabbit in her arms, can see the BAR that extends from Clyde's arm. Tall Henry stands on the far side of the car, his shoulders above the roof.

The laws jounce slowly toward them, paying more attention to controlling their bikes on the uneven surface than to the black automobile with yellow wheels. They obviously intend to provide assistance to Sunday drivers with engine trouble, not apprehend notorious criminals.

When Clyde turns to Henry and says softly, "Let's take 'em," Bonnie knows he means to kidnap them. She's at once annoyed that this will mean they'll miss their rendezvous with their mothers and pleased at the opportunity for fresh company. The explosion beside her makes no sense. Nor does the sight of the lead policeman and his bike toppling sideways onto the road.

"What the hell?" Clyde whips a quick, furious look at Henry.

The second cop fumbles at his chest pocket and removes a handful of shells. Bonnie sees one dribble from between his fingers and bounce onto the road, while he struggles to unstrap a sawed-off shotgun from behind his seat. He's a small man and young, and her instinct is to retrieve the dropped shell for him and to help him steady the bike. No, she says to him in her mind. Go. Go! The words are so loud in her head that she feels as if she's shouting them, but no sound is coming out.

It's Clyde who speaks. "Stop," he says. "Leave it."

But the young law doesn't leave it. He's jackknifed the shotgun over his arm now, and he's pushing the shells in. Another escapes his shaking fingers and falls to the road. Clyde's shoulder shifts.

"Stop!" she screams, her voice finally pouring out, rough as the whiskey she's been downing.

But the men pay no attention to her.

Now both laws are on the ground, the small one on his back, as if sunbathing, the large one in a pose of exaggerated contortion, the way a child might fall in a game of Ring Around the Rosie.

From the other direction, a car appears, driving toward them on Dove Road. Clyde turns and steps into the road, his scattergun erect, and the machine stops with a shriek and then spurts backward, its wheels clawing at the dirt.

◆

Incredibly, behind them, a stream of bullets bangs out, as if the motorcycle cops have only been playing possum. Bonnie ducks, shielding Sonny Boy's body with her own. But when she turns to look, it's Henry she sees in the road, standing over the two policemen. He's riddling them with his BAR, and their bodies jump in response to the assault, as if the bullets are bringing them back to life.

◆

Bonnie could not have balanced on her good leg and wielded the BAR in that fashion, but it makes a good story in the papers the next day to say it was the woman who went back and shot the fallen officers. On the following day, the paper reports that the woman was heard to laugh as she did so, laugh and crow at the way "his head bounced like a rubber ball." The article adds that the fiancée of one of the officers wore her wedding dress to the funeral.

"It's a bunch of bunk!" Bonnie tells the rabbit. "I didn't do it. I wouldn't do it. That isn't me."

But who will believe her? And is the distinction between the person who would and did—Henry Methvin, to whom she refused to speak for the rest of the day—and herself great enough to matter?

She would never have let Clyde write that letter declaring her innocence, but the possibility had remained. Now it's gone. In a way, she feels more innocent than ever before—what Henry did was monstrous, and she's not a monster—but at the same time, she knows she's guiltier than she's ever admitted. She sits sandwiched between them on the front seat, Clyde on her left, Henry on her right. To an observer, they are all one.

CHAPTER 72

"You gotta do what I say," Clyde said, "not go following your own damn ideas."

Henry, his voice high with indignation, argued that he'd followed Clyde's order, but Clyde refused to listen. "We ain't killers. I oughta turn you in. Get me and Bonnie out of this."

Behind his spread fingers, Henry looked scared and on the verge of tears.

"Don't be so hard on the kid, Daddy," Bonnie said. "He made a mistake, but what's done is done. We just got to go forward now."

◆

They drive, not exactly forward, but in their usual zags and loops for the next five days, stopping only for a few hours in the deepest night, so that Clyde can get a little sleep. Just after midnight on the night of April 6, Clyde pulls onto the shoulder of State Road, outside the town of Commerce, Oklahoma. Rain has been sluicing against the dark windows for hours. They haven't dared to drive anywhere near Dallas, so Sonny Boy is still with them, and the skirt of Bonnie's red dress is covered with the fine white threads of his fur.

Bonnie watches first, then Henry. It's his job to wake them at dawn, but within half an hour of his watch, he falls asleep. When Bonnie awakens, the rain has stopped, and the sun, burning white behind a thick layer of gray cloud, reveals that they're parked among heaps of black slag beside a mine. It's much too late.

To accommodate Sonny Boy on her lap as she slept, Bonnie had placed her whipit beside her on the seat, but it has slipped to the floor.

She bends to retrieve it as Clyde starts the engine. When she sits up again, a black sedan has appeared on the road. It slows as it nears them and pulls over.

"Fuck!" Clyde guns the engine, backing away at top speed. Behind the windshield of the other car, four eyes widen in surprise.

For a second or two it seems they'll escape; they're traveling fast and the black sedan remains fixed. But then a back wheel catches in the mud, and the car slides right. Both rear wheels spin in the slickness, gouts of mud slapping against the chassis.

As the laws—one beefy with a big white moustache, the other tall and slim—get out of the car, they appear to be laughing.

She raises the whipit to the windshield, aiming it not at one or the other, but in the general direction of both and of their smug, unyielding car. "What's so funny?" She's shrieking, but it's doubtful her voice carries beyond their own closed car.

The laws' first shot shatters a headlight; the second rips a long wound into the metal of the hood. Clyde slithers from the car and lifts his scattergun in one motion, but he's slow compared with Henry, who's running toward the other car, shouting as he goes. The big man with the moustache falls sideways, blood blooming from his neck. Then the slim man clutches his head with a grunt and sinks to his knees. In moments, Clyde has one hand on the slim man's shoulder, the other under his arm, and is helping him to his feet, urging him forward, away from his car and toward theirs.

"Help me," Clyde snaps at Henry, when the man stumbles. "Put your gun down. Get him in the car."

From behind the slag heaps, people creep out to investigate the noise and another car comes up the road. Over the course of the next half hour, Clyde and his BAR direct a strange dance of coercion and helpfulness. With Bonnie behind the wheel and a borrowed rope around the bumper, the new car struggles to drag the Ford out of the mud, while Clyde, Henry, and four other men, including the wounded officer, who's obviously disoriented, push, shouting instructions and encouragement at one another, until the rope breaks.

Clyde swears wildly but doesn't give up. He stops other cars as they appear: does anyone have a chain? Bystanders offer suggestions: "You got to back her up." "She needs more weight in her." "No, she needs to lighten up." "Ain't nobody got a board?"

Clyde is about to abandon the V-8 and take one of the other cars he's waylaid when a truck comes along carrying the necessary length of chain. Even once they're free, they can't go far. The rain has caused mudslides all along the mine-ravaged earth, and another stuck car blocks their way. Clyde and Henry push it free, while Bonnie, her whipit in one hand and a cigarette in the other, waits in the back, guarding the injured lawman.

Although the blood continues to trickle around his ear and into his collar, his eyes seem now to be focusing. She watches him scan their arsenal. "Impressive, ain't it? You best tell your friends to quit coming after us, if they know what's good for them."

"Am I crazy?" he whispers. "Or am I looking at a rabbit?"

"That's Sonny Boy. Isn't he sweet?"

"I'll bet he is. There's nothing better than a rabbit stew," the officer says.

"That's the most disgusting thing I've ever heard!" Bonnie flicks her butt out the window to free one hand so she can lay it protectively over the rabbit's back. "He's a present for my mama!"

"If I gave something like that to my mama, she'd put it in a pot," the officer says.

"Not a white one!" Bonnie pulls Sonny Boy tight against her thigh until he squirms.

"Meat's all the same." The officer shrugs.

Bonnie shakes her head. "My mama'll love this rabbit. I'm going to give her a whole white menagerie. She's gonna have a white goat, a white duck, a white kitten . . ."

"How about a cockatoo?" the officer asks.

"What's that?"

"One of them talking birds. Like a parrot."

"Do they come in white?"

"I seen a white one once."

"Then I'll get her one of them, too." Bonnie lowers the gun. They're driving fast now, free of the mud, the mines, and the law on the ground with a bullet in his stomach.

"You shoulda let us run," Clyde says. "Then you wountna got your-self shot."

"I gotta take action when I see fit," the law says. He wipes at his forehead and then examines his hand, as if surprised by the blood on it. "I'm the chief."

"The chief!" Clyde nods approvingly. "Y'all got some good shots off, you know. A couple of them bullets came real close."

"I'm responsible for that man you left bleeding to death back there."

"Oh, I reckon he'll pull through, Chief," Clyde says. "I been shot plenty of times."

"We're going to die soon, too," Bonnie says. "If that makes you feel any better. Not the kid." She nods at Henry. "He's going back home to his mama and daddy."

"Only thing he's good for is getting us into trouble," Clyde says.

"He's trying his best," Bonnie says. "But me and . . ." She pauses. "Do you know who we are?"

"I believe I do."

"What's your name, then?"

"Boyd. Percy Boyd."

"Well, Mr. Boyd, you know when the sun is down, but it's not dark yet? You know how the edges get all soft and blurry, like someone's put a screen in front of your eyes?"

"I don't follow you," Boyd says. "Maybe it's my head." He reaches for the spot where the blood is beginning to coagulate in his hair, but Bonnie bats his hand down.

"Better not touch that. Listen, I'm trying to tell you something, Percy." She slides forward on the seat and leans into the front with her hand out. "Gimme my glasses, Hank." Henry passes her a soft leather case from the glove compartment from which she removes a pair of steel spectacles with small, round eyepieces. "These were right here in the car," she says, "like God put them in. I didn't even know I needed glasses until I tried these on. And now it's like the whole world's been cut out with a razor. Maybe that's how you see it all the time. You got good eyes?"

"Yes," Boyd says, "although I'm not seeing too good right now." He begins to lift his hand again, but Bonnie grabs it and holds it down.

"There was a time when I thought we were going somewhere. I didn't know where exactly. I just thought there was some place up there that we could get to and be happy." She's lit another cigarette and gestures with it toward the windshield. "But then Buck got killed and Blanche got hurt and locked up and W.D. got so scared he don't want to be with us again. And then my babies, who hardly even got to be alive, died, and I'll tell you . . ." She pauses to pull smoke into her lungs. "I wished I was them, dead before I lived this life. It was like dusk all the time, everything gray and dim and sorrowful. That sad time of the day, you know?" She looks expectantly at Boyd, until he nods.

"But it's gotten so I know what's coming," she goes on, "I can see it, clear as can be."

"What's that?" Boyd asks.

"*Boom!*" Clyde shouts suddenly, so that they all jump.

Bonnie frowns. "That's not the part I dwell on. I think about the part afterward. No more driving, no more hiding, no more being scared."

"Whyn't you just give yourselves up, then?"

"Mister Boyd, we're just like everybody else. We'd rather live until we die." She pats the seat beside her. "Let's quit talking about this now and get you cleaned up. You put your head down right here."

With her right hand, she uses the hem of her nightie to dab Mercurochrome onto his wound, while with her left, she keeps a cigarette going. She binds his head with one of her old stockings. "We've seen a lot worse," she says. "That'll heal quick."

"I got twenty-five dollars on me," Boyd says. "What do you say we get something to eat?" It's now early afternoon, and they've driven nearly the length and breadth of Kansas.

"I ain't taking your money." Instead, Clyde pulls over beside a gumball machine in some little town and, with a twist and jerk of the screwdriver he always carries, empties its pennies into a bag.

A little farther on, they send Henry into a diner for food and soda pop. The newspaper he brings out with the lunch has already printed an account of the shootout in Commerce on the front page. Bonnie is identified as a "cigar-smoking gun moll," and Cal Campbell is dead.

"Sorry," Clyde says, handing the paper to Boyd.

"I suppose he was a good man," Bonnie says. "The ones who get killed always are."

"Eight kids," Boyd says. "And no mama."

"A man's got that kind of responsibility, he hadn't ought to be working for the laws these days," Clyde says.

Around one a.m., Clyde pulls a short way down a wooded road and stops the car, but Bonnie shakes her head. "It don't look right, letting him go off with all that blood on his shirt. You give him one of yours, Daddy."

While Boyd changes his shirt, Bonnie selects a tie for him. They make him try one of Clyde's jackets, but it's too small. Bonnie insists he take Henry's instead.

"This is for the bus," Clyde says, handing Boyd ten dollars.

"Don't forget," Bonnie says, "go right to the doctor in the morning and get that head looked at." She lifts the rabbit to her cheek. "Would you do me a favor? If we're killed, would you see that my mama gets Sonny Boy?"

"Anything else? You know the press is going to be all over me for this story."

Bonnie brightens. Percy Boyd can tell those reporters that they have it wrong. She and Clyde aren't mean and dirty, the way the papers say. They didn't intend for any of those men to get killed. If people know who she really is—

But she can't think how to explain it, and Clyde is impatiently tapping the steering wheel. "Tell them I don't smoke cigars," she says. "I never smoked a single one."

CHAPTER 73

Oriented as they now were toward Louisiana, they chose an east Texas town for their next family gathering. The Barrows brought fried chicken and a pile of newspapers, one of which had published a letter from Raymond Hamilton, disavowing any connection to the Grapevine and Commerce shootings. For that, Clyde could hardly blame him, but Raymond, typically, also managed to get in a few digs about Clyde being capable of robbing only gas stations and grocery stores.

"He's just jealous," L.C. said, gleefully showing off several cartoons. In one, Pretty Boy pouted that Clyde was getting all the attention, and in another, Sheriff Smoot Schmid snored while a young man with big ears and a blond woman with a cigar poked their heads out from under his bed. To be so famous as to be recognizable in the few squiggles of a caricaturist's pen was worth being associated with the hated cigar. Bonnie regretted the loss of her scrapbook, but Henry Barrow shook his doleful head.

"I don't like it," he said. "He'll get you sure now."

In fact, West Dallas had heard that a Ranger named Frank Hamer had been hired specially to track down and kill Clyde and Bonnie.

"I'm worried," Emma said as she and Bonnie, who clung to her mother like a worn-out toddler, trailed after the sleek bunny while the others were enjoying the chicken. "They say Rangers don't have to stay around Dallas or even in Texas but follow you wherever you go."

"He's still a law," Bonnie said, "and Clyde can outrun any law there is."

"You're too old for that," Emma said.

"For what?" Bonnie narrowed her eyes, homing in for the argument.

"For thinking you're different from everyone else. I don't say he ain't run pretty good so far, but look at yourself!" She gestured to show she meant every part of Bonnie from her twisted leg to her ragged hair. "The both of you are worn down—me and Cumie can see it, even if you can't—and them Rangers are just warming up. If men like that decide they want something, there ain't nothing you or me or even Clyde Barrow can do about it."

"Well, then I guess we'll die!" Bonnie said.

"It's not just you that's suffering. It's all of us. They won't leave us alone. I can't use the telephone without wondering who's listening in. They even drug Cumie into the station for questioning. Kept her the whole afternoon and made her feel like trash."

"Clyde won't stand for that."

"What's he going to do?" When Bonnie was silent, Emma took her chance. "We think you should go to Mexico. The Barrows and me, we agreed. It don't take much money to live down there, and we know you got some. You stay over the border, and they can't touch you."

"But, Mama, then I won't be able to come be your bonny Bonnie." With her fingertips, Bonnie smoothed the wrinkles in her mother's forehead.

"I'd rather know you're alive than see you dead!" Emma began impatiently to brush Bonnie's fingers away, but thought the better of it and gathered them in a tight grip.

"Clyde can't live like regular people, Mama. And I guess I can't, either. That's just how it is." Bonnie shrugged.

They both cried, while Emma embraced her daughter. The integrity of Bonnie's words comforted her, even if she hated their import. This was, at least, clear and honest thinking. But Bonnie, typically, had to ruin it.

"We're fixing to get us a little house, Mama," she said, her eyes glowing in their hollow sockets.

"A house?" Thrown off guard, Emma let herself be drawn in.

"Yes, over in Gibsland. It's so pretty and comfortable in Louisiana. And we're safe there, because it's all Methvins."

"Folks in Louisiana may not be like those in West Dallas."

"We can trust them, Mama. They got us to thank for getting Henry out of Eastham."

"And for making him a fugitive."

Bonnie shook her head. "They don't do nothing but help us, Mama. They invite us to all their parties, just like we're family, and Ivy Methvin says he can find us a little house to buy with nobody knowing. When we have our place, I promise we'll just live quiet," Bonnie went on, blithely contradicting her argument against going to Mexico. "Clyde'll fish and loaf, and I'll write my poetry. We figure you'll only be able to slip in to see us at night for the first little while, but if we stay low Texas'll get tired of paying that Ranger. Then you and Billie and the Barrows can move to Bienville Parish, and we can all be happy. Wouldn't that be wonderful?"

"It would be wonderful, darling," Emma said, scooping up the white rabbit before he could disappear under a huckleberry bush.

CHAPTER 74

In May, they returned to Bienville Parish with money stolen from a bank in Iowa, a saxophone, and a nearly new V-8 with wire wheels, plucked from a driveway in Topeka. Unlike the black car with yellow wheels, this one was inconspicuous, an elegant matte gray-brown with a warm greenish undertone, the color of an unpaved road.

During the days, they drove through the warm air deep into the piney woods, making-believe that they were searching for a house to buy, delighting service station attendants and delivery boys with Baby Ruths and peanut patties. In the evenings, as the sun lingered, they joined the various Methvin relations and friends who lived in the summer almost as Bonnie and Clyde did, picnicking daily at various spots around Black Lake and roasting their meals on campfires. Flush and famous, Clyde and Bonnie were honored guests who readily passed out five- and ten-dollar bills and entertained children with fast rides in their big car. When, one evening, a Methvin cousin, face aglow in firelight, announced that she was pregnant, Bonnie pressed her own abdomen. "So am I!" she exclaimed. It seemed possible, given how happy and replete she'd been feeling.

◆

May 6, 1934

They took advantage of their nearness to Dallas to make another visit, although this time, Henry Barrow stayed home.

"He says I'm only encouraging you to get shot, coming out here like this," Cumie told Clyde. "He says if we don't show up, maybe you'll stay away. But I told him that'd make you drive right on down Eagle

Ford Road to find out what was what, and what did he think would happen then?"

"Look at this one, Mama." Bonnie was thrusting some new photographs in front of Emma and gushing about the fashions she was sporting in them: a fur jacket with a shawl collar and a little cap—"I'm going to get you a jacket like the one I'm wearing there, Mama. The fur is so soft, you'll just want to pet yourself the whole goddamned day." She'd cinched one of Clyde's ties around her waist in another. "Myrna Loy did just like that in *Movie Mirror*."

Emma murmured the approbation that Bonnie demanded, but the pitifulness of this display pained her.

"I've got a new poem for you, too." Bonnie unfolded a thin piece of writing paper and tried to press out the creases with her red nails.

Emma only glanced at the page of schoolgirl script, entitled "The Trail's End," before refolding it.

"Read it now, Mama. I think it's the best I've done."

"It's too dark. I'll read it when I get home."

"Then I'll read it to you. I want to know what you think. Y'all listen," she said, interrupting a conversation on the far side of the fire. "This is about me and Clyde."

It was a stout defense, elevating Bonnie and Clyde to legend, blaming the law for harassment and false accusations and the press for sensationalism, praising West Dallas—"Where the women are kin / And the men are men"—for its support. The end, however, referred to the wages of sin. Bonnie held a pregnant pause, which would have earned Miss Gleason's approval, before pronouncing the final line—"But it's death for Bonnie and Clyde."

"What the hell's wrong with you?" Clyde said. "Why would you say that to our mamas?"

"Why not?" Bonnie said. "It's what we're all thinking. Why not say it?"

"Bonnie, you hush up . . ." Emma began.

"I'm sick of being scared all the time, wondering, will it be today, tonight? Sometimes I just want it to be done. I think about lying on the divan at home, with you and Billie and Buster around me, and it just feels so restful and peaceful, like a cool, night breeze. Mama"—she gripped Emma's arm fervently—"promise when it happens you'll bring me home and let me lay peaceful for awhile."

"It ain't gonna be peaceful. We ain't going down without a battle, and we'll take a few of 'em with us, like you say there." Clyde gestured at the poem.

"Clyde," Bonnie frowned, refolding the paper, "that's the talk that's upsetting. No one wants to think about all those guns and shooting. Anyway, as long as we stay in Bienville Parish, we'll be all right. We never see the laws there at all. You'd think they were staying away on purpose, letting us have the place."

"Well, then, you stay put," Emma said.

◆

May 20, 1934

But they had to go into Shreveport. Gibsland didn't have a dry cleaners and the pregnant Methvin cousin craved chicken salad with green grapes from the Majestic Café.

While Henry went inside to buy lunch, Bonnie and Clyde waited in the car, soaking in the buttery sun. When a police car cruised by, the officers inside didn't turn their heads, but Clyde knew better than to wait and see if they'd been recognized. He jackrabbited away from the curb.

Of course, that made the cop car spin and the siren scream, and for a few minutes Bonnie shifted her gaze at least two dozen times between the V-8's hood ornament, a straining greyhound, and the menacing eyes behind it. But the distance between them stretched steadily until the V-8 broke free. It was nothing, an incident that, had they ever seen their mothers again, they would not even have thought to mention. Obviously, they didn't dare go back to the café for Henry, but they had a plan in case of separation: they were to meet at Ivy and Avie Methvin's.

"Goddamn laws owe us lunch," Clyde said.

If Henry had paid and left the café with his bag of sandwiches, no one would have connected him with the car that had bolted. But Henry disappeared, which made an impression on the waitress who was left with four unclaimed chicken salads and three bottles of cold soda pop. She identified him in a photograph that two members of Frank Hamer's posse—Bob Alcorn and Bonnie's old friend Ted Hinton—showed her the next day. Sooner or later, Alcorn and Hinton guessed, Clyde and Bonnie would be on the road to Ivy and Avie Methvin's place.

◆

May 22, 1934

But not yet. Encountering the laws in Shreveport had reminded Bonnie and Clyde to be wary, to stick to the back roads that petered out at abandoned logging camps, became marshy, mosquito-clouded trails to creeks and lakes, or climbed the ridges into stands of pines and tangled underbrush. They had their favorite spots along these routes, some halfway across the state, clearings through which the sun shone bright enough at midday to discourage mosquitoes, and they played house in these, spreading a blanket beside the car to serve as bedroom, living room, and kitchen. For an hour or so Clyde cleaned the guns, while Bonnie first fooled with the accounts, counting and rearranging stacks of bills, as she determined how much to bestow on their families and the Methvins; how much they needed for gas, food, and dry cleaning; how much they could save toward a cabin. When she was satisfied with her figures, she read over the copy she'd kept of "The Trail's End." The meter was off, making a few of the lines clumsy, and she wanted the poem to be perfect.

When he tired of the guns, Clyde took his sax from the trunk. Years ago, Nell's husband had taught him how to attach the reed and shift between octaves, and lately he'd been practicing every day, developing power in his cheeks and lungs and working out the notes. Bonnie found the process difficult to listen to; her ear kept trying to follow a tune, but just as it got going, it ran off the road.

"Da, da, da; DA, da, DA; da, da, BRAHHH," the instrument squawked.

The big, black animal burst from the underbrush, so suddenly that Bonnie thought for an instant that it was death itself come for them. But when it stopped about ten feet away and stood baying, she could see it was only a dog.

"Don't shoot!" she cried, throwing her hands in the air to stop Clyde, who'd dropped his instrument, grabbed his scattergun, and stood aiming it at the poor creature.

"Black Boy, what you got?" a voice sang out. Twigs snapped and leaves rustled a little distance away. "You found a squirrel?"

"Come on over here," Clyde said sternly. "Here's your dog."

"And here's your squirrels," Bonnie said, as a skinny boy in a brown cap broke into the clearing.

He stared but, like the dog, stood his ground, dropping his hand to the animal's neck. "Quiet, Boy."

"What's your name?" Clyde had lowered his gun, but his voice remained hard.

"Robert," the boy said. "Robert Brunson."

"Do you know who we are?"

Robert shook his head.

"C'mon, guess."

"Rich folk?" the boy ventured, his eyes skimming the piles of bills Bonnie hadn't yet bothered to put away.

"You ever heard of any bank robbers?"

"I heard of Pretty Boy Floyd."

"You ever heard of the Barrow Gang? Bonnie and Clyde?"

Robert stood silent for a moment, thinking. "Maybe."

"Goddammit!" Clyde stalked to the car and yanked open the back door.

"Daddy, don't scare him."

"Look at this." Clyde produced a newspaper that detailed on the front page Frank Hamer's mission and the huge rewards on offer for the capture of Bonnie and Clyde. He shook it in front of the boy. "Can you read?"

Robert nodded. He accepted the paper and held it for some seconds—it was difficult to know whether he was reading or just allowing a decent interval to pass—and then handed it back.

"We're them," Clyde said. "Bonnie and Clyde. We rob banks."

"Bring your dog on over here," Bonnie said, patting the blanket beside her. "I want to pet him."

Together the boy and dog advanced tentatively to the blanket.

"Clyde, take a picture of Robert and me and this pretty dog," Bonnie said.

"Someday," she said confidingly to the boy, "this'll be a story you'll tell your grandchildren. The day you met Bonnie and Clyde. Now I'll take a picture of just you that you can give your mama."

"You think you'd want to rob banks?" Clyde asked.

"No, sir."

"I could learn you like that," Clyde said, snapping his fingers.

"He's a good boy," Bonnie said. "Leave him be."

"Is your family hard up?" Clyde said. "Do you want some money? Here." He grabbed a handful of bills and thrust them toward Robert. "Take as much as you want."

But the boy cringed, as if the money were on fire.

"How about a shotgun?" Clyde selected one from the blanket. "This here's a good gun, a long sight better than the one you got there."

"No, thank you."

"You'd better give me your address, so I can send you these pictures when they come out," Bonnie said. She turned the copy of her poem over and wrote what the boy told her on the back.

"Can I write back to you?" Robert asked.

"I wish you could, honey, but we don't have an address. Just V-8 Ford, Some Road, USA."

CHAPTER 75

May 23, 1934

"Don't eat that now," Clyde says. "We'll stop someplace after we get Henry and have a picnic."

So she rewraps the bacon, lettuce, and tomato sandwich as well as she can with one hand, while with the other she keeps the Remington from sliding off her lap as he speeds around a curve. She clamps her knees around the Crush, but a splash of orange darkens her red dress. "Do you have to drive so fast?"

It's 9:15 a.m. Humidity hangs in the air, but the breeze streaming through the open windows is watery and cool. The gravel crunches smoothly under their speeding tires so that it sounds as if they're driving beside a racing river.

Bonnie plays with her glasses, nudging them off her eyes and then pushing them back again, blurring and sharpening the landscape.

"Isn't that Ivy's truck?" Clyde nods at a Model A in the distance. It's at the top of a long rise and seems to be stopped. It's in their lane but facing toward them.

"Must have a flat," Bonnie says, when they're close enough to see that the truck's jacked up, its right wheel off the ground. She fluffs her hair out where her earpieces have caught it.

Their acceleration slakes as Clyde relieves some of the pressure on the gas pedal. "Where the hell's Ivy?"

Both of them study the truck as they pull into the other lane, draw even with the engine, and idle for a moment. Something about the situation—maybe the direction the truck is facing or the absence of the driver—seems wrong.

When the semiautomatic gunfire sizzles through the air and crashes against the door, Clyde should be gunning the engine, but instead his head falls between the spokes of the steering wheel, and the car only inches forward. A barrage of rifle fire, amounting to more than 150 slugs, cuts through Bonnie's scream, her final exhalation.

The V-8 continues to move, as if the pummeling bullets are forcing it on. It gains speed as it rolls down the hill, veers to the left, and finally comes to rest against the embankment, but those inside the car are unaware. Although she still holds her sandwich, Bonnie does not feel the bullets that Frank Hamer pumps into her through the rear passenger window and those he adds, just to be sure, through the windshield. She does not see the wisps of gun smoke that float around the V-8, a detail she might have referred to in a bitter poem as her and Clyde's version of heaven, nor does she know that she has made it into the pictures, a 16-millimeter film Ted Hinton takes of the posse inspecting what will come to be known as the "death car."

◆

"What do you have to say about the way they shot your daughter?"

Emma learned of Bonnie's death from some eager newspaperman over the phone. She'd always believed she'd be ready for the event, but when it finally occurred, an icy blackness suffused her veins, and she fainted.

She wanted to go to Arcadia with Buster to claim the body, but he said that the way people were mobbing the place would make her sick. "They're treating her like a carnival attraction," he complained. "They say there's not even a sandwich left to eat in that town."

It made Emma unhappy to think that Bonnie would be pleased to be the center of so much awful attention, but at the same time, she was sorry that Bonnie could not enjoy it. "I suppose people just have to have a little excitement," she sighed. "They can't help theirselves."

"You're not going to be able to bring her in the house," Buster warned. "The crowds'll knock the door down."

"That boy stole every bit of peace that girl could have had," Emma said. "You tell them Barrows that he's not getting any more of her. She's going to be buried beside those babies that she loved, so she can watch over them. That's what she would have wanted."

Emma almost fainted again the next day, when Bonnie's body arrived in Dallas. The funeral parlor had done its best to clean up the blood and piece together the ragged edges of her skin, but embalming fluid oozed from the bullet holes and so much of her flesh had been torn away that most of the mutilation was irreparable. Almost more disturbing was the discovery that souvenir hunters had hacked off her hair in random places. Still, the twenty thousand people who filed past Bonnie laid out in her pale blue negligee that afternoon were mostly well-behaved. When Emma heard that the police had had to eject an overly raucous crowd from the funeral home that the Barrows had chosen, she further congratulated herself on her decision to separate Bonnie from Clyde.

It was well after dark by the time she and Buster could have the body to themselves and do their best to create the quiet hour that Bonnie had envisioned the last time Emma had seen her. Billie could not join them, having been jailed for allegedly shooting the patrolmen in Grapevine on April 1. Gently, Emma lifted the white veil she'd arranged over Bonnie's face to disguise the worst of the damage. She closed her eyes and pressed her own face against a few inches of unmarred skin and imagined that under the oily smell of the makeup and the chemical odor of the embalming fluid and the sulfurous whiff of gunpowder that permeated her daughter's hair she could still detect a trace of Bonnie's light, girlish scent.

In writing this novel I've been faithful to all the facts known about Bonnie Parker's life and the circumstances of her crimes. But because so many details of Parker's life are unknown—as are, of course, her emotions and thoughts—I've interlaced the few facts with my own inventions. Parker and Barrow's crime spree was reported in local newspapers, and accounts in those papers are often unreliable and contradictory, as are the reminiscences of her contemporaries, which were often elicited years after the events. When my sources differed in their account of an incident, I chose the version I judged most plausible. When I encountered differing but equally plausible accounts of an event—for instance, Parker and Barrow's first meeting—I chose the one that best fit my narrative purposes. To give the novel shape and, particularly, to keep it moving at a reasonable pace, I had to omit some interesting anecdotes and several of Parker and Barrow's myriad robberies and kidnappings, so while my story is accurate within the limits of the paucity of facts, it's not exhaustive. And, inevitably, I've made errors in fact and in judgment.

I visited nearly all the locations I depict—from the compact, isolated West Texas town of Rowena, where Parker was born, to the winding road south of Gibsland, Louisiana, where she was killed. Some sites had changed so much that they no longer resembled the places that Parker had experienced—the Red Crown Tavern beside a two-lane road in Platte City, Missouri, where police mortally wounded Buck Barrow, had been obliterated by Interstate 29 and acres of fast-food outlets and gas stations. When I visited the area west of Dallas once known as Cement City, where Parker grew up, the Southwestern Portland Cement plant and the housing it had built for its workers were gone, but a smaller cement plant remained and the locality retained the feel of a place on the edge, too empty to be urban, too industrial to be rural. The schoolhouse on the hill with a vaguely arabesque entry that Parker is said to have attended was boarded up and surrounded by a chain-link fence when I saw it, but the building has since been restored and the acreage across the street filled with big-box stores.

Many buildings, townscapes, and landscapes remained very much as Parker must have experienced them. The Barrow's Star service station and home on what was once Eagle Ford Road in West Dallas was derelict, but substantially undisturbed. The calaboose in Kemp, Texas, where Parker was first jailed, still stood; the business district surrounding the downtown square in Kaufman, where she was involved in her first burglary, had hardly changed; and, not surprisingly, the ornate courthouses in Dallas, Denton, and Waco continued to appear imposing. The site of the abandoned amusement park in Dexfield, Iowa, where Buck and Blanche Barrow were captured, was only more overgrown. Most haunting was the garage apartment that the Barrow Gang rented in the Joplin, Missouri, neighborhood, which looks from the street exactly as it did in 1933. Although the highways and the vehicles on them had changed enormously, the views out the car window of worn towns and long horizons, of soil that shifted from brown to red, of majestic banks of cloud against a brilliant blue West Texas sky endured.

Among the many books and articles that I consulted, the most helpful were those of Jeff Guinn and John Neal Phillips, both of whom are obviously the experts on this subject. Guinn's *Go Down Together: The True, Untold Story of Bonnie and Clyde* exhaustively sifts the evidence on all aspects of Parker and Barrow's story from context to personalities in a highly readable, somewhat hard-bitten style. With graceful prose, Phillips delves even more deeply in his focused account: *Running with Bonnie and Clyde: The Ten Fast Years of Ralph Fults.* Both books include copious notes and insightful commentary on sources. In *My Life with Bonnie and Clyde* by Blanche Caldwell Barrow, edited and meticulously annotated by Phillips, Blanche Barrow's strong and lively voice conveys not only details of the months she spent as a member of the Barrow Gang but also the language of the time. Wonderfully evocative of the era is *Fugitives: The Story of Clyde Barrow and Bonnie Parker*, compiled from interviews with Emma Parker and Nell Barrow, arranged and edited by Jan I. Fortune and first published in 1934.

The documentary *Remembering Bonnie and Clyde*, directed, written, and produced by Charles T. Leone, provides an intimate perspective, including the reminiscences of Clyde's younger sister Marie and of several other contemporaries, as well as the footage Ted Hinton took of the scene after the posse had killed Parker and Barrow. Frank R. Ballinger's website at http://texashideout.tripod.com/bc.htm was invaluable for its extensive, and often irreverent, collection of photos, clippings, and artifacts. Finally, while the most casual Internet search reveals debate among Bonnie and Clyde aficionados over nearly every detail of the pair's lives, the blog http://bonnieandclydeshouse.blogspot.com/ convinced me that Bonnie's cousin, referred to as "Bess" in *Fugitives* and all subsequent accounts, was, in reality, called "Dutchie."

The poems "Suicide Sal" and "I'll Stay" (the latter quoted in its entirety) were among the collection of verses that Parker composed in the Kaufman County Jail, which she called "Poetry from Life's Other Side." She wrote the ballad "The Trail's End," also known as "The Story of Bonnie and Clyde," shortly before her death. All other verses attributed to Parker in the novel are my attempts to imagine what she might have written. Parker's elocution piece, "Gertrude, or Fidelity till Death," is by Felicia Dorothea Hemans, whose poetry often appeared in contemporary compilations of elocution pieces.

ACKNOWLEDGMENTS

I'm immensely grateful to Jon Zobenica, who was overwhelmingly generous with his remarkable talent and his time and helped me to separate wheat from chaff. I thank my perspicacious agent, Jennifer Rudolph Walsh, for suggesting that I try writing about someone real, and Greer Hendricks, who first acquired this book, for her enthusiasm and confidence in me. If the opening chapters don't drag and if I've stuck the landing, it is thanks to Peter Borland's keen editorial sense. Astute readers with exceptional psychological insight, Jennifer Stuart Wong and Cynthia Davis helped me fully develop Bonnie Parker's behavior as a child and her relationship with her mother. I thank Barbara Faculjak for her perennial willingness to read and reread early chapters. So that I could fully research this book, Nick, Ben, China, Raccoon, and Cyrus Schwarz endured thousands of miles in a hot and not particularly fresh minivan; I am grateful to them all. Finally, Ben curbed my instinct to render the tedious and repetitive aspects of Parker's life tedious and repetitive on the page. He remains the best reader I know.